SUPERWORLD

SUPERWORLD

PART FOUR

BENJAMIN KEYWORTH

Podium

Podium

SUPERWORLD

PRELUDE

I cannot live like this.

It is Tuesday, and I have not slept. I can feel that lightness in my bones, the blur at the back of my vision, but now, sunlight creeps beneath the curtains, and I know the time has passed for sleep. I must get up. I have spent the whole night thinking about how to prepare for this morning, mind churning over and over words and movements and scenarios. I can do this. I have to do this. Liang has gotten away with it; Liang suffers no consequences, and if he can kill without meaning, then surely, I can just speak . . . Surely I can have one moment . . .

I am already moving long before my alarm sounds. I barely glance at the cameras because there is no one mad enough to intrude here, and I do not run on the treadmill for fear I might fall. I shower, scrubbing furiously with soap and gel. I struggle to recall in which order I apply the skin products. I dry every inch of me, hurriedly dress, then check, check, check, and check. Every button is sealed. There are no holes in my gloves. I am clean, I am clear, this is the best suit I own, and I . . . I can do this. I can do this. I will approach her. Just one tiny step. Just one sliver of time.

Please, God, let me have this.

I can do it. If I am prepared, if I am ceaseless in my vigilance, if I just keep my distance, then it will all be fine, no worse than going to work or any other . . . People do this, people talk to one another; it can happen. It will be alright.

I sit in the kitchen, gloved hands splayed atop the marble benchtop, unable to eat, unable to drink. Eventually, I manage to force down some water, which seeps into the cracks beneath my lips and teeth and churns dangerous nausea in my stomach. There is no thinking of doing anything but steadying myself. There is no thought of anything but the plan. My place is set. Her place is set. Glasses ready in the cupboard, cold water in the tap.

"Morning," I whisper to no one. "Morning. Morning. Morning."

Finally, 10:15, her van pulls up. My hands clench so hard it feels as though the tendons are going to snap, like my entire body will rip to pieces. *Breathe*, I tell myself, *try to breathe*. My forehead trickles with sweat, a single traitorous droplet.

The doorbell rings.

I close my eyes and count to eight, then force myself to swallow one last breath and rise from the kitchen stool, striding down the hallway to meet her.

I open the door, and there she stands, the same as ever: radiant.

"Morning," she smiles, and it is all I can do not to collapse.

Emily.

"Morning."

She glances down at the boxes she has started stacking by my door. "What's in these?" she asks. "They're heavy today. At least some of them."

"Weights," I answer, rushing in almost before she's finished the sentence. "For the gymnasium. Exercise. I'm working on getting stronger."

"Aww." Emily laughs. "That explains it. Felt like I was carrying rocks. You don't need it, though, Quin. Look at you!" She playfully taps me on the arm, over the fabric of my coat.

The world tumbles. The window of skin beneath my shirt where she touched me heaves with sensation, burning, and I could swear it almost glows. It is like my entire arm has gone numb. My first true human contact in over ten years. I struggle not to fall.

Emily does not notice. "Well, guess your workout starts here," she continues, turning back to her van, curtain of thick red hair flicking behind her. "I'll bring them over if you want to move them inside? Or are some going in the garage?"

"Here, please," I murmur, and it claws out more like a gasp. Emily remains unperturbed.

"Okey dokey. Back in a sec."

She hums as she walks away, and the moment her back is turned, I reach out to the doorframe for support. Causal touch, just like the forums talked about. She likes me. She likes—

My head is thundering, and my chest is about to burst. A high-pitched ringing screams through my ears. I realize I am watching her go, staring at her like a madman, and it is only through ceaseless vigilance and panic that I am able to break my gaze and turn back to the boxes that, to appear normal, I must continue to move inside. I cannot let her know the effect her touch has had on me. I cannot let her realize I am a freak.

Load by load, I move the boxes into the kitchen. Emily returns to the doorstep, making several trips, always having more ready for me whenever I come back out, a perfect synchronous little relay. Already in tune with one another.

"Phew," she says when we are finished, wiping sweat from her brow. She smiles at me with those soft pale dimples, those beautiful emerald eyes. "That's the lot of them."

"Thank you," I manage to get out. "You're so helpful. Really, thanks."

"Aww, shucks, don't mention it. You're doing half the work. Half the folk I deliver to want me to carry stuff all round their houses."

Somehow, the moment seems right. I extend my hand back through the doorway toward the kitchen, heart pounding in my chest. I can do it. Controlled risk.

"Can I offer you a drink?" I say, doing my best to smile without seeming sinister, to be approachable and kind. "A glass of water?"

"Oh, that's nice of you, Quin, but I don't want to impose."

"You wouldn't be. Really. It's hot. I'd feel rude otherwise."

Emily laughs. "A true gentleman. Well, alright, just one."

"Only if you want to," I stumble to add, the words tumbling out before I can stop myself. "It's okay if you're busy; I know you've probably got other—"

"Water would be great." She smiles, and I think she genuinely means it. She steps inside, past my outstretched arm, and I panic not to recoil as she comes close.

It's happening. Oh my God, it's happening.

Mechanically, as if in a dream, I follow Emily into my home, watching with trembling hands as she sits down at a stool against the kitchen bench. The house is bright—the curtains all open. Sunlight streams, safe and serene.

"Such a nice place you've got," Emily remarks, her gaze wandering over my cabinetry, the interior prearranged and immaculate.

"Thank you," I manage. I circle around the island, giving Emily a wide berth, and place myself opposite her on the counter. "I have a lot of time to clean."

For an instant, I curse myself for exposing my pathetic lifestyle, but Emily just laughs, seeming to take it as a joke. I force myself to smile, trying desperately not to sweat. I turn around, shaking hands opening the kitchen cupboard.

"You could teach me a thing or two. My place is a pigsty."

"Maybe we should live together," I murmur, and only a moment later realize what I've said. My fingers clench around the glass.

"Sorry? What's that?" Emily glances up.

"Nothing. I mean, I'm sure it's not that untidy."

She laughs. "Well, you say that." A brief pause as my trembling hands press the glass to the fridge, to the cold-water dispenser. One, *gurgle-gurgle*. Two. "Oh, aren't you a star. Thank you."

I turn, one glass in each hand, and force my face into a benevolent smile.

"You're very welcome." I reach forward, placing Emily's cup upon the benchtop, the filtered water sparkling pure and clear.

And then it happens, in the space of a second.

Instinctively, she reaches forward to take the glass from me, to be polite and shoulder some of the burden. My eyes flick up at the movement, and my mind, so focused on setting the glass down and immediately backing away, explodes in a sudden surge of panic. Instinctively, I recoil. Instinctively, I flinch. And as Emily's fingers brush the top of the glass, my own gloved hand slides from the bottom, and the vessel drops like a stone onto the benchtop.

KRISSSH.

A cascade of crystal noise, shards and water flying everywhere. Panic suddenly consuming every part of my body, screaming humiliation, incompetence, retreat. My gloves are wet, the bench is wet, water sprays onto Emily, and there is a stinging in my eyes, heat rushing across my face, and I look like an idiot, a fool—

"Oh my God!" Emily exclaims. She stands up. "Oh my God, Mr. Q, I'm so sorry! I didn't mean to—I'm so—"

"No!" I almost shout, reeling back, desperate—desperate to undo, unable to believe my own carelessness, my ineptitude, slick gloved hands fumbling behind me for a cloth. This wasn't how it was supposed to go; this isn't what she was supposed to think. "No, it's not your fault; it was me. I'm sorry—"

"Let me, hold on—" She's already reaching across the bench, pulling off some sheets of paper towel. "Let me, I can do it. Just give me a second; I'll—"

"No! Please, no, just stay where you are. It was me; I can—" I turn back to her, suddenly terrified. "Did it get you? Are you okay?"

Emily shakes her beautiful head, almost laughing. "No, seriously, I'm fine; it's just water. I'm so sorry; I'm so clumsy. You were trying to be nice—" I can barely hear her, shame burning all over as I reach across the counter, frantically mopping at water and glass. My gloved hands slide near her.

Suddenly, Emily gasps.

"Quinten—Oh no! Your face!"

And it is like time itself freezes. I look up, my arm partway across the benchtop, and I see Emily gazing across at me, her features arranged in a bouquet of exquisite sympathy that makes my very heart want to weep. Her emerald eyes glisten in the morning sun. Light trickles atop her freckles and luscious autumn hair. I am a measly creature before her, groveling as she deigns to reach across. As my heart stops, I assume for some reason that she is reaching for the cloth I am holding.

She is not.

Before I can move, Emily reaches over, and with bare fingers, brushes the cut on the side of my face.

GROUND ZERO

My dearest Caitlin,

I hope this letter finds you well and succeeding in whichever marvelous endeavor you are currently applying yourself. I read with fondness and astonishment the stories of your work in Ireland; was this truly the same little girl who used to tear around my waiting room? The papers rarely mention your name, of course, but I recognize your handiwork. I still remember a certain someone imperiously commanding children twice her age to go door-to-door collecting cans for the winter food drive. Those so-called leaders have no idea what they are up against.

To the purpose of my letter. Many thanks again for referring Walter to me for observation and assessment these last few weeks. I know this cannot have been an easy decision, and I am honored to have your trust in this most sensitive area. Rest assured there will be no written report of my examinations beyond this letter, nor were any records taken or my other staff involved. As far as the secretaries are concerned, my niece's husband simply passed through and stayed a few days to help an aging woman around her home, as any well-bred gentleman would. (Though I caution you perhaps to be careful, dear, and keep a keen eye on your beloved. You should hear how some of those hens clucked over his broad shoulders and chiseled jaw. He's less likely to stray than a puppy, mind you, but you shouldn't doubt the cunning of some foxes.)

Walter presents as he always has: kind, affable, and slightly bashful at being the focus of attention. He remains an exceedingly polite and obedient young man, and I am confident that if I had ordered him to single-handedly renovate the practice or repaint every wall, he would have complied without hesitation. He talks of you constantly and with rapture, and clearly misses your mental connection, though I would caution you about relying on telepathy too much, dear, lest strangers wonder why the two of you hardly talk. We're also not sure of the long-term side effects—so again, be careful.

Walter reports his symptoms—and I use that word for lack of a better one—with acceptance, indifference, and an absence of concern. He confirmed, as you suspected, that he has not slept since the Aurora in 1963, and I have no reason to disbelieve him. He reports no feelings of tiredness nor delusions, auditory or visual hallucinations, or feelings of anxiety or dread. He scores perfectly well on assessments for short- and long-term memory, spatial reasoning, concentration, and logic, and has a functioning conversational awareness of social and current affairs.

He shows no signs of dementia, confusion, lethargy, emotional irregularity, poor judgment, or any other effects usually derived from lack of sleep, and indeed reacted to the whole process of being questioned with long-suffering amusement. He simply said that he does not feel the need to sleep anymore, as one might say that they are no longer interested in golf. I did not share with him my intense unease at this statement, nor the truth of total insomnia in the usual course being universally followed by death.

Other observations were no less remarkable. You may already be aware of this, but Walter no longer requires food. When I put this observation to him, he agreed that he continues to eat out of habit, but at times forgets and can go several days without consumption. This was then confirmed over a half-week period while he stayed with me; clearly, the man no longer feels hunger. He is also, as far as I can tell, impervious to injury; with his permission, I tried both knives, bullets, and even dropped a bowling ball on his feet, which may as well have been a pillow for all the harm it caused him.

The energy around his body exudes itself in a substantive yet intangible barrier approximately one-fifth to one-quarter inch from his skin, which is warm and seemingly impenetrable to the touch, but I think you likely already knew that. He also, very disturbingly, does not seem to need to breathe; when I asked Walter if he could hold his breath, the stopwatch ran to an hour before I simply gave up, and he appeared absolutely no worse for wear at any point.

His physical strength is quite frankly ridiculous, and his endurance obscene. On our second day, I sent him running laps around the lakebed, and I am confident that if I had not returned at sundown, he would be running still. He sits in an ice bath quite comfortably, and his body temperature remains a healthy ninety-eight degrees. He is immune, it seems, to nearly all physical constraints and limitations, and physical exertion slides off him like a hand off silk. This is to say nothing of his powers of flight and energy expulsion, which are well-documented enough and not, I think, the reason why you sent him to me in the first place.

Diagnostically, as far as I can see, Walter is in perfect physical and psychological health. Indeed, from reviewing old photographs and pictures, I suspect he may be identical to how he was immediately after the Aurora, i.e., not having aged a day. I could not draw blood, as no needle I owned was capable of piercing through his barrier, but he obliged me by removing a few hairs, and what limited tests I could run on those returned healthy and robust. I see no signs—and I am usually a good judge of these things—of underlying mental instability or some kind of physical "wave" waiting to crash. His eyesight is good, his hearing fair. Excellent lung capacity. I made him pee in a cup like a schoolboy, and his urine was remarkably clean and well balanced.

X-rays and other scans were useless, as whatever energy he puts out prevents them penetrating, not that I'm overly concerned about his internal physiology. I suspect we could lock Walter Reid in a room with every disease known to man and he would come out smelling like roses; there are likely few pathogens on Earth that could survive whatever nuclear reaction is currently taking place inside his body.

So it is, as you suspected, greater than simply a transitional change. These abnormalities do not fluctuate, and Walter does not seem capable of turning them off, besides perhaps lowering his barrier a fraction. This is in itself unusual, although I have not told him so. He is a sweet man, and I do not wish to worry him—nor you, for that matter.

I hesitate to write this final part, dearest Caitlin, but after some agonizing, I feel I must. Walter's condition worries me, not for physiological reasons but for psychological ones. The need to sleep, the need to eat, advancing age, breathing, fatigue, the inescapable threat of harm— these are fundamental aspects of human existence that unite and humble all of us. The implications of Walter's powers, more than any ability I have ever seen, untether him from these vulnerabilities. This causes me deep concern, and I cannot help but fret that he unknowingly teeters on the precipice of believing he has ascended beyond mankind.

We have, my dear, been astoundingly lucky that it was Walter of all people who manifested these powers, as in my view, it is only his innately simple, docile temperament that has thus far prevented his change into a real, perhaps unstoppable threat. The dear man remains simply aloof to his own potential, bless him, and content to remain in subservient bliss.

Though I hope this letter provides you some immediate reassurance, it would be a disservice to you, and perhaps all of us, not to be explicit. You must remain vigilant. A change to Walter—a psychological trauma to him—risks toppling a house of cards far heavier than I think most people appreciate. As an undiplomatic corollary to this, young Miss née Alba, I must in particular warn you that if you ever think of stepping out on this man, you risk not being simply an adulteress but someone who actively places the good of humanity beneath the scintillation of their loins.

That may not be something you wish to hear from an old, irrelevant woman, but fast times can fill fast heads with fast notions, and I want to impress on you the extreme importance of remaining faithful to your vows. Walter's condition troubles me enough in a calm, well-meaning fellow. I shudder to think of the consequences in a man less mature or afflicted by rage or trauma.

Continuing love and success in your commitments,
Yours faithfully,
Dr. Adeline Price

Her name was Emily Charlotte LeBeau, and she had never considered her bad luck.

She had friends and a family out there, though sadly, she'd been disconnected from both of late. This was not intentional. Her mother had left when she was young, gone to marry a man lousy with excitement, and her father, though caring, had never truly been able to move on. Little Emily had grown up at his knee, around the blue crab fishery where he worked, pitching in to sort, catch, or carry boxes when she wasn't staying with her grandparents up in Baton Rouge. They had a skip they took out trawling for shrimp or crawfish on weekends, and one time, Emily had found an injured baby pelican tangled in fishing line, which she'd cut free and nursed back to health.

It might have been that bird, Pepper, that set Emily on the path toward veterinary science, or maybe the constant injuries sustained by her grandparents' two dogs, Duck and Gordon, black-and-white-patched basset hounds with heads so full of love, the family often said there was no room left for brains.

She'd been an outgoing girl, humble, gregarious. Never afraid to muck in when something needed doing; never shy to stay back or clean up. At eleven, she'd manifested the power of floramancy, which always made her pa say she should be a gardener, but Emily preferred animals. Besides, she always riposted, the two went hand-in-hand when you thought about it. By the summer of her fifteenth birthday, her grandparents' big backyard was so green and chock-full of perfect bird habitat that Emily's Memaw joked they should start charging folk to come and admire it.

Emily'd done alright in school, was doing okay in college. Academics were never her strongest suit, but she could knuckle down with the best of them and only really did the whole partying thing as much as was socially required. She'd moved out early on because the college she'd gotten into was out of town, and though living with her pa was good for the most part, there were still days when she'd come home to find him stoned out of his gourd and crying, begging Em to help him contact her mom. Emily wanted no part in his schemes or his wallowing. She had other family filling the space her mother had left, and no desire to disturb the foolish woman with the love she'd so casually thrown away.

At twenty, Emily had taken up with her then boyfriend, a gangly, curly-haired econ major named Josh. Josh had aspirations of being a musician and the ability to crush diamonds with his teeth, but he veered between artistic endeavors and the desire to make money hand over fist. He was funny, chatty, and quick-tempered, and the two got along like a house on fire, or so Emily had thought. Only a few months prior to her death, Emily had discovered that he'd been cheating. The revelation broke her heart, but in hindsight, it was typical—Josh did always seem to believe, without reservation, that he was entitled to everything and all.

Unfortunately, Josh was local to their college, and when he and Emily had split, the ties binding him to their friends had run older and deeper than hers. These aftershock betrayals had hurt Emily almost worse than the original schism because she felt like she had shown these so-called friends naught but love and loyalty. Regardless, the knowledge of Josh's cheating clearly carried insufficient toxicity to poison most wells. Emily was tough, however, and had endured abandonment before, and likely could have weathered this latest round of other people's failings, too, were it not for the second hammer blow: her college was kicking her out.

Far more than Josh's betrayal, *this* Emily did not understand. There'd been an incident, sure, where perhaps she'd held a dog down a little firmly, but the shih tzu's owner had been completely unreasonable and more overanxious than the pooch. Yet, somehow, the woman's complaint had stuck, then soured, then spread, until finally, the university had found it all too difficult. Far easier to drop a student than fend off a maniac. They had no loyalty to a nameless girl.

Devastated and alone, Emily had moved back in with her pa, but his old, scarred heart brushing up against her newly wounded one had only led to conflict. She'd half left, half fled, with little more than a pain in her chest and a backpack over her shoulder. Nothing seemed to be going right, so Emily had done what her heart told her to do, to sail solo into uncharted waters, and followed a job ad to a new city to regroup and recover. And she had been recovering.

In a homey yet frugal one-bedroom apartment overlooking a train line, she'd filled a home with houseplants, painted mugs, and a secondhand corduroy couch, and watched *Simpsons* reruns while pretending to study. Her old connections, though frayed, began slowly to mend. She'd called her pa, and they'd talked long and exchanged sorrys. A few of her old friends had reached out. Her expulsion was on appeal, and she'd had positive talks with a local veterinary school, who'd indicated their incredulity at a fourth-year being expelled for a complaint of that nature. Her job set good hours and paid hard cash, and she loved the routine and chatting to her regulars. She'd woken up that Tuesday morning in September thinking only of the bright blue sky and how later she might see about going swimming. Emily was a good swimmer, a great diver. Her eyes never stung.

The man who killed her did not know this, nor would he ever. All he knew was that she was there, unmoving, on the floor of his kitchen. Thought eluded him, as did calm and stable breath. There was little for him to do but sob and rock Emily's body desperately, clinging to her weight, her fading warmth.

The sounds of his cries carried through windows he'd opened a thousand years ago to let in light and ventilation, the girl's delivery van sitting abandoned outside. That his agonized wails would raise concern and curious alarm in his neighbors did not occur to him. Nothing occurred to him, for his fracturing mind had room only for Emily, and the sight of her eyes staring empty into the abyss.

Matt slept fitfully; Jane not at all. She had, on his insistence, dragged down the mattress from the destroyed bed in the guest room, flopping it in a heap of tangled bedding in the corner of Azleena's computer lab. Matt had slept partially wrapped up atop the sheets, passing out almost immediately despite the overhead lights, the constant pitter-patter of the genius on her keyboard, and the low mutterings passing between her, Helen, and Jane.

When Matt awoke, it was to the stale heat of long-running electronics and the room looking as he had left it—tawny brown wooden walls, windows with blinds drawn down, public-use computers running along the sides, plus Azleena's setup in the middle. The biggest change was that somebody had been kind enough to dim the fluorescent lighting—that and the sight of Jane's golden cape pacing back and forth. She'd changed back into her uniform and was interspersing her constant marching with only the occasional muttered word or heavy breathing, none of which boded well.

"Ugh," Matt groaned, half from stiffness and half to announce he was awake. He stretched his arms over his head, sending his spine through a series of satisfying cracks as, across the room, Jane spun around, locking onto him with piercing eyes. That his girlfriend hadn't slept all night would have been Matt's initial evaluation of her, save for the fact that Jane hadn't slept any night in the last six months, which rendered the description kind of moot. He ran cold, clumsy fingers through his tangled hair and rubbed the poor excuse for sleep from his eyes.

"Hey," Jane grunted, striding toward him. Over at the computer desk, Helen's cybernetically enhanced head peered up, but Azleena gave no indication she'd heard anything, remaining fixated on the screens. The lumbering close-shaved technopath and dainty dark-haired genius were in pretty much the same exact positions in front of Azleena's computer they had been when Matt lapsed into unconsciousness, and neither had changed clothes. "Are you okay?"

Matt interpreted this as paranoid speak for asking how he'd slept. Physically, he was the same as ever—still just some midsize brown-haired white dude, though there were a few scratches on his hands from where he'd crawled through rubble at the apartment yesterday, and his ears still rang a bit from the sirens and explosions. Mentally, Matt was a bit shaken, adrenaline still spiking a little whenever an errant thought reminded him of how close he kept coming to dying. Yet, his years of mental training persisted, and functionally, Matt had everything pretty much under control. And now that they had the USB drive from Lionel—the assassin turned whistleblower—and access to the mystery server it drew from, Matt finally felt like they were close to getting some answers. Answers, please, and then resolution. And then an end to the chaos and a return to mundane normality. Maybe. *Please.*

But as for sleep? "Not bad," Matt replied, stretching his stiff legs out and somewhat mashing the untucked sheets. "Bedframes are over-rated." A more skittish man might have had difficulty falling asleep in a semi-lit computer room with a genius and a technopath muttering and clacking away relentlessly on a keyboard while his large, jittery girlfriend paced and mumbled dark curses nearby, but Matt had always been a deep and easy sleeper. He'd fallen asleep watching *Die Hard* at the cinema once, plus had slept through a hotel fire alarm, which his family were always fond of reminding him about.

"Where're we at?" he asked, climbing somewhat unsteadily to his feet and directing the question over Jane's shoulder to Azleena. His girlfriend moved beside him, arms crossed, and Matt squeezed her bicep in substitution for a hug. Over six foot tall, especially in her Dawn boots, Jane was athletic and lean, with long bronze hair, sharp—he thought—attractive features, and a large spikey *E* tattooed on her right cheek, which was either normal tattoo black or a variation of living gold depending upon how much of the power of Dawn she was currently releasing.

At present, though not actively streaming light, the mark had taken on the color of a flat sunrise, which Matt did not need a lifetime of studying human behavior to interpret. The glowing *E*, pearlescent white body of her uniform, gold cape, boots, and gloves, and the gold symbol of breaking day emblazoned across Jane's chest presented the tall empath in stark contrast to Matt's own appearance, which was disheveled gray track pants, a maroon pajama shirt with a triceratops on it, and bare feet (because what kind of weirdo slept in socks).

Azleena—the wafer-thin, dark-haired genius currently responsible for the Legion of Heroes' operational organization, security systems, technology management, information dissemination, research, and collective music piracy—did not glance up at Matt's question but instead maintained laser focus on the three computer screens arrayed in front of her. Legs tucked beneath her atop the seat of her computer chair, strands of long black hair sticking to her forehead, the genius was clearly twenty-thousand leagues deep into document trawling, and the fact that she was still at it after six hours or so boded ominously for the weight of the haul.

"We are balls deep," Azleena answered, a very incongruous statement coming from a ninety-pound girl who had at best given puberty a light slap. "I'm not making preliminary conclusions."

"Can't or won't?"

"Won't," she replied. Beside Matt, Jane's lips twitched into a frown. "I'm not unintentionally strapping myself to anything. Besides, you"—she pointed without looking at Jane—"have the habit of charging off at the first hint someone has wronged you. You are not blowing up cities over this. We have to be very, *very* careful."

"Why do we have to be careful?" snapped Jane, bristling a little at Azleena's entirely correct assessment. "It doesn't matter who's responsible. Whoever it is, they're dead. Them, their lackeys, their whole operation."

"One word," replied Azleena. "Money." This time, she actually turned in her chair to stare at the pair of them, Helen continuing to interface quietly with the computer in the background. "This is the only conclusion I'm willing to draw right now, but it's not so much a guess as a certainty. Whoever is behind the attacks on you is spending money. Like, an incalculable amount. Not literally," she was quick to add, seemingly unable to stop herself. "I can calculate it. But in common parlance. They are spending a proverbial ton of money acquiring and utilizing a diverse, niche, and quite frankly baffling array of resources."

"How much are we talking here?" Matt asked, feeling his stomach churn. Unconsciously, he crossed his arms across his chest in a half self-hug. "Millions?"

Azleena shook her head and swung back to the computer, lips pursed as if sucking on something sour. "Billions. There are transactions in here for things I don't understand. Diamonds. These people are selling diamonds—truckloads of them—and I have no idea why."

"Diamonds?" Matt said, incredulous. "I'm being hunted by diamond miners?"

"You're being manipulated by someone with access to what looks to me like half the world's diamond reserves, not to mention gold and any number of other precious metals. Which makes absolutely no sense, because surely the majority of those diamonds would be tied up in, you know, jewelry." She squinted at the screen, seemingly torn between irritable and insulted. "Why would anyone have a multibillion-dollar diamond horde just sitting around?"

"Maybe we're up against a dragon?" Matt joked. Beside him, Jane's head slowly turned, and she fixed him with a razor-thin, letterbox glare, which Matt chose to interpret as her way of saying she found him adorable.

"At this stage, I would take *dragon* over the other options," Azleena muttered darkly.

"I mean, at least if it was a dragon we could hit up Celeste and have a sick dragon fight."

"Government," growled Jane, ignoring Matt's sheer raving idiocy. "It has to be the government."

"Multipronged," piped up Helen, who'd clearly been listening, though so far not contributing to the conversation.

"Exactly," Jane agreed, nodding the buzz-cut technopath her thanks. "Attack from the courts, attack from the radicals, attack from the FBI. Force Matt into giving in to them. Cover every angle."

"It's not like the government to be that organized." Matt frowned, feeling troubled. Yet, he had to admit it seemed plausible.

"We can't discount the possibility," Azleena said. "And because of that, I'm not making any conclusions until I've reviewed everything and talked strategy. With more than just you, Jane. No offense."

Jane grumbled under her breath but nevertheless raised no further protests. She could, it seemed, temporarily preserve her calm, at least within the safety of Morningstar's walls.

"So what do we do in the meantime?" she asked the genius. "Just stay put?"

"I could use some breakfast," Matt suggested. As usual, everybody ignored him.

"Things need doing," replied Azleena. "North Korea's going to need more attention. And you still have a regular schedule. Herd's in bed at the moment, but you've got a full day mapped out."

"Matt's coming with me," Jane stated. For the second time, Azleena's eyes pulled away from her computer, and she fixed them both with an inscrutable, unblinking stare.

"Is that wise?" the genius asked, with only the tiniest hint of exasperation.

"Come on," scowled Jane. "You're sitting here talking about some international conspiracy, someone spending billions of dollars, and you still think the Academy's safe? You think there's absolutely no possibility, not even a shadow of a doubt, that one of these new Acolytes might be a sleeper; that we haven't onboarded a rat?"

"I think that's highly unlikely," Azleena replied, her voice monotone. Yet, the genius's expression wavered as she turned over the possibility. "Although I guess not impossible. And potential ties of this nature aren't something we actively screened for . . ."

"Exactly," said Jane. "No offense to you or any of the newcomers, but as far as I'm concerned, everyone who came in post Detroit is a suspect."

"As much as I dislike paranoia, I think Jane's right." Matt grimaced. Beside him, Jane's face flowered in surprise.

"You do?" she asked, staring at him in disbelief. "You agree with me?"

"It has been known to happen." He paused to let her process her shock, which converted a moment or two later into an expression of quiet self-satisfaction, before turning back to the others. "It only takes one, right? I mean, probably not you two"—he indicated Azleena and Helen—"since you're the ones who helped uncover this, but the rest . . . What do we really know?"

"A lot," Azleena complained.

"Yeah, but do we know enough?" Matt replied. "Do we know with one hundred percent certainty their whole background prior to coming? Or forget infiltration; are we absolutely certain none of them could be turned? Sad to say, but it sounds like there's a lot of money on the table. And it's not like my existence and the Legion's necessarily aligns."

"The Legion is going to protect you," Jane growled, glaring at him and then at everyone else for good measure.

"Right," Matt said, "but is it such a stretch to imagine one person in the world's foremost team of superhumans being a bit worried about the possibility of someone out there having human DNA? The greater good and all. Some of that conspiracy stuff is convincing. Besides"—he glanced between all three—"it's what I'd do. Helen's right: multipronged.

It's logical. If my blood can't be obtained legally or voluntarily, why not by coercion? Create a threat, force us to respond to it. So, think about it; play that scenario out. Our home gets attacked, where do we go, logically? Here. Then what? That's easy—at some point, Jane leaves, and I'm left wide open. Well, somewhat semiopen," he corrected, seeing the dark cloud cross Azleena's face.

"I intensely dislike this line of conversation," the genius muttered, though she followed that statement after a moment's hesitation with, "but only because it's plausible." She eyed Jane and Matt off. "Is dragging him everywhere better, though? It's out in the open."

"It's random." Matt shrugged. "Less people know in advance where Jane's going. And if someone makes a move, she can break off. Unless we're looking at, like, the end of the world, she's probably not going to have her hands so full she can't protect me. And if we're all going to die, well, then we have bigger problems."

"Hilarious," replied Azleena, flat and sarcastic. "Yet, sadly, I follow. There are no completely safe options."

"Exactly."

"In that case, you're taking my bug-out bag." The genius leaned over to her left, forcing Helen to step back, and pulled open the large bottom drawer of her computer desk. Azleena reached inside and drew out a black polyester backpack with drawstrings, the kind a regular person might get as a freebie for joining a new gym. She wheeled over in her chair, pushing across the floor with her dainty legs, and held the bag up to Matt, who took it with mild to medium confusion.

"Your what?"

"My bug-out bag. Small, portable devices to assist survival in imminent danger. Physically," she said, casting her gaze over Matt with a keen, empirical eye, "we're actually somewhat similar in our practical uselessness in combat. Except you're also an idiot."

"Thanks," Matt said, trying not to take that too personally. He weighed the bag in his hand, feeling a variety of different-size objects jangling around inside.

"You're welcome," replied Azleena, spinning back to her computer. "I'll also build you a mech suit."

Matt's head snapped up from examining the bag's contents. "Excuse me?"

"A mech suit. A mechanized suit of armor." Still locked onto the screens, Azleena's face split into her rare goblin grin. "It's something of a genius tradition. The armor protects from external dangers and—"

"I know what a mech suit is," Matt replied, having indeed watched cartoons. "I just . . . um . . ." He glanced at Jane for support, finding her completely unperturbed, as though they were discussing used-car prices. "That's . . . Thank you?"

"You'll love it," Azleena assured him with a dismissive wave. "It'll be classic, something Mentok would've approved of. Bulletproof, flight enabled, missiles—"

"I don't know if I need—"

"Plus, it'll cover your face, hide your identity. Nobody will think twice to see a Siegfried accompanying Lady Dawn."

"What's a Sieg—"

"And it'll make you taller," Azleena stated, nodding over her shoulder at Matt like she expected that to meet his approval. Matt just looked concerned.

"Is there something wrong with my hei—"

"Thick boots, lumbar support, a decent visor." The genius was not even vaguely listening to him at this point. "I think a comfortable seven feet. Six and a half, if you want to be inconspicuous."

"As a giant killer robot?"

"Or we go big." Abruptly, Azleena stopped talking, peering off into space with her head cocked and one eye slightly squinted. "Really big. Mechazord. *Oh.*" She sounded suddenly, almost sexually, excited. "With a body hole right in the center."

"Azleena, please, no fifty-foot robots," Matt pleaded. "I'm getting enough attention as is."

"Quiet, idiot. Let us do what's best for you."

"Stop calling him an idiot," Jane growled. Azleena completely ignored her.

"Enough," the genius demanded, waving aggressively behind her. "No more talking. I've got too much to do. Matt, take the bag; familiarize yourself."

"How—" Matt started to say, but then his phone pinged. He glanced down to find a text message enclosing an instruction manual.

"No more questions," said Azleena. "Unless it's about what color you want your robot. Jane, I've sent you your itinerary. Liaise with Herd. Helen, coffee." Azleena turned back to the computer, her small eyes dark and gleaming. "No sleep this week."

INTERLUDE

Her eyes are open, and there is nothing in them; my mouth is open, and there is only screaming.

I touch her. For the first time in our lives, I touch her, really hold her, cradle her limp, cooling form. Time passes in fits and starts, and my body moves without reason. I have neither understanding nor consciousness. I am crying, I am holding, I am pacing, I am shrieking, I am pounding her chest with useless fists. I have wrapped my mouth around red, motionless lips, and I am breathing air into them. I am gagging, I am vomiting. I am breathing faster than I thought possible. The room is spinning, a suffocating blur, the walls falling in around us. I cannot think. I do not hear. My flesh is not my own; I renounce it.

No, no, no, please live, live, live—

Somewhere, a small voice mumbles that it is pointless. Somewhere in the far distant recesses of my mind, I understand what is lost can never return. It is a whisper in a hurricane. I am not my thoughts. I am not my soul.

My fingers rake track marks down my cheeks, and my trembling hands have blood beneath the nails. I do not care; I cannot see. I clutch her soft, unmoving body with the utmost care and reverence, then so tight it feels like every bone should break.

"Emily," someone with my voice is moaning. Broken, mournful, weak. "Emily, Emily, Emily . . ."

So beautiful in death. She is not dead; she is just sleeping. This is a fairy tale, she just needs a handsome prince. Not me, I—I am a criminal, a murderer, I will kill myself. Please shoot me, oh God, make me a stone. Do not bury her; she cannot go below the ground. She isn't hurt—she isn't—

Somewhere, knocking, knuckles on a distant door. An American voice asks in English if I am okay. I am not here, so I do not answer. I am dead, I know, with Emily. My body has simply yet to catch up.

Take it back. Take it back. Return her to life, God, and I will never speak to her again. I will rot in the darkest prison until the sun weeps black. Take my hands, my eyes, my soul, just please return her. Return her. Return—

There is another thought, somewhere in the darkness. There is a hand that is connected to my body. It moves on its own, the world it fumbles through blurred by tears, yet . . . it holds a phone. It is dialing a number. Characters nostalgic to my swirling, aching brain.

I look down, and the body I am cradling is my mother's. I am ten years old. The world is shrinking, I am shrinking, the colors are rippling, and the corpse is growing larger, features melting, sinking into the floor.

Digital ringing. A click—

"Liang, please, it's Em—"

But I cannot even say her name. Nausea overwhelms me. My fingers tremble on the red End button, and the link to the world beyond this room is severed. I cannot speak. I cannot breathe. There is no life in this emptiness. We are alone, the two of us, and this is not real, this is not—

Time passes. Does it? There is no instant, no eternity. I feel her weight in my arms, against my body, and I cry—broken, animal sounds—for she has left me, and nothing I do will make her return.

Far away, a distant pop. Another knock on the door, more voices, more shouting, beyond my home and comprehension. I cradle her. I cradle her. A sudden bang, the sound of a door slamming, and suddenly, footsteps approach, almost at a run, and in the kitchen hallway is—

"Jesus Christ. Qiang."

My stomach churns, and my eyes are lead, but I manage to look up. A figure I know stands in the doorway, clutching the wall, reeling in shock. He has my face if I were fat and prideful. A different haircut, an expensive fade, touches of product. Why have you come, corruption? Why have you opened the door and let in the hateful world?

"What have you done?" my brother whispers. He glances frantically over his shoulder, back down the hallway, out the front door, to where middle-aged American strangers peer curiously inside. I do not care; I do not notice. They are the light of far distant stars, not arriving for millennia. Liang's footsteps hurry over tiles and floorboards, and I hear the door slam. I close my eyes and cling to Emily, whispering faithful sobs into her neck. My tears pool damp upon her cold skin.

"What are you doing, you idiot?!" Liang hisses, and I realize he is once more standing in the doorway. I look up, and there is a familiar madness in his trembling eyes. The dark bags under them. The grinding of his teeth. "Get away from her! Get up!"

It seems an eternity before my tongue finds Cantonese. "She's dead," I whisper. "Liang, please . . . you have to . . . I didn't . . ."

"Get up, you filthy idiot. We must burn her; we must hide before the neighbors see, the—Where is your phone? Have you called the authorities, your government contacts? We need to get ahead of this and—"

"She's gone," I say, and the moan escapes my lips, the last petal on a dying flower. "Gone. I don't . . . I cannot . . ."

"You have ruined us," Liang mutters, standing shaking in the doorway. He jerks forward as if to reach out to me, but then stops himself, his eyes wild. "Qiang, you inept, useless dog, you've ruined everything; you've—"

Finally, my eyes break free from Emily and manage to crawl their way up. I see him, really see him, for the first time since his arrival. I see him and I realize he is there.

"Brother?"

"Yes! It is me, you moon-brained idiot. Stop clinging to the dead girl, we have to—" He runs his hands through his short hair. "We have to . . ."

"Bring her back." Suddenly, Liang's tirade falls silent. He stares down at me. I stare up at him. Every part of me shakes, and the room swims in tears. "Please. Please."

"Bring back the delivery girl?" my brother snaps. He gnaws at his lips, his eyes as wide as saucers, endlessly kneading over and over with his hands. "Are you out of your goddamn mind? No, no-no-no-no-no, we have to run; we have to go, quickly. I-I-I have brought a teleporter, loyal, she can—Where is your Disruptance? Turn it off, we can—to the mainland, safety. The Party, they will protect us; they will—"

"Please," I whisper, and in that moment, I look at him and will every shattered shard of my being toward him, trying desperately to make him understand. "I love her."

Abruptly, Liang falls silent. "You love her?" he finally mutters, and then suddenly, his voice rises, incredulous and hot. "You love her?! The *diǎo* delivery girl?! *Lǎomǔ kǎn jiā chǎn,* who cares if you love her, I'm not going to—"

But as his words wash over my ringing ears, a memory suddenly rises, an ice-bound dagger stabbed into the back of my mind. Suddenly, I am returned there, to the kitchen, to my body. Slowly, I gently slip Emily's head from my lap and stand, trembling, pulling myself up by numb hands on the kitchen counter until I am at full height, staring, equal to Liang. My eyes never leave his, welded onto him now, refusing to let go. Emily's body lies between us on the floor.

"You did," I whisper, and the words uncurl as frozen thorns around my throat. "You did, for your love. I remember. You took another—and I promised. I let you betray our promise; I let you get away with it, and now . . . and now . . ."

Suddenly, I scream. **"BRING HER BACK!"**

Liang flinches. "No, are you out of your—"

"BRING HER BACK!"

I reach forward, and Liang stumbles backward. "Get away!" he cries. His pupils are black holes of greed and panic, and his skin is scabbed and haggard. And I see it now. I understand what he is. I see his degeneration and debauchery, and in that moment, something breaks. Shards of pain turn to iron, and bloody violence surges through my soul.

I lunge for him, hands outstretched, every tendon on fire, every fiber of my being screaming to hold him down, to force his hands upon her. He shouts and scrambles, slipping back, feet scrabbling on the rug, and suddenly he is running, and I chase, screaming through a red haze—

Bam! Liang slams open the front door and goes tumbling down the front steps, sprawling in a heap where the footpath meets the lawn. I stalk through the doorway, shoulders hunched, shaking, sucking air between my teeth. The sunlight burns; there is a ringing in my ears, and the smell of cold and death intertwined with grass and passionfruit. Emily's hair. Somewhere, there is movement and sirens, somewhere voices, but I do not hear, and I do not see. I only have eyes for my traitorous worm of a brother, slithering on his belly toward the freedom he has wasted his whole life.

No more.

Liang is screaming in delirious Cantonese. He scrambles between the strangers arrayed on my front lawn, who watch, standing like bowling pins atop the grass, their mouths agape. My so-called brother has fallen to the left, and to the right before me stands a black-suited African woman, her face plastered in an expression of shock and concern. Between them, astride the thin concrete footpath, two police officers slowly advance between my brother and I, their hands held out and cautious. The fat, soft-brained Americans spaced out behind them murmur in their shorts and T-shirts, cattle sensing slaughter with monotone fear. To my mind, it is not real, a moving picture. Naught but enemies to overcome.

I tear my hands from their gloves.

"Hey," the male policemen says in English. The female turns, reaches down toward my brother, eyes flicking worriedly between the two of us. "I see you're angry. Let's all—"

I do not let him speak. I roar, some noise between a shout and a gurgle, and I lunge for Liang, who shrieks and backpedals across the grass. He scrambles to his feet, staggering toward the black-suited woman, screaming, "Get me out of here! Get me—!"

I launch forward. Everything is a ringing blur. Diamond flows over the policeman's body, and he steps toward me, between us, extending a hand. My fingers wrap around his wrist. Instantly, he falls.

"Mike! Holy—"

He drops, cast aside, and my eyes burn only for Liang as the policewoman's hands fumble for the weapon on her belt. Barely a distraction. I sweep forward, and my fingers brush her neck, and suddenly, all light vanishes from her eyes. Her strings are cut, and she falls, crumpled, silent. Somewhere, fat Americans scream. I do not care. Liang is scrambling, pushing himself back toward the dark woman in the darker suit, clambering desperately to his feet as I scream—

"MURDERER!"

His hands flail, clutching wildly to her jacket, almost dragging her down trying to pull himself up.

"BETRAYER!"

He has found her; he is clutching her hands and shouting, and she has closed her eyes, fervently mouthing something where moments ago she could do naught but stare at me in terror.

"I WILL TELL EVERYONE!"

Liang leans back, and I lunge forward. In an instant, that final instant, my hands close around his collar, and suddenly, there is a lurch as something pulls me by the hips, and I am hurtling, hurtling, darkness pressing in on every side—

Bam! The darkness ends, and we are no longer in suburbia. A wide, open arrow of lightboards and buildings, skyscrapers, glass, and concrete, an intersection of two roads heaving with gridlocked honking buses and cars. The smell of waste and traffic, people walking and chattering everywhere, in their hundreds, their thousands. For a second, Liang staggers, thrown by the teleportation, his face pale, trying to get his bearings. I know where we are; I know it from pictures. New York City, Times Square. The information is there, crystal clear atop my predator brain, present and irrelevant. I care only for one thing.

My worthless brother turns and stumbles backward, sees me there, opens his mouth to cry something, his fingers still gripped white to the teleporter's coat. The words never leave him. I grab them both.

And suddenly, the world around us is not life and color but screams and burning gray.

Flashbang. Wire. Space blanket. Decoy. Smoke cloud. Stink pellet. One by one, Matt withdrew the items from the bug-out bag, placing them gingerly on the armory bench beside him, checking back on his phone with each one he removed so as to cross-reference them with the user guide. He wriggled his arm around the bag's depths, feeling for anything he'd missed. This was like a Christmas stocking for psychopaths.

"Yes, I can hear you." Azleena's voice buzzed in his clear plastic earpiece. Matt could almost see her up in the lab sitting in front of her computer, speaking into a little microphone tucked beneath her chin, her dry hands and dark-ringed eyes continuing to scan back and forth, undistracted by what Jane was saying on the other end. "Check, check, check. No, Herd has the coordinates." Standing at attention a few feet away from him, Will Herd, teleporter, flashed them both a nod and a stiff grin. "Satellite looks clear whenever you're ready. No hostiles on approach."

Laser pointer, Matt counted out, ration bar. Remote-detonated explosive. *Oh, good.* A pair of metal ice-cream-cone-shaped stabby things. Wall climbers? Wall climbers.

"You know me having to climb anything is just synonymous with me falling to my death, right?" he said, holding up the cone stabbers to show Jane.

"Pack that away," she snapped back at him, already on her feet. Matt couldn't tell if the tension in her voice was giddiness or nerves.

They were in the armory, the Legion's underground arms depot and one of the few things to survive Klaus Heydrich's mansion-leveling blast half a year ago intact. Aboveground, a small molehill of a bunker led down to a long, low concrete hall, which inside was lined with rows upon rows of Legion body armor, looming in its custom crimson and gold. The whole place stunk of disinfectant spray and cold. Matt hadn't liked it the first time he'd come here, and he sure as heck didn't like it any better the second.

At least this time he got to wear civilian clothes. Jane was suited up as Lady Dawn, obviously, and Will was wearing his standard gloveless Legion armor, its only change since Matt had last seen it being that someone had painted on the front chest plate a black eagle clutching a banner saying *F*** Nazis*. Matt, on the other hand, was wearing jeans, a gray T-shirt, and a brown leather jacket that made him look as if he was on his way to the hardware store and very effectively hid the bulletproof vest he was wearing underneath. The only indication that he was in any way connected to the Legion of Heroes might have been the earpiece nestled in his right ear, although that was clear and difficult to see from a distance. Well, that and the fact that he was a very white man about to teleport into a very North Korean civil war zone.

Trying to reassure himself that this was the only way and only temporary, Matt repacked the contents of Azleena's goody bag, which the genius had assured him dismissively back at the computer room would not go off or explode no matter how much they jiggled around.

As he did, Will moved away from the entrance toward the tunnel leading out of the armory and beyond the range of Morningstar's Disruptances.

"Ready when you are," the teleporter said, slipping Matt a somewhat sad, sympathetic grin.

"Wait," Azleena's voice came suddenly. "Hold." Matt saw Jane frown and both her and Will's hands go to their earpieces. "Wait, wait, wait. Abort. Abort, abort, abort."

Matt's stomach fell—because for the first time since he'd known her, Azleena's voice rang with something resembling panic.

"What?" Jane demanded. "Is there a problem with the landing?"

"No. Hold on." Matt heard furious typing. "I'm getting reports . . . You're being redirected. Giselle's coming. Wait. Will, I'm going to need multiple jumps."

"Az?" the teleporter asked, voice laced with concern. "What's happening? What's going on?"

"Priority alert. Multiple calls from New York. I'm scrambling everyone; it's Ana Bloodbane."

Beside him, Jane's eyebrows furrowed in confusion. "What?"

"Wait," said Matt, frowning. "The corpse lady?" He turned to Jane. "Didn't you just have some girl a few weeks ago who was—"

"This isn't a copycat. We've got hundreds of dead in a ten-block radius, and I . . ." The genius's voice abruptly stopped. "No," Matt heard her murmur. "That's not right. I . . ." Azleena's voice snapped back into focus. "Go, go! Will, I'm resending you coordinates. As soon as Giselle—"

She didn't get a chance to say anything further because at that moment, the armory doors exploded back on their hinges and something too fast to see shot inside. In the space of half a second, Giselle Pixus, speedster leader of the Legion of Heroes, was standing beside them, breathless in her Legion colors.

"Run," she urged, and together, they sprinted toward the tunnel.

* * *

They popped into existence in the streets of Manhattan, stomachs churning as the world reoriented itself. Beside her, Jane saw Matt lean over a little, coughing and rubbing sulfur from his eyes, but otherwise, he seemed unaffected. She turned back to the city they'd teleported into.

"What the hell . . . ?"

Before them lay a shattered, twisted landscape. The streets were in ruins—buildings broken, cars overturned, fires burning, craters in the pavement, shattered glass—everywhere, signs of devastation. Yet, far from being abandoned in the wake of some disaster, the city before them churned with movement. Jane took an involuntary step back. Her eyes widened, and for a few moments, she could do nothing but stare as her mind reeled, struggling to take in simultaneously not one but three impossible sights.

"Mother of God," Giselle whispered.

The first thing Jane saw were the people. Men and women and children of every race and age and attire filled the streets in front of them, lurching from side to side, spasming, seemingly stuck in place. For a moment, Jane's mind marked them as zombies: reanimated bodies stumbling with that stereotypical stagger of a corpse under someone else's control. But an instant later, she was hit by the screaming. Horrible, delirious screaming howling from thousands of mouths, not some sort of undead moan but the shrieks of living people, a cacophony of agony, broken fingernails drawing bloody down a blackboard. And something else was wrong. These people weren't decaying. There was no rot, no mortification on them of the kind borne by truly dead creatures, though there were bodies. Hundreds of bodies lay motionless on the asphalt between those still standing—rotting, motionless, or reduced to husks.

And then, before Jane's horrified eyes, one of the stumbling people erupted with power. Then another, then all of them, each person firing or arcing or slamming out around them with an ability as if a pulse had suddenly raced through the city streets, freeing the tormented from their paralysis for a single solitary moment to move, unleash, and destroy. Some staggered forward, some stumbled backward, some shivered in superspeed, while others swung wild arms billowing fire or ice or acid, or screamed and smashed their hands into the pavement.

Yet, as quickly as the movement had come, it ended, the devastation flinching, the delirious, shrieking people freezing in place once more as if some great unseen gravity had suddenly reasserted itself. Their powers faded to twitches and dribbles, dripping from eyes or mouths or fingertips. And then came another pulse. And then another. Every few seconds, the deranged superpowered horde moved again, only to immediately stop, paralyzed. And all the while, their voices wailed in torment, the sound of it howling between the buildings, a horror wind curdling Jane's very blood.

Second, she saw the monsters.

Because the screaming people did not stand alone. Among them, interspersed between them and the corpses, no less paralyzed and no less deranged, stood warped beings some five, ten, twenty feet high. Abominations. There was no other word. Creatures with multiple heads, multiple arms, splattered with scales or spurs or tufts of hair, whose flesh bulged wide and rippling and blubbery, or taut and sinewy and laced all over with veins. No two were the same: some spilled out as broad as they were tall, some teetered on multiple crooked legs, some were a uniform color, some a patchwork of different flesh tones, some with skin stretched or bleeding or pierced by protruding bone spikes.

Jane saw a monstrosity of skinless red muscle fifteen feet high, with patchy scales of what looked like human teeth; an armless creature with a dozen long beige tentacles hanging loose across the ground ending in bone-white blades; a ten-foot midnight horror crawling spiderlike across the asphalt on seven crooked, spindly limbs, body spiraled with rapidly blinking eyes; a bulbous heap of pale flesh wider than a truck, its vast sides splitting again and again in gigantic gnashing mouths.

And from these monsters, too, flared powers. But not just one. Lightning arced between bone spears erupting down a twisted spinal column as clawed hands clutched orbs of fire. Mutant flesh shimmered and shifted to metal, to rock, to crystal, air or water, blurred unrelenting with superspeed, or sunk intangible into the ground. Twin mouths drooled with acid as the head beside it howled with hypersound as bodies bristled with wings or fur or antlers. Abominations grew in size and divided. Some floated in midair, ashen limbs dangling like seaweed, while others clung to buildings or shattered the streets around them, their own feet slamming and breaking and regenerating with every shuddering step.

Like the people, the monsters stood stuck in place, only able to twitch and surge free in a sudden pulse of movement every few seconds or so. And like the people, too, every mouth they had—the ones not gurgling with some kind of power or substance—screamed without pause. The noise coming from the creatures was more inhuman, reeling from high-pitched piercing shrieks to low guttural rumbles. Every sound was pain, and it underscored the cacophony of human screaming like a vast, demented orchestra erratically crashing their instruments beneath a terrible a capella song. The whole scene was a nightmare of twisted flesh and power, devoid of sanity or reason, and it awoke in Jane an existential terror she had never before felt, not once in her entire life.

The third thing she noticed was the bubble.

"What the hell . . . ?" Matt whispered. All Jane could do was rub her eyes.

The world they were watching—the twitching mutant monstrosities, the screaming, paralyzed people, the shattered streets, the devastation—all of it loomed before them like they were looking through the bending screen of an old broken television. Everything, from the air to the buildings to the people to the freaks, shimmered behind a patchwork of gray and color, shifting and changing as though encased in a giant monochrome soap bubble. It was as if someone had dropped a giant mirrored lens across the street in front of them, and it was through this shifting looking glass that Jane and the rest of the rapidly appearing Legion now viewed reality—or at least, reality in one direction.

They were a few hundred feet away from the barrier, surrounded by untainted police barricades and squad cars, and here, all color remained normal. It was only ahead, beyond some stark yet invisible line, where the colors of the world warped and twisted—a ring of desaturation extending horizontally in either direction where inside lay the trapped people and abominations, rippling in patches of gray and technicolor and screaming unceasingly into the void.

"Yo," said Will to Jane's left, his voice shaking, uncharacteristically high, "could Ana Bloodbane do that?"

"Hey!" someone called before anyone had time to answer. With great difficulty, Jane tore her eyes away from the impossible scene and looked behind her to see a police officer frantically waving. "Get back!"

Then she heard it. From inside the bubble, the world of patch-work monochrome, a sound rang forth like the ringing of a bell or a great hammer striking an anvil. Suddenly, a ripple raced through the surreal world, and everything shifted. The dead bodies—the ones that moments ago had lain motionless, desiccated, or dismembered between the living—suddenly began moving, crawling, their limbs repairing, flesh flowing back and reattaching, stumbling to their feet as their unpeeling mouths abruptly opened into cries from resurrected vocal cords. Powers erupted, and all of a sudden, the dead were whole again, old again, young again, a myriad of ages, all screaming—and around them, the living twisted too. Some shrieked and shriveled, falling on their knees, disintegrating into corpses; others gasped for air as their bodies rapidly aged; yet, before her disbelieving eyes, Jane saw others getting younger. Adults sobbed as lines sucked back into their faces, as their limbs shrank, as they reverted to children, then babies, and then, for some, nothing.

Awake yet trapped in this terrible fever dream, Jane could do nothing but watch as hundreds upon hundreds of people collapsed into pools of blood and viscera, while around them, others rose from nothing, and corpses struggled back to life. And all the while, the monsters around them shuddered, continuing to mutate further and further, growing ever more twisted, ever larger.

There was no explanation, no reason, no pattern—only horror. Ten thousand denizens of New York City staggered through the streets in front of them engulfed in waking hell, shifting between life and death.

And then, the bubble of corruption pushed out.

Jane recoiled.

"Nope," said Matt, immediately scrambling backward. "Nope, nope, nope, screw that!"

The field, the desaturated patchwork, whatever you wanted to call it, advanced in a sudden surge toward them, claiming another five feet in every direction like the mouth of some gigantic toothless mollusk intent on swallowing the earth. Everything that had been alive or dead inside it now began changing, twisting and mutating in the same surreal horror as that which had already been claimed. Jane watched as a bird collapsed to bones while a rat remerged from blank pavement, its mouth open in a voiceless squeal as it reassembled from a bloody stain. The colors twitched, the gray shapes shifting, and those who had been unborn grew to life again, the dead unfurling back through decades, the living crumbling to death. It was chaos. Pure, horrifying chaos. And through it all raced flashes of a thousand powers, and the air rang with a ceaseless whirlwind of screams.

Jane had absolutely no idea what was going on. But it was very, very bad.

Beside her, in the Legion's colors, Giselle's face was as pale as porcelain. "Get clear!" she yelled at the police, and in a rush of air, she vanished, the blur of her racing back and forth through the streets, sweeping over stragglers, survivors. Will swore something frenzied and disappeared in a pop, only to reemerge a few moments later farther away from the gray zone transporting more Acolytes. All around them, figures in crimson and gold flashed into existence, the Academy's teleporters deploying the Legion en masse. Jane swung her eyes around, heart hammering, as a vision from another world returned to her.

A twisting pit, darker than the stars, swallowing all life in existence.

"Stay here!" she roared, shooting straight up into the air as Matt took cover behind a police car, a comet of blazing gold burning in defiance of the seething gray. Jane climbed above the city skyline, beneath the clouds, until she was hundreds of feet clear of the monochrome field, until she could clearly see—

Mother of God. It was a dome, an enormous shimmering bubble wobbling precariously atop the Earth, all color within it warped or drained. As she watched, looking down upon this aberration spanning a radius of ten blocks, another humming peal rang out, and Jane stared in horror as the bubble seemed to suck in, almost drawing breath, before once again expanding, its borders pushing infinitesimally out. Even up here, she could hear the people and the monsters screaming. There must be thousands of them—tens of thousands. Writhing, teeming. Surging through lifetimes in seconds, dying from old age then suffering it in reverse, all while beside them, hellish abominations continued to mutate, growing further heads or hair or teeth or limbs, mutating beyond insanity.

Holy crap. Holy crap. Holy crap.

Jane dropped back down to where they'd landed, slamming so hard into the ground she sent cracks running through the pavement. A moment later, Giselle sped back into existence beside her, Will racing to join them from behind the police lines mere moments after appearing with more Legion and some of their black cratelike weapon kits in tow.

"That's the last of them!" he shouted. Giselle nodded, her eyes wide and frantic.

"Police are fanning out around the city," she reported. "Army's mobilizing. I've spread our teams as best we can around the perimeter. Azleena, order everyone to stand by and prepare to move back. Clear the buildings, pick up stragglers and strays. Nobody touches that barrier. I repeat, *nobody* touches that goddamn barrier."

"Copy."

"There's something in there," Jane reported, wind racing through her hair, her eyes wild. The three of them turned to face her, Matt pale, Will shaking, Giselle's jaw set. "In the middle. I think I see it."

"What is it?" demanded Giselle.

"I don't know. But the energy's spreading out evenly from the center."

"What the hell is going on?" Matt cried. Around them, law enforcement and now soldiers were streaming in all directions, shouting their own orders, though their eyes returned always to the Legion, gravitating nervously toward the pockets of crimson and gold. The police officers near the four of them in particular edged progressively closer, straining their ears over the screams and shouting to hear what was being said by the Legion's leader and Lady Dawn. Jane ignored them—now was not the time.

Suddenly, a gale buffeted into them, the wind surging as the bubble shivered, sucking in then expelling out in the same second a surge of foul-smelling air. The gust carried a swath of leaves and loose newspaper past them, only to shoot back a second later into the field, where they too rotted and blossomed and disintegrated. The debris landed at the feet of the nearest abominations, which as Jane watched, shuddered with twisting new limbs, bones pushing through skin, tumors erupting from its torso.

"What is this?!" Matt repeated, eyes bulging with terror.

"I don't know," swore Jane. "But I'm stopping it."

She turned toward the bubble.

"CLEAR!" she shouted, and to a man, everyone rushed to obey her, the soldiers and police officers falling back behind Jeeps and squad cars as Jane faced the encroaching nightmare head-on. Out of the corner of her eye, Jane saw Giselle and Will drag Matt clear, the human not really resisting, merely standing with his mouth open and staring flabbergasted at everything going on. Jane forced her focus forward. Shifting her feet, she locked her knees, bared her teeth, and cupped her hands behind her, releasing the barrier that restrained the power of Captain Dawn.

Suddenly, the air crackled with waves of golden light as burning, rippling power coalesced between Jane's palms. With a wordless cry, she spun, firing a torrential blast of energy, the air swirling wild as a searing beam erupted from her hands and slammed into the gray-stained field. She poured through more and more power, and to her utter relief, Jane watched as the bubble slowly began to buckle and then fold, pushed inward like a pillow punched in by a fist. Yet, the retreat was sluggish—every inch the light pushed forward the field resisted, and when after a moment Jane lowered her hands and let the golden beam fade, the surreal energy inside began immediately creeping back out, slithering toward the ground it had previously claimed.

She glanced over her shoulder, cupped hands still wafting wisps of energy, breathing hard as Matt, Will, and Giselle rejoined her.

"Okay!" said Will, his face drenched in relief though his voice still rang unnaturally high. "Positive! We have movement!"

Giselle leveled her gaze at Jane.

"Can you maintain fire?" the speedster asked.

"Until the sun dies out," Jane promised. Her breath was coming hard, but the heat inside her veins did not waver. Matt squeezed her shoulder in wordless support. "I've got to get close, though. I've got to go in."

Matt's face fell. "Into the death bubble?" he asked, sounding worried.

"It's not a bubble," Jane told him. "Something's releasing energy. I can feel it; it's everywhere inside, coming out nonstop. But Dawn's stronger. I can push through. Give me time, and I can reach whatever's in the middle, find a way to—"

But whatever Jane was going to say was suddenly and irretrievably cut short, as from behind them came a horrific, bloodcurdling scream. The four teammates spun to find one of the police officers—a bald, hooked-nosed man—pointing toward the gray zone. They followed his finger.

To where, on the very edge of the barrier, one of the abominations had emerged.

"Kill it!" someone cried, their voice rising to a fever pitch. Beside her, Giselle cursed, and Will involuntarily stumbled.

At the outer ring of the bubble, where the untainted world met the field of shifting gray, a monster crawled toward them, its body a jumble of crooked limbs protruding from a torso the size of a car. As Jane watched, the creature's locks of rust-colored hair, which extended some twenty feet in tendrils from its shoulders, stabbed into the street, throwing up chunks of asphalt as it dragged itself along, pulling its back half out from the bubble. The second its body was free, the creature reared on its hind limbs like some kind of horrific bulbous centipede, roaring from three misshapen heads as searing liquid metal belched from openings across its belly. The ground around it shivered, shimmering into mud, as all around the creature giant icicles erupted, frozen spikes the size of a person.

Jane had only pushed the bubble back a few inches—but the creature had been mere inches from the border. Now free, its myriad eyes swung around in delirious fury, and it abruptly surged forward.

"JESUS TAP-DANCING CHRIST!" she heard Matt shout, but Jane did not hesitate. She raised her hand, took split-second aim at the abomination, and unleashed a stream of golden death. There was a deafening *boom*, and the creature's screams abruptly fell silent. Jane lowered her arm, the monster reduced to ash.

"Okay," she said, turning back to Giselle, the remains of the monstrosity blowing away behind her. "Complication."

"The field's keeping them in place," said the speedster, running her hands through her hair. "If we push it back, those things are exposed."

"And they are *pissed*," Matt added.

"If I'm blasting it, I can't be blasting them," said Jane. Giselle swore, glancing back at the police and soldiers behind her, as well as the spread-out pockets of the Legion.

"Right," she stated. Giselle rolled back her shoulders and cracked her knuckles. "Looks like today, we kill monsters."

"Is it always this wild outside?" asked Matt incredulously. Everyone ignored him.

Giselle put her finger to her ear. "Az," she said, "You following?"

"Always."

"Spread the word; defensive lines. I want armed flyers and anyone who can hit long range on a rooftop. Meteormancers cleared for Category Five, but keep it contained to the top of that dome. Some of those things can fly."

"Copy."

"You!" Giselle shouted, rounding on the nearby police and military members who had been edging toward them, faces pale and weapons clenched. "Get on your comms! You're under Legion jurisdiction now; you listen to what we say when we say it. You reinforce our lines. Got it?!" The cops and soldiers wilted under her gaze and began quickly nodding. Jane watched as several reached trembling for their radios or gave frantic hand signals to distant comrades.

Giselle continued, undeterred. "You are doing one of three things!" she barked. "You are clearing civilians! You are falling back when we tell you! And you are taking aim at anything that comes through that barrier, and you are killing it dead!" She paused, allowing the message to be relayed. "This is as simple as it gets, people! If it scares you, annihilate it! Make your powers useful! Make yourself known!"

In the city beyond, the bubble pulsed.

"Jane?" Giselle called.

"On it." She began striding forward, palms glowing gold. Matt hung back, staying near Giselle.

"Az," the speedster called, hand once more flicking to her ear, "see if you can bring a satellite over and link military comms. I'd prefer—"

Suddenly, Jane's ear filled with static. She came to a halt in the middle of the street, glancing back over her shoulder. Giselle had stopped midway through giving instructions, furiously poking at her own earpiece.

"Az?" she repeated. "Azleena? Come in. Morningstar, do you copy? Morningstar. Hello."

"That's not good," Jane heard Matt murmur. Beside him, over at the police barricades, the speedster had taken out her comm-link and was swearing furiously while prodding at it. Her eyes met Jane's, and their gazes swept together over to the shimmering bubble. Giselle aggressively waved her on with one hand while simultaneously beckoning Will over with the other.

"Jump back to the Academy," she heard Giselle tell him. Jane turned with some hesitancy back toward the undulating gray field. She continued to advance, her palms aglow. "Something's wrong with comms. See if it's on our end, or what the—"

"Got it," interrupted Will. Jane glanced unconsciously once more over her shoulder in time to see the teleporter screw up his eyes.

Nothing happened.

Jane's heart dropped.

Will opened his eyes. "I'm disrupted," he said. His brow furrowed, and he rapidly blinked. "I'm disrupted; why am I disrupted?"

"Morningstar, come in, Morningstar, I—You, yes you, in the vest, is your radio—Give it here, I— Hello? Hello, come in, anyone. Hello—"

Jane stood frozen in place. In front of her, another haunting peal rang out from the field.

"JANE!" Giselle shouted, rounding on the empath and stabbing viciously with her finger. "THE BUBBLE!"

"Right." Jane turned reluctantly back to face the gray zone, continuing with slow steps forward. The unnatural barrier rose a hundred feet in front of her, shimmering in swirling colors. *Focus. Delegate and prioritize; one problem at a time.* Jane advanced until she was only about a foot away from the edge of the bubble, the horrors beyond it shifting in unnerving, desaturated color. She took a deep breath, golden energy swirling around her, and tensed her hands.

With a final moment's hesitation, she glanced back over to where Matt, Giselle, and Will were still standing. Giselle's hands were raised, and Jane could see her shouting as, beyond her, teams from the Legion broke into a run. Will pointed in the opposite direction to the bubble before turning and vaulting over a police barrier, running frantically away from the battle site. Matt was just standing there, his mouth closed, watching everything. His eyes met Jane's. Despite the worry plastered all over his face, he forced a small smile and gave Jane a thumbs-up. She took a deep breath.

Matt's head exploded.

"NO!"

Jane barely heard the gunshot. One second, he was standing there, smiling. The next, there was just this *pop* and an explosion of red shards where his head had been. Blood, bone, and brain flew everywhere. The police officers yelped, instinctively diving for cover, leaving only Giselle—standing rigid with shock three feet away, blood drenched all over her hair and face and armor—beside a body without a head.

Nothing moved. For a moment, the wind stopped, the screaming stopped, the world seemed not to breathe. Jane's hands shook, her head swimming, ringing and light, breathing faster, faster, faster. All thoughts of the bubble and the monsters fell to dust, forgotten. There was no danger. There was no war.

There was only Matt, headless, teetering in slow motion . . .

. . . and collapsing to the ground.

He landed with a muffled thud.

And Jane screamed.

Screamed and screamed and screamed, light exploding off her, flinging back the field, the police cars, annihilating everything, a tempest of blinding fury which expanded, vaporizing half of New York and—

NO.

Without thinking, without caring, without a single thought for the Child or fate or consequences, Jane lunged for the swirling sapphire vortex between her fingers and hurtled back, tearing her mind free from reality and her body free from time. In an instant, the nightmare infinite engulfed her, gouging strips from her flesh, screaming into her soul—but Jane screamed back. All her anger, all her fear, all of it screamed out until her lungs were close to bursting, until her breath churned blood and fire, her fingers raking against the endless colors, clawing threads, clawing black. It was not instinct this time that filled her; this time, it was rage. Jane knew what she was doing, knew the danger, knew the pain— she just didn't care.

The infinite weave, the endless possibilities, all of it spun out from her consciousness, binding around her eyes and wrists and throat in shining wires, dragging her down—but Jane tore them all away. Screaming in fury, she ripped herself free, howling defiance at time, screaming hate and pain and blood—

Until her burning hands clenched around a moment, and she wrenched herself back through the veil.

"Yo," said Will to Jane's left, his voice uncharacteristically shaky and high, "could Ana Bloodbane do that?"

Reality rushed back into focus, and Jane's head snapped forward, gasping like she'd been drowned. She spun around wildly, looking wide-eyed either side of her. They were still in the streets of New York. The field of undeath still loomed before them, a motley gray bubble sinking deep into the Earth inside of which writhed an endless sea of people trapped in cycles of birth, decay, and aging, and monsters mutating into grotesque forms.

And Matt was still there, beside her. Alive. Intact.

Jane staggered, her vision swimming. She grabbed Giselle by the arm.

"We're under attack," she gasped. Panting, Jane doubled over, wracked by sudden nausea, feeling like her head was about to explode. Her eyes danced with patches of light, and the world swam with false color, her ears ringing, her mouth suddenly bone-dry.

"Jane?" she heard Giselle ask, her voice flush with alarm. Somewhere beyond the spinning world, she felt the speedster's hands grab on to her, trying to hold Jane upright, Giselle's blurry face a mask of concern. "Hey, hey, you alright? What the hell is—"

Jane shook her head, her knees shaking, trying to keep her legs straight. To her left she heard Matt's worried muttering, and a moment later, she felt him slip beneath her arm, holding her upright. But support wasn't what Jane wanted. Gritting her teeth, she clenched down hard with the arm Matt had maneuvered himself under, locking him in place as she threw out a rippling transparent energy field, ready to deflect anything within ten feet.

"Back," she hissed. She stumbled, limping away from the bubble, forcing her head up, looking for Will. Her eyes locked onto the teleporter, causing him to flinch. "Morningstar. Go. That's an order."

"Belay that!" Giselle barked, aggressively pushing Jane free. She stepped beside Will and stared at Jane, expression ripening into incredulity. "You're not going back; what the hell are you talking about? Look around you; this is a crisis, we need—"

"I'm coming back," Jane snarled, baring her teeth. "There's a gunman here; they've got sights on Matt." She heard Giselle gasp. "There isn't time. We're about to lose communications, teleporting, I— I don't know, maybe something about the barrier is—"

"Or this is a kill zone," Giselle murmured. She stared at Jane, her face hard. "How do you know?"

"There's no time to explain," replied Jane. She forced herself upright, the light inside her burning against the nausea. "Trust me. Get him safe, and after this is done, I'll tell you everything."

For about two seconds, Giselle did not move or speak, only stood stock-still with her mouth half open, frozen in the midst of saying something. Her eyes bored into Jane's, and for a moment, Jane could only guess at the wheels turning, the thoughts racing inside the speedster's head.

Then Giselle's mouth snapped shut, and her hand shot to her earpiece.

"Az," she ordered, "get Nat spinning up a psychic link; we're about to lose comms. Accelerate deployment. Military, LE, they're under our jurisdiction; have them clear civilians and make their powers known. I'm sending Will back with Jane and Matt. I want a satellite overhead in five, and your best guess as to what the mother-loving hell we're dealing with in ten. Matt stays with you. You"—she jabbed a finger at Will's chest—"you take them back, you get my info, you strap it to her"—she pointed at Jane—"and you drop her outside the Disruptance zone, wherever the hell that ends up being. I don't care if she's got to fly down from orbit, I want her back, and I want to know what we're up against." She glared between the two of them. "Got it?"

"Wait—" started Matt, but Jane didn't need to hear anything more. She nodded in unison with the teleporter, grabbed Will's wrist, held tight to Matt's shoulders with her other arm, and gritted her teeth.

"Go!" she shouted. "Go!"

A moment later, Will closed his eyes, and the wind and screams of the twisted city were replaced with crushing dark. The sensation pressed in around her for a moment, then the pressure vanished, and Jane opened her eyes to find them at the end of the Legion's armory tunnel.

Suddenly, her ear filled with hissing. Beside her, Matt tapped the side of his head.

"Anyone else getting a bad line?" he asked.

"Goddamn, you weren't kidding," Will muttered. He pressed his finger to his earpiece. "Giselle? Giselle, come in, you—"

"She's dropped out," came Azleena's voice. "They all have."

"Just then?"

"As of two seconds ago."

Will swore. "I'm going back." He scrunched up his eyes, but to Jane's delirious surprise, nothing happened—the teleporter did not vanish, only continued to stand there in the tunnel with a clenched expression, a thin wisp of sulfur smoke rising from his back.

"I'm blocked," said Will, opening his eyes. There was fear in them.

Jane shook her head.

"It can't be everywhere. Figure out where the barrier is, get as close as you can. I'll get the info and come find you."

"Hurry," Will urged. He started climbing the stairs to the outside, heading toward the edge of the grounds and the forest, leaving Matt and Jane facing back toward the armory in the other direction.

"Meet you out front," said Jane. The teleporter gave her a quick nod and was up the stairs and out the rear hatch before anyone could say anything further.

Immediately, Jane's shoulders sagged. In the dark of the tunnel, she staggered forward, gloved hand clutching for support against the rock wall, her mind and body churning.

"Jane?" Matt whispered, urgent, terrified. "You okay? What's happening?"

Jane shook her head, fighting fresh waves of nausea, trying to burn the tremoring feeling from her bones. She reached deep into the power of Dawn and let the golden energy suffuse her, lighting up the tunnel, feeling the sudden rush prop her up. "It's a trap," she finally managed to get out. She urged Matt forward, and they broke into a loping run, boots pounding on the earthen floor. "Someone shot you. The moment I stepped away, they just—"

Even through the echoes of their footsteps, Jane heard Matt catch his breath. "Who?" he whispered.

"I don't know. I couldn't see, but they were far away, and I just—I did it again." They ran onward through the darkness. Matt remained silent. Jane glanced over, seeing his empty expression. "Are you angry?"

For a few seconds, Matt said nothing. "Right now," he answered finally, grimacing, "I'm alive, and we've got bigger problems."

Jane's heart soared. Right then, though she felt like puking, she could've kissed him. "Agreed."

They ran as fast as their legs could carry them. By the time they came through to the armory bunker, Jane's nausea had disintegrated, and she grabbed Matt by the hand and pulled him forward. They slammed out the doors and raced in a sprint across the Academy grounds, Matt doing his best to keep up with Jane's rapidly increasing pace. They hurtled inside, past a dozen shocked and confused Acolytes, and ran round and round the stairs until they reached the door to the computer room. Jane barged inside.

". . . and if you tell me to turn it off and on again, I swear I will—" Azleena's voice abruptly cut off at the sight of them. "Wait, hold on, Jacqui. What the actual"—the genius turned to the pair and unleashed a stream of virulent curses—"is going on?"

Jane strode forward. Behind her, Matt doubled over, panting, one hand against the doorway.

"Freaking cardio," he muttered, though a moment later, he moved into the room proper. Jane rounded Azleena's desk, no longer sick or tired, instead alert and fully restored, her tattoo glowing.

"The landing site is a kill zone," she explained. "Someone almost shot Matt. There's a field there of some kind of energy that is making people age and mutate and die over and over. That's either interfering with our comms, or—"

"Or it's our missing wave disrupter," the genius finished. She fixed Jane with a piercing gaze. "This field. I received initial reports. People are aging and dying?"

"And de-aging and resurrecting and turning into babies and bones and puddles of pre-baby goop," Jane confirmed. She shook her head.

"Except that's only half of them. The other half seem to be growing unnaturally, like parts of them are randomly overdeveloping, or other whole people are growing inside them, and it just keeps happening and happening until they're freaking twelve feet tall with four heads and tentacles."

"Holy hell. Is it Bloodbane?"

Jane shook her head. "I don't know. I don't think so. Unless she's wildly upped her game." Her eyes burned into Azleena. "These bodies aren't combining. They're changing, growing. And they're alive. They're using powers. None of Fleshtide's corpses ever did that."

"No matter how big they merged," Azleena agreed. "Can the field be penetrated?"

"You can walk into it if you feel like becoming a deathless monster. My energy repels it. I'm pretty sure I can bring it to heel; I've just got to get close and really lay into it—"

"Jane," she heard Matt murmur. Jane glanced over to see him standing in the middle of the room, his face pained. "You have to go back."

"I know," she replied. "Give me a second. You heard Giselle; we don't understand what's happening. The more I tell Azleena, the better—"

"I agree," the genius interrupted, staring over at Matt. "This has about a dozen aspects I don't understand, and it may be we make things a thousand times worse if we just charge in."

But for some reason, this only made Matt look more distressed. "There isn't time," he whispered.

Jane scowled, annoyed—but something about his expression made her stop halfway through a rebuttal. Matt was scared. Really, really scared.

"Azleena," Jane ordered, looking down at the little genius girl. "Do you have a mech suit?"

"Yes, what of it?"

"Matt needs to get in."

"It's mine," the genius protested. "It's not calibrated for him; the interface is beyond his intellectual capabilities. He'll either be unable to move, or it'll fry his brain."

"It doesn't have to work." Jane scowled. "He literally just has to stand there, here, with you, while I go back to New York. In case someone tries to shoot him."

"Wouldn't it be preferential for him to be able to move?" Azleena asked with an exasperated shrug, but at that same moment, something on her computer beeped, and the genius swung back around in her chair.

"I've got a satellite coming into alignment," she told them. "Wait two seconds, and you can bring my theories to Giselle."

"Jane," Matt whispered. "Please."

"Human, shush," Azleena snapped, rising out of her chair to glare at him over the screens. "What do you think is going to be more useful, Lady Dawn flying in with no knowledge and backup, or Lady Dawn knowing what she's doing? Have a teaspoon of goddamn patience."

Jane hesitated, torn between the girl's glare and Matt's silent plea. She knew Azleena was right—objectively, Azleena was right—so why did the look on Matt's face trouble her so much?

"Matt, it's fine," she reassured him. "The bubble's growing, but it's only by a couple of feet every few minutes. Giselle is down there with the Legion; they can see what's going on, and they can keep backing people to safety. They can—"

"There," cut off Azleena. "Feed established. Come on, clouds, move. There, we've got—" An image appeared on the screen, a bird's-eye view of New York City. In its center, around what looked to be Times Square, shimmered a mottled gray dome, an infected blister rising from the planet's skin.

"What in the—" Azleena's ferocious swearing trailed off the rest of her sentence. "Look at that. What even is that? It's like nothing I've ever—" On the other side of the computer, multiple windows were popping up, black lines of characters streaming down. "This is impossible. Half of these readings are nonsense. There must be electromagnetic interference; this is—Wait. I've seen this before."

"Jane," Matt whispered.

"You have?" Jane urged Azleena, ignoring Matt's pained pleas. "Where? What is it?"

"Jane."

"Not exactly like this," the genius responded, the words gushing out in a torrent, almost a stream of consciousness, "but similar in their unsimilarity, lack of cohesion with regular forces, resistance to measurement. It upends conventional understanding, and then you're left with absolute illogic breaking not just human ability but physics. I—" Her words skidded to a halt, and she spun to face Jane, her eyes swirling with a touch of madness.

"Charles and Edward Lewis. The Brothers Darkness. The combined ability to create and control actual physical dark rather than simply the absence of light. Nothing anyone could do could touch it; it was like an enveloping, nongravitational black hole. Even Captain Dawn struggled, until in the end, he was swallowed by it, and I guess fully unleashed his powers or something and finally managed to break through, but . . . but the energy reacted the same way, this unnatural field that was somehow penetrable but reactive, affected but resistant to the power of Dawn, like two forces of equal measure recognizing each other and being able to interact and—" Azleena's mouth froze. "Bloody hell," she murmured slowly, drawing shaking, shallow breaths. "It's a Divine."

Jane's heart skipped a beat. "I don't—"

"It has to be," Azleena said, rounding on her. "It has to be. Look at this; one power covering dozens of city blocks? This is one of a kind. This is Divine power. This is Dawn-grade—"

A sudden red pinging on the corner of her screen sent Azleena's words stumbling to a halt. Her brow furrowed as she turned and clicked on it, her expression becoming incredulous.

"Intruder alert?" she cried. "Intruder alert, why are there—Why are there three different groups of intruders on my freaking grounds?!" Azleena's hand flew to her microphone. "Cykes, heads up, we've got company. Link up the skeleton crew. I'm texting you locations—Jesus Christ, they're in the armory. Did someone let them in? Did you—?"—she rounded on Jane, her eyes wide—"Did you see anyone?"

On the screens in front of her, beside the satellite image of New York, security camera feeds flashed with images of people in combat gear racing through the tunnel with assault rifles. Jane gritted her teeth.

"Dammit," she swore, and she spun toward the door, preparing to run back outside. Her gaze swept over Matt, standing alone and unmoving in the center of the room, staring out the window, his eyes wide, his face blank.

"Too late," he whispered, and the words dripped like cold poison from his lips.

Suddenly, on the feed across Azleena's screens, the bubble pulsed. As Jane turned, breath catching in her chest, it began rippling from the center, shivering, before the rippling stopped. The energy grew tense, seeming for a moment to almost become firm.

Then it exploded.

On the satellite feed, a wave of gray shot out, and suddenly, Azleena's comms were live again, erupting in a horrifying cacophony over her speakers as hundreds of voices simultaneously shrieked and screamed. Jane could only watch, heart hammering, as a shock wave of corruption spread across the Earth in a ceaseless, relentless circle, enveloping first Manhattan, then New York, then, as the video feed pulled back, the surrounding county and—

"Oh God," Azleena whispered. And as she turned and joined Matt's gaze out the window, suddenly, to the east, in the distance, they saw the sky had grown dark. Jane's eyes widened. In the center of the room, Matt slumped, the light dimming, mumbling something indistinct as he stared into the encroaching apocalypse.

NO.

This time, when Jane stepped back, there was no feeling inside her—only horror, only gray. She floated in sudden silence, in endless darkness amidst infinite color, seeing through an eye the size of a postage stamp as a wave of undeath flowed out and smothered the entire world. It was not her desire to go back this time that drove her—it was her only choice. Hardly any fractals screamed, for her thoughts were empty, momentarily devoid of emotion. Her hands were transparent crystal, her mind a mound of colored salt dissolving beneath black, endless waves. Shock, despair, held her together. And an understanding of where to go. A used path re-trodden. Cold fingers digging into an old wound.

She opened her eyes.

"Yo," said Will to Jane's left, his voice uncharacteristically shaky and high, "could Ana Bloodbane do that?"

Jane's eyes snapped open. Almost instantly, she doubled over, hurling a stream of vomit onto the windswept pavement. Shouts of concern rose up all around her, plus cries of surprise some way back from among the police. Jane staggered forward, falling to one knee. Her head was spinning, ears pounding with straining heartbeats.

"Jane!" she heard Matt shouting. "Jane!"

Back in New York. The same street, the same moment, the same— She forced her eyes up, her head swaying, the edges of her vision so blurry they bordered on black. She struggled to stay upright.

"It's okay," she tried to murmur. "I'm okay."

Once more, the doom loomed before them. Once more, the wall of patchwork gray, swirling life and sucking undeath, the hideous screams of the twisted and the damned. Divine. Divine energy. There was a person at the center of this. Another being almost as powerful as her.

Jane curled her lip and spat out a thick wad of blood. *Almost.*

She pushed to her feet, surging golden power through every fiber of her being, fighting to hold her shoulders straight. "I'm fine," she told them. "Something I ate. Sorry. Just getting it back up. I'm fine." Ahead of her, the bubble pulsed and inched forward. Jane felt, more than saw, the others take an involuntary step back, all save for Matt, who'd bent down to help her.

Beside her, in the Legion's colors, Giselle's face had turned pale as porcelain. "You okay?" she asked in evident concern. Jane nodded, and reluctantly, Giselle moved away, gaze lingering on Jane as she turned to face the people nearby. "Get clear!" she yelled at the police, then in a rush of air, she vanished, the blur of her racing around the streets. Will swore something nervous and disappeared with a *pop*, only to reemerge a few moments later farther away from the gray zone transporting more Acolytes. All around them, figures in crimson and gold flashed into existence, the Legion deploying en masse.

Jane swung her gaze around, heart hammering, consumed by visions of futures past.

"Hey," Matt whispered, sounding worried. His face pressed gently against her cheek. "You okay?"

He reached for her hand. Jane took it, feeling the nothingness within.

"No," she whispered, too soft for anyone else to hear. "I can't. We keep . . . You're in danger."

"What? How do you—?" Matt's face grew white, and Jane saw him quickly take in her sickened state, the terror swimming in her eyes. "Time travel."

"Yes."

"What happened?"

"This is round three."

"Jesus."

"I can't do another," Jane mumbled. The golden light flowing through her felt like ceaseless air trying to inflate a fluttering tube man riddled with holes. "I'm sorry. I just can't."

"Jane, no. Don't—"

"We have to . . . We have to . . ."

Suddenly, Giselle sped back into existence beside her. A moment later, Will also appeared behind the police lines with more crimson-clad fighters and the Legion's black cratelike weapon kits in tow. He dropped hands and raced to join them, vaulting a barricade.

"That's the last of them!" he shouted. Giselle nodded, her eyes wide and frantic. Matt and Jane exchanged silent glances.

"Police are fanned out around the city," Giselle reported. "Army's mobilizing into parts. I've spread our teams as best we can around the perimeter; Azleena, order everyone to—"

"Wait," Jane's pained voice crawled out, cutting the speedster off. Giselle turned to her, face worried.

"Jane?" she asked. "What? Are you still not feeling good?"

"No, I—That's not important." Jane shrugged out from underneath Matt's arm, trying to stand on her own. Her swaying eyes fixed onto Will and Giselle, and she stared at them, pleading. "Please. I need you to listen. We don't have much time. Just listen, please. Don't say anything."

Giselle fell silent. She and Will exchanged glances then looked at Matt, who quietly nodded. Giselle touched her ear, turning off her comms.

"Go."

"We're under attack," Jane told them, and to their credit, though Giselle and Will both blanched, neither interrupted. "They're getting in place. They've got guns; they could be aiming at us right now." As she said it, Jane gritted her teeth and groggily pushed out her barrier, flaring the energy to protect against incoming projectiles. "I don't know how, I don't know who, but they're trying to kill Matt." She paused, surveying their faces. "In a few minutes, that field is going to expand," she said, pointing at the shifting gray barrier. "I can stop it. But it'll take everything I have. While I'm doing it, I can't protect—"

"Fine," said Giselle, quickly catching on. "Will, jump them back to Morningstar; you can get Azleena's take on all this and—"

"No." Again, Jane interrupted, shaking her head, her chest heaving. "The second I leave here or walk away from him, you lose comms. A Disruptance field goes up."

"Over the entire—?"

"Over the entire city, yes!" Jane almost screamed. "Shut up, just shut up and listen. If I go back, this spreads! Everywhere!" She gestured wildly at the gray shimmering wall. "Everybody loses. Everything dies!"

"Okay," replied Giselle, thinking fast. "So just Matt goes back, alone."

"No!" Jane wrung her hands together. "Last time, they . . ." She shook her head. "They're tracking him, okay? If he goes anywhere away from me, they're just going to follow, and they'll—"

"They're tracking him?" gaped Will. "How?"

"I don't know!" Jane shouted, throwing up her hands, almost tearing her hair out. "I don't know! Maybe through your jump scars; maybe someone's betrayed—It doesn't matter, okay? This is a trap! This is a trap!"

For a moment, the four fell silent. Fifty feet away, the screams of the Deathless intensified as the barrier let out another spine-tingling peal.

"Okay," said Giselle. "Alright. So you handle the bubble; Matt stays here. We protect Matt."

"Except the second I start pushing it in, those things will be released," replied Jane, gesturing toward the monsters. "You can't fight them and keep him safe."

"Okay, so maybe just a few of us—"

"No!" Jane wanted to scream. "It won't be enough. We can't trust—They'll have thought of—I can't—" The words died upon her lips as she gazed up at Giselle, her mouth metallic with the taste of blood. "Sound a retreat."

"What?" Giselle yelped.

"Have the Legion retreat!" Jane was almost shouting. "Protect Matt, stay around him. I can do this; if any of those things come near me, they'll get incinerated and—"

"And leave the rest of the city to die?" Giselle's voice rang high with disbelief. "Jane, there are thousands of people here!"

"I don't care!"

"I do!" The speedster's eyes flicked to Matt before returning to focus, unyielding, on Jane. "I am not abandoning thousands of people!"

"Matt will—"

"One life cannot outweigh thousands!" Giselle shouted. "Tens of thousands!" Her voice lowered, and she turned to Matt, flushed but unashamed. "Matt, I'm sorry; I love you, but—"

And to Jane's utter horror, Matt shook his head. "You're right," he said. "There's no choice."

"No!"

"Jane." Matt's voice was firm. He turned to her, his face stony. "There isn't time. It's simple math."

"But you—"

"Every person out there," he said, "is someone's son or daughter. Someone's friend or girlfriend or dad or mom. I can't let them die for me. They shouldn't die for me. They wouldn't—" He abruptly stopped. "Giselle's right. The Legion's supposed to save everyone."

Silence—horrible, trembling silence—swept through the group. Jane's chest heaved with shaking breaths, her arms quivering, despair clawing at her throat.

"Then what do we do?" she whispered. For a moment, no one said anything.

And to her utter amazement, it was not Giselle that answered but Matt.

"You said it yourself," her boyfriend murmured. Jane looked up at him to see an odd expression creeping over his face. "It's a trap."

Suddenly, in the middle of the windswept streets, facing down death and abominations, Matt Callaghan laughed and straightened his shoulders. "This is a trap," he repeated, and he shook his head. "It's the only thing that makes sense. Whoever"—his lips twitched—"is out to get me, this is their play. How? Who the hell knows, but we're boxed in." He paused, glancing between the three of them. "Way I see it," he continued, "we've got three options." Matt held up his hand and began counting on his fingers. "Option one, I stay and they kill me. Option two, I leave and they kill me—"

"We don't—" Giselle began, but Matt cut her off.

"They will. It's the only logical outcome. Because I'm either here or there, here or at Morningstar, hiding among the skeleton crew. Which means they're ready for it, which means they're waiting. Ninety-nine percent of the Legion is here, and my family is there, and I'd bet dollars to donuts I know how that plays out. Maybe they've got a team standing by. Maybe it's the same one they've got here. It doesn't matter; this is too well planned. Wherever I go, they're coming for me."

"That's two choices," murmured Will.

Matt counted off a third finger. "Well, option three is Jane and I both go back and the world dies, so let's maybe leave that one in the reject pile." He turned to Jane. "The communications blackout, the Disruptances. How long will it take them to go off?"

Jane saw the truth behind his question. "It varies. Different times."

Matt nodded. "They're controlling it," he said. "Waiting to spring the trap. Which means this party doesn't start until we want it to. Well," he corrected himself, looking over as the gray bubble ominously lurched forward, "within reason."

Jane swung an arm out and blasted the field with a beam of golden energy, causing it to flinch back. "So what do we—"

"We've got one shot," Matt continued, glancing from Will to Giselle, then finally her. "They've accounted for you, and they've accounted for the Legion. But there's one thing they haven't accounted for."

"What?" asked Giselle.

At that, Matt's chest swelled, and he fixed them all with a wild, defiant grin. "Me."

There was a moment's silence. The three of them stared at Matt like he was crazy. Matt's gaze never wavered.

"You need to save the world," he said to Jane, then to Will and Giselle, "You need to save humanity. Let me save me."

"Matt"—Giselle shifted, agitated, from foot to foot—"I love the positivity, but didn't Jane say they have guns?"

"And superpowers," Will added.

"Yeah, mainly superpowers," the speedster agreed. But Matt shook his head.

"We've got surprise. They don't know we know about them. Plus, I've got this bag with"—he held up Azleena's backpack—"a whole bunch of goodies, and—and I only have to hide. That's the whole thing. Time's not with them; it's with me, and all I have to do is run and hide and survive just a little, and I can wait for you to come save me."

He glanced between the three of them. "Giselle, go give orders while comms are still up. Will, help get people into position while you can. I'm good here. I can do this." He met their eyes, and for the barest moment, the two Legionnaires hesitated. They exchanged glances.

"I . . ." Will began, but stopped before the word went anywhere. Sweeping his gaze over the chaos around him, the teleporter blew out his lips, then shook his head and gave Matt a shaky salute before disappearing into the ether. Beside him, Giselle pinched the bridge of her nose, then opened her eyes and fixed Matt with a sad, proud smile.

"Your vest's the wrong color," she told him. Then she drew a deep breath, leaned forward, and wrapped Matt in a suffocating hug. A moment later, she pulled back, kissed him on the cheek, and vanished, leaving only a gust of wind. Jane felt her shoulders shaking. Matt turned to her.

"It's fine," he murmured. It sounded honest, but Jane knew he was lying.

"I can't," she whispered. "I can't."

He squeezed her hand. "Do you trust me?"

"No," Jane sniffed.

"Smart." He leaned in close, trying to hold her gaze, trying to smile. "This'll work."

"Are you sure?"

"Not even slightly." His mouth twitched into a trembling smile. "But what's life without a little risk."

"Everything's out of control."

"That's life, isn't it?" Matt said sadly. "Sometimes, you've got to let go." His hands clenched softly around hers.

Behind them, the bubble groaned. They both turned to look at it.

"We're out of time," said Matt. He turned back to her. "On the count of three, burn white, bright as you can." Matt tightened the strings on his backpack, drawing it tight against his shoulders. "Blind them if they're watching."

"Don't do this," Jane whispered.

"It's my choice," Matt replied. He forced a smile. "And I gotta say, it's a goddamn good one. After this, I want one of those bird badge thingies."

Then he kissed her, hard on the lips, and Jane's shoulders slumped. They let go.

"Count of three."

"I love you."

"I love you too. One. Save the world."

"Run. Run like hell."

"You goddamn better believe it. Two. Bright now. Bright as you can."

"I'll come back for you."

"I know you will." For the briefest flash of an instant, Matt's eyes gleamed with something resembling defiance. "Three."

Jane threw up her hands as Matt squeezed shut his eyes, and the air around them exploded in white light, burning, blinding, a supernova in the middle of the street. From behind them, in the police line, there came shouts, cries of shock and sudden pain, and in an instant, Jane felt Matt push away.

LIFE AND DEATH

Getting to Know Home Super-Security Systems
safehome.org, copyright 1999

Your home should be your sanctuary. It's the place you return at the end of the day for comfort and safety. For most, this involves having security systems installed to protect against common types of superpowers that could be used to access their home.

Understanding more about the different systems, their features, and technology will help you make a wise choice when it comes time to purchase. This guide covers those home security products designed to specifically protect against powers (in addition to general home security systems and accessories, which you can find in our list here—give it a click!). It also shines a light on factors you may not have thought about (but that are important!). And of course, we break it down into clear language and easy-reference sections. Enjoy!

Disruptances™

- **Core Function**—A clever device developed by the Department of Defense in the 1970s, it stops teleportation into your house. An absolute necessity and a legal requirement for many homeowners.

- **How It Works**—Once plugged in, a Disruptance puts out an invisible energy field, similar to wi-fi. The science behind how this field works is complex, but in practice, as long as the Disruptance remains powered, it will prevent teleporters appearing in the protected area.
- **Key Features & Tech**—Disruptances come in a variety of sizes, ranging from small and portable to bulky and able to cover a football field. When buying, you should have the measurements of your home ready so that you know which options are most suitable. Most states will require you to have a Disruptance installed and working (like smoke detectors), and although it's possible to opt out, it can be difficult to get home and contents insurance without one. Luckily, government rebates are available when purchasing Disruptances for most homes.
- **Add-ons and Integrations**—Many current Disruptance models will come with a backup battery and tell you on the box how long they'll keep working in the event of a blackout. Most include optional anti-phasing technology, which will prevent people from walking through your walls. You can also integrate Disruptances into your home security ecosystem to get automatic alerts if anybody tries to teleport through one.

Entryway Speed Limiters ("Clackers")

- **Core Function**—Small moving rails that are installed on the inside of outer doors and windows. They prevent the entrance they are attached to from being opened at superspeed.
- **How It Works**—As a window or door moves, the rail of the Clacker (named for the quiet noise they make) moves along a series of notched teeth. If this movement is too fast, the mechanism locks firmly in place for a fraction of a second. A Clacker is not a substitute for a lock or for locking your doors and windows but is instead designed to stop anyone opening an unlocked door or window too fast for the people inside to react.

- **Key Features & Tech**—Many Clackers are targeted to homeowners who want to avoid paying for professional installation. These DIY systems include easy-to-follow instructions and can be installed with screws or adhesive. The internal mechanism works on gears and springs and does not necessarily require power.
- **Add-ons and Integrations**—Higher-tech Clacker sets come with a Bluetooth battery component and can send an alarm signal if someone attempts to open them too fast. There are also models with entry sensors that can be temporarily turned off by swiping a fob, should you have a speedster in your family who wants to regularly go in or out. It's highly recommended to place a Clacker on every outer entryway and on all opening windows.

One-Way or Tinted Windows

- **Core Function**—Glass made or treated to allow those inside to see out but those outside not to see in. Having this kind of glass in your windows protects against telepathic intrusion.
- **How It Works**—A lot of the strength of an intrusive psychic connection comes from making eye contact. Having windows people outside cannot see through means telepaths outside your home will have a much harder time interacting with any minds inside.
- **Key Features & Tech**—N/A
- **Add-ons and Integrations**—For a premium, windows can be installed with antipathic lensing that reflects a telepath's focus back onto them, causing uncomfortable feedback.

Smart Detectors

- **Core Function**—Fires or break-ins often happen when the homeowner is away, rendering the traditional smoke detector useless. But a smart detector not only sounds the alarm—it also senses for abnormalities in the environment and can send real-time alerts to your smartphone.

- **How It Works**—The app-based device installs in just minutes with plug-and-play ease. Anytime you need to access, monitor, or control the detector, just open the app and everything, including the nature of the alert, is set out right there for you.
- **Key Features & Tech**—Smart detectors come equipped to detect for a range of changes to the local environment, including sudden spikes and drops in temperature, electrical pulses, seismic vibrations, ultra-high light or sound, noxious gases and (obviously) smoke.
- **Add-ons and Integrations**—Most smart detectors offer seamless integration with third-party platforms. More advanced models can also function as motion sensors, able to be turned on and off using a keypad or remote and sensing for movement on both the visible and invisible spectrums.

Matt Callaghan ran.

As the streets of New York rang with gunfire, shouting, and explosions, the howls of wind and the cries of the undead, as soldiers in military fatigues and policemen and crimson-gold warriors raced in every direction—Matt ran. Behind him, the blinding white of Jane's flare darkened into burning gold, and a shock wave rippled through his clothes as a beam of energy shot out of her and slammed straight into the Divine field. Matt did not turn, did not look to see if Jane was succeeding, if she was pushing the corruption back. He simply ran, heart pounding, as fast as he could go.

He vaulted a police car, swerved a signpost, and with a crack, a section of sidewalk a foot away from him exploded. Gunshot. They were on him. Matt never stopped, forcing his burning legs forward with breathless energy, zigzagging this way and that, dodging on instinct, unpredictable. He hurtled around a corner into an open, abandoned Chinese restaurant, racing past half-strewn chairs and tables into the kitchen, around steel benches laden with food left forgotten and out the back through an open flyscreen door into an alleyway, around one corner, two corners, three and—There. Another open door. Matt sprinted past a dingy-looking bathroom, slammed through a swinging door, and skidded into the snack-laden aisles of a convenience store. He slid to a halt and dropped to a crouch, panting and pushing his back up against one of the shelves, packets of chips crinkling behind him.

Just had to hide. Just had to lose them. *Don't have to win, just keep on living.*

Matt breathed hard, forcing air down deep into his burning chest. He could do this. He could do it. The city was chaos, these idiots had cut off their own communications, they couldn't teleport, and there were a thousand places he could be. Once they'd lost sight of him, he could've gone in any direction. What would he do? Where would he go? A normal person would panic, keep running, maybe back out into the streets, trying to get as far away as possible. *No. Outthink them. Do the opposite.*

Matt pulled his knees to his chest, glancing around the empty store, heart racing, making doubly sure he wasn't visible from the outside. He wasn't—the aisle hid him from view. *Just wait. Wait.*

And then, beneath the sounds of distant fighting, beyond the bangs and screams, Matt felt it, worming into the back of his mind.

Telepathic contact.

Matt Callaghan. A woman's voice—cold with a hint of laughter. *You cannot run. We'll find you.*

Crap, Matt swore. He felt the tendrils of the psychic's connection wrapping around the base of his skull. Unlike the amateur back at the apartment, this telepath did not try to see his thoughts or take possession, made no attempt to make their connection firm. She was just waiting there, keeping the barest touch on his presence. Sensing where he was, relaying it to the rest of them.

She was their spotter.

Surrender, the psychic's voice cooed. *You cannot escape. We're coming for you. We'll make it quick.*

You'd like that, wouldn't you, Matt thought back, opening his mind just a fraction. *If I just gave up. Well, too bad so sad. Didn't expect Jane's flashbang, did you? And you're never getting inside my head.*

Laughter echoed down the psychic link. *You are outnumbered. Outmatched. What can you do, little boy?*

I escaped your kill zone.

It won't matter. He could feel the voice smiling. *We're still stronger than you.*

Everyone always is, Matt replied, defiant. *That's what makes me special.*

He severed the connection, though he could feel the telepath's gaze lingering on the back of his skull. Matt pulled himself to his feet, turning back toward the rear door. And despite everything, his mouth split into the barest hint of a smile.

This telepath was good, he knew; a professional. Unlike the one who had attacked him back at the apartment, she knew not to throw herself unprotected into Matt's mind, was wary of his defenses, and was keeping little more than a thin, monitoring link. But she'd made one fatal error. With network connections down, she was fulfilling multiple roles—spotter for Matt, lookout for danger, and her team's communications link.

She may have been a competent psychic, but she was also confident in her abilities, used to being the dominating mental force. And like every person with every power who'd ever gone up against him, she couldn't help it: she underestimated Matt. And unbeknownst to her, while she'd been talking and seeing through him, he'd been reaching and seeing through her. The river flowed both ways if you knew how to swim it. And while Matt hadn't been able to see the psychic's thoughts, who she worked for, or even her name, he had felt, like a blind man tracing down woolen strings, the other minds she was connected to.

There were eight of them. Eight people out to kill him.

And now, he knew their powers.

Matt raced into the next aisle over, scooped up bottles of cooking oil and deodorant, and sprinted for the rear door.

* * *

Ninety degrees around the curve of the monochrome field, Giselle Pixus could see the power of Dawn blazing in a golden torrent. From this distance, Jane's power shone like a second sunrise, blasting unrelenting into the gray corruption, burning slow and ceaseless, pushing the field back. Step by step, inch by inch, Giselle could see the bubble buckling inward around the billowing light, folding in, drawing back the perimeter.

But for every foot the undead zone retreated, another wave of those trapped inside it was unleashed.

There were two sorts. The first were still human, or at least humanoid. Deathless, undead, whatever you wanted to call them, they were still ostensibly people, and once free from the power of the field, collapsed into a heap if they were very old, or crawled away crying if they were very young. Her concern was those in the middle— the ones who staggered out as walking corpses or white-eyed adults, their faces twisted in mad, directionless pain, moaning and bristling, with powers flaring at anything that came near them, repairing and refusing to die.

But they were not Giselle's biggest problem. That honor went to the second category, the ones who'd been stuck in the colored patches inside the motley bubble or who, otherwise, through some distinction Giselle couldn't see and didn't care about, right now were afflicted not with cycling undeath but endless unnatural growth. These were the monstrosities, the Cronenberg-esque mountains of bubbling, lumpy flesh and protruding bones, with hair longer than their bodies, seven-jointed fingers, multiple heads, and spidering legs. Anywhere from five to forty feet tall, no two were the same, and many of them seemed to be growing as multiple people—three, four, five bodies melted and melded together with flailing arms and legs and eyes. They were terrifying to look at and petrifying to hear, their fleshy throats warbling cacophonous, disharmonious medleys of guttural wailing and moans.

But most horrifying of all were their powers. From each one of these abominations—Chimeras, Giselle was mentally calling them—streamed abilities. Multiple powers. A body turned to iron while fire bellowed from the mouths of its twin heads. One monster blurred with inhuman speed, arms lengthened to ten-foot rocky ropes, while telekinetic debris ripped from the street around another mountain of perpetually growing fat. A creature with an acid-drooling, ten-foot jaw shimmered and turned invisible, and beside it, a three-legged, thirty-foot titan lumbered slowly forward, a shock of telepathic pain reverberating through its heads every time one of its twenty-toed, oil-drum-sized legs pummeled into the ground.

And they were coming for them.

Whatever was happening inside the zone clearly inflicted terrible agony upon these monsters. As their bodies changed, as they grew younger or aged or mutated or died, they were paralyzed, unable to do anything but wail inhuman screams while they were wracked by flux. But the second the field fell back, the second they were exposed and free, the changes ceased. The bloodcurdling shrieks swung in pitch, dropped in volume. The agony of constant change disappeared, replaced with the agony of unnatural existence, and as far as Giselle could see, the latter of those two nightmares was a lot less incapacitating and a lot more inciting toward frenzied rage.

She'd done two laps around the bubble, getting everyone she could clear, helping other Legion members get in place. They stood spread thin now, around the entire twenty-block circumference, sentinels of crimson arrayed behind makeshift barriers, between pillars and abandoned cars. Some of the police, some civilians, and the military had joined them, while others had fled or focused on helping the vulnerable. They stood interspersed along the Legion's battle lines, blue and white and khaki, blazing powers, aiming guns. An army of superhumans, suddenly so small and mundane and insignificant against a horde of so much worse.

A group of seven crimson warriors stood behind Giselle: Neil Lomachenko, Becky Sandstrom, Editha Reyes, Carla Black, and the Acolytes Gabbi, Monique, and Nour. Everywhere around her, she saw pale faces, clenched fists, and sweat trickling down brows. In the distance, there came the shrieks of children, a school group and their families being rapidly loaded into a bus. Giselle's eyes swept back to the monstrous onslaught, and though her heart hammered, her lips curled.

"LEGION!" she shouted, and she threw into her voice every ounce of conviction, every iota of fury and self-belief. "YOU ARE THE BEST!" A shout went up around her. "YOU ARE THE BRAV-EST!" The cry rang louder.

Around the curve of the field, there came a blinding flare, and the golden light intensified.

"PROTECT THE WEAK!" she roared. "PROTECT THE INNOCENT!"

Carla raised her hands and threw Giselle two half-foot silver rods, drawn from the black weapons crates the Legion had brought with them. She caught them both in midair, twisted the bands atop the grips, and the hilts shot out into seamless titanium blades.

"KILL THE MONSTERS!"

A mighty roar surged all around her. At that moment, the dead zone moved, and the enemy broke free.

Faster than a bullet, at the head of the Legion reborn, Giselle Pixus charged forward, a crimson blur.

The alley abutted a construction site. Matt raced inside through the gap to the left of the green sliding entrance gate, which had been left abandoned and ajar.

He knew what was coming. He knew what they would do, what to expect. His shoes pounded onto an unfinished concrete staircase, up one floor and then another, backpack jostling in front of him, hands churning desperately through it.

Find a place, find a place, find a—

His fingers closed around what he needed, and Matt yanked the backpack closed, swinging it back over his shoulders. He flew up the stairs two at a time, then sprinted out the stairwell into a long concrete room, empty save for construction lights and pallets of building material. His chest heaved, his forehead slick with sweat, his breathing ragged.

Cardio, he could almost hear Jane nagging. Cardio, cardio, cardio.

Without stopping, Matt raced down the hallway, slamming the three-inch-long cylindrical device from his backpack straight into the left-hand wall. He heard a crack, a hissing pop, and a thud in the concrete opposite. Matt didn't stop to look back, only kept running, racing through the empty doorway on the far side of the room.

"Found you." A voice, a female voice, curling singsongy and purring behind him. Matt skidded to a halt, stopping just beyond the doorway, and turned around. A smirking woman dressed in US military gear over thin, friction-proof khaki leggings had appeared as if from nothing, grinning at him down the other end of the hall. Late twenties, athletic, arms bare, she had brown hair shaved down at the sides and cut to a short mohawk on top. The woman smiled, meandering lazily forward as if she hadn't a care in the world, her thumbs tucking casually beneath the shoulder straps of her bulletproof vest. Matt stood stock-still, silent, staring her down, banking on not getting shot. Speedsters didn't carry guns, Giselle once told him. Why bother, when you could run faster than bullets?

"Did you think you could get away?" the woman laughed. "Really?"

"S-S-Stay back," Matt stammered. He took a clumsy step backward. The speedster laughed.

"I don't know why so many people struggled with this," she chuckled, and in an instant, her body blurred as she shot toward him.

Sl-ick.

Matt had only enough time to sidestep out of the doorway before the speedster sailed through, continuing right past him before hitting the far wall with a fleshly thud. The lifeless body sank onto the concrete, sliding onto the ground with barely a noise, blood rapidly pooling from above its lower jaw where the woman was now missing the top of her head. Matt glanced back into the corridor in time to see a bloody mohawked scalp plop down from where it had impacted above the doorway, watching as a few drops of gore dripped onto the floor from the thin, taut, almost invisible line of anti-speedster wire he'd laid out.

"Maybe next time," he said coldly, all trace of fear and stuttering vanished. Matt turned, leaving behind the half-headed corpse, and sprinted deeper into the abandoned building, feet pounding on the concrete.

One down. Seven left.

A vortex of undeath whipped around Jane as she gritted her teeth and pushed.

Step by step, she forced herself forward, inch by inch, a torrent of blazing energy burning from both hands. The air whirled and blasted around her, the sound of crashing power deafening, the light bright enough to blind. In front of her, the gray energy swirled and twisted, ceaseless in its resistance, relentlessly surging outward from whoever stood at its center, but still unable to stand before her might. A half step. Another one. The power of Dawn slammed into the monochrome gray with such intensity that it billowed back behind her, engulfing her in golden flames, annihilating everything within a hundred yards. The policemen had retreated. The Legion was fighting the hordes. She stood alone in death and corruption. A lone, unstoppable force.

Inside the bubble of Divine power, distorted figures stumbled and moaned. A few lurched toward her as she drew nearer, only to be vaporized instantly by the burning light. Jane bared her teeth, pushing harder. She could do this. She was stronger. She just had to keep going . . . She just had to keep . . .

Hold on, Matt, she begged. *Hold on.* With a wordless roar, she threw out everything she had, and the storm around her raged gold.

You'll pay for that, the psychic whispered.

Matt raced around an unfinished corner of concrete and steel cabling, his eyes darting wildly, searching for anything he could use.

Sorry, he thought back sarcastically. *Were you friends?*

You can't escape us.

Watch me try.

He had time now, precious moments to work with. The speedster would have raced on ahead, and now, the other assassins would be hurrying to catch up, slower on foot but no more so than him. He had maybe a two-to-three-minute head start, a tiny window for preparation. Think fast, think smart. Speedster, telepath, strongman, cryomancer, teleporter, diamondmorph, electromancer, invisible. One dead, the teleporter and telepath probably not fighting. That left five.

Matt skidded to a halt, staring hard at a small room stacked with tarp-covered pallets, picturing himself cowering behind them. It was a good place to hide. He kept the image, the location fixed firmly in his brain as he sprinted around the half-constructed hallways, up open concrete stairs, over barrels, and around. Twenty-four stories, he knew, from having glanced upward at the stairwell. Twenty-four stories of space and corners, of retreating farther and farther up. Make them work for it. Make them pay.

He grabbed two buckets, raced back past his hiding place, slid a round device from the bug-out bag beneath one of the tarpaulins, then sprinted for the far staircase.

He's hiding. Eastside room, construction storage, fourth floor.

Beneath his helmet and balaclava, the man who called himself Jackson nodded. *Clever boy.* Run then stop, run then stop, throw some smoke and mirrors so they overshoot, then go back while they chase a phantom up and up. Smart kid, smart strategy. Many of his men had been dismissive, even contemptuous, of the challenge Matt Callaghan might pose. After all, he had no powers; how could he possibly be a threat? They were fools. Matt Callaghan had survived a lifetime without powers, outsmarted some of the world's most powerful people with naught but cunning and tricks. Besides. Jackson's father had been special forces in the aborted war in Vietnam. He knew exactly how much death an unpowered enemy could inflict.

Unfortunately for Matt Callaghan, he had one disadvantage the Vietcong had never suffered. They could see into his mind.

Up the stairs, he relayed. His thoughts transmitted to Blaine, and the psychic redirected them out. They stormed wordlessly up onto the fourth-floor walkway, weapons raised, the concrete shell still open to the elements on one side. A flicker of movement caught his eye, and Jackson spied a shadow move atop the fifth-floor staircase. The diversion. He waved Lone Star and Calder forward, motioning for them to investigate.

Don't charge after it, he ordered. The cryomancer stalked forward behind the invisible soldier, his rifle and gear mere shimmers beneath his veil. Calder's footsteps kicked up small swirls of dust, but otherwise, the man was a ghost.

Images floated into his head from the invisible man's eyes. *Something silver next floor up. Something moving. Looks to be a space blanket hanging over the stairs.*

Back here, Jackson told them. *Eli, Pierce, the storeroom.*

His electromancer and the diamondmorph soldier, Pierce, a towering six-and-a-half-foot brute, moved with muffled footsteps toward the open concrete doorway. Both men kept their rifles slung over their shoulders, Eli's hands sparking, Pierce's body turned glittering and indestructible. Jackson followed a few feet behind, his weapon raised, wary.

Got him, he heard relayed through Eli's thoughts. Jackson's mind flashed with an image of a small square room with walls of half-finished sheeting, the same one Blaine had sent now filtered through

Perspex goggles. Cubes of bricks covered in tarpaulins, along with metal beams and other junk. The pallet the farthest away had its tarp pulled slightly out. Low enough to cover a curled-up human.

Eli nodded to Pierce, who grinned and raised his rifle, aiming at the tarp. The electromancer slunk forward, weapon shouldered, hands outstretched, sparks jumping silently between his fingertips. He crouched low, and then, with a victorious cry, ripped away the tarpaulin.

To reveal the end tucked under a bucket, and a red flashing orb.

"NO!" Jackson screamed, but in an instant, his words were swallowed by an explosion. The building shook, dust and debris flying everywhere, stray shards of metal and brick, and suddenly, the storage room no longer had an outer wall. Jackson staggered, mentally reeling in shock as soulwrenching pain ripped through him, a sudden gulping darkness as Eli's death ricocheted across their mental link, as it had a few minutes ago with Chrissy. Around him, he saw his team stagger, screaming and clutching their skulls—and in that moment, Jackson saw the shadow of the silver space blanket part, and the torso of a boy lean upside down from the fifth-floor landing, a black detonator in his left hand. And in his right—

That looks like a— Jackson's swirling brain tried to muster, but in that instant, Matt Callaghan took aim and shot the laser pointer across the room, square into one of Pierce's diamond eyes.

"Argh!" the huge man screamed, staggering, flailing blindly as the red piercing beam of energy shot into his iris, unable to escape, pinging endlessly inside. Agony echoed back through their psychic connection as the big man wailed, stumbling backward, his flesh reverting to normal in an attempt to halt the damage, his hands clutching at the smoking ruins of his eyes.

Through their psychic connection, Jackson felt Blaine curse and begin hastily redirecting the rest of the team's perceptions, thrusting them into Pierce, trying to help him see—but immediately, Jackson felt something wrong. As the sensation of his teammates swelled, another force exploded outward, and suddenly, Jackson was overwhelmed with visions of a shadow hurtling toward him; something dark, terrifying, huge. In front of him, he saw the same thoughts hit Pierce, and before he could even think, the big man yelped, stumbling back toward the building's edge, instinctively away.

Jackson shouted a warning, but before he could do anything, Pierce's feet caught on a chunk of debris and he tripped, sending his lumbering body flailing backward into open air. The soldier hurtled down into the exposed construction site, and Jackson's stomach lurched as the sudden sensation of falling piled on top of their mental pain. A second later, the sound of Pierce's rapidly fading screams abruptly ended, cut off by a horrific wet snap and the crash of glass and meat.

A fresh surge of agony blared red through their psychic connection. Wails echoed up from below. In the fifth-floor stairwell, Matt Callaghan's thoughts flew free from the team's connection, and he swung his torso clear half a second before a staggering Jackson raised his gun and let loose a stream of bullets, the shots deafening, flying wild.

"Get him!" he screamed. "Get him!"

The Chimera roared, fifteen feet tall, and Giselle slammed into it like a linebacker.

"AUUUGGHHH!"

The abomination staggered, stumbling from the force of the impact, but Giselle was already moving, clambering at impossible speed over and around, stabbing flesh, stabbing eyes, stabbing everything. In the space of a second, the creature gurgled and collapsed with a thud onto the asphalt, lava dripping uselessly from one of its many open mouths, a tower of bleeding wounds.

Behind her, three soldiers fired round after round at a twitching, shimmering Chimera with four legs at ninety degrees to one another and fingernail scales running over every inch of its mutated form.

The bullets sank into the creature's body, leaving oozing bloody holes, but then, the jaws on one of its heads lolled open, and a flood of liquid metal spewed forth. The soldiers cried out, but the moment before the molten stream could hit, it cut around them, diverted by an invisible force.

"Help!" One of the Acolyte telekinetics, a blonde seventeen-year-old Gabbi, stood locked in place ten feet away, sweat desperately pouring down her forehead. Behind her, a crystal-clawed Deathless lurched toward her, swinging wild its glistening talons. Giselle blurred, slicing the bloodless corpse in a hundred places and hurling it back toward the bubble. The body skipped like a stone, landing a few feet from the retreating barrier where, slowly, it rolled over, and again began crawling forward, new ribbons of flesh flowing down the tendons Giselle had cut. The speedster swore.

"I can't hold—!" Gabbi screamed, but at that moment, the dreadlocked Acolyte Monique leapt over an upturned police car and brought her force fields to bear against the molten metal stream. One of the soldiers plunged his hands into the earth, raising a barrier of stone, and together, the three of them pushed the silver torrent back around onto the Chimera, coating it in the burning liquid, the creature continuing to vomit even as it sizzled and screamed. In moments, it was silent, a horrific hardening statue of gray metal and smoldering flesh.

Woosh. A shard of serrated steel shot past her, but Giselle was already moving, snatching pieces out of the air and directing them away from her students. A hundred feet away, a telekinetic Chimera hissed as its mind tore fist-size chunks from the buildings around it, laser beams slicing out in random directions from every one of a dozen body-embedded eyes, cutting through stone and street and steel, cleaving everything nearby.

"BRING IT DOWN!" she screamed. In an instant, Giselle felt the order relayed to Natalia in her position atop one of the buildings. Suddenly, the clouds above them darkened, and the Chimera was pummeled by a blast of wind, pushing away its projectiles. There was a crack, a flash, and in the middle of the city streets, bolt after bolt of lightning rained down, hammering into the creature, annihilating it in a meteorological artillery strike.

Thirty feet away, Helen's mechanical arm hurled a tiny Malaysian boy toward a twenty-foot Chimera behemoth slowly advancing with rapidly whipping hard-light tendrils, its fully steel body impervious to harm. The boy, Nour, shot underneath the titan's bulbous legs, wrapped his hands around its foot, and phased the titan ten feet into the ground, where it suddenly found itself struggling, its lower half encased and unable to move. A dozen stumbling white-eyed Deathless in a myriad of states and ages lurched toward the phaser, but Giselle was faster, skidding between the tentacles, scooping the brown-skinned boy up into her arms, and running him back to Helen.

"PUSH THE HUMANS BACK TO THE BARRIER!" she screamed; she didn't have time to think if the command made sense because, suddenly, she felt a scream of pain go up from a group of distant Acolytes, and then she was running, hurtling as fast as her legs could carry her, around the other side of the bubble, through a thousand disparate wars.

On the far edge of the city, Giselle slid to a halt, breathless, taking in the scene. Fifteen or more Chimeras, a horror show of flesh and limbs and gnashing teeth, advanced upon a cluster of five Acolytes; one healer, Delores, kneeling over and whispering desperately to a new boy, Adam, whose crimson armor had been pierced through the chest by a three-foot spear of bone. The other three, Cameron, Kane, and Leticia, stood screaming, trying to hold off the advancing monsters. Cameron's silver-stained hands scrambled for everything he could reach, rubble and asphalt turning to steel at his touch; as soon as it was changed, Kane ripped it up off the surface, magnetically bending the metal into thick conical spikes, dropping them straight into the hand of Leticia, who threw the door-length missiles at the advancing monsters like a belt-fed machine gun.

Some shots took out a leg, a head, all finding their mark somewhere, but it wasn't enough. Because as each one of the creatures fell, the abomination at their center—a bloblike, flesh-toned beast some thirty feet wide—shot out a fleshy sucker and pulled in the pieces of its kindred's corpses, growing larger, growing stronger. Pieces of bone and steel began shifting out beneath the surface of its wriggling body, lightning sparking between the teeth on one of its heads, and every hit the Acolytes scored on it only glanced off its fleshy mass, swiftly regenerating, almost immediately repaired.

Giselle steadied herself and raised her daggers, praying to a clearly effing absent God, then bent low, preparing to charge. The second before she did, a figure in black leapt in front of the students, putting himself between the Chimeras and their prey. Soft and lean, with thin dark hair, Charles Farrington advanced on the creatures with a snarl, flames spreading from his fists, engulfing his arms, his entire body. In an instant, he rose, a being of pure flame, and with a bellowing roar of "DAWN!" he snapped his hands forward and unleashed cataclysm.

Fire, a forty-foot wall of fire, exploded from the burning figure, engulfing the advancing Chimeras, the sound of their screams swallowed by heat and howling winds. The fire spread in a tsunami, an unstoppable wave, slamming through everything before it and smashing against the dead zone wall. Giselle shielded her eyes, the tips of her hair curling as the flames rose hundreds of feet into the air, a towering, winged inferno. Finally, the fire faded, leaving only the still-burning figure of Charles Farrington standing before the Acolytes, staring down a runway of annihilation and ash. Buildings on either side dripped melting stone, the ground glowed molten, and of the regenerating Chimera, there remained nothing.

Charles glanced at Giselle, gave her a curt nod, and on they both ran.

Matt raced up the concrete staircase, the sounds of shouting and footsteps ringing out beneath and behind him, sprinting as fast as his legs could carry him into the upper levels of the building's shell. Wind howled through unsealed walls, and in the near distance, the world shook with screams and explosions, twisted inhuman moans. But still, Matt ran, unrelenting.

How did you—?

You think you can see into my mind? Matt spat. He leapt over a block of bricks, sprinting inward toward one of the few doors that had been installed. *You think by now, I'm winded or frightened or panicked, that my thoughts are starting to leak? That I can't use you? You're nothing. I beat Klaus Heydrich bleeding in the desert, with broken bones torn through my thighs. You think you're better than me? You're NOTHING.* And he believed it as he thought it with every fiber of his being, and on the other end of the connection, he felt the telepath flinch.

This is impossible.

This is discipline, Matt sneered. *This is talent. This is passion and fear and anger and knowing that I only have to outlast you useless idiots for a few minutes more.* He paused. *Do you fear for your life, you worthless piece of crap? Can you abandon this fight whenever you want to? Because I do, and I can't. So which one of us do you think is more motivated, is going to push that extra effort to ensure they're not destroyed? Fear me.* He glared down the connection at her, a searing beam of rage. *I want to live.*

He paused, skidding to a halt in a narrow corridor, turning to face the door he'd come through. Matt's hands rummaged in the bug-out bag for what he needed, and he waited, breathing heavily, thirty feet away from the entrance as footsteps raced toward him.

"There!"

The door slammed open and through it came first seemingly no one and then, a split second later, the cryomancer, a tan, chisel-jawed twenty-something with movie-star stubble and a cleft in his chin. Both of them yelped, flinching in surprise as from atop the door fell the second bucket Matt had collected, filled to the brim with cooking oil. Their boots slid, but this was not a cartoon, and the men, though momentarily off-balance, did not fall, instead steadying themselves and swinging their guns around toward Matt, the invisible one now visible underneath a splattered coating of oil.

The bucket of oil was stupid, schoolboy nonsense. The stun grenade primed in Matt's hand was not.

Matt had barely a second's opening, but he needed nothing more. He lobbed the flash grenade, dove behind the corner, and shut his eyes.

"ARGH!" the two attackers screamed, clutching their faces, and the tiny corridor suddenly turned deafening as they fired wildly, bullets ricocheting into the concrete and gouging chunks from the floors and walls. "Flashbang!" the cryomancer screamed, but though they both lurched and stumbled, clawing at their eyes, neither seemed truly harmed.

Matt picked up the flare he'd taken from his bag, twisted the top, lobbed it sparking around the corner, and changed that.

Privately, Matt had been hoping the stun grenade might ignite the oil—the bright, blinding stuff inside did burn hot, and if it exploded in the right place could cause burns. But his aim hadn't been perfect, or maybe the canola oil wasn't as flammable as he would've liked.

The flare had no such reservations.

Instantly, flames erupted over the soldiers, and their cries of discomfort became hysterical shrieks. The invisible assassin, suddenly visible, had the sense to drop and roll, wildly slapping at his shoulders, but the cryomancer had taken the brunt of the oil bucket over his head. The flames raced, and when—in a fit of panic—his hands spluttered with ice crystals, the oil fire suddenly hissed and exploded, the ice racing through water into steam and splattering everything nearby in searing flames.

Matt did not stay to watch, even as he heard the cryomancer gurgle and collapse, already racing toward the stairs, up another level, around and around and around. He leapt the last three steps and sprinted into a room of bare concrete devoid of outer walls, with nothing between him, the open air, and a sixty-foot drop. The burning war zone of New York City spread out before him, meshes of exposed metal bars reaching like unnatural fingers through the concrete floor and pillars toward the gray, windswept sky.

You'll pay for that, the psychic whispered. Matt scowled at the nothingness.

Haven't you learned to shut—

CRACK.

A fist-size chunk of concrete exploded out of a support column five feet from Matt's head. Matt yelped, leaping behind cover as he was showered in a hail of dust and gravel. He scrambled on all fours, clambering to push his back flat against one of the pillars, squeezing his limbs as close as possible to put the support between him and the outside world.

CRACK.

A tremor raced through the square column, the bullet thudding into the other side and burying itself into the concrete and metal. Matt slid down into a crouch. *Crap.* He was on the east side of the building. The sniper.

Yeah, okay, psychic, he had to concede, *you got me on that one.*

There came another distant CRACK of gunfire, and Matt's heart skipped a beat as another dent exploded in the floor not six feet from him. He was trapped. He couldn't move. Even if the sniper was too far away for the bullet to go entirely through the concrete-and-steel girder, even if he ignored the threat of ricochet, one step out from behind this pillar and he'd get a brand-new hole in his abdomen. *Crap. CRAP!*

Matt breathed hard, his hands shaking, and in a rush of terror, his heart leapt to his throat as behind him, from the staircase, came the sound of more footsteps, of ripping fabric and of the invisible man slamming into the stairs below him and screaming, incoherent with rage.

* * *

Will Herd, teleporter, crouched behind an abandoned car in the streets of New York, listening as his friends fought for their lives. Breathing heavily, dust slick across his armor, he peered out at the chaos around him, feeling helpless as the carnage unfolded.

Disruptances. Some sick bastard had raised a Disruptance field as soon as he'd brought in the last of the Acolytes, trapping nearly the entire Legion in place. It was like Matt had said. If he'd jumped him back to Morningstar, they would've chased after them, shutting the door behind them to keep the Legion bottled up. Will swore under his breath, chancing another glance out at the battle beyond, watching as a roaring man with arms of bladed crystal hacked a horde of Deathless fiends to bits.

This was not how he had envisioned this fight going. This was not how he envisioned any fight going. Will should have been able to jump as he pleased, bring in reinforcements, ferry wounded, move people to better positions, help them set up overlapping fields of fire to best keep these freaks at bay. But he couldn't. For the last ten minutes, Will had been sprinting, block after block, away from the fighting, struggling against the lead weight of the Disruptance atop his powers to no avail. The Disruptance covering the city was huge, military grade, a billion dollars' worth, or else a thousand networked little regular ones overlapping anti-teleportation bubbles into the street. Teleportation only, it seemed, since he'd seen Nour phasing through the ground earlier. Freaking hell.

He had come back, run back, when he couldn't find a gap in coverage. And now, Will was stuck in the middle of a superhuman war zone, unable to use his powers, while only a few hundred feet away, the Legion battled and rampaging mutant abominations screamed.

This was a shame. A real damn shame. Because Will Herd was a good teleporter. A very good teleporter. Very quick, very precise, very fit.

But the difference between a good teleporter and a great teleporter was not how well they could jump. It was being useful for more than just teleportation. It was about being proactive, not just sitting there gormlessly because someone had turned a Disruptance on, twiddling your thumbs and going, "*Ah, well,*" while your friends fought and bled and died.

And as he crouched there surveying the situation, leaning his sweat-stained forehead around a car, listening to the roars and rushes, the explosions and gunfire, Will heard a crack off in the distance unlike any of the other sounds around him. A distinctive boom, deeper, louder, and thicker than other weapons, and coming from way higher up. A high-caliber rifle. Not one of theirs.

What had Jane said? *They've got guns. They're trying to kill Matt.*

Will's mouth curled into a scowl. He glanced up briefly, ensured the coast was clear, then leapt out from behind his cover, sprinting across the dust-blown street and sliding onto his knees behind one of the Legion's weapons boxes. He slammed his fist on the silver button, causing the lid to slide open and expose the crate's contents. Will stood up and leaned over, pulling out a heavy black case.

You know what also made him a great Legion member, just generally? Liking guns. So many superpowered people forgot about guns and were really just not prepared to deal with a sudden gaping chest wound appearing from half a kilometer away. Those people were shortsighted. Guns were fantastic. Will loved guns.

Grabbing the black case with both hands, the teleporter sprinted toward a nearby hotel and its internal fire escape, racing for the stairs.

Farther. Farther! Jane pushed onward, the roaring in her ears deafening now, the weight of Divine undead power pressing in from all sides. Only a few blocks now. Only a few more blocks!

Golden light streamed from her hands, from her mouth, from everything, her eyes and cheek and hands burning unstoppable, radiant, as she plunged farther and farther in, each step harder and heavier than the last. But she did not relent. She would not relent. The howling winds reached a fever pitch, the power of Dawn rushing and burning not just the very air but her body and thoughts, surging through every atom of her being, shaking with the fury of the sun.

The light flared high and unbreakable, burning against the shifting gray as Jane pushed forward, a storm of all-consuming gold.

Bam! Will kicked open the door to the hotel rooftop, clutching the black case tight. His breathing was ragged, his brow slick with sweat, but in the space of a moment he inhaled deeply, flushing the fire from his lungs. Will broke back into a sprint, darting between the exhaust vents and air-conditioning units of the paver-clad roof, sweeping his eyes over the city and the destruction toward the northeast buildings, where—

There! Two figures in standard-issue military green, lying prone atop a building, facing west ninety degrees away from him several stories below like malicious, distant slugs. Will slid onto the ground, slamming against the half-foot ledge running the circumference of the rooftop, then set down the black case, flicked up the clasps, and threw the lid open.

Hello, old girl, he wanted to say, but there was no time for sweet re-seduction. He grabbed the lower receiver, flicked up the two front legs of the rifle stand, pulled out the locking pins, grabbed the upper receiver, extended the barrel out, pulled back the spring, slid the two receivers into one another, slotted the locking pins back into place, and snapped a cartridge up into the body of the weapon. And then, in a matter of seconds, Will Herd was sitting pretty on a hotel rooftop, aiming at his enemies down the distinctive square-nosed barrel of a .50 Barrett M82A1.

Up here, he chuckled, squinting through the pre-attached scope, peering down. He couldn't see where they were aiming, the angles were all wrong, the asymmetrical, aesthetically slanted roof of the hotel rising sharply up and blocking that direction. But he didn't need to. The two would-be assassins were too focused on their quarry to notice Will's rifle gleaming above and to their right.

There were two, he saw through the telescopic lens; one with a long-barreled rifle, which looked to be an AWM, and the other with a pair of black binoculars. The shooter was a man—pale skin, cropped black hair. The spotter was a woman, white and tanned, with a blonde ponytail. Will took aim, steadied his breathing, and adjusted for drop and wind. "I would like to solve the puzzle," he whispered to no one in particular.

He fired.

BANG.

Five hundred yards away, the head and upper body of the black-haired man exploded like he'd gargled a stick of dynamite. The M82's recoil slammed hard into Will's shoulder, and a spent fifty caliber casing the size of a pencil flew out the side of his gun. Will took a deep breath and leaned back in, taking aim at the other assassin. Through the round constraints of the scope, Will saw the blonde ponytailed woman silently scream and roll, scrabbling away from her partner's suddenly lifeless body. He tilted the barrel, following her movement—and then saw through the scope as her head snapped up toward him, as she saw his muzzle gleam, and as her fingers flew to her temple.

Die!

Pain. Telepathic agony. The rifle dropped from Will's hands as, suddenly, the world burned, searing-hot talons of pain raking down the inside of his mind. All at once, he was five again, he was three, he was every moment of silence from his mother and his father's dis-appointed stares, and he was reeling, tumbling down into oblivion, but—*No!* Will gritted his teeth, pushing the intrusion back, forcing his walls up, clinging to—What was it he had to cling to, from those afternoons with Matt and Wally? He couldn't remember; she'd taken him by surprise, and though Will reached desperately to marshal his thoughts, for mental defenses, he felt himself slipping, felt his con-centration starting to fail—

I THINK NOT.

Suddenly, another voice, a towering thunderhead, came roaring into his mind. A third person—a familiar, indignant fury—rushed to surround Will's consciousness. Through the Legion's long-distance psychic connection, a cyclone of black and feathers and ivory swept through his mind and into the interloper's, picking up the petty blonde psychic by her mental throat and slamming her choking into the ground.

KNEEL.

In a world of endless white, the titanic specter of Natalia Baroque rose, a swirling, shadow-robed leviathan unfurling wings of bottomless darkness that shook and gleamed with a thousand ebony eyes. The enemy psychic screamed, and through the connection she had foolishly made with Will, the woman he now knew as Blaine could do nothing but shriek while the colossus of Natalia's mind lunged down, tearing with claws of black-veined porcelain and pounding her consciousness into the dirt.

Back in reality, Will gritted his teeth, the world suddenly shifting back into focus, though his mind still reeled with the force of Natalia's counterattack. He sat up, shook his head angrily, spat out blood where he'd bit his tongue, shrugged the gun's stock back into the crook of his shoulder, took a deep, jagged breath, aimed once more down the scope—

—and blew the bitch's brains out.

Suddenly, the shooting stopped. Crouched behind his pillar, his head between his hands, Matt felt a wave of sudden panic flow through the psychic connection, then a surge of fury, then hysterical, abject fear—then nothing. The connection went dark, all sensation fading from the back of Matt's skull. His mind raced, sifting through the thoughts. It didn't feel like they'd pulled back; it felt like they were gone.

Screw it, Matt swore. *Now or never.* He leapt from behind the pillar, running as fast as his legs could carry him, racing in an erratic zigzag for the other end of the building. No shots came. But though Matt's chest swelled with a surge of excitement, his relief was short-lived, because the delay had cost him seconds, practically all his precious head start. As he rounded the corner, he heard the invisible man shout, and Matt sprinted, desperate, up the stairs to the higher levels, around and around and around.

Only two left. Only two.

The sound of rapid gunfire shattered his concentration, bullets ricocheting off the stairs and walls, punching lines of concrete holes. *Screw me, screw me, screw me*—Matt darted to the right, feinted left, in and around another bare shell of a room, swinging Azleena's bag back in front of him and pawing desperately for something, anything.

His hands closed around the stink pellets, and he threw them on the ground, not even bothering to aim, just launching them behind him in the path his attackers would take. He shot around a corner, and a second later was rewarded with angry shouts and the sound of coughing. But bad smells would do nothing. Matt had bought himself a few seconds max.

Think. Think! There, on the far corner of the building, abutting the jagged patchwork of unfinished floor, a blue tarpaulin fluttered over another pallet of bricks. *Go, go!* Matt sprinted over, skidding around the gap leading to open nothingness, heart hammering, lungs burning. Tearing off the tarp, he wrenched it over the hole in the floor, slamming down bricks on every corner and then running, his hands fumbling, scrabbling in the bag for the decoy projector that just this morning he'd let scan him to create a passing 3D likeness.

The false image sprung to life, showering Matt's surroundings with refracted images of himself and flickering patterns of light. Matt sprinted, device in hand, pelting down the length of the room, then sliding on his heels and slapping the projector on the ground, facing toward the other end of the building and the tarp he'd just laid down. Footsteps pounded on the staircase below him, and Matt barely had time to hit the Play button, sending the intangible figure running, before his pursuers caught up.

With any sober consideration, through anything less than a pain- and adrenaline-soaked haze, the image wouldn't have been convinc- ing. The movement was too stiff, the footsteps too light, the colors and sway of hair and clothes disconnected from everything around it. But the soldiers who raced up the half-built stairwell drenched in sweat and thoughts of murder did not see the image through unfiltered eyes. They saw it through fog-stained goggles, through burning muscles and churning rage and a million years of predator instincts tracking the rapid movement of prey, all shapes and approximate sizes.

Matt did not see the invisible man come first up the stairs, but he heard his footsteps, heard his screaming and the deafening bang of bullets erupting from his rifle. He heard him swearing, saw his footprints in the dust as he sprinted toward the decoy, giving chase, enraged at his shots doing nothing, boots pounding closer and closer as Matt's image crossed the tarpaulin, ran free across to the other side—

And then, Matt saw the blue tarp give. He heard a scream, a thick, cracking thud as the thin plastic sheet pulled free of the meager bricks, and the ensnared shape of the invisible man plummeted, hur- tling down the side of the building, his screams fading rapidly into nothingness. And then, far below, there came a crunch.

One.

"DAMMIT!"

Matt spun, and there, on the other end of the building, stood the final soldier—a piston-necked, barrel-chested bear of a man, his ruddy face smeared with a shadow of pockmarks and stubble and pure, frozen fury in his eyes. His head spun from where he'd watched his companion fall, toward the shimmering light of the hologram, and to Matt, not three feet beside it.

He snapped the barrel of his weapon up. Matt dove.

Bam-bam-bam-bam.

Pain. Sudden, excruciating pain in his right arm, his bicep, but Matt shoved it from his mind and refused to feel, his legs pounding on the concrete, hurtling around corners, hurtling upward. Ever, ever upward, blood streaming between his fingers, toward he knew not where, with only one man giving chase.

But almost no more tricks.

The Chimera rose, its spidery mutant body covered in tawny hair, its seven arms swinging lashes of fire, deafening sound erupting from all four of its split, bleeding lips. Yet, as it cantered forward, a shadow reared above it, the dragon roaring, shining brilliant red, its claws as big as a man's waist. In an instant, its jaws slammed around the creature and shattered every bone in its brittle body with a sickening, shrieking crunch.

The defenders cheered. Celeste whipped her head around, savaging the limp monstrosity like a dog shaking a rabbit, then pivoted, rearing on her back legs and slamming through lines of Deathless with her spiked wrecking ball of a tail. She flung the broken Chimera away, a bloody, shattered rag doll, and bellowed so loud the ground trembled, a victorious, defiant roar.

"HOLD!" Giselle thundered. "HOLD!"

All around her, the Legion were winning. Bloodstained, panting, but unbroken they stood, shouting incoherent war cries and unleashing wave after wave of hoarse, delirious power at the abominations who dared survive. All around the dead zone now, battle lines held, drawn and unyielding; barricades of risen earth and foot-thick ice, steel, shining force fields, and shields of fused car doors. All throughout the barriers, through opening portholes and closing gaps, projectiles and energy rocketed: flares of rifles, defiant shouts, and screaming death. As a single-minded team flanked by soldiers and civilians, the Legion tore through their enemies, slicing apart the Chimeras and pushing back the Deathless: the former dwindling in number; the latter blasted into crawling wrecks that no matter how quickly they repaired were never fast enough to get back on their feet.

"FIRE!" Giselle roared, a part of her no longer knowing what she was shouting. "FIRE!"

Celeste's enormous ruby wings unfurled, and she beat a thudding retreat up and out of the line of fire. With a barrage of filthy swear words, the Acolytes around Giselle filled the no-man's-land with a hail of powers and bullets. The Deathless stumbled, collapsed, tumbling. The Chimeras roared.

"WITH ME!" the Legion's leader cried, and though her lungs burned and her legs ached, she once more vaulted over the barricades, two other speedsters falling in formation behind her, racing together, three crimson blurs, over to one of the last remaining Chimeras, fifteen-foot wide and covered in chitinous plates. The speedsters flew over and around it, shining knives finding every crack in its armor, every weak point. In the space of a heartbeat, they were running back, blood gushing out of the creature as it staggered onto the sidewalk, a water balloon pierced with a thousand pinpricks. The creature once more began to divide, replicating, but this time, the defenders were ready, and bolts of lightning pummeled down upon it from the skies.

Almost there. They almost had it. On the far side of the dead zone, hundreds of feet away, Giselle could see the golden light of Lady Dawn pushing inward, so far inside the monochrome bubble the gray was almost wrapping back in and around. But Jane was still there—still going. And like a slow-moving beacon carrying all their hopes, with every step the light advanced, the field of gray grew smaller, the number of new abominations exposed growing less and less. All they had to do was hold. Just a little longer. A little more.

"FOR HUMANITY!" Giselle screamed, and all around her, fists punched into the air, the earth shaking with mighty roars. "FOR THE LEGION! FOR THE DAWN!"

Through the golden hurricane around her, through the briefest gap where the gold washed against the gray, Jane saw it. The famous crossroads—the sign-lit streets. Times Square, twisted into a patchwork of colorless aberration, all traffic within it stopped, its people stumbling, forfeited of their souls. And there, in the middle, the center of the pulsing. The source of the energy radiating out like a thundering heartbeat, shuddering and remaking the world.

She had expected a person, someone kneeling and unleashing madness, or some child come fresh into their power and unintentionally releasing horrors untold. But to her shock, instead Jane saw two people, or what looked like two versions of the same person, stumbling, the storm swallowing up the shout of their voices. Locked together, fighting. Killing one another, over and over again.

They were both men in their early twenties, both Asian, both lean. One, dressed in the tattered remnants of a suit, staggered with strands of dark hair falling over jet-black eyes, screaming hoarse nothings, wild and delirious. The other—in a torn, filthy white jacket—shouted back at him, equally incoherent, his eyes not black but pure white. Suddenly, Jane thought she could somehow hear their voices over the howl of the churning storm. Because they *were* the storm.

Whatever was happening to them, whatever was happening between them, their pain and chaos was exploding outward, rippling through the fabric of reality in rhythmic, pulsing thuds. As Jane gritted her teeth, pushing desperately forward, she saw the black-clad twin fall upon the body of the white one, gripping his shirt with both hands and slamming his head into the pavement. Yet, the ivory-eyed twin did not die. Instead, he shrieked words only God could understand and slammed his fist into the chin of his counterpart, hard enough to break wrist and bone, yet there was no crack, no splintering, no blood.

In the eye of this surreal storm, two photonegative clones beat each other to never-nearing death, oblivious to the destruction billowing around them.

Jane bent her knees, driven low by the force of the whirling energy, and once more threw back her chest and shouted, the power of Dawn roaring with her, the light bellowing its unyielding answer. Through the heart of the storm, she bore down toward the Divines, advancing by inches, bearing the power of the sun.

Matt leapt the final staircase and skidded to a halt atop the empty rooftop, with nowhere left to go.

His vision swam. His legs were lead. His chest had stopped heaving, simply content to seize, clenching in a vain attempt to stop his lungs from collapsing in on themselves. He stumbled forward, lurching toward the edge of the building, free hand clutching loosely at his injured shoulder. He was . . . Well, oh *wow*, he was losing a lot of blood. This, ugh . . . This was starting to become something of a habit.

"Jane . . ." he murmured, stumbling with staggering footsteps. "Any time now . . ."

In the distance, he could see her still fighting. How could anyone not? The light of Dawn shone like a star, like the Aurora Nirvanas, a golden maelstrom of energy burrowing into the corrupting gray. She was so close to the center, the entire field now buckling around her. She'd almost done it. And he was almost not dead. Almost. So close.

But there was nowhere left to run. No more silly bullcrap. Beneath him, behind him, the footsteps coming up the stairs had decreased into a steady, relentless thud, following unwaveringly along his erratic, bloody trail. *Thud. Thud.* One foot in front of the other, the murderous gait of a predator slowly stalking its prey, savoring the fear, the trapped moments sweetening the killing.

Matt winced as he shrugged off Azleena's bug-out bag, the weight of it now depressingly empty as he held both strings in one hand. What was in there now? A protein bar? A smoke bomb? Those cans of deodorant he'd picked up? He'd had some thought of turning those into makeshift flamethrowers, but Matt no longer had a flare, and he didn't have a lighter. Also, the blood on his hands kept slipping, and he was having trouble seeing straight.

None of those were going to do anything. The smoke wouldn't even slow him down; the bag itself? Maybe if he could get it on the attacker's head and then play dead man rodeo, with only one working arm and a significant amount of blood loss. Sure, seemed doable. The deodorant and the rations? Well, the man coming to kill him might be smelly or hungry. But Matt guessed the final soldier was probably not the type to be deterred by petty niceness; otherwise, he probably wouldn't have been picked to assassinate him in the first place.

Oh God, I'm thinking nonsense, Matt thought, reeling. May he die as he lived, the king of stupid tricks, having exceeded everyone's expectations. There were worse ways to go.

Desperate, Matt once more bent his working arm down and rummaged inside the bag, feeling desperately for something, *anything*, he could use.

Wait. His fingers closed clumsily around something that felt like a metal ice cream cone, groping around a handle. He fumbled in the bottom of the bag, feeling another, then drew one of them out. Ice-cream-cone-shaped stabby things. Like a little umbrella or mushroom of solid silver with an aggressive point on the end and a handle. Wall climbers. Matt almost laughed out loud. The roof was completely bare. He wasn't facing any walls.

Except—

Suddenly, Matt had an idea so monumentally stupid it couldn't possibly fail.

He broke into a loping run, sweeping his gaze around the surrounding buildings. Directly in front of him, on the short side of the rectangle, there was only empty air, but on the long east and west sides . . . skyscrapers. Other buildings—fully constructed ones—each taller than this, separated on his left by a thirty-foot gap, and on his right by a mere forty.

Could he do it? Was he strong enough? Dexterous?

In a rush of understanding, Matt suddenly realized that either way, he was dead. So why not go out in a blaze of idiocy? Why not make this stupid ape traipsing up the stairs work for his goddamn murder?

Matt stuck the ice cream stabber between his legs and hurled the smoke grenade down the stairs before flinging the bag away, forgotten. As he heard the soldier cough and swear, heard his footsteps hasten, Matt gripped the wall climber with his working hand and ran toward one side of the building.

Die how you lived, Matt told himself. *Stupid plans and mind games.*

The man who called himself Jackson stalked up the last of the stairs and into open air, his labored breathing mixing with the rush of wind buffeting his helmet. He pushed through the smoke, the distraction harmless, the flexible filter in his balaclava purging the smog before any could be sucked down into his airways. Cold gusts whipped at his hair, the small gaps around the back of his neck still exposed to the elements, his rifle raised, his steps quick now but cautious. A frightened rat would bite when it was cornered. Unless it had nothing left to bite with. Unless it was merely scrabbling for time as the wolf drew close.

The smoke cleared—the roof was exposed. Jackson glanced around him, swinging the muzzle of his rifle yet seeing nothing but empty concrete. The man's breathing quickened, and his eyes bulged. No. NO! How?! He'd come so far! There was nowhere to run; the boy had nowhere to hide. He couldn't—

Jackson's eyes fell on the buildings either side of him, looming forty, fifty stories tall, waiting across a gap stretching an entire street. No. It was impossible. He could have done it with his superstrength easily, but the boy? Wounded, dripping blood, chased down, and run ragged? Yet maybe, with an adrenaline surge . . . with no baggage and just the right amount of wind . . .

His eyes came to rest on the human's backpack lying abandoned on the rooftop, the blood trail running from one side of the roof to the other.

He did it, Jackson swore. *That crazy human bastard, he really—*

The squad leader's head swung either side of him, judging the distances of the gaps. The one on the left was smaller. If the boy had jumped, that would've been his best shot. Jackson stalked over to the ledge of the building, dropping the tip of his gun before peering over. There was no one clinging to the skyscraper on the far side. And in the street below it . . . carnage. Debris; chaos. He could see several people moving, some laid out and motionless, a few dead . . . Was Callaghan one of them? Had he been so desperate, so foolish, maybe preferring to go out on his own terms, to go out by his own hand . . .

Jackson's grip tightened around his rifle. No. This wasn't over until he'd seen his corpse. He'd have to . . . He'd have to get back down there, pass as a regular soldier among the bodies, and—

Suddenly, a thought hit him, and Jackson stopped. All day, he and his people had been underestimating Matt Callaghan, even when they had been consciously trying not to. What had he learned? What did he understand about his quarry? The boy was ruthless. The boy was cunning. But most of all, the boy understood people. Got into their heads with this keen, uncanny insight, and in a moment knew how to make them see what he wanted, drew from them a reaction, manipulated their response.

An empty rooftop. A discarded bag. A thirty-foot gap, and a twelve-story drop. All pieces of a puzzle Jackson had easily brought together, united by a common thread: desperation. But he had *assumed*; he had assumed desperation. He had assumed panic. He had assumed wrong. Matt Callaghan never panicked. Matt Callaghan lied.

Slowly, Jackson lifted his gaze up from the street on the left of the building and swung his rifle back toward the right. Toward the other side, the other street, and the forty-foot gap. Logic said only a fool would've tried it. Yet, misdirection fed on logic.

He strode across the rooftop, boots cracking on the concrete. In the distance, the light Lady Dawn was blasting against the unnatural gray shone like a second sun, a lighthouse warning Jackson against impending death against the rocks. But she was occupied. His brief had guaranteed she'd be occupied—they all would—until the gray bubble went down.

Jackson put one foot on the building's edge, sweeping his gaze over the city below. More carnage, more fire and destruction. He bent down.

There, two feet below him, dangling one-armed from the side of their building from some sort of mechanical piton, hung Matt Callaghan.

"Gotcha," the soldier smiled.

Jane was five feet away from them. Four.

All around her, the grayness pressed, smothering her, howling, but the light inside Jane blazed its fierce defiance, almost blinding as it burned, a boiling golden storm. Somehow, though she advanced step by agonizing step within a forty-foot ball of shining fire, the two men did not notice her. They just kept fighting. Fighting and fighting and fighting. And with each word they screamed, each fist they struck into the other's face, another surge of power raced out, crashing into the other's body, who like an echoing bell, pulsed in turn, the twin waves merging and amplifying in endless corrupting horror.

Twins. They were twins.

"STOP!" Jane shouted, but they could not hear her—or did not want to. She clenched her teeth and forced another step forward, the wind around her so violent now it threatened to bring Jane to her knees.

"STOP!" she cried again, but it was hopeless. Even as she watched, the brother with eyes consumed by white sunk his teeth into his ebony-eyed sibling, and a fresh wave of desecration ricocheted off them.

They could not hear her. But Jane didn't need words. The light of Dawn burned inside her, and its relentless hum soared above the pulsing, screaming shadows, thundering to be heard.

"ARRGGHHH!"

Jane roared, pushed almost flat against the ground—and then, with a wordless shout, the light around her exploded, brighter than it had ever been. In that moment's space, she lunged upward—

And grabbed both men by the neck.

Suddenly, their gazes fell upon her. Abruptly, the twins stopped shouting, and as one, their heads turned, moving despite the strength of her grip to level inhuman stares at her, one set of eyes unbroken white, the other seamless black. Their faces twisted in unblinking fury—identical, flawless opposites—and as one, she felt them rise, glaring down at her with utter contempt, as if they were gods torn from some predestined war. They snarled, and it was as though her fingers clutched around primeval forces, the people they once were consumed by whatever power raged inside, hell-bent on nothing but isolation and the other one's death. In an instant, the full force of the gray, the impossible tempest, descended on her, reverberating one off the other, no longer reeling haphazardly around the men's conflict but focused entirely on Jane, howling to destroy her and no other.

The horrible sound—the hurricane shrieking—grew impossibly louder. Suddenly, though the light of Dawn still burned, it was a flame flickering against the wind. Slowly, the twins stepped forward, their mouths open into voiceless maws, and inch by inch, Jane sank to her knees. For the first time, around their necks, her barrier wavered. Suddenly, the wave of obliteration swept through the golden energy and disintegrated her gloves.

And all of a sudden, she felt them.

And it was as if all time had stopped.

A pool. A pool of deepest black in an endless hall of white. Utterly unbroken, bottomless, a perfect circle of ink sinking down into eternity. Yet, was it a pool, or a reflection of a pool? The inside of an eye or the darkness surrounding one? Was the white outside the black outside the white outside the black outside the—

Suddenly, Jane's mind was hurtling back an impossible distance, to the dawn of time, to the edge of eternity. And from this distance, feeling both of them simultaneously, twin screams swirling and echoing off each other, she saw it. Black coming from white coming from white coming from black. It looked gray because, from a distance, the distinction blurred, so close it grew impossible to separate. But the powers were not gray. They were black and white—they were opposites—and divided, their song was agony, anger, annihilation. Yet, as Jane felt them here—together, synchronized, in concert—she knew they were two halves of the same whole. Death and Life. A shattered circle, never meant to be divided. They belonged together, only for fate to tear them apart.

And suddenly Jane knew what to do. As the searing pain of life and death and creation boiled through her fingertips, as her flesh blackened and grayed and sparked, she moved in her mind a coin she had not rolled for eons, letting it slip between her fingers, disintegrating into the abyss. Electromancy, one of her two remaining mortal powers, fell abandoned into nothingness.

And with her bare hands clenched around both men's necks, Jane Walker *took*.

Suddenly, the wind stopped howling. The twins blinked, and the gray-circling energy stuttered as the storm fell quiet. In the center of Times Square, Jane's eyes turned black. Black as the depths of midnight.

She snarled.

And the brothers collapsed.

The soldier leaned over the side of the building where Matt dangled, his lips twitching into a smile both bloodthirsty and wry.

"You gave me quite the runaround."

"Screw . . . you . . ." Matt answered. Droplets of blood were trickling down his right hand, and his left, the one holding on for dear life to the wall climber, screamed as though it was going to pop out of its socket.

Beyond them, the city roared. The wind whipped. There came distant gunfire and explosions. But in this tiny space between them, on this rooftop, none of that seemed audible. They had two feet of emptiness. Two feet of peace.

"You were great," the man called Jackson smiled—because all of a sudden, Matt knew his name, knew things he hadn't realized, visions he'd never stopped to sort through. The psychic; it must have been. Memories echoing down the line. "If it's any consolation. Honestly, kid, I'm actually going to be a bit sad to kill you. If I had ten guys with your balls, hell, I'd be unstoppable. But, well, the bill comes due."

"Bill these . . . nuts . . ."

Jackson sighed and pulled off his helmet, shaking free his short brown hair. The helmet clattered on the concrete. "You sure you want those to be your last words, little man? You sure you don't want to beg for something more?"

Matt's teeth bared, his vision swimming. His left hand was spasming around the climber, the tendons in his arm shrieking. His entire right side was numb.

"Who?" he managed to gasp. The words fell from Matt's mouth and tumbled twenty-four stories to the asphalt below. "Who . . . did this? Why?"

"Ahh, buddy," the killer sighed. "This isn't one of those tales. This isn't the part where I tell you everything and your friends rush in and you make some heroic getaway. I don't even know, to be completely honest. I do a job, and then I get paid. Everything beyond that's just dressing." He laid the tip of his rifle on the building's edge, casually facing Matt's forehead. "I'm going to shoot you. And you're going to fall. And nobody is going to save you, and I'm going to walk out of here and go home and collect my payment. With seven more shares than anticipated."

"You . . . talk a lot . . . for a man . . . who almost . . . lost."

"Well," said the soldier, "just so happens you've caught me in a loquacious mood. I don't know, maybe it's the fact that on the ride home, I'll have no one to talk to. I don't quite know whether to thank you for that. Eight shares is far more than one, to be certain, but at the same time, I didn't mind some of those kids. They had their uses. Once you got past the stupid."

"You're . . . wasting . . . time . . ." hissed Matt. Tendons in his arm clenched and strained.

"Oh, I've got time aplenty," Jackson smiled. "I know things no man should be knowing. I knew where you were going to be. What you were going to do. And I know that up until the moment that gray bullcrap"—he pointed to the distant field—"disappears, I have all the time in the world."

All of a sudden, the ground beneath them shook. The wind suddenly changed directions, rushing in toward the center of the gray sphere, and it was all Matt could do to hold on for dear life as he was buffeted against the side of the building. Jackson crouched, swinging an incredulous stare toward the dead zone, letting the wind rush over his shoulders.

There was a moment's pause, a breathless hesitation, as if all the air had been sucked into the center of the bubble, reduced now to a single city block.

Suddenly, the gray disintegrated. A shock wave, visible even from this height and from this distance, rippled out in a perfect circle from the center of Times Square, rushing through the streets and cars and the thousands of abominations slowly shambling between them. All of a sudden, from the city below, the cacophony of chaos fell silent, leaving no screaming but the pain in Matt's shoulder, and no wails beyond the whispering winds of death.

Matt stared over the city with watering, disbelieving eyes. The patchwork gray field had vanished, leaving only a single solitary force in its center—a pillar of shining light.

Matt and the mercenary glanced at one another, Matt still dangling there, one shot away from death. Jackson's hard-jawed face was blank. Matt's lips curled into a savage grin.

"You . . ." he hissed, "lose . . ."

For a moment, nothing happened. Matt swayed from the embedded climber, one arm hanging uselessly, suspended in midair on the side of a twenty-four-story building, unable to climb up, unable to swing down, struggling for consciousness and breath. Below him, the wind whipped through the New York City streets, swirling leaves and papers and clouds of dust. For a moment, the world seemed to hold its breath. Jackson could only stare, shocked, off into the distance at the sudden silence, the sudden absence of doom.

"Yeah," he mumbled blankly. "Guess I do."

Then he threw his rifle to the side, reared up to his full height, raised his arms, and slammed them down into the rooftop.

It took three hours, but eventually, they found his body beneath the rubble. A broken corpse among a city of broken corpses, though this one not ruined by undeath's ebb and flow. Two of them, a pair, the muscle-bound soldier and the pale brown-haired boy. Both dead, their bodies shattered, crushed under twelve stories of falling concrete as the entire building collapsed around them.

Jane Walker stared numbly down at Matt's lifeless, ashen body. His bones were cracked, his limbs limp; the back of his head split open like an egg. Somehow, though, his face had survived, unbroken. Powdered in white dust, his features painted as if in some ancient ritual—a peaceful corpse in a nameless urban tomb.

Nobody said anything as they brought him to her, as they laid him at Jane's feet. Suddenly, the Legion's victory seemed muted, their triumph over the inhuman monstrosities soiled by the blood drying behind Matt's skull, the dust on his tiny broken corpse. Jane stood over him, gazing down at him, her mouth closed, barely seeing.

She had done what the Time Child wanted. She had sacrificed Matt Callaghan to save the world. Even now, as her vision swayed, she could feel the timelines floating around her, silk threads spinning into alignment. A strange calm pooled beneath her eyelids, an otherworldly, tearless peace. Two Divine halves were now unbroken. She had crossed some invisible threshold she could not undo.

But which she didn't have to.

"Heal him," she commanded. Jane turned to the Acolytes, the assembled crowd, directing her gaze to Editha, the small, mousy-haired medic who once a thousand years ago had tended her mortal wounds. Not anymore. Nothing remained to hurt her.

The healer paled and glanced at Jane, standing there in her white and flowing gold, her unyielding eyes blue-gray. They could burn with other colors now, though Jane did not share nor use them. But they had all seen.

"I . . . Miss . . . Jane, there's no point. He's gone; there's—"

"Just do what I say."

Reluctantly, the small woman conceded. She shuffled forward, knelt by Matt Callaghan's corpse, and pressed her palms into his flesh.

Slowly, as the minutes ticked by, Matt's wounds knitted together. Bones shifted back into place, gashes sealed over. After a time, the body was whole. Pale, silent, unmoving—but whole.

Editha stood. "There," she said, her voice for once lacking its usual authority. "He's healed. I've done it."

"Good," Jane murmured. She stepped forward. "Now, stand aside."

The circle of dusty, bloodstained maroon-and-gold soldiers stepped backward, not one of them saying a word. To her right, Jane saw out of the corner of her eye Giselle clench Will's hand.

"Jane—" their leader mouthed.

"No," Jane simply replied.

And then, her eyes turned white.

On the shattered streets of New York City, surrounded by ash and rubble, Matt Callaghan awoke, gasping for air, his chest seizing forward, fingers clenching, color rushing back into his cheeks. He awoke to a gray-blue sky and a legion of crimson warriors standing over him, staring down with expressions of mingled horror. But his eyes beheld only the towering, imperious being at their center. The shadow of white and gold that loomed over him, her face drenched in darkness, her hair swirling bronze in the sun.

Matt stared up at Jane and whispered.

"What have you done?"

THE BROKEN MIRROR

REPORT OF PSYCHOLOGICAL ASSESSMENT
Confidential

NAME: Wallace Edmund Cykes

DOB: 22/12/1978

DATE OF ASSESSMENT: 7/1/1997, 17/1/1997, 21/1/1997

DATE OF REPORT: 7/3/1997

STATUS: Intake

— NOT FOR DISTRIBUTION TO PATIENT –

CURRENT MEDICATIONS: Nil.

PSYCHOLOGICAL HISTORY: None.

SUBSTANCE USE: Recreational alcohol, cannabis, psilocybin, lysergic acid diethylamide, 3,4-Methylenedioxymethamphetamine.

Mr. Cykes's toxicology was clear on all occasions of testing, and while he admitted openly to past substance use, he stated he was happy to "give it up if the Legion wanted."

FAMILY HISTORY: Mr. Cykes's mother was 29 and his father 31 at the time of his birth. Mr. Cykes's mother, by his report, suffered postnatal depression and has received treatment for anxiety. He reports that his maternal grandfather had problems with alcohol. He also reports a paternal uncle who may have suffered bipolar illness but is not aware of any specific diagnosis, only that he was "a bit nuts." He has a cousin with an addiction to prescription opiates.

BACKGROUND: Mr. Cykes reports a supportive home and no trauma in his childhood. He states that his family have always been aware of his sexuality and that this has never been a problem for them. Mr. Cykes reports having a strong cohort of friends at various stages of his childhood, and that he still keeps in touch with many of them.

Mr. Cykes reports his earliest telepathic experiences as a child at age 6 as being able to hear his parents' thoughts. When asked whether this was distressing, Mr. Cykes replied in the negative, and stated that when the noise grew overwhelming, he sought solace from the family's beagle, up to and including when she passed away when he was 8. Mr. Cykes spoke with some fondness about the dog and stated that sometimes he "could still feel her there."

PHYSICAL PRESENTATION: Mr. Cykes presents as a neat, intelligent, engaged, and well-mannered individual. He showed no resistance to questions around potentially sensitive subjects and displayed no negative responses when challenged on his answers. He engaged openly with the interviewer regarding complex and philosophical issues and seemed keen to converse. His stated reason for wanting to join the Legion is "because I think I may as well; I'm good enough," and when challenged that this might be insufficient responded, "That's fine. If that's the way it is, then so be it." He appeared healthy, well-rested, and in good spirits across the duration of the interviews.

MENTAL PRESENTATION: Mr. Cykes's mind presents upon examination as exceptionally active and vibrant. His Thought Clarity is graded 1.01 Flawless.

His Malleability is graded Excellent. His Thought Color is Full Spectrum. His Imprint Diameter from outside thought patterns is <0.1. Mr. Cykes uniformly scored in the 99th percentile in practical assessments of Telepathy Levels 1 through 6. Due to the exceptional nature of these results, Mr. Cykes's examinations were repeated by the writer at each interview and the results verified by colleagues on 17/1/97 and 21/1/97 (reports annexed as 'A').

CONCLUSION: Mr. Cykes is an exceptionally gifted telepath of a caliber rarely seen at this or any other center. His thoughts are of a strength, scope, and clarity practically unprecedented in professional practice, and his mind is the most resilient the writer has examined to date. Any attempts by the writer and other colleagues to contest mentally with Mr. Cykes proved fruitless. Mr. Cykes possesses an unwavering foundation of identity and self-assurance that borders on (in a traditional understanding of superego) incongruence with human nature. In the initial stages of interview, the writer held concerns that Mr. Cykes's lack of natural self-doubt may be the result of narcissism or delusions, but upon repeat examination, no basis for either diagnosis has been found.

It is the opinion of this writer, having now examined Mr. Cykes three times, consulted with senior colleagues, and reviewed the existing literature, that Mr. Cykes has, unbeknownst to himself, his school, or his parents, undergone Precocious Manifestation. In telepaths, the early development of powers is near-universally disastrous, as the afflicted child's mind is underdeveloped and unable to process the experience of external thought patterns. In clinical practice, this writer would have anticipated telepathic manifestation at age 6 to be acutely detrimental and have required immediate intervention to avoid serious developmental delays, mental damage, and suicidal ideation.

Despite this, Mr. Cykes neither presents with nor reports any of these symptoms either historically or otherwise. On the contrary, Mr. Cykes's presentation is one of a highly functional and mentally robust young adult. Noting the competing view of Dr. Fawley (report annexed as "B"), it is the opinion of this writer that in seeking mental shelter within his childhood dog, Mr. Cykes's mind may have unwittingly shaped itself to some degree to mirror his companion's, thereby permanently acquiring aspects of canine psychology, in particular a profound sense of optimism and self-assurance. Such experience, as well as Mr. Cykes's current presentation, is highly unusual and demands further study.

RECOMMENDATIONS: Mr. Cykes is RECOMMENDED for recruitment by the Legion of Heroes. In addition to his mature, stable presentation and exceptional telepathic aptitude, his psychological makeup offers hereto-unexplored opportunity for research into Precocious Telepathic Manifestation, treatment of prepubescent telepaths, cross-species telepathic connection, and early mental plasticity. It is the unanimous verdict of assessing physicians that Mr. Cykes be offered immediate Acolyte placement and fast-tracked to full member status.

There was a crash, a tremor, then Matt was falling. The sky fled from his reach, though his hand scrabbled to grasp it, his pale fingers closing around nothing. There was a rising in his stomach and a lightness in his limbs, and the buildings grew tall on all sides, a forest of looming mirrors. Abruptly, all movement ceased; there was a sudden, momentary flicker of blinding pain—

And then nothing. Darkness.

Then he woke up.

"Huuuuuuuhhhh—"

Matt's eyes snapped open. All at once, every one of his senses came rushing back, overwhelming, clamoring to be heard. The sounds of the city: of swirling wind and whispered murmurs, distant sirens, rumbling vehicles, and the far-off *thack-thack* of helicopter blades. The dry smell of dust, of sweat, heat, and garbage, of acrid smoke, and across his tongue, the taste of metallic blood. The feel of his heartbeat—rhythmic thuds which had never before been absent and now returned—shocking, unceasingly loud. The hard, rough surface of the road pressed into his back, the scrape of coarse asphalt rugged and grating beneath his fingertips. Bright images assailed his eyes. The gray-blue sky, the buildings craning their necks down to stare at him—the circle of people doing the same.

Have you ever felt peace? True, absolute, infinite peace borne of the total abandonment of care and self and purpose? In that moment, that darkness, that was what Matt had known. Peace. Devoid of thoughts, devoid of feelings, devoid of life. It was nothing he had ever experienced, yet it was there now, an indelible pinprick inside his memory, a nanosecond of true black. Or maybe an eternity. Time had not mattered; no, had not existed. There had been no change, no gain, no loss. It had not been rest but utter release, devoid of dreams or sense or weariness.

Slowly, Matt sat up, seeds of panic blooming within his rib cage, a feeling of such abject wrongness, because he—he could feel again; he could breathe again. No, he shouldn't . . . His eyes strained against the light, and his breath strained against his lungs, and he . . . he was *wrong*. Everything felt wrong, messy, wet and hot and dry and cold and loud and rough and painful, and he was tumbling, he was choking, acidic saliva threatening to close his throat as his fingers scrapped against reality.

He lifted his gaze to find Jane standing over him, and in that moment, Matt knew without knowing where this terror stemmed from.

"What have you done?" he whispered. For no man was meant to know nonexistence. No man was supposed to return, carrying that black splinter in his mind.

Matt sat on the remnants of a collapsed brick wall, feet on the footpath, keeping his own quiet, downcast counsel as the Legion's healer, Editha, examined him. Throughout the city, emergency services had arrived in force, the National Guard and the Army marching in detachments down the streets, fixing damage, attending to the wounded. Most of them didn't spare Matt a glance, though the few who did lingered for a confused second look. The day's chaos and death shrouded Matt's normal celebrity beneath a veil shared by every other civilian survivor; silent, distant-eyed, caked in dust and drying blood.

"Open your mouth," Editha requested. Matt complied, obedient yet resigned, as the small healer stuck in a wooden tongue depressor. "Say 'ahhh.'"

"Ahhh."

"Good." She put the strangely pleasant-tasting stick away, then felt petite fingers around underneath his jaw. "Glands feel fine." Editha placed the back of her hand on Matt's forehead, then held his wrist and began counting. "No fever. Pulse . . . eighty. Bit low, considering."

"Considering I was just dead," Matt noted, making no attempt to restrain his bitterness.

"Yes," Editha replied, her voice level and dry. "Considering that." She withdrew a small hammer with a triangular beige plastic head from her pocket and tapped first one and then the other of Matt's knees. "Reflexes fine. Pupil dilation . . ."—she pocketed the hammer, drew a pen-torch and shone a light in his eyes—"normal." The healer paused and took a step back. "How do you feel?"

"Physically or mentally?"

The corners of Editha's mouth twitched in what was either minor amusement or the beginnings of a frown. "Perhaps the wrong question." She considered him for a moment, one hand perched tentatively on her dainty waist. "You seem fine. Normal, even."

"Thanks."

"Is there any pain?"

"Physically or mentally?" Matt repeated darkly.

"Either." The seriousness of Editha's tone didn't waver. "Anything abnormal." She glanced behind her, perhaps making sure they were alone. "This is new territory for me too."

Matt let out a small sigh.

"I'm . . . unsettled," he told her finally. "Jittery. Having trouble marshaling my resources. But nothing hurts. I can see clearly. I hear fine. Everything's moving."

"Nothing's numb?"

"Nothing's numb. I don't have a headache. I don't feel hot."

"Any insatiable desire for human flesh?"

Matt glanced up at her, a bit taken aback. The healer's face split into a small, apologetic smile.

"Black humor. Sorry."

"No," said Matt. "It was funny. I'm just . . . I guess I'm struggling to get in the mood."

"Understandable." Editha glanced again over her shoulder. "Look," she said, turning back to Matt, "if it's any consolation, as far as I can tell, you're perfectly healthy. When I put my hands on you, I don't get the sense anything's broken. Usually, you can tell. Everything points to you being in normal human condition." She paused. "Do you feel like you're missing your soul?"

Matt made a face. "Is that a standard ER question?"

"Are you a standard ER patient?"

"Good point." Matt let out a deep sigh, then reluctantly gave it due consideration. "No," he eventually answered as a Jeep full of khaki soldiers drove past, huddled around one crimson-clad figure in their center. "Everything feels . . . okay."

"Okay," replied Editha. She looked down at him, her expression torn between sadness and knowing. "I guess we're just left with the big disturbing nonmedical questions then, aren't we?"

"*Yeppp.*" Matt shifted his legs and slid his hands beneath his thighs, rocking slightly forward, gazing off down the broken streets, the smoke and rubble. Editha grimaced.

"Look," she told him, "I've got to go heal other people, but I'm booking you in for another consult in twenty-four hours. We need to monitor for changes. Plus," she added, half joking, "I've watched a lot of Romero movies."

"Very reasonable," Matt replied. He indicated with his chin over toward the battle zone. "Were there many wounded?"

"On our side? A few. Bunch of cops panicking and getting themselves injured, though others made a good accounting. Most of them have been taken care of. It's just . . ."

Editha's voice trailed off as she shifted in place, decidedly uncomfortable. Matt's brow furrowed.

"What? What's the issue?"

"The healing's not for the living." Editha's mouth was a hard, thin line. "We're doing everyone from the gray zone."

Matt's face paled.

"Yeah," said Editha, mirroring his expression. "That's about my take on it too."

"What happened to them?"

"After the shock wave? Every single one of them dropped dead." She hesitated, thin lips twitching. "Well, dropped more dead. Actually dead. They stopped moving." The healer gave a small shrug, as if trying to convince herself they were discussing nothing more worrying than an interesting case of kidney stones. "The work's actually not that difficult. I thought the big ones were all going to require surgery, but if you keep healing them long enough, they just sort of . . . shrink back to normal."

"Normal and dead."

"Oh yes. Very much dead."

"I'm guessing there are plans to change that," Matt murmured. He gazed off over the now quiet devastation, searching listlessly for a figure of gold and white.

"You guess correct."

They lapsed into silence.

"This feels wrong," Matt muttered.

"I'm sure not going to get much help from the AMA advice line," Editha replied, keeping the reply decidedly neutral, though it sounded like she agreed.

In the distance, the pearlescent figure Matt had been searching for broke away from a group of Acolytes and soldiers. Matt watched as her eyes swept over the battlefield and found him. She began marching forward. Editha followed his gaze.

"I better go," she said, watching Jane approaching. Matt shook his head.

"You haven't done anything wrong."

"Not a hundred percent what I was concerned about." She flicked Matt a quick, guilty glance. "Not that I'm saying anything. I know you two are—"

"Were. In a past life," he muttered darkly. The corner of Editha's mouth flicked in a subtle grimace as Jane crossed the last of the gap between them, gold cape billowing in the wind.

"How is he?" she demanded, leveling a stare at the healer.

"Perfectly healthy," Editha reported. "No issues."

"Good. They're getting the bodies laid out."

"I'll get right to it." With only a single discreet backward glance of mingled concern, the small healer set off toward Times Square and the field of greater disaster, leaving Matt and Jane alone.

For a few long seconds, the couple remained silent and apart from one another, Matt sitting on the brick wall averting his eyes, Jane standing looking down at him, her hands on her hips. Finally, Jane broke the silence, her voice laced with warmth and worry.

"Hey," she said, "are you alright?"

"I'm fine."

"Do you want someone to take you home?" The moment the battle was over, the citywide Disruptance field that had been preventing teleportation had just . . . stopped. Whoever was behind all this had either destroyed the device or devices, or simply turned them off.

"What home?" Matt replied, the words perhaps coming out angrier than he might have wanted. Jane frowned.

"Morningstar. Obviously."

"No, thank you."

"You'll be safe there."

Matt kept his mouth closed to prevent any of a thousand burning comebacks leaping unbidden from his tongue. Instead, he forced himself to swallow, looked up, and met Jane's gaze.

"You're resurrecting the monsters?" he asked.

"I'm resurrecting the people," she corrected, sounding a bit annoyed. "The waves were mutating them. I can fix it."

"'Fix it'?" Matt asked, incredulous. "Resurrecting dead people is 'fixing' now?"

"They weren't supposed to die," replied Jane. She sounded a little taken aback at his resistance. "They just got caught up. They're innocent bystanders."

"So we're resurrecting anyone who's innocent now?"

"I'm sorry," Jane said, scowling, "are you annoyed at me for not killing people? For not letting—hell, I don't know, however many thousands of mothers and fathers and children die because they just happened to be in the wrong place at the wrong time? Isn't this exactly what you were arguing, like, four hours ago?"

Matt stared at her, his hands balling into fists between his thighs and the crumbling ledge. "How the"—he swore—"can you not see how slippery this slope is?"

"Oh, come on," Jane sighed.

"Being Dawn wasn't bad enough. Time travel wasn't bad enough." Matt was too angry to even say Pokémon. "Now you're controlling life and death too? You're the Grim"—he swore again—"Reaper?!"

"That's not fair," said Jane. She leaned forward, raising her hand halfway, as if about to start shaking a finger at him, then seemed to think better of it. "I'm making it right. This power killed them; it makes sense—it's . . . fair—that it brings them back."

"Oh, so you're deciding what's fair now?"

"Oh, well, screw me for not leaving a city full of orphans!"

"What's next?" Matt cried, hands clenching on the brick wall, feeling as if he was about to launch to his feet. "Seriously, what's next? You going to resurrect every victim you find? You going to resurrect that little acid girl's family? How about James, huh? Nancy, Chino, Selwyn. Hell, let's go dig up Mentok and the old Legion—let's go dig up your mom!"

The cloud that descended over Jane's face was darker than any Matt had ever seen. "Be careful," she whispered, her eyes narrowing. "Be very, very careful."

"Or what?" Matt replied, throwing up his hands. "You going to put me back to sleep? A little bit of time-out in deadland before you resurrect me so that I learn my lesson?"

"For your information"—Jane scowled—"it doesn't work like that."

"What doesn't? Enlighten me, oh angel of mercy."

"Will you stop?" she said, rubbing her forehead with an exasperated sigh. "I'm trying to tell you. This power . . . It's not like that. It's more . . ." Jane hesitated, clearly struggling to find the words. "Conscious? Temperamental? It doesn't . . . It's hard to explain, but you can feel . . . I don't know. It likes it when things are balanced somehow. It doesn't want to be used lightly. I don't know; I can't explain . . . But the people who are dead here are fine because it did that. It damaged them, so it's fine with fixing them, see? But if someone's been dead for ages . . ."

"Listen to yourself," Matt said, appalled. "You're talking about powers as if they're sentient. About life and death and resurrecting people like it's a . . . jigsaw puzzle." Matt chewed his lips, resisting the urge to launch into more aggressive criticism, instead forcing himself to pause, to close his eyes and draw in a long, deep breath.

"Jane," he said, trying his best to keep his voice level, "I love you. And I . . . I mean, I appreciate what you . . . I . . . I appreciate being alive. I really do. And I know you're just trying to help. But you are in so, so deep right now it's gone past the point of being worried." He paused, staring up at her, pleading with his eyes. "Let's compromise, okay? I get what you're saying about the dead bodies. I agree, that makes sense. This . . . life, death, whatever power caused this, okay. Use it to fix it. Okay. I concede. But then please, please give it up. I'm begging you; I'm actually begging you. I will get down on my hands and knees and"—he swore—"beg you . . . just get rid of it. No good can come of this. We are . . . so far from Kansas. We are waist deep in weirdness; two hundred yards on the wrong side of the line."

Jane's thin eyebrows furrowed, and she stared at him like the very suggestion was ridiculous. "I'm not giving it up," she replied. "What if something else like this happens? What if the twins get loose again?"

"The . . . The guys who were in the center? I thought you killed them."

"I did." Jane shrugged, nonchalant. "But I'm going to resurrect them. The power doesn't like them not living. And they just sort of got . . . caught up fighting." She shrugged. "Honestly, I don't think they really understood what they were doing, how their abilities interact. It's one ability, really; sometimes, this happens with twins. It was just unfortunate it was a power like this, and—"

"Jane," Matt interrupted, still aghast. "I don't care about obscure superhuman biology. I'm telling you, fix the mess they made, then give the power up."

"Come on." Jane sighed, her hands going to her hips. The way she said it made it sound like she was having to re-explain a shellfish allergy she'd already told him about. "You know I can't give this up."

"Why not?!"

"Why?" snorted Jane. "Look around you! What the hell do you think just happened? Do you remember a team of soldiers setting this crazy, city-leveling trap to try and kill you? Do you remember being at the bottom of a collapsing building? No," she said, and the dismissal in her tone made it clear she found the idea preposterous and that her decision was final. "I'm keeping it. You didn't want me time traveling? Fine. This is how I'll protect you."

Matt was at a loss for words. "Jane," he spluttered, "you can't—"

"What?" Jane snapped, annoyed. "What's the problem? Whoever sent those men after you is still out there, and until I find them, you're not safe."

"So once you find them, you'll let it go?"

"No," Jane sniffed, wrinkling her nose. "There'll be other dangers. What does it matter?" She glared at him. "You don't want to die, and I'm not going to let you. I thought this would be a good thing! You don't have to be scared."

"I *am* scared!" Matt cried, throwing up his hands. Without realizing it, he rose to his feet. On the other side of the street, he saw people turn and look toward them. "Jane, I'm terrified! You're not letting me—"

"What? What am I not letting you do?" Jane shouted, her own hands rising, equally incredulous. "What life am I stopping you from leading? What have I ever done except try to help?"

"You're not listening!"

"I *am* listening!" she cried. "You said it was dangerous to travel through time. I did it anyway, and I was *fine*, but who cares about that? Matt always knows better, so I'm *listening*." She laced the word thick with derision. "I've found another power. I've found another way!"

"Good, so you're going to give up time travel?"

Jane fell abruptly silent, her mouth open. For a few moments, she worked her jaw, but no words came out.

"I knew it!" Matt exclaimed, throwing up his hands. He stabbed at her with an accusing finger. "This isn't about me; it was never about me! This is about power! It's about control!"

"Oh, as if you—"

"You can't let go!" he cried. "You've got to be in control of everything: everybody's lives, everything aligning to your little vision, and—!"

"That's not fair!" Jane countered. "You know that's not fair! You're so hung up on this . . . *normal* bullcrap, you can't see the bigger picture; you can't see—"

"You're playing God!"

"I'm protecting you!"

"YOU'RE NOT GOD!"

"WELL MAYBE I SHOULD BE!" Jane's roar echoed across the city streets, the sound reverberating off the skyscrapers. Across the road, the onlookers who had been trying to eavesdrop flinched. Matt paid them no heed, his scowl reserved solely for Jane, who met his gaze with equal fury, her eyes gray-blue and burning. "Maybe I've had enough of suffering for other people's choices. Maybe it's time I set things right."

"Absurd," Matt spat, shaking. "Absolutely absurd. I'm going. I can't do this. I can't—" He moved to push past her, but Jane stepped in front of him, blocking his way.

"Where are you going?" she demanded, holding a hand to his chest. "Stop being an idiot. Where are you going to go?"

"Away!" Matt shouted. "For a walk! Anywhere! Outside!"

"I'm coming with you!"

"No!" he cried, and though his girlfriend towered over him in every way, he nevertheless pushed her aside. "Leave me alone!"

"It's not safe!"

"What does it matter?!" Matt shouted, turning on his heel to face her, throwing his hands up in an incredulous expression as he walked backward, away from her. "It's not like anything can hurt me; it's not like you won't just *bring me back to life!*" He swore hot and furious, muttering dark curses under his breath as he continued to storm away, small pebbles of concrete crumbling beneath his feet.

"Matt!"

"No."

"Oh, for God's—" Jane rolled her eyes so hard it moved her entire head. Matt just kept walking. "I'm sending someone with you!"

"I'm fine!"

"No, you're not! It's not—!"

"Fine!" Matt shouted. "Fine! Send Celeste! At least she's capable of changing!"

"Oh, screw you!" cried Jane.

"Screw yourself!" He spun back and flipped her both middle fingers, a gesture that in the moment felt incredibly petty, unhelpful, and profoundly satisfying. Jane watched him go, the expression on her tattooed face torn between exasperation, anger, and shock. Matt paid it no heed, continuing his furious march, storming on toward the deserted city, with nowhere left to go.

Jane strode through the front doors of the Academy some hours later, alone, daylight and her indignation having faded, her sense of self-righteousness having not. As she stepped into the halls, she passed dregs of exhausted Acolytes, some dusted in grime or blood or still wearing dirty armor. They huddled together and whispered as she approached, though most fell silent when she got closer. Some stood to attention, some just stared, some saluted. Those that motioned to her, Jane met with curt nods. She was right, she thought as her boots strode across the powder-blue carpet. She knew she was right. And if Matt couldn't see it, well, that was his problem. She'd keep on saving him anyway.

Jane made her way up the stairs and around to the third-floor computer lab, not bothering to change out of her uniform or give the many people staring at her an errant thought or the time of day.

"What've you got for me?" she demanded, striding without announcement into Azleena's command center. The genius was, as ever, behind her computer screens, wearing what Jane noted with approval were the same clothes she'd been wearing this morning.

"A study on monozygotic twins," Azleena replied, glancing up. "That theorized that in rare cases, congenital superhuman abilities could manifest in complementary asynchronous phenotypes."

"Azleena," Jane sighed in monumental exasperation, rolling her eyes, "it's just me."

"Oh. Right. Sorry. You were right. What you were saying on the comms before. Seems like identical twins sometimes each share half a normal superpower."

"Great."

"Much more interesting is the fact that you were able to combine them, at least internally," the genius murmured. She peered up at Jane with the expression of a scientist considering dissection. "That warrants further research."

"Can it wait?"

"Yes. Obviously. Probably today's least interesting development." She flicked open new windows on her screen as Jane strode around the computer desk to be able to see them. "Cleanup operations are well underway. Crews are under strict orders not to dispose of the bodies." Azleena glanced at her. "I've informed the authorities that the cause of the wave was an Aurora Nirvanas–style prototype some mad scientist cooked up illegally in their basement. Consequently, the dead bodies are not 'dead,' simply in a 'Six Day Slumber' style coma. They're being moved to hospitals for 'monitoring,' i.e., for when you get around to seeing them."

"Very nice," Jane complimented her. "Well done."

"Thank you. I thought it circumvented questions of a more metaphysical or religious nature, as I assumed you had no desire for a conversation with the Pope."

"You assumed correct. What else?"

"Qiang and Liang Cao Duan," the genius continued, "have been moved to one of our secure storage facilities in the Appalachians. They have their hands covered and bound, they're being telekinetically floated everywhere, and each has a personal neutralizer staring holes into them around the clock."

"Excellent. Do we know what they were fighting over?"

"There's been no interrogation."

"Good. I'll go and see them when we're done. Next?"

"Of Matt's attackers," Azleena sighed, "we have nothing. No, that's not entirely correct. We have pulled out eight bodies from a collapsed Department of Agriculture and Fisheries construction site. They've all been identified. I'm still running the list of names, but my initial impression is that they're mercenaries. Mostly ex-military guns for hire; I presume pretty high grade and pretty expensive to be taking on this kind of job. I suspect once we check their bank records, we will find large wire transfers."

"Trace their every movement," Jane demanded. "I want to know everything."

"I will try, but it may be difficult," Azleena replied, the words dry. Her small head turned, and she fixed Jane with a raised, meaningful eyebrow. "Seeing as all of them are dead."

Jane raised her own eyebrow just an inch. "Interesting. Let me consider that."

"Good. On the communications blackout front, we can confirm the device recovered from one of the nearby buildings matches the one stolen from the Department of Defense lockup some weeks ago."

"I put two and two together."

"Well, just confirming." The genius paused. "I haven't had time to go much deeper into those server records Matt procured for me. I'll get around to it, but—"

"No, I understand," Jane interrupted. "Higher priorities. Find time when you can."

"Time is the one thing we geniuses never have enough of." Azleena tilted her head slightly as she said it; Jane got the impression the girl was deliberately averting her eyes.

"Something you want to say?"

"Not in this context," Azleena replied, "but I would be keen to schedule a discussion." She paused and returned to her screens. "Other than that, um . . . Well, there's no classes tomorrow. Everyone's on general R&R."

"They can do what they like," Jane said, indifferent. "That's a matter for Giselle."

"I'll leave it to her, then. What else. The DoD and the State Department both want to debrief; I'm ignoring them. Media are having a field day, but the marketing teams says it'll come out as good PR. The mayor of New York wants to give us the key to the city; I'll add it to the collection. The Eastborough Baptists have declared the end of days, same as they do every couple of months. Oh, and some beauty pageant hotel owner is suing us—I've flicked it to legal." She paused and glanced up. "I'm still working on Matt's mech suit."

"It can be a lower priority." Jane didn't know whether she said that because she was less worried about Matt dying now or because she was still angry at him for storming away. Maybe both.

"Where is he?"

"Taking some time."

For a moment, Azleena was silent. "Doesn't he need to come back?" she eventually asked.

"Not immediately," Jane replied, trying to sound indifferent. "Celeste is with him. If he's going to be a princess, she can be his dragon."

"Oh, that reminds me." Azleena turned back to her computer. "I have to forward some emails to her. She's had three requests for paid appearances at Renaissance fairs."

"Wonderful," drawled Jane, who genuinely did not care. "Unless there's more, I'm going to interrogate the twins."

"Giselle will want to come with you. Hang on, let me just send . . . She'll meet you in the grounds."

"Good." Jane strode out without a backward glance. As she did, a little voice inside her head that sounded suspiciously like Matt reminded her to say *thank you*, but Jane had heard enough from Matt for one day. She shoved the voice aside. Azleena was doing her job.

Jane marched back down the stairs and through the corridors, ignoring again the Acolytes' whispers and stares and salutations, along with those who shouted thanks or clapped or held out their hands for high fives. Jane didn't need them. She didn't need any of them.

She hiked down the long grassy hill for once instead of flying, finding something cathartic in the stomping of her boots, and found

Will and Giselle waiting for her by the tree line, speaking in low whispers. As she approached, their conversation slid to a halt.

"Hey," said Giselle. She gave Jane a smile, but it was stiff. "There you are. What a—What a day, huh?"

"It went well," Jane replied simply, her mouth staying taut. "Let's get this over with."

"Jane, I—" The Legion's leader glanced between her and Will, seemingly unsure of what words she was trying to stammer out. "I think . . . There's been a lot of . . . Do you need to . . ."

"What I need," Jane snapped, "is for everyone to stop wasting my time and to go talk to these prisoners."

Giselle and Will exchanged further glances, the former opening her mouth as if to say something, the latter staying deliberately silent. Eventually, Giselle seemed to think better of it. Jane took Will's arm, her hands still bare, as she hadn't gotten around to replacing her gloves. The teleporter recoiled slightly.

"Hang on," he said, completely unnecessarily, and once more, they were transported through a tunnel of darkness pushing in on all sides.

They reappeared atop a mountainside, at the summit of a small dirt path leading back down several hundred feet into a waiting forest below. A bus-size metal door lay before them, embedded into a semicircular wall of concrete that was itself sunk into the mountain beneath a shady rocky outcrop. The sun was setting. Without any preamble, Giselle stepped up to the metal door and knocked three times, causing it to open and allow them all through.

"Welcome," came a voice, familiar though somewhat strained. "Welcome, do come in. Welcome to my mountain abode."

"Hey, baby." Will smiled, pecking the waiting Wally on the cheek. Giselle greeted him the same way, while Jane just grunted and made no physical contact. The psychic ushered them all into a low room that was mainly concrete, a few folding chairs and table, a makeshift kitchen, and a small television with a DVD player, closing the door behind them. "Big day."

"No rest for the wicked," the teleporter replied.

"I've put on a pot of coffee."

"Where are they?" demanded Jane, looking around the small bunker. "I don't see them."

"They're in the back," Wally explained. "We cleared out a few old storage rooms, Midas'd in some glass. One-way mirrors. Not the fanciest, but—"

"It'll do," interrupted Jane. She turned to the psychic. "Have you talked to them?"

"Beyond checking if they wanted coffee? No. Kabir and Waverley are still neutralizing, but neither seems to be doing anything to escape. One keeps crying." Wally looked around, his eyebrows furrowed. "Where's Matt?"

"Taking a goddamn walk," Jane snapped. "Where were you?"

"What do you mean?" The psychic looked taken aback.

"Today. You weren't at the battle."

"I was in the skeleton crew," Wally replied blankly. "At Morningstar. People always hang back to guard the Academy; you know this."

Jane grumbled something under her breath but was unable to articulate her objection any further. She had known that, actually.

"Besides," Will chimed in, "it's not like I could've come get him."

"Exactly," the psychic agreed. "And Natalia handled it."

"Handled herself well, actually." Will grinned.

"Of course she did," Wally laughed. "Mad bitch, when has she ever not?"

"Enough," Jane snapped. "Take me to them. Let's get this over with."

The three Legionnaires exchanged glances, but after a moment, Wally gave a small flourishing bow and began leading the way. He led them through a low steel door and into a tight round-roofed concrete hallway, where two doors stood to the right beside large, out-of-place panes of glass. Two Acolytes, a dark-skinned boy and a bushy-haired white girl, stood against the wall opposite, standing to attention as they stared through their respective windows.

Jane stepped up to the wall before the two neutralizers, looking through both mirrors at the men detained within. Both sat at rectangular metal tables, their hands bound in thick mitt-like restraints and handcuffed to the back of their chairs. The one on the right, the one with the torn white jacket and buzz fade, was just staring blankly, not saying anything. The one of the left, still all in black and with strands of black hair dangling down his face, was openly weeping.

"They haven't said anything?" Jane asked, looking between the Acolytes and Wally. All three shook their heads.

"The one in white has been considering asking for a lawyer," said the redheaded psychic, "but he keeps thinking better of it. The other one . . ." Wally shrugged. "He's only thinking about a girl."

"You've read their minds?"

"I've done some . . . light digging," the psychic replied. "Figured while they were sitting here, it couldn't hurt to have a gentle . . . ruffle around?"

"Is that legal?" Will asked, one eyebrow raised in mild concern.

"Is what legal?" Wally replied airily. "There's no evidence these men have been telepathically examined. Not a single blip or errant thought. I don't know what you're talking about."

Jane clenched her eyes closed. For some reason, even though he was being helpful, she found the psychic's playful tone extremely irritating.

"So what can you tell us?" she demanded, glaring at the twins—though of course, her words did not carry into the sealed cells, and neither man could see her.

"They're Qiang and Liang Cao Duan." He pronounced the names *Chang* and *Lee-ang*. "Twin brothers, in case that wasn't obvious. Liang works—or worked—for the Chinese Communist Party as their state executioner. He can bring the dead back to life by touching them, but doing so causes someone else nearby to die. Qiang was recently rented out to the American Department of Justice. His power's the opposite: he kills anyone who touches him, and then a few seconds later, someone comes back to life. Which is ironically what started this all." Wally paused and looked at Jane. "He killed a girl."

"Right," said Jane, chewing the word.

"Accidentally. Anyway, Liang is a drug-fiend party boy, and Qiang needs about twenty years' worth of hugs and therapy before he can reengage with society. Which one do you want to talk to first?"

"Which one's going to be most useful?"

"Qiang at this point has essentially no emotional barriers," Wally advised her. "If you went in there and asked him to cut you out his organs, he'd probably do it, and in my view, you'd be liable for duress. Liang might be a little more recalcitrant. Although he's got a deep sense of having screwed up." The psychic paused. "If you're going to talk to him"—he nodded at Qiang—"be careful. He's fragile."

"I don't care."

Wally frowned, but before he could say another word, Jane strode over and opened the door, barging into the black-clad man's room. The riveted metal door swung shut behind her, blocking out all sound, replacing the noise of the bunker's halls with the prisoner's sobbing, which continued, oblivious to her entry.

"Do you know who I am?" Jane demanded. She loomed over the Chinese murderer with her arms pushing down against the steel table. "Do you speak English?"

It took a few moments, but eventually, the black-clad twin's sobbing ceased, and the man looked up. Behind lengths of lank hair, his eyes were no longer pitch black but normal white with brown irises. The edges were red from crying.

"Yes," he murmured.

"Yes to what?"

"Yes. Both."

"Good," said Jane. She pulled herself into the seat opposite him, the only other chair at the rectangular metal table. "Your name's Qiang."

"Yes."

"Do you remember what happened?"

"I . . ." Fresh tears leaked from his eyes. "Some of it."

"Which parts?"

"Before we got to New York. After that . . . it's . . . blurry." He hiccupped, then gazed up, slow revelation dawning. "You were there."

Jane already knew that. "What happened?" she demanded. "Why were you and your brother fighting?"

She had expected some supernatural answer: that they had gotten too close together, that in close proximity, unknowingly, they had triggered some reaction in powers, the force of Divine polar opposites. She had not expected Qiang to slump forward and start crying again.

"I killed her," he moaned, almost a whisper. Fresh tears trickled down his cheeks. "I killed her. I dropped the glass; it's all my fault."

"Glass? What glass? What're you talking about? Who did you kill?"

"I . . ." Qiang hiccupped again. "She used to deliver things to my house. I-I invited her inside. I-I loved her, but she touched my face, and—"

"And your brother was angry at you for killing this girl?" Jane pushed. "You both knew her?"

"No," the broken man whispered. "He didn't . . . A few weeks ago, his own girlfriend, Melody, he . . . He used . . . He revived her. I begged him to do the same. He refused. I . . ." His head dipped further. ". . . I *couldn't* stand it. I just wanted her back. I wanted him dead." Fat tears leaked from the corners of his eyes. "I'm so sorry."

"If a mistake's been made with the girl, I can correct it," Jane said, dismissing the problem with an errant wave. "Did anyone speak to you leading up to the conflict? Did someone tell you to go fight your brother?"

"No," Qiang replied, sniffing. He looked back up at her, confused. "What do you mean correct it? She's dead."

"I have your power," explained Jane. "Yours and Liang's. If you tell me where the body is, I can arrange for it to be collected, and I can revive her. We're doing the same to everyone you killed in New York."

Qiang's breath drew in so sharply it could've punctured a lung. "You can . . . fix her?" he asked, leaning forward, his eyes wide, pulling unconsciously against his restraints as though he didn't dare believe.

"Yes." Jane sighed, trying not to grind her teeth. There was nothing new about this. She didn't care about some dead delivery girl. "You're missing the point. Other things happened while you and your brother were fighting. Stuff that made it seem like the whole thing had been planned. What do you know about that? How can that be?"

"Planned?" asked Qiang, and his mouth puckered as if he'd tasted something sour. "None of this was planned. I didn't mean to. I ruined . . ." He stared back at her, desperation shining on his tearstained face. "But you can do it? Please? You can save Emily?"

"I can save whoever I—" Suddenly, Jane stopped. For something had just snagged in her brain.

She abruptly stood. "Thank you for your time. Someone will be in shortly. Goodbye." Jane turned on her heel and strode out into the hallway, slamming the door behind her before the man could eke out another word.

"Do we have a connection up here?" she demanded of the Legion members assembled outside. Giselle and Will glanced at Wally, who shrugged.

"Probably out on the hilltop," he replied. "Until something more permanent gets put in. Why?"

"I need to speak to Azleena."

"Okay. Why?"

"The fight was over a girl."

"Okay," Wally repeated, shrugging. "Are we . . . Is that outside the realm of possibility? I know it's a huge disaster, but isn't that kind of a universal human truth? Earth-shattering things stem from trivial causes?"

"It's not the fight that bothers me," said Jane. "It's her."

Without further explanation, she pushed past them, leaving the twins to their holding rooms and the neutralizers on guard. She strode through the bunker, back out through the door, and into the open cleft of the mountainside. The second Jane smelled fresh air, she pressed her finger to her earpiece.

"Azleena."

"Copy."

"The girl in the server records. The one there were so many documents about, whose life they were trying to ruin. Who was it? What was her name?"

High atop the mountain, staring out over the valley below, Jane's head spun with a sensation that wasn't vertigo. She knew the answer already; she remembered it from last night, though the conversation felt as if it had been in another lifetime. Even so, Jane clung to the possibility that her memories were false, that she'd misheard or misremembered, though she knew the hope was in vain. She had no doubt. She didn't even need to hear the genius say it.

"Emily?"

"The fight was orchestrated."

They were all, the five of them, back at the Academy, in Azleena's computer room. The Cao Duan twins had been left in containment at the mountain, under guard but almost forgotten. Later, they would have to be dealt with; someone would have to figure out what to do with them. Right now . . .

"I'm still in preliminary review of the documents," said Azleena. She turned in her chair to look at Giselle, Jane, Wally, and Will. "But there's no mistaking it. The same group behind the attack on Park River Arms targeted this girl." The genius's face was grim. "We have to assume their goal was for her to seduce—well, that's the wrong word. *Infatuate* Qiang. That's the point of the psychological profiles. His browser history. Somebody put him in the path of a girl they knew would fuel a disproportionate reaction, who would trigger an irrational attachment in his psyche."

"That's impossible," Giselle protested. "It doesn't make any sense. There's too much coincidence. Someone knew Qiang was going to drop a glass, and Emily was going to touch him? That his brother was going to appear? That they were going to be panic-teleported to New York? That's ridiculous."

Azleena shook her head. "You don't understand. It's not just Qiang they were manipulating: it's Liang too." She turned back to the computer, opening up a series of items on the screen. "They have records of his every move. Psychological profiles of women, just like they did with Emily. They identified this girl, Melody—I mean, Chu Mey is her Chinese name—who was his type and had an existing drug problem. They've been playing on their vices for months." Azleena clicked through more windows. "Higher-potency drug drops. Keeping police off their and their dealers' backs. A clear pattern of encouraging use in two addictive personalities, which pretty much sooner or later is only going to result in one thing."

"But again," said Giselle, "how the hell would they know that? How the hell would they know what this guy was going to do let alone when we would do anything?"

The genius shook her head, staring at the speedster with wide, unblinking amber eyes. "You've got to stop thinking about this as planned down to the last detail. It was meticulous, yes, but in broad, key elements. Adaptable. Qiang, suffering severe isolation, inevitably having some kind of breakdown. Liang, with his drug abuse, inevitably running into overdose, paranoia, or problems with the law. Two volatile elements, and all you've got to do is wait and watch and make sure, somehow, they end up in the same room."

Azleena turned back to the screen. "I don't know how they predicted the reaction once they did finally come into contact, but maybe it's not a stretch to think that if a man who kills by touching and a man who brings people back to life make direct contact, something bad will happen. For me, that's the biggest hole. How whoever planned this knew there was going to be a reaction of this magnitude, rather than just, say, both of them dropping dead."

"Because it's happened before." Wally suddenly stood straighter, withdrawing his forefinger from where it'd been pressed against his lips. "When I was listening to their thoughts earlier, both of them kept thinking back to the sensation of touching each other, the gray waves, this field, this house . . ." He looked around at the other four. "I assumed it was just feelings of guilt at the time, interspersed with memories of New York, but what if it wasn't? What if previously, they . . ." His voice trailed off, looking horrified. Giselle and Will looked sick.

"Our missing piece," said Azleena with a grimace and a nod. "That settles it. They're Chinese nationals; the record is likely hidden. But I'm certain if I keep digging . . . Both their parents are listed as deceased. I'm guessing sometime after their powers manifested, they made contact, and . . ." She let the thought trail. "Their powers wouldn't have been as strong back then. Maybe the emotional turmoil wasn't as bad. Maybe they were able to break apart before the effect spread, but the Chinese government still found them. Maybe there's still a record somewhere."

"Jesus," Will breathed.

"From there," Azleena powered forward, laying her theories down like a hand of cards, "it's simple. They have the communications blocker ready to go. They organize the attack on Matt in his apartment to flush him out and back to Morningstar. And then, it's simply a matter of waiting for the disaster to go down." She paused, looking at each of them in turn. "The Legion deploys in force, as it has to. Dawn is tied down matching Divine with Divine. And then, irrespective of whether Matt is with Jane or stays at the Academy, they have a team on standby waiting to deploy, and a citywide Disruptance net waiting to close the door. Simple."

"Simple?" Wally asked, incredulous.

Azleena rolled her eyes. "Alright, not *simple*. But clear. Logical. Flexible. Adaptable to coincidence and shifting circumstance. This was all a play for Matt's blood."

"The only thing they didn't account for was him being so slippery," said Will, shaking his head in wonder.

"And Jane being able to bring him back." Azleena paused, hesitating to give voice to the elephant in the room. "As far as I can see from my brief foray into the literature, nobody has ever tested an empath's ability to combine complementary twin powers. It's completely unprecedented. If it wasn't for that and the mercenary team being so ineffective, everything would have gone like they wanted."

Giselle swore—a vicious stream of curse words that caused everyone else in the room to look away from her and was entirely uncharacteristic to how she usually spoke.

"Who?" she demanded, staring wide-eyed and angry at Azleena. "Who could possibly have done this?"

"I don't know," the genius replied, looking quite unhappy to have to say it. "The documents don't have that. I need more time to go through everything and cross-reference with external data to begin mapping out an indication. But thinking through it logically, our suspects are simple. The Chinese government and the American government." She paused. "Both knew about the twins; both had the resources. Both obviously want Matt."

"But they were trying to kill him," Giselle protested. Jane barely heard her—there was a ringing in her ears. "That doesn't make sense. If they wanted to develop an anti-powers vaccine, wouldn't they need his blood?"

"Lots of blood in a dead man," pointed out Azleena. "Seems pretty logical that was step two. Kill him, harvest samples. Until Matt kept getting away."

"Jesus," Giselle lamented. She held her forehead with her hands. "Okay. Step one. Get Matt the hell back from his moonlit strolling."

"Already on it," replied Wally, his phone to his ear. The room sat in breathless silence as they listened to the muffled dial tone.

Ring-ring.

Ring-ring.

"He's not answering." Wally frowned. He turned to Jane. "You try."

Hands shaking as if in a dream, Jane slid her phone from her pocket and scrolled to the picture of Matt, the first starred number. The phone trembled as she held it on speaker.

Ring-ring.

Ring-ring.

"Hi, this is Matt Callaghan. Sorry I can't take your call. Please leave your name and number and—"

Jane hung up.

"Voicemail," she whispered. For a moment, it felt like nobody could breathe.

"Celeste," Azleena practically shouted. "Someone call Celeste." Giselle did, her fingers moving faster across her Kinetic phone than it was possible to keep track of.

"It's ringing too," she told them, then: "No answer." Her face paled. "What the hell—"

"I let them go," Jane whispered, unheard.

"Get a search team. Jump to New York, and—"

"I let them go," she whispered again. There was a screaming in her ears, a ringing intertwining with the burning power of Dawn, and without realizing it, wisps of golden light began trickling down Jane's face. "I let them go."

"Send out a general alert. I want the last people to see them; I want—"

"Wait!"

Azleena's shout rang through the computer room, and suddenly, everyone—including Jane—fell silent. All four of them turned to look as the small genius leaned forward in her computer chair, her eyes racing, finger touching her ear.

"They've found him," she whispered, breathless. Jane's heart suddenly leapt—only to drop back into fear a moment later as the girl's thick eyebrows furrowed. "He's in New Orleans?"

"He's getting *hammered*?!" Wally almost shouted, and when he ran his hands through his red hair, he did it so hard it looked like he was going to tear clumps out. "I am having a freaking *heart attack,* and he is off with that dragon-breasted skank drinking voodoo daiquiris!"

"The police have picked him up," Azleena relayed. Giselle spun on Jane and Will, eyes ablaze.

"Go," she demanded, jabbing a furious finger toward the hallway. "Right now. Go pick his stupid ass up and bring him right back here. I don't care about the cops, hold them back if you have to. I will sort it out later, just go!"

Will and Jane were already running, halfway through the doorway, when Azleena once more let out a wordless cry.

"Wait!" They spun back, and again, Jane's heart dropped—because the genius's eyes were no longer incensed and bewildered but trembling, wide, and terrified. "Something's wrong."

They emerged on an empty street, on the outskirts of the bayou, in the blue-black dead of night. To the right ran a row of rundown, darkened houses—single story—their yards carved out with warping chain-link fences and marred by uncut grass and rusted children's toys. On the left stretched an expanse of swampland, the thicket of low twisting trees standing waist-deep in water straddling the flat slope down from grass to mud.

The street—a single-lane road and a sidewalk—ran parallel to the wetlands, an unimportant border marking the edge of mankind's development. Most of the far-spaced streetlights stationed at set junctures along were blown, flickering only occasionally from darkness or just not working at all. Only one truly functioned, throwing out a cone of seedy orange light onto the bitumen. That was the one the police car was parked under.

"Matt!" The instant they arrived, Jane spun, looking for him, only to find the two officers standing outside their squad car, one hand on either of Matt's shoulders. Instantly, the power of Dawn flared to life all around her, and she stalked toward them, lips trembling with golden fury, hands balled into fists. "Get away from him, you—"

"Whoa!" the nearest policeman said, recoiling, arms flying up in surrender. "Be cool, be cool, we called it in!" He was a fresh-faced Caucasian man, and he and his partner, likewise fit but African American, both looked too young to be police. They held up their hands under Jane's advancing glare, her eyes blazing, and took a step away to either side, leaving Matt free. With a sob, Jane lunged forward, burying her face in his jacket.

"I'm sorry," she whispered. "I'm so sorry—"

She pulled away as Giselle, Wally, and Will's footsteps caught up behind her, her hands holding both of Matt's shoulders. "Let's go home. We can talk about everything, I promise. I just—I was so worried you were safe, and—"

Suddenly, Jane's voice skidded to a halt. She stared forward, her face frozen, hands still clutching Matt either side of his jacket.

"Matt?" she whispered to him. "Matt?"

Her lover's body moved. His jaw worked. Soft mumbling trickled from his mouth, and his face shot through with occasional twitches. But his eyes—his eyes were glazed. They didn't see her. They didn't see anything. They stared off into the horizon, trembling and delirious, taking in nothing.

"My name is Matt Callaghan," she heard him mumble. "I am human." Pause. "My name is Matt Callaghan. I am human."

With a slow, creeping sense of horror, Jane released Matt's arms and took a step back. Matt did not follow her but instead just stood there, swaying on the spot, his face twitching, his expression blank. He did not move.

Behind her, Jane heard Will curse.

"What did you do to him?" she demanded, winds of fury erupting as she rounded on the policemen, who had backed off slightly to stand against their squad car. Again, the rage in Jane's voice and the light pouring from her eyes sent the two men stumbling backward, tripping over desperate platitudes, holding out placating hands.

"Nothing, I swear!" said the foremost one. "We found him like this, I promise. Darnel, you'll—Back me up!"

"Absolutely," swore the other officer. "He was like this when we found him. We got a callout, someone saying there's some drunk guy stumbling around their neighborhood. We didn't think anything; I mean, it's New Orleans, what the hell you expect. But we show up thinking we just gonna give some sumbitch a night in the drunk tank, then . . ." His nervous words trailed to nothingness. "I couldn't believe it, man, when I saws who it was. I called that Legion hotline, spoke to the lady right away."

"Took us a while to get through," the first officer chimed in. Jane swept her volcanic glare onto him, and he quailed, though a moment later, her gaze shifted inevitably back to Matt, and she could do nothing but look on in curdling panic as he stood there, delirious.

"They're telling the truth," Wally confirmed, moving to her right. The psychic narrowed his eyes. "This is wrong. I can hear his thoughts."

Jane spun to face him. "What?!"

"I can hear his thoughts," Wally confirmed. "Like profoundly, they're everywhere; they're . . . broken." His freckled face paled, a sickly orange in the streetlight. "He's mentally shattered."

The dread in Jane's chest billowed, and the entire world spun around her head.

"Officers," she heard Giselle saying, coming to stand to the other side of her. As if in a dream, Jane felt herself stumbling back. "I'm Giselle Pixus, speedster, Legion of Heroes."

"We know," said the foremost officer, sounding slightly stunned. "I got you on a T-shirt. Chris Simmons, hyperdexterous. This here's

Darnel Drexler; he can make oil outta things. It's a pleasure to meet you, ma'am."

"Likewise. When you picked up Mr. Callaghan, did you happen to see a girl with him? Or an animal? Any sort of animal, big or small. Even made up?"

"Made up?"

"Like a dragon."

"Wait, like a dragon-dragon?"

"Exactly."

Silence.

"Miss Pixus, I don't mean no disrespect, but I'm fair certain I would've noticed a dragon flapping around when we rolled up on this here stretch of nowhere."

Jane could barely hear them. She could barely hear or see anything other than Matt and his blank, distant stare, his brown eyes empty of recognition of her or anyone else.

"Matt. Matt, can you hear me?"

"My name is Matt Callaghan. I am human."

"He's been saying that since we got here."

"Got his wallet on him, his phone. Confirmed his ID."

"I don't know what to tell you, ma'am. Maybe he got into some bad Indian Hay."

"You think he's drugged?" Giselle asked.

"I don't know. I mean, he likes to smoke, but—" Wally started.

"Yo." Will's voice, laced through with concern, suddenly cut across everyone. Jane tore her gaze away from Matt's face and swung her eyes over to the teleporter, who was standing behind her staring at Matt with concern.

"Yo," the teleporter repeated. "He's got something in his hand."

Five pairs of eyes swung downward. Under the dirty glow of the streetlight, Jane could see . . .

"He's right."

"Looks like a bit of paper?"

"Matt, sweetie." Giselle bent over him, forcing a smile both gentle and kind. "Can you let go of the paper? Can you let go, please?"

"My name is Matt Callaghan," he muttered. "I am human."

"Okay," the speedster said with false sweetness. "Just gonna . . . reach in and . . . get this out . . . There we go." She pulled back and straightened, the scrap of paper coming with her. Whatever it was, Matt released it without much resistance. Giselle uncrumpled the scrap—no bigger than the bottom of a torn-off notebook—and as she read it, her face paled. She turned to Jane, and without speaking, handed her the paper. Jane took it with clumsy fingers, her head swimming, cupping the scrap of paper in her hands so that it lay words up, facing her, like some kind of sick communion wafer. It was slightly yellow, cream—the bottom of some torn document.

But Jane didn't care about the color. She only cared about the name.

In what would have been the bottom right-hand corner, below a box's edge, a tiny footer, size eight font.

Area 60—Port Lions—Alaska
Property of the United States Government
Classified restricted. Not for public release.

"Holy—"

Jane could barely see. She could barely hear what was being said. All around her, the cold night suddenly burned like wildfire, and she was clenching her hands, stumbling out from beneath the orange streetlight into the darkness, away from Matt, the Legion, the police. Her teeth clenched, her head pounded, and a thunder roared in her chest as every fiber of her being surged with building, blinding rage. Golden light dripped from her eyes like mercury. Vapors of energy wafted between her teeth. Every power inside her howled, *howled*, to be unleashed upon the world in cataclysm, and her shoulders shook with fury, screaming to be set free.

"Jane?"

She could go back in time. She could prevent—but no. It had been hours now, stretched out gleaming black and unbroken, and on top of it all now sunk the power of life and death, the black-and-white clouded orb, light as air yet smothering . . . Her mind was too drained. She had to . . . She had to . . .

"Jane?"

Suddenly, Jane screamed. Screamed, roared, a raging wave of fury and light exploding out of her, blasting into the car, knocking down everyone but Matt, slamming a crater into solid Earth, breaking every window in the street. Energy whipped around her like a hurricane, and in an instant, Jane bent, gathering every ounce of wrath, then with a shattering *BOOM*, she shot upward, a burning golden comet, up into the clouds, faster than a jet, faster than a missile.

Heading northwest.

"Get the president on the phone."

In the darkened night, Giselle's command rang out over Morningstar's infirmary, the speedster striding forward, blurring to turn on the lights. Row upon row of white linen single beds, a lot of them occupied, stretched out before them, their occupants blinking up with blurry eyes.

"Private room," Giselle demanded, pointing at the healer, Delores, who had stumbled out of the medic's station looking bewildered and as if she'd likely been asleep. Her gaze darted from the leader of the Legion to the stumbling figure of Matt—whose shoulder she was clasping—to Will and Wally's hard, fearful faces following close behind.

"I don't—"

"Did I stutter?" shouted the Legion's leader. "Private room!"

The larger woman tried to stammer, but a moment later, she simply quailed and scurried off under Giselle's furious glare. The speedster turned back to Will.

"Go!" she cried. "Run, what are you waiting for? Go to Azleena, get her—Link me up a call." She spun on Wally. "Jane's still not answering."

"She's turned off her phone."

"Jesus freaking Christ! Okay. How fast can she move?"

Wally stared at her, incredulous. "How the hell should I know?"

Giselle mashed her knuckles into her temples, forefingers massaging the black bags under her eyes. "Okay. Will. Another question for our genius. How freaking fast can Lady Dawn move, and how long do we have before we're at war?"

Will ran off without a second glance. Giselle sucked a deep breath between her teeth.

"Get him to the room." With Wally's hand on his other shoulder, the speedster and the psychic wheeled Matt past the rows of hospital beds, their battle-damaged occupants sitting up and rubbing their eyes, squinting at the source of the commotion. On the far side of the infirmary, Delores's shaking hands were struggling with the keys to a small square examination room. Giselle resisted the urge to kick in both her and the door.

Finally, the room was unlocked, and Giselle and Wally dragged Matt inside. The Legion's leader deposited him—swaying—on the muted green examination bed while Wally hurried over to close the blinds.

"Healer," Giselle demanded, clicking her fingers at Delores. The woman's chubby face paled.

"I . . . I'm on night duty."

"Great," the speedster replied, jabbing her finger at Matt. "Patient. Nighttime!"

"I . . ." the medic stammered, "I need to go get Editha."

"So help me God—" But the big healer was already stumbling away, running back across the infirmary with a pace Giselle had rarely seen her achieve. Wally put his hand on her arm.

"It's alright. Editha's a better fit, anyway. She's good at toxicology."

"I know that," snapped Giselle. Immediately regretting the hostility, she took a deep breath, closed her eyes, and again rubbed her temples. "Sorry. Sorry. It's getting the better of me." She breathed out, lips in an O. "Good leadership. Goooood leadership."

"You're doing great."

"I'm doing dog crap. Why the hell did I take this job?"

"Because you are the absolute best person for it, and I love you."

"Thanks."

"My name is Matt Callaghan. I am human."

"Feels like I haven't slept in a week," said Giselle.

"Day just doesn't seem to end, does it?"

"Freaking . . . undead monsters and conspiracy theories and disasters and—You know what I was doing last year?"

"What?"

"Running on a salt flat. Practicing really, really hard at running on a salt flat."

"The more things change."

"My name is Matt Callaghan. I am human."

"I should apologize to Delores," she sighed, clutching her forehead. "When did I get so rude?"

"About the time dead people started coming back to life."

"My name is Matt Callaghan. I am human."

"Yes, thank you, Jane, thank you just so, so much for that. Thank you for everything. I swear, one day I am going to strangle that girl so hard they'll write sapphic poetry."

"You do just want to slap her around sometimes, don't you?" said Wally, the corner of his mouth twitching.

"Worst part of her getting that stupid Dawn power: nobody will ever properly slap her around again."

"My name is Matt Callaghan. I am human."

"And you!" Giselle snapped, rounding on Matt, sitting on the sheer green medical examination bed, his expression still glazed and distant. "As soon as you recover from this, I am going to castrate you!

What the hell were you thinking? 'Oh, I know what goes great after a long day of life and death: a quick trip to the Big Easy! Couple'a po' boys and bourbon! Gonna mosey on down like it's Mardi Gras.' Honestly!" She threw up her hands. "I am just so through."

"It's Celeste I'm mad about," Wally said darkly.

"Oh yes, Celeste!" Giselle cried. "Possibly dead, possibly passed out in a bowl of gumbo, possibly having sex somewhere with some furry pretending to be a dog. I am going to sell her to the freaking glue factory!"

At that moment the door opened, and Editha, the petite mousy-haired healer, stepped in.

"What happened?" she asked.

"We don't know," Giselle replied. "The military got him. Some sort of drug? But he's not getting any better. And he doesn't seem to be responding."

"There's something wrong with his brain," Wally added, his expression worried. "I keep telling you: I have seen Matt wasted, and his thoughts have never been like this. They're practically leaking out of his ears."

"Some sort of hallucinogen?" Giselle asked the healer as she strode over toward Matt. "A narcotic, maybe? Poison? Electroshock?"

Editha leaned in, flicking the silver penlight from her top pocket and shining it in both Matt's eyes. "Pupils are responsive, but they're not following anything around him."

"I noticed."

"Not to cause undue alarm," the healer started, glancing Matt over, grim, "but my main concern wouldn't be any external interference. This man was dead this morning."

Giselle and Wally both paled. "I hadn't considered that," the speedster admitted.

"Well, I've got a few movies that might be worth watching," Editha replied, the words dry, not looking away from Matt. She pocketed the light. "I'm going to see what I can feel."

"Do it."

The healer put one hand on Matt's wrist and another on his neck. She closed her eyes, her brow furrowing, her lips a thin frown.

"I'm not getting anything."

"There's no heartbeat?" Giselle gasped.

"No," Editha scowled. "His heart's fine. His body's fine. I'm not . . . There's nothing wrong with him. Nothing's responding when I try to heal."

She closed her eyes and pushed against Matt's skin for a few more seconds before releasing him and stepping back.

"There's nothing wrong," she repeated. "Nothing's happening." Wally moved his confused gaze between doctor and patient.

"So what?" asked the psychic. "He just needs to sleep it off?"

"No," Editha replied, her face blank. "I'm saying there's nothing bioactive in his system. He's not injured. He's sober." She glanced between Giselle and Wally's disbelieving stares. "When you go to heal someone, you get feedback, a sense of how much is broken. If you're good, you can sort of get better at listening to it and eventually figure out what's wrong. If he was intoxicated or somehow poisoned, I'd be able to feel it and treat it. But I can't. I'm just hitting a wall. The health bottle is full, so to speak."

Wally stared at her as Giselle felt the pit of dread in her stomach deepen.

"Matt?" she asked trepidatiously. "Matt, honey? Can you hear us? What's going on?"

"My name is Matt Callaghan. I am human."

"So if his health is fine," Wally asked, "what's wrong with him?" Editha fixed the human with a pained stare—then once more, leaned forward with the penlight; only this time, she was not looking in Matt's eyes but in his ears, his nose. She pulled the skin down beneath his eyelids.

"Rupturing of the capillaries," she said quietly.

Wally's indignation was titanic. "The Bleeds?! The freaking Bleeds?! You're saying psychic—"

"I'm saying it's the only explanation!" Editha snapped back sharply, retreating from Matt and once more tucking her pen away. "Patient presents unresponsive to healing, no outward physical injury, severe mental impediment and fugue state, and ruptured pericranial vasculature. You tell me what it sounds like!"

Wally blew air through his lips, leaning back and holding the base of his head between his hands, but he said nothing. He could only stare at Matt with renewed, sickening concern.

"He needs an MRI," Editha told them, taking another step away, shaking her head, almost fearful. "I need to consult other physicians. We need metrics."

"Can you compare his blood toxicology?" asked Wally.

"To what?" replied Editha. "He never let anyone take any."

"Taking blood might be problematic," Giselle agreed. "The rest—Go." She dismissed the dainty medic with a weak wave. "Make whatever arrangements you need." The healer hurried out, closing the door behind her. Once again, Giselle and Wally were left alone.

There was a moment of horrible, horrible silence.

"My name is Matt Callaghan. I am human."

"I know, buddy. It's going to be okay." Wally turned to her. "What're you thinking?"

Giselle gnawed on a knuckle, staring at Matt with roiling concern. "I think Jane's going to destroy the US military."

"We have to warn them."

"They're being warned. Azleena will tell them." She put a hand over her face, and it took every piece of her remaining strength not to break down and cry. "Oh, Matt. I'm sorry. I'm so sorry. We screwed up. I should've . . . I should've been more assertive; I shouldn't have let Jane—"

"It's not your fault," murmured Wally. He slipped an arm around her shoulders. Giselle lowered her head and drew three deep, shuddering breaths, then sat back up, hiccupped, and wiped her eyes. As she blinked, she noticed Wally still staring at Matt as the human sat there, rocking, mumbling his mantra.

"Wal—"

"I don't believe it." The psychic's words were almost too quiet for her to hear.

"What?"

"I don't believe it. It can't be true."

"Wally." Giselle's voice was pained. "Editha's right. It's the only thing that makes sense. They picked him up, those"—she let slip a few violent swear words—"bastards, and when they had what they needed, they broke his mind so he'd never be able to tell anyone what they'd done. Maybe they didn't even mean to. Maybe he just fought back too hard." She sniffed. "It's a miracle he managed to snag that bit of paper. His last sane act. He must have known. He must have known." Her vision blurred, and she reached forward to take Matt's hand. It was warm and rough. "You were so brave. Nobody ever said that to you, but I always thought . . . you were so brave."

Her touch brought no response. Giselle let Matt's fingers drop and retreated back to sitting, staring at the linoleum floor, speckled white and green, the color of seaweed. After a few moments, she forced herself to look up, swallowing and blinking away tears, trying to push down the pain—only to find Wally leaning in toward Matt beside her, his eyes narrowed, shaking his head.

"No," said Wally, and there was something in the way he said it— the anger, the certainty, the absolute confidence—that made Giselle's breath catch. "No. This is wrong."

Suddenly, the psychic rounded on her, eyes ablaze. "They broke his mind?! He fought back too hard?! Matt Callaghan—Matthew frigging Callaghan—who fought Natalia *unaided* to a standstill, who kept any trace of his identity secret from me, *me*, for six months? Who mind-gamed the Black Death—the Black"—he swore—"Death, alone and under threat of torture. You're telling me some government psychic, some *federal employee*, broke that man, mentally, to the point of only being able to say his name and power in half a day? No." Wally shook his head with a vehement fury Giselle had rarely seen. "I refuse to believe it. Something else is going on here. I know it."

Giselle could only stare. "Like what?" she asked.

Wally scowled. "I don't know," he told her. "But I intend to find out."

He rose. "Lock the door," Wally commanded. His eyes bored into Matt, unblinking and determined. "Tell Editha to delay her tests. I'm going in. I want to see exactly what's happened."

Giselle knew little more about telepathy than the basics they taught at the Academy, but even she was horrified. "You're going to free dive into a shattered mind?"

"I'm going to help my friend," Wally growled.

"You'll lose yourself! The madness—"

"I know who I am," the psychic muttered. "No amount of insanity will change that."

"My name is Matt Callaghan. I am human," Matt murmured.

"I don't want to—"

"I know Matt," swore Wally. "I know me. And I will pull him back from a million pieces before I let him fall into the void. So sit down and shut up."

Then, without another word, the redheaded psychic grabbed Matt's head on either side, pressed their foreheads together, and stared into the human's soul with fierce, unblinking eyes.

She descended from the sky in a ball of golden flame.

From a distance, she heard the alarms sounding, heard the soldiers shouting, saw them running and screaming orders, moving weapons into place. It didn't matter. Her eyes ablaze, Jane unleashed a bloodcurdling cry and let loose a burning golden torrent, scorching everything in sight.

She slammed into the ground, the shock wave shattering a fifty-foot crater, and all around her, soldiers screamed—traitors, murderers—screamed at her to stop and raised their guns and pow-ers and fired, fired—

Jane howled, and in an instant, light exploded around her, hurtling back the farthest, vaporizing those who were close. Snow fell in blind-ing flurries, turning to steam before it could touch her, annihilated like everything else as she launched blast after blast at everything she could see. Men fell, tanks exploded, buildings, vehicles—

Khaki blurs raced at superspeed, helicopters rained fire, figures circled in the distance, but Jane could not see them, and she did not care. Everything was gold and pain and anger, and if it moved, it died before her as her palms spread wide, bringing annihilation, bringing searing death.

He was in a soft, violet space, floating through the cosmos.

Inside Matthew Callaghan's head, Wally Cykes opened his eyes and stared out into ruined chaos.

The stars shone, a remnant nebula. Patches of synapses, memories shredded and hazing, clouds of knowledge and belief torn asunder, left adrift. Pinpricks of white and green, orange and blue, flashing brief among the purple dream and vanishing, antimatter destroyed by night. Wally floated down. There was barely anything left here, no structure, no sense of purpose, only scattered debris, a supernova's corpse.

[I remember the frozen sun]

He sank into the ruined starfield, between pieces of floating rubble, bricks and glass and floating doors. A tinkling of beads, a reflection in a lake. He could go through them if he wanted—there would be mem-ory on the other side. Wally ignored the whispered promises. He sank down into the synaptic currents, whirling, pulling in every direction. There was so much to know. So much to explore. A trillion sensations if he would only drift, sparks and feelings of paramount importance, primordial, unwavering. *Come, embrace true understanding. Bridge the infinite abyss between all people. Experience. Understand.*

[Take me back. Take me back]

Wally held his mind loose, the mantra weaving soft bands of being around his diving bell consciousness. He whispered as he sunk, the same old songs, the same old colors that had always run through him. *I do not need your mind. I am happy with my own.*

He floated past spinning mirrors, slivers of memory, potentially deadly and intoxicating in their detail, but ultimately carrying nothing clear, nothing solid. Wally had not known what to expect in this ruined world—a mind so damaged, scoured open—but he had not expected this. Such desolation. So empty.

[What a gift for the chosen one]

There had been forces at work here. Telepathic forces, that much was obvious, for a mind did not shatter this severely under its own pressure. He drifted with purpose through the purple cosmos, a universe spread silent and open where mind and memory should have been. A shard of rubble drifted past him. A key, a flower, a droplet of water, tiny specks in the stardust. Fragments that murdered and pleaded and promised something much greater, seeking him, seeking an understanding mind, longing to be known. Wally slid them gently aside. He was not here for them. He was here for what they'd broken from.

[Heart attack. No way back]

An underwater river flowed beneath him, dark ink blue, violet midnight. Swift and strong, it ran beneath the detritus, its currents rippling, the weightless surface of a world below which leviathan stirred. The River Styx; death, insanity. An infinity of thought and fear strong enough to sweep another mind away.

Wally held calm to his soul and sank gently beneath the waves.

[Oh. The madness comes]

Inside, the navy current swirled, dark and thundering. It would take him here; no, it would drag him there; no, he would become it a thousand times over—but Wally refused to be stained, unwavering, and he would not be swept away. He moved a calm hand, and the current split before him, twin streams of the river parting around his consciousness like a stone, as if it had always been that way, as if it had never known. The ink clouds cleared, forming sapphire pools and royal blood. He gazed down upon what lay beneath the surface.

[I've got nowhere left that I can run]

A wall. Wrought and twisted over, a thousand vines of turquoise crystal curved into a sphere, a planet, shining smooth and intertwining with neither beginning nor end. For a moment, Wally's heart beat faster, and he marveled at it, the exquisite craftsmanship—this moon a thousand shades of blue, indigo, cerulean, magenta, witch-hour diamond—clear and color bound as one. Could it be? An organic construct? A sublime palace of the mind. Yet, as Wally floated closer, he saw the veins of iron lacing through it, the almost invisible sutures. The meat glue.

Then he remembered. This sphere shone blue. Matt Callaghan's mind was green.

[I could sleep for days]

Open now, Wally thought, and his thoughts hardened. *This is not you.* His fingers traced the crystal curves, unbroken glass smooth and twisting in tree trunks bigger than his body. It was enormous, but size was relative.

Open now. As he stared upon the orb, he saw the writing running through it, frozen blue electricity, lightning trapped inside a bottle. "My name is Matt Callaghan"; "I am human."

Woven into every turn of it. Every fiber.

Open.

[Maybe when I find just such a mysterious place]

Wally bared his teeth and dug his hands into the glass fold between the tendrils. They could not move; they were hard as diamond, perfect blue, unbreakable. But Wally's grip did not yield. There were no truths. No thoughts born indestructible. This was nothing but ideas—free and malleable, whether in his mind or a thousand—and he believed, and he knew—

BEGONE.

In a surge of blinding light, Wally Cykes threw down his barriers and unleashed his own mind like a spear-tipped prism, piercing inward, the clouds of violet dust blasting away before a glaive of light of a million colors. The crystal cracked, the barrier shattered to sand—

And Wally saw in.

The psychic started back with a gasp.

"Hhhhhuh!"

"Hey!" Giselle was suddenly beside him, hands clutching his shoulders, steadying. He was back in the doctor's office. The infirmary. Wally glanced around, his eyes wild, finding the door open and both Editha and Will standing behind him, the healer staring fretfully, the swarthy teleporter's face a tormented mask of concern. Wally pushed to his feet, stumbling a step, breathing fast.

"Wally. Wal! Hey! What happened? You alright?"

The psychic shook his head, the dim color of the real world reasserting itself. White walls, blue chairs, green-and-white floor. Plastic medical trays, yes, with all their equipment, bandages, vials, sterile wipes. The sage green examination bed, where a man sat with light skin, short milk-chocolate hair, and the occasional freckle. A man he recognized.

"What is it?" Giselle asked, clinging to his arm. Wally steadied himself, allowing himself to lean on her while gravity fell back into place. "What's in there? What happened to Matt?"

And in that moment, Wally laughed, a hollow, bitter bark utterly devoid of merriment; a swirling cocktail of fury, contempt, and utter, savage disgust.

"I have no idea," he answered, eyes locked on the man in front of him. "That's not Matt."

Matt Callaghan's eyes flickered open, and he saw only darkness. His limbs were heavy, his tongue dry, his head spinning. The taste of something—something dizzying, something cloying, something utterly disgusting—lined his mouth in a foul film. His nose felt as if someone had poured baking soda and vinegar into it. Matt coughed, spitting out a bubbly hack of who knows what, and tried to sit up, groaning as his mind reeled dizzily between ceiling and floor.

I am in a room, his groggy consciousness concluded. It was cold, and there was . . . there was this smell, like old trees . . . No, the sweet offense of a distillery . . . No, a hardware store. It was tough to tell. No light shone directly above or around him, but as Matt's eyes adjusted to the dark, he could see the faintest sliver of a glow slipping through the cracks of a vague square over in the ceiling. His hands touched . . . earth—no, dirt, maybe, and for a mad second, he thought he was back in Cassandra Atropos's basement, about to look over and see a mad eyeless woman peering over at him and cackling.

But he was alone. Matt groaned and attempted to roll over, only to find with a sudden clank that there was something stopping him. He tried to move his hands over to feel what was restraining him, but abruptly stopped as he found himself unable to move his wrists. Matt strained his eyes and stared down, attempting to see through the gloom. A matte surface, thick and cold, slightly darker than his skin, rested on the ground beneath his leg. Matt tried to move his arms again, listening. The chain clinked.

Manacles. Wrought-iron chains and wrought iron manacles, one on each wrist. Clumsy, blind in the dark, his mind still recovering, Matt felt around groggily with his shoe, tracing part of one chain along with his toe. It descended into a metal floor plate, from the ridges of which Matt could guess was probably bolted to the floor. *Sex dungeon*, a gadfly thought proclaimed with baseless confidence, aggressively unhelpful, causing Matt to groan and shoo it away.

He reached for his pocket. No phone. That made sense. No wallet either, from the feel of things. *If I have to reapply for my ID . . .* But Matt dropped that thought, as it was clear that was not presently his biggest problem. He squeezed his eyes closed in an attempt to push back some of his headache and shuffled his legs back so he was sitting up. He still had his shoes on, his jacket, the same clothes. So they hadn't stripped him; they'd just . . . God. Matt's head pounded like he'd been on a seven-day bender. Whatever they'd hit him with—whatever form of rapid anesthetic—it put you to sleep much more pleasantly than it let you wake up. He rubbed his eye socket, gawking into the dark.

A part of Matt told him he should be scared. But despite the depths of his predicament, he wasn't. Fear was unhelpful, and death, it seemed, was no longer permanent. Besides, Matt remembered how he had gotten here.

There were footsteps up above, thuds that shook flecks of dust from the floorboard ceiling, and Matt tracked with his ears their path as they approached. There was a *clonk, clonk, clonk* of steps descending down some stairs, and then a scraping noise, the sound of rusty hinges. The light-tipped square swung open, and a blinding brightness suddenly assaulted Matt's eyes. He shielded his gaze, squinting as a figure came toward him, a shadow in front of the light now streaming into the cellar.

Slowly, as Matt's eyes adjusted, the room became visible—the low, uneven dirt floor, the dusty wooden ceiling, the cobweb-strewn brick supports rising like the crawlspace beneath some house, and gigantic, eight-foot-diameter brewing barrels curved around in a semicircle against which Matt's back now pressed, forming the inner wall. Matt's gaze swept over all of it—the chains, the metal floor plate, the distant, shuttered vent at head height . . . and slowly, as light streamed in behind him, his captor.

"You . . ." Matt breathed.

His eyes widened, and suddenly, the figure came into focus.

"Wait . . . you?"

A MAN OF FAITH

Our planet is a lonely speck in the great enveloping cosmic dark. In our obscurity, in all this vastness, there is no hint that help will come from elsewhere to save us from ourselves.

— Carl Sagan, *Pale Blue Dot: A Vision of the Human Future in Space,* 1994

"His name is Donald Blackmore."

In the small chamber of the doctor's office at the edge of the infirmary, six members of the Legion of Heroes stood silently as Wally Cykes explained the truth.

"He's a paranoid schizophrenic from Albuquerque. He's a shapeshifter. Someone has taken this man, broken down his mind, and crushed the bleeding pieces back together into a single, unshakable belief: that his name is Matt Callaghan, and he is human."

"My name is Matt Callaghan," the poor, shattered creature whispered, rocking atop the doctor's bed. "I am human."

"Do a blood test," Wally insisted, pointing at the two healers, Delores and Editha, who were standing at the entrance to the examination room wearing matching expressions of utmost horror. "It'll show you. He's a shapeshifter. He's holding on to Matt's form because it's the only thing left remaining in his mind."

"Mother of God," Giselle whispered.

Of all the years she'd known him, she had never known Wally's face to bear such fury.

"There are no words," the psychic breathed, and his eyes burned so intently into the fake Matt Callaghan that for a moment Giselle was worried Wally was going to leap up and tear the imposter apart. But the telepath's rage wasn't directed at him. "There is no place in Hell for the scum responsible for this. This act—this atrocity—goes against every code of psychic ethics, every shred of human decency. If it takes me to my dying day," he swore, "I will hunt down whoever did this, and they will burn for a thousand years inside a prison of their own mind before they ever see the inside of a jail cell."

Behind him, Will laid a quiet hand on Wally's shoulder. The telepath did not respond to the touch, only continued staring forward, teeth clenched, fists balled in utter, unyielding anger.

"Stay here," Giselle said quietly. "Help. See to him. Fix the damage."

"I'll try" was Wally's only response.

The head of the Legion turned to the rest of them: Azleena, Editha, Delores, Charles Farrington, and Will.

"We fell for the decoy," she reiterated to them. "We have to assume the Port Lions note was a fake. Unfortunately, it's bait Jane's currently swallowing. Where are we on stopping her?"

Azleena's small, round face remained blank. "Do you want the good news or the bad news?" the genius asked.

"What's the good news?"

"The good news is that we have located Jane."

Giselle blew a sharp breath across her bottom lip. "Let me guess the bad news."

"It would not take a genius," the small girl replied. "On the plus side, the president is no longer asleep and suddenly very willing to talk."

"He knows it isn't us?"

"He does, and he is as concerned about stopping Jane as he is about the media never getting word about any of this."

"I don't even know if that's a silver lining."

"What are our options?" Charles Farrington asked. He stood in the doorway, his arms folded, dressed in a compression suit in his usual uniform black. "How can we subdue her?"

"The power of Dawn has two real weaknesses," Azleena explained, "neutralization and telepathy. Telepathy is off the table, since Jane started taking Psy-Block. Neutralization requires time, proximity, and for Jane not to notice her powers diminishing while it happens. It's practically impossible." The genius paused. "Unless someone's hiding another Divine in their back pocket."

Giselle disregarded that last suggestion. "Contain her, then," she ordered. "Lead Jane somewhere deserted."

"It might be possible," conceded Azleena. She pointed to the shapeshifter Blackmore. "As much as I hate to suggest putting this man through any further trauma, perhaps if Jane thinks the real Matt Callaghan is still under our control, we could lure her away from populated areas with the appearance of a threat."

"Absolute not," Wally growled.

Giselle rubbed her forehead. "I thought it wouldn't come to this," she said heavily, "but I can't say I hadn't considered it." She sat up straighter, staring at each of them in turn. "There's a contingency I've been working on. An empath out of Boston. Touch-based like Jane, I've contracted him to remain on standby holding four powers: neutralization, superspeed, invisibility, and flight. He's not particularly good at any one of them, but put them all together . . ." She let her words trail off. "He might be able to keep up with Jane undetected long enough to make a dent."

"You are full of surprises," Azleena said, eyeing Giselle with something approaching approval.

"I read a lot of *Batman*."

"That's great and all"—Will frowned—"but that's presuming he can keep up with her and she doesn't just hit him with force from all directions like she did Klaus Heydrich."

"I said it was *a* plan, not a good one," Giselle grumbled.

"For the love of God, this is Jane we're talking about," said Wally, throwing his hands up. "She was saving all our lives twenty-four hours ago. She's our *friend*. Can't we just *explain* it to her? Can't anyone make her see reason?"

"The person most likely to do that," Azleena said, glancing over once more at the imposter, "is unfortunately currently not present."

The group lapsed into silence.

"Which raises the second question," Giselle said after a few moments. "Where the hell's the real Matt?"

Pastor Phillip Fredericks stood at the base of the cellar stairs and stared down at Matt, his face blank.

"You're awake," he said simply, and for once, there was no emotion in his voice, no conviction, no rapture. The words simply fell dead at the pastor's feet, cold and empty, and from the light leaking in through the trapdoor, Matt could see the bare dispassion long settled in Fredericks's eyes.

"I'm going crazy," Matt whispered. The priest did not respond. Instead, he walked over with slow, deliberate steps and bent down, checking Matt's chains and manacles.

"What do you want?" Matt demanded. The barest flicker of annoyance passed over Fredericks's face as he tugged briefly against one of the steel plates bolted to the floor. The metal did not move. With a grunt of satisfaction, Fredericks rose.

"Be quiet," he muttered, turning away, moving back toward the staircase. Matt's mind churned rapidly.

"I get it now!" he cried. "I get it! I understand!"

The tall man's footsteps halted. He paused and straightened his back, rising to his full height—an imperious six and a half feet—rolling his shoulders and cracking his neck. When he turned, the gray, unblinking eyes Matt had once seen stare at him with such kindness were filled only with simmering fury and contempt.

"Really?" he said quietly. "You 'get it'?"

"Yeah," replied Matt, a little breathless. He tried to sit up straighter against the frame of the timber barrel, though the chains prevented him from rising very far. "I do. It's been you all along. You've been working with the government."

The cult leader stood silent, framed by the light of the staircase, his features engulfed in shadow.

"All along, you've been playing me," Matt continued, "pretending to be harmless. Playing on my need to be liked. But I should've seen it sooner. You hate powers. You'd like nothing more than for my blood to get out, to rid the world of the superhuman." Matt leaned toward Fredericks wearing a breathless, triumphant grin, chains straining against his wrists. "What did they promise you? Abilities for good, God-fearing Americans only? A sole nation of superpowers? Or did they sweeten the deal somehow? Put you over a barrel? You've got a daughter they're holding? Assassins coming for you? You got gambling debts?"

When the pastor did not answer, Matt laughed. "It doesn't matter. I should've seen it all along. Of course the group that thinks superhumans are a sin is going to be trying to help destroy superpowers. No cure for the gays, but there might be a cure for freedom, right? Of course you were onboard. Self-righteous, inbred, pea-brained, sanctimonious traitor. Your God isn't real, and if He is, He hates you."

Matt closed his mouth and let the stream of words fade into damp darkness. With nothing more to go on, he'd hoped his tirade alone might bait Fredericks into getting enraged, maybe revealing more, but the pastor just stood there, silent, absorbing Matt's insults without so much as a ruffle of his gray-streaked brown hair or a shift of his thin, frameless glasses. The words washed over him, and then they faded into oblivion, and the two were left with only the cold, dark basement between them, the smell of dirt, of long-drained alcohol and rot.

"You know nothing," Fredericks muttered, and without another word, he turned back toward the staircase and ascended into the light. The heavy wooden trapdoor slammed shut behind him, and once more, Matt found himself engulfed in darkness.

The cellar remained silent for a few seconds save for the distant *thump, thump, thump* of the pastor's retreating footsteps. Matt traced their path along the ceiling by sound and by the dust shaking from the floorboards. When they had retreated into nothingness, his face split into a smirk. Matt glanced down.

"Alright," he said, tapping his finger three times firmly against his chest. "I think it's time."

As Matt spoke, a tiny speck leapt off him, and from the dank floor of the darkened cellar, a second shape began to grow.

Several hours earlier

Matt Callaghan wandered aimlessly through the empty streets of New York City, fuming at himself, fate, and the entire world.

It was not, despite his frustration, entirely lost on Matt the uniqueness of his situation. Rarely in the hundreds of years since its inception had New York ever been so utterly deserted—its workers gone, its storefronts vacant, its citizens evacuated beneath a looming supernatural threat. It would be a good day or two, Matt guessed, until people returned in significant number, until the all clear was given, until the city was confirmed safe. He had a rare opportunity, a chance he might under other circumstances have relished, to wander these normally bustling streets practically in isolation, with only rubble, rubbish, and the occasional yowling cat or cooing pigeon to disturb his peace.

Well, except for Celeste. The faunamorph clopped behind Matt at a steady distance about ten feet away in the form of a moose, keeping her long brown face pointed discreetly downward and maintaining a respectful gap. Matt appreciated the space she was giving him.

Someone else might have been tempted to try and make small talk or "keep him company," but Celeste could read the room well enough to stay quiet. They plodded along together in silence, and at times, until he inevitably glanced around and caught a glimpse of thick flat antlers, Matt could almost pretend like he was alone.

Matt's stomach felt sick, and his thoughts swirled. He shouldn't have shouted at Jane. Again and again, their conversations kept getting away from him, and . . . and God, she was trying to help him. She was doing her best. And what she was saying, ultimately, about using the death powers to undo damage was in many ways not totally unreasonable, so long as it was restricted to individuals; it was only when one stood back and stared at the bigger picture that the terrible, tremendous implications became apparent. All she saw were trees; all he saw was forest. Jane was trying her best to save him. Was he trying his best to save her?

Matt ran his hands across his face, over his eyes, through his wind- and dust-strewn hair. The problem was that it was all just so endless. So frustrating. One disaster after another, lurching from home to broken home, never reaching any sort of resolution, no end to all these threats. He had beaten one Godlike being, only to seemingly incur the wrath of another. He had convinced Jane not to abuse one terrifying power, only for her to absorb a different one. He had escaped two hit squads, but it seemed only a matter of time before another one came after him.

"ARGH!" Matt bellowed, a wordless roar of frustration that echoed out into the gray, empty streets, scattering a flock of pigeons and causing Celeste behind him to raise her lumbering head. Matt flapped his hand back idly at her, waving her moose worry down.

When would it end? When would he finally—*finally*—be free of all this? He still had no idea who was behind it, what they were planning, if it was the Child or some other antagonist out to get him. Heck, the thumb drive . . . was that something the Time Child would have done? Would a time traveler even need . . . ? But it was impossible to know. Maybe after Azleena had gone through the data, he tried to console himself. But even then, there was no guarantee she'd find the answer. No guarantee they could stop whoever was behind this, that they wouldn't escape or regroup, or that someone entirely new might not simply take up their murderous torch. And there was no guarantee the Time Child or Time Children wouldn't keep hunting him, no matter what Matt attempted, keep pursuing their nebulous quest to free Matt from his protective tethers and leave him lying in an unmarked grave.

How could he fake his death now, when everyone knew Jane could just resurrect him? How could he possibly escape to another life with all this bullcrap pressing in around him, refusing to let go, refusing to let him be? Staring between the buildings, despondent, it was like Matt could see his future stretching out before him: no freedom, no happiness, to be ping-ponged back and forth between life and death like a cat toy by the Godlike forces who wanted to maintain him, and the Godlike forces who wanted him dead. He just wanted his old life back. He wanted to go back to being normal.

The absurdity of the situation suddenly hit him so hard that Matt actually stopped dead in his tracks. He let out a sharp, painful, incredulous bark of laughter, completely devoid of humor or mirth. Normal? *Normal?!* He was walking through an abandoned metropolis being followed by a moose, having just been dead an hour ago, after *Home Alone*-ing a team of mercenaries while his time-traveling, star-eyed girlfriend battled forty-foot monstrosities in a break from her usual job of kidnapping foreign leaders who could talk to fish. He had broken into prison to speak to a comatose robot man, there was at least one poster child for the Aryan Brotherhood tracking him across dimensions, and he had drunk beer and mind-gamed a geno-cidal super-Nazi on national television.

He was a nineteen-year-old self-made multimillionaire; he was in the Legion of Heroes. He'd been on Leno. And before that? Everything had been a lie. The deception, the clairvoyancy. He'd deliberately duped budding superheroes. At thirteen, he'd tricked the US government. He'd shoved a drugged crow into a backpack and thought it was a solid plan.

He could beat the greatest psychics in the world. He could outsmart literal superpowered people with nothing more than a few tools and quick thinking. He had stared down the choice between staying safe and saving others, and had run headfirst into death. And he'd do it again, Matt realized. In a heartbeat.

He was not normal. He would never be normal.

What the hell even was normal, anyway?

Suddenly, it was like a veil had lifted. Suddenly, something clicked. All along, for so long, Matt had been holding on to this idealized version of what his life was going to be, feeling betrayed, feeling forgotten, slighted by things he could never seem to have or never seem to get back. He'd placed so much weight on normality, so much obsession over everything he wasn't, that he'd never once stopped to realize who he was.

There were things in life he would never have; things in life he would never have again. Simplicity, anonymity, normality, maybe even peace. But in their place were other things worth having. Money, status, celebrity. Health, luxury, excitement—a voice to change the world. Camaraderie. People—wonderful, brilliant people—who shared, who wanted to share in his life's maddening battle, who would fight for him until their knuckles bled and save his life with their dying breaths. Friendship. Companionship. Purpose. Intelligence. Cunning. Identity. Love.

Matt's chest clenched as his vision suddenly swam. What was he going to do? Was he going to stay fixated on all the things he couldn't have—a dorm and dog and a white picket fence—or was he finally, *finally* going to let go? To accept that this was his existence? And it might not be the life he'd always wanted, it might not be everything he'd always dreamed, but it didn't matter. Because he could either accept the truth and make the most of it, and find joy, and seize upon all that was good in the world, or he could spend the rest of his life wasting away, pining for a day that would never come.

He was not safe. He was not normal. And he could either grow the hell up and accept that or be miserable until the end of days.

You either play the hand you were dealt, or you complain about the cards.

In the empty streets of an unbeaten city, Matt Callaghan wiped his eyes free from tears, drew in a deep, swelling breath, and for the first time—the first actual time since all this nonsense started—knew exactly what he had to do.

"Celeste," he called, turning to face the moose. The giant deer tilted its huge, gormless antlers, and as Celeste continued forward, her body shifted, and she came to a halt three feet away from him, returned to human form.

"Wassup?" she asked once her body was once more human. "Everything okay?"

"Better than okay," Matt replied. He beckoned her close and lowered his voice. "I have a plan." He paused. "You like horses?"

"You goddamn better believe it." Celeste shrugged.

Matt fixed her with a victorious grin. "How about Trojans?"

For the first time since he'd awoken in this basement, Matt was glad of the gloomy, oppressive darkness. There were many things he needed in his life right now, but seeing Celeste morph back from a flea was absolutely not one of them.

"You were right," the girl said once her face had reverted from a long, stabby thing and whiskers. "They took the bait."

"Of course they did," gloated Matt, grinning into the darkness. "They were always going to. Imagine you're a secret group of big, intense conspiracy people, your mercenary team has just screwed up royally, and you see your target just walking around all undefended and alone. They probably watched me storm off and thought they'd won the lottery."

"How did you know they wouldn't just shoot you?" she asked. Matt shrugged, the movement barely visible in the dim light.

"Just a hunch," he replied. "Besides, if they did, Jane would just resurrect me."

"So casual."

"I'm trying this new thing called acceptance."

"Oh, babe, that's so sweet. Good for you." She glanced around at the empty basement. "So, dragon, right? I'm busting you out of here?"

"Not just yet. I think you go rat to dog to bird to pay phone. Get the hell out of here and go bring the cavalry while I stay here looking vulnerable."

Even in the dark, he could see Celeste's concerned grimace. "You sure you're going to be okay?"

"Please," Matt scoffed, "I've already been dead once today. Besides, this interrogation is going swimmingly."

"You're chained up."

"And he's just where I want him. Go. Let's catch this bastard in the act. The only thing I like better than seeing what a man's hiding is catching him with his pants down."

The faunamorph fixed him with a grin. "Sometimes, I really get what Jane sees in you."

"You're only saying that because it's dark. Go on, get."

Celeste flipped him a two-fingered *peace*, then with a sudden rush of fur, she vanished, leaving Matt alone and chained to the floor of an earthen basement, listening with a triumphant smile to the rapidly disappearing scurry of tiny rodent paws.

Deep in Azleena's computer lab, Giselle's cell phone rang. The speedster turned away, putting her back to the genius and the rapidly flashing computer, and squinted at the unknown number. A landline; probably a telemarketer. Sigh. She had to answer it. Worst part about being leader of the Legion: nothing could ever just be ignored.

"Hello?"

A sudden rush of excited, familiar chattering erupted from her speaker. Giselle's eyes widened.

"Celeste?!"

All around the room, all work abruptly stopped. All eyes turned to her: Farrington, Will, Azleena, Helen, a dozen or so other recon-useful Acolytes.

"Where the hell—?"

Giselle's words cut off as the voice in her phone rattled. Immediately, she reached back to the staring crowd and whipped a finger through the air.

"Sedgwick, Kansas," she called out. "We have a location." Giselle turned back to the phone, covering her ear as the room burst into electric commotion. "Uh-huh. Yep. Got it. Slow down. Okay. Roger. Hold on." Giselle cupped her hand over the receiver as the black-clad figure of Charles Farrington stepped over, his expression set, his chin held high.

"What do we need? Who are we taking?"

"All of it," Giselle commanded. "Everyone who's standing; anyone who's awake. Matt is one of our own. We are going to rain Hell down on this son of a bitch the likes of which he can barely dream, and then he'll see what happens when you mess with the Legion of Heroes."

"SUIT UP!"

Jane stood in the ruins of Port Lions and stared with burning eyes at the ashes in her wake.

"ARGHHH!"

More. More. Destroy them all; any who dared to touch him. The searing light of Dawn blazed out from her in roiling waves, never ceasing to rest, never needing to stop. Around her, blackened shells of vehicles, of trucks and tanks and helicopters, and bombed-out building remains sat smoking between mounds of ash and scorched skeletons.

Some had run. Some had begged. Some had tried to stop her. It didn't matter. Nothing did. They had hurt the person she cared about, and this was the only way to stop it. This was the only way they'd learn.

In the distance, there rang more sirens, more shouts, far-off rumblings—reinforcements yet to arrive. Let them come. They swarmed from underground, and though Jane had scorched everything atop the surface, she knew the snake's true body lay beneath. She would purge them all, all of it. Let them see what it meant to hurt him. Let them spend the last seconds of their miserable lives learning the consequences of his blood.

"Oh my God."

Jane's head snapped around, her lips curling in a snarl. At the top of the blackened crater, crimson against the drifting smoke, stood Will. His eyes were wide. He stared down at Jane, at the devastation, face mangled in unmitigated horror.

Jane would have none of it.

"Either help or get out of my way," she spat.

"I . . . I . . ."

"I don't want to hurt you, but I will," she promised. "I'm done with mercy. Done with restraint."

"Please," Will begged, "you've got it wrong."

"Have I?" Jane snarled, turning on him. "These aren't the ones who've been hunting him? Who've been pursuing him? Who hurt him?" She turned back toward some distant bunker. "No. I don't care if it's wrong. I'll burn it all before I let them get away with—"

"We've found Matt."

Jane's words stopped midsentence. She spun on her heel, cape cutting a swathe through the ash, and glared up at the teleporter.

"What do you mean you found him? He's already—"

"The person we found on the side of the road—that wasn't Matt. It's an imposter. A decoy."

Jane's heart leapt to her throat.

"A decoy?"

"Yes."

"Then where—"

"That's what I'm trying to tell you. We've found him. Please. Stop this." Will held out his ungloved hand. "I can take you."

Jane's head spun. Suddenly, the light around her decreased its intensity. An imposter? A decoy? That meant she'd been . . . The paper had been . . .

Suddenly, Jane was turning her gaze, staring at the destruction all around her. The ruined buildings, ruined vehicles, ruined lives. She had attacked . . . She had attacked . . .

NO! This was what they wanted. They had put that note there to control her, to manipulate her, and now these bodies were on their hands, their—

"Where is he?" she demanded, launching in furious strides up the side of the crater toward Will, who recoiled, shrinking. "Where are they?"

"I can take you there," the teleporter repeated, again holding out a trembling hand. "If you'll just—"

"Yeah, right," spat Jane. "How can I trust you? How do I know you're not just here to stop this"—she gestured behind her at the devastation—"and teleport me into the sun?"

"I'm not . . . You don't trust me?" Despite the fear in his eyes and the smoke of death billowing all around them, a part of Will actually looked hurt. It was a ploy, Jane knew, all a ploy. She ignored it.

"You don't trust me?" she demanded. "Give me the location. I'll go there myself."

"I . . . Okay. No problem." Will hurriedly reached into his back pocket and drew out a small scrap of notepaper. An address in Sedgwick. Kansas.

"It's Pastor Fredericks," the teleporter explained, words falling from his mouth like rotten teeth. "The Eastborough Baptists. We don't understand why, but—"

But Jane listened not another moment. With a resounding boom, she launched into the air in a blaze of golden fury, abandoning Will and the military, leaving ashen destruction in her wake.

Down in the darkness, Matt was finding it difficult to mark the passage of time. For a few minutes, he tried counting, but unfortunately, after he got a bit past three hundred, he got distracted by boredom and found himself losing track. He then settled instead for feeling around with his hands at the chains binding him and the metal plates drilled into the ground where they were attached. So far, his fingers hadn't been able to discern any loose bolts or weak links, but Matt remained optimistic that with time, he could find something. Some unexpected edge. Privately, he was a little surprised at how nonchalant he was about this whole capture and imprisonment situation. Guess the whole "grim reaper girlfriend" thing had its benefits.

There was a low familiar *thud, thud, thud* across the floorboards above him. Instinctively, Matt followed with his ears as the footsteps swung around on approach. Internally, he hoped that it might be literally anyone other than Pastor Fredericks—the priest had seemed uncharacteristically taciturn the last time around, and Matt wondered if another Eastborough practitioner might not prove more forthcoming.

But Matt's hopes were in vain. When the cellar door opened, it was again Pastor Fredericks who descended, silent and clutching a tall glass full of clear fluid. Matt tilted his head to demonstrate confusion, but the pastor continued to say nothing, merely stopping before Matt and holding out the glass.

"Ah, yes," Matt said, grasping the vessel with both hands, careful not to drop it. "Everyone knows you can't donate blood without at least ten cups of water."

Even in the dim light, the pastor stared down at his prisoner with withering contempt. Matt suspected he was already beginning to regret his kindness, if that was indeed what the water was.

"Drink," Fredericks commanded, little more than a grunt. Matt made no move to do so.

"How do I know it's not poisoned?"

The pastor's lips curled. "If I wanted you dead, you would be."

"Yeah," conceded Matt. "Suppose so. Though, I gotta say, there's been some evidence to the contrary."

"You know nothing. Shut up."

"I know a few things," replied Matt. "Well, *know* is a strong word. More like educated guess. My guess is that you're working with someone, maybe the military. My guess is that they want my blood, to harvest it, anti-powers, blah blah blah. They were just going to kill me and take it at first, but then, that failed. Since I seem to be having a little dying problem."

The priest continued to glare at him, his eyes narrowed.

"Am I getting close?" Matt continued, turning his head but never leaving his gaze. "Am I getting warmer? See, now I figure you're in a bit of a predicament. You want my blood, except, you know, you can't take it without me noticing, and you can't kill me to keep me quiet. Which really only leaves one option, and you're looking at it. Captivity. If you want my blood, and you don't want anyone to find out you took my blood, you have to keep me imprisoned, and you have to keep me alive."

Fredericks remained silent, still standing at the foot of the staircase, staring. Matt overdramatically rolled his eyes.

"Oh, give it a rest with the brooding silence! You do not scare me! I am not worried about you! You are an idiot with a plan that's doomed to fail, and you know what? You better get used to the sound of my talking because as long as you keep me down here, I am going to be doing *a lot* of that."

In the light of the trapdoor, Matt could see a vein twitching in Fredericks's forehead.

"Do you even believe in God?" Matt laughed, voice brimming with disdain. "Is any of this real? Do you guys actually worship the toilet bowl I crap in, or was that all just a scam to—"

"Shut up!" the pastor roared, and suddenly, Matt's world reeled as in the space of an instant, Fredericks lunged forward and slammed a fist into the side of his head. Matt staggered, the darkness swirling around him with sudden pain as the pastor reared up again and again and pounded his fist into Matt's face. "Shut up, shut up, shut up! You stupid, arrogant, blabbering imbecile; you think you know anything?! You think you understand?! Shut up!"

Fredericks stumbled back, blood dripping from his knuckles, leaving Matt to gasp and whimper, his ears ringing, spots dancing before his eyes. "You know nothing," Fredericks whispered. In the shadows of the cellar door, his eyes shone, utterly mad. "Nothing. Not you, not anybody . . ."

All of a sudden, to Matt's pained, groggy bewilderment, the priest fell to his knees and began crying. Through a throbbing haze, the left side of his face bloody and swollen, Matt could only watch in disbelief as Fredericks curled into a ball, wracked by endless, shaking sobs.

"I have to . . ." he whispered, the words skittering from his mouth like rats squirming through a crack. "I have to do it, but I'm scared, but I . . . I have to."

"Have to do what?" Matt whispered, forcing the words from his bleeding tongue, his jaw numb and mouth still screaming at him. Fredericks drew a long, abrupt sniff and looked back, still crouched, clutching his knees.

"You wouldn't understand," he murmured, hunched shoulders suddenly stiff, staying dead still on his toes like a taut, teetering boulder. "None of them understand, they're all . . ."—he sniffed again—". . . all fools, cattle, idiots, waddling about their meaningless lives without thinking . . . without knowing . . ."

Slowly, he shuffled backward, climbing to his feet, pushing from the dirt with a small step, gazing unfocused around the corner of the curving basement and its empty barrels, staring mournfully off into the dark.

"The military," he mumbled. "Pfft. Ants clambering over rocks. Governments, societies, everything we've built—none of it matters, none of it . . ." His voice trailed into nothingness, and for a few moments, no sound came from between his hulking shoulders. "It was me," Fredericks murmured. "Just me. Only me. Guided, yes, but alone. No footprints on this path, Christ our Lord, child-fake-legend. Only I walk it."

Watching the clearly disturbed man muttering incoherently into the darkness, Matt's brow furrowed, a reaction he regretted a second later as pain shot through what felt like a cracked eye socket. He gritted his teeth and forced himself to push further. "How . . ." he breathed, the words coming through thick and bloody. "How did you . . . ?"

The pastor barked a short, joyless laugh. He shook his head, not turning around. "Money," he said. "Just money. So simple, so pathetic, and yet, it just . . . turns all keys. Opens all doors. Our broken world; this broken system. All men have prices, and I paid them. I paid and I paid and I paid, buying every one, a thousand little pieces. All King Solomon's gold. Meaningless. Trinkets. It'll all be gone."

Matt's head swam as he forced himself to listen intently to every word Fredericks was saying, but it didn't make sense. They were talking billions of dollars here. Phillip Fredericks wasn't some secret billionaire; he didn't own entire countries or half the stock market. He was just some irrelevant old preacher with like a few acres of land. Maybe if there was oil . . . but the idea was absurd. It was all utter nonsense.

"All that," Matt fumbled out, "All that . . . to kill me? Why?"

Fredericks rolled his head back, staring at the ceiling as he let out a great, frustrated sigh. "Endless," he almost shouted. A part of him seemed almost pleased to be talking, to finally be releasing all these pent-up, boiling thoughts. "Just endless self-obsession, these delusions, this—" The pastor suddenly rounded on him, lunging forward, jabbing a finger an inch from Matt's face.

"You are a fool," he snarled. "An unfit, clownish child, so obsessed with your own existence that you cannot *for a moment* picture a world that doesn't revolve around you." He stepped back, throwing up his hands with so much force they almost struck the ceiling, half his face illuminated in the light of the stairs, eyes fevered and insane. "It has never, *ever*, been about you. You were a pawn. An instrument." Fredericks paused as his arms sank back down to his sides. "It was always her."

In the cold, earthen dark, Matt felt his face pale.

"Jane." The words were barely a whisper. "You're trying to kill Jane."

"Kill?" Fredericks's manic laughter bounded off the walls around them. "Oh no. No, never, and she will never . . . No." He turned back toward Matt, his eyes wide, unblinking, gleaming. "I'm not going to kill her; I'm going to help her. And I have, and I have; it's all gone as He said, as He promised . . ."

"Who?" Matt asked. Yet, somehow, he already knew.

"The Child," the pastor muttered. "The pale, all-seeing Child. He came to me in my weakest moments, and He laid it out for me: what I must do, the only way . . ."

He spun back to look at Matt, eyes burning in the shadows. "It's okay. Shh, it's all okay. Listen. We're at the end now. I'll let her wade and rage, and then I'll reveal, and she'll come racing back, as only you could make her, as only you motivate . . ." He let out a psychotic, high-pitched chuckle. "So hard to tame. So indomitable. Yet so predictable. So predictable. For you."

"It's okay," pleaded Matt. "You don't have to hurt her."

Fredericks recoiled as if stung by the very thought. "Hurt her?" He scowled, voice curdling with offense. "Hurt her? You don't understand; I'm not going to hurt her."

Abruptly, he fell silent, and his entire body slumped, as if he was sinking slowly underwater.

For a few moments, there was only silence. The world seemed to hold its breath.

"Do I believe in God?" the pastor murmured, turning away, so low it was almost difficult for Matt to hear. Suddenly, the fire and the fervor in his speech had vanished, replaced by this emptiness, this bleak, mournful sorrow. "I did. Once. Born in it." He sniffed, hiccupped. "Raised with it. All my life, all my . . . I studied. Oh yes, studied and studied. I knew. Thought I understood, could cite with precision the canon, a hundred, oh Lord, generations of learned men. With fire, you see, with . . . They were all wrong. This sinful world. Disbelief, debauchery. I knew the truth. I knew his words. I knew my place.

"And then, I went on television," he stated, mouth moving silent between breaths as if whispering back to every echo. "And I was ridiculed by this . . . atheist, this fat, smug man who . . . And everything he said made me so angry, and I left those lights, that room, and I went home, and I tore through tome after tome for what I knew must be there, for the answer, to denounce him . . .

"But the more I read," Fredericks murmured, "the more I yearned, the more I could not get away . . . I . . . I was learned. I was logical. Six thousand years of arguments, and I . . . And all of them are wrong."

In the cold, empty cellar, the great priest began to rock. "We are alone," he whispered. "It is all random. There is no meaning; there is no purpose. We are a speck in unyielding darkness. We will . . . We are dying, our planet is dying, *everything is dying*, and at the end, there is nothing. There is nothing. There is only . . ."

He sucked wet air between his teeth, his chest rising and falling with fast, shallow breaths. "There is no God," Fredericks whispered. "There is no one guiding us, just coincidence and our own misdeeds; a hundred billion light years of dust and nothingness, and to dust we will return, and of dust we all began, and I cannot stop . . . I cannot . . ."

And for the second time since Matt had awoken, Pastor Phillip Fredericks broke down crying, collapsing on the ground in a heap, curling into a fetal ball that rocked his giant frame with shakes and sobs, the deep gurgling of horror and the wet sucking of breath.

Matt stared at him wide-eyed, his heart hammering. "I . . . It's okay," he murmured. He tried to lace his voice through with compassion and understanding, to calm, to reassure this insane, unhinged man. "It's going to be okay."

"You don't understand," Fredericks whispered, alone in the weeping dark. "There is no God."

And suddenly his head snapped up, and from beneath his arms, he bored into Matt with a demented, bloodshot gaze.

"There has to be a God."

Giselle materialized in Sedgwick, Kansas, with a team of twenty crimson-clad Legion members to find Celeste arguing with an overweight police chief in black, outdated SWAT gear and, to her shock and dismay, the Eastborough Baptist compound already surrounded. Not content to wait for introductions, Giselle dropped her grip on Enrique, one of the Legion's junior teleporters, and marched over to where the faunamorph was standing opposite the chunky gray-haired man with a walrus-like mustache.

"And I'm telling you, you need to wait for—"

"I know what I need, missy, and it ain't your—"

"Hi there, hi," Giselle interrupted, fixing both of them with a wide, forced, aggressively amicable smile. "Giselle Pixus, speedster, Legion of Heroes. What, ah, what's going on here?"

"Chuck Brady," the police chief replied before Celeste could get a word in otherwise. "Sheriff of Sedgwick County. I eat things. And I could ask you the same thing. This is an active crime scene."

They were standing on a grassy strip beside the sidewalk, to the east of which lay a parking lot, a nail salon, and the remains of a dilapidated mini mall. Across the double-lane road to the west lay a wide block suburban property, in the center of which stood a large, mostly single-story brown Ranch-style house surrounded on the street sides by a waist-height chain-link fence and about a quarter of a football field of flat-mown lawn. Around the edge of this lawn, approximately a dozen local law enforcement officers, dressed in black SWAT tactical gear and carrying assault rifles, had taken up position aiming at the house's windows, from which no movement was visible. The police chief, who looked to be in his midfifties to early sixties, followed Giselle's gaze as she took all this in, his face set in an expression of smug satisfaction.

Giselle did not have time for this. "Sheriff," she said, not so much turning on the sweetness as upending the whole syrup bottle, "thanks so much for getting here as quick as you did."

"Well, what can I say, miss," the fat man replied with a bemused smirk. "When we roll, we roll out."

"Exceptional. Well, it looks like you've done a great job keeping everything under control, and you have our sincerest thanks, and we are ready to take over."

"Oh now," Sheriff Brady said with a brief stroke of his mustache, "I don't think that'll be necessary. We're already set to go." He waved a hand high above his head to one of the SWAT members. "Your little friend has explained it all to us; I know this Fredericks fellow, and we are more than ready to take him down."

"It is my strong preference—" Giselle began with all possible politeness.

"Well, I'll take that into consideration, missy," Brady cut her off. "But your friend here called us first, and we're here first, and we're gonna do our jobs."

Feeling the heat rising in her cheeks, Giselle fixed Celeste with a look that could have melted diamonds. "You called them?"

Beneath her gaze, the faunamorph withered. "I thought . . . they would be closer . . ."

"And you thought right, miss," said the sheriff, slapping Celeste hard on the back. "Quick as a flash we were, much quicker than you Legion folks. Don't know why anyone bothers paying you."

"We're NFP." Giselle smiled through gritted teeth. "Sheriff, I'm sorry to do this, but I'm going to have to pull rank. This is Legion business. Have your men pull back."

"Legion business?" Brady scoffed. "You got a boy trapped in a ranch house with a kooky old man; you call that Legion business? I call it simple kidnapping, and I feel I've got a county judge who might agree with me."

Giselle never let her smile waver. "The law clearly states—"

"I know the law, miss." That statement, Giselle knew with utter, seething certainty, was patently false. "Thirty years I've known the law. I want tips on the law from you, I'll ask."

The Legion's leader drew in a long, calming breath. Then she smiled. "Azleena," she said into her earpiece, "could you please get the relevant criminal codes for our good friend here and send them through to me?"

"I don't care what you show me on no phone." The sheriff shrugged. "This is my crime scene; I'm in charge of it."

Giselle turned around to the Legion members assembling behind her, the force of the smile now physically hurting her face. "Enrique," she said sweetly, gesturing to the teleporter, "would you be so kind as to head back to Morningstar and get those printed. It might help if we've got the legislation in front of us."

She turned back to the walking butterball of a man and tried to set her words down as firmly and politely as possible. "Mr. Brady. Sheriff. I apologize if it feels like we're storming in here, stepping on your toes. But we're not looking to steal any thunder; we're here for one of our own. You know what I'm saying. You know who's in there. You—"

"Powerless human, way I hear it," the sheriff spat, hocking a loogie onto the grass. "Minor celebrity, but not one of you lot; couldn't possibly be." He cocked his head back toward the spread-out SWAT team. "Now, you just hold tight there and don't get your panties in a twist; we'll have him out and safe all lickety-split."

They were running out of time.

"Sheriff," Giselle said, pursing her fingers together in front of her as if in respectful prayer, "let me make myself abundantly clear. We are not state, not federal. We're the Legion of Heroes. Now, I respect that your men have made the effort to come out here today, but when it comes to who's better suited to handling the situation, the Legion—"

"Legion?" Brady scoffed. "I don't see no Legion." He swept his gaze over the Acolytes arrayed behind Giselle. "I see a bunch of children, most not old enough to drink." He leveled the speedster with a patronizing smile. "I've been a hostage negotiator for twenty-three years, missy. When I need a bunch of college kids come tell me how to do my job, again, I'll holler."

It was a testament to Giselle's utter professionalism and the commitment she felt to her organization's reputation that she did not immediately, despite approximately thirty-six hours without sleep, supersonically stab this man in the neck. Instead, she just smiled, bent her head slightly in a gesture of grating genuflection, and turned, smile still straining the muscles in her face, back to her team.

"We," she announced sunnily and through barely gritted teeth, "are going to let the locals try first."

"What?" exclaimed Natalia, pushing her way through, her mascara-tinged eyes bulging with absolute indignation. "We're waiting?" There were similar sounds of annoyance and dismay from the rest of the group.

"Are you serious?" asked Celeste.

"I am serious," replied Giselle, doing her absolute best to keep her voice level. "Just as serious as I am about the fact that when we get back to Morningstar, you, Celeste, are going to write me a two hundred-page essay entitled 'Why Law Enforcement Calls Us. We Do Not Call Law Enforcement.'" The speedster's head tilted to the side as she spoke, her wide eyes fixed on Celeste the entire time in a way that made it abundantly clear where Giselle's tolerance lay for one more word of protest. Celeste wisely shut up.

"Spread out," Giselle commanded, smile vanishing. "Set up a perimeter, defensive positions, give the locals a wide berth. I've had enough surprises for one lifetime." At that moment, Will and Wally appeared, carrying another ride-along Acolyte crew. "Spread the word." She strode over, directing questions in unbroken succession to one and then the other. "Where's Jane? How's your patient?"

Will looked surprisingly pale. "She's on her way."

"Why didn't you teleport her?"

"She was worried it was a trap."

"Good, that's just great," said Giselle. "So we have essentially a complete breakdown of trust. Fantastic. You?"

"Blackmore's under observation by Delores."

"Fine. That's a long-term project, anyway." Giselle marched away from the greater host of Acolytes, motioning Will and Wally to follow. She also flicked a firm nod at Natalia and Charles Farrington, and though it burned her to do so, Celeste. The faunamorph thankfully had the good sense to at least look sheepish.

"Alright, look," Giselle said, keeping her voice low as they formed a loose huddle away from the prying ears of the sheriff. "Until the entire bench of the Supreme Court comes down and convinces that moron that we actually have jurisdiction, I am not going to push this. I have had about my fill of Legion members attacking American peace officers for one day, and I am not letting this get blown up all over the news." As she said it, Giselle could see over Wally's shoulder two white vans approaching down the street, from their markings carrying what looked to be camera crews. "Not now, okay? So we let Sheriff Braindead over there have his shot at playing hero, and we see how it plays out. Best-case scenario, they get Matt, they all jack off, and everyone goes home. Worst case, they get Matt shot, and well, it seems like for some reason we don't care about that anymore."

"Yeah, I mean, what's the worst they can do?" Natalia shrugged. "Kill him?"

"PASTOR PHILLIP FREDERICKS," a lanky police officer standing over by Sheriff Brady shouted at the house via megaphone. "COME OUT WITH YOUR HANDS UP."

If Giselle still had a bridge of her nose to pinch by the end of the day, it would be an absolute miracle. "In the meantime," she stated, "I want the five of you—six, you're in on this too, Azleena"—she said, touching her earpiece—"looking for ways into that building. Safe ways." Giselle paused. "Options. Teleportation."

She looked at Will, who threw a quick glance at the building and squinted his eyes. A small plume of sulfur wafted up from the small of his back.

"Disruptance."

"Typical. So no phasing either."

"Not unless they've skimped."

"Unlikely. At the very least, though, it means nobody's going out that way."

"Agreed," said Farrington.

"Invisibility then," suggested Giselle. "Sneak someone in to recon and ID."

"Advise against it," crackled Azleena's voice. "I'm looking at the video feeds. Those cameras hanging from the awnings have thermal sensors. They'll see us coming." The genius paused. "Very expensive for a suburban church."

"Nat, Wally?" Giselle asked, turning to the psychics. "Who do you sense inside?"

"Dozens of people." Natalia scowled. "It's like an entire Podunk family."

"You know how these cults love communal living." Wally sighed. At that moment, though, the front door of the complex opened, and a stream of men in plain shirts and trousers and women in ankle-length dresses poured into the front yard, running frantically toward the police line.

"Oh crap, oh crap," swore Giselle, but it became immediately apparent that they were neither under attack nor were these suicide bombers—every member of the congregation had their hands up, several were screaming, and all appeared absolutely panicked. As they reached the edge of the property, the SWAT members lunged forward, surrounding and hurrying the civilians away with a probably unnecessary amount of force.

"They're just letting them through," hissed Giselle, her voice rising, incredulous. "They could be anyone; they could do anything. They're just—"

"They're being detained," Wally reassured her. His hand was on his temple, as was Natalia's. "And I'm not getting any animosity or pushback. Nothing but panic."

"Same," Nat confirmed.

"Alright," breathed Giselle, turning back away from the rushing crowd, who were being chaotically herded into the back of police vans. "Where does that leave us?"

"There're still two people inside," Natalia said, her dark eyes squinting. She scowled at the complex for a few seconds. "I can't get through. Psy-Block."

"Psy-Block," confirmed Wally.

"The pastor and who, Matt?"

"WE KNOW YOU HAVE MATTHEW CALLAGHAN WITH YOU. RELEASE HIM, AND YOU CAN WALK AWAY FROM THIS UNHARMED."

"Maybe he dosed him?" Celeste suggested. Giselle turned to her.

"What about you?" she demanded. "You got us into this mess, can you get us out of it? Go mole or . . . something? Rat? Get Matt out?"

"He didn't really want to get out." Celeste shrugged. "He wanted to catch someone. He wanted to get everyone here."

"Well, everyone's here now, mission accomplished," growled Giselle.

"I don't know how much more *in the act* this pastor can be," Farrington added.

"Why don't we make this simple?" Giselle sighed. "I run in. Azleena, find me a door or window without clackers. I'll run in, carry Pastor Fredericks away, then somebody with some bolt cutters go and free Matt in their own damn time. Sound good?"

"It's either that or we drop someone big or heavy from space," said Will.

"My way has less squishing. The whole point is to get the pastor and whatever evidence he's got intact. Matt too, preferably." She turned toward the house, cracking her shoulders. "Alright, here we go."

"Wait!" Azleena's voice cried suddenly in her ear. "Don't!"

Giselle paused midstep. "What?" It was rare for the young genius to sound so urgent, let alone so alarmed. "What is it?"

"I'm cycling through Helen's bodycam," Azleena said, and the six of them glanced over to where the technopath cyborg was standing on the Legion's perimeter, facing toward the house. "I'm picking up something above the front lawn. There's—I need someone to go and take an air sample. Not Giselle!" she practically shouted.

The group of senior Legion members exchanged glances, then Will shrugged and strode over past the Legion and the police line, ignoring the shifty glares the SWAT team gave him. He stopped at the foot of the grass, reached into his back pocket, and pulled out what looked to be an empty sandwich bag. The teleporter swiped it through the air, then glanced back.

"YOU HAVE FIVE MINUTES TO COMPLY OR MAKE YOUR DEMANDS KNOWN."

"I'm sending Helen." Giselle nodded, though she knew the genius couldn't see, and a few seconds later, the bulky, short-haired half-robot girl stomped over. Wordlessly, Will handed her the bag.

"Analyzing." Helen's robotic hand had retracted and transformed into what looked almost like a metallic satellite dish, which enveloped the bag like a snail's mouth swallowing paper. "Analyzing."

Over the comms link, the genius swore. "I knew it. Giselle, do not run in there."

"What?" Giselle replied, her hand going to her ear. "Why?"

"The entire field is covered in electrostatically suspended silica crystals," Azleena explained. "The second you go in at speed, it'll shred every inch of your body, and the instant you breathe, it'll tear apart your lungs."

"Suburban church, huh?" said Wally, his expression dark. Azleena did not sound amused.

"This is high-grade military ordinance," she continued, the words tumbling through their comms. "Not for commercial sale, bleeding edge. I thought I saw something strange on the in-depth cameras, but I didn't think—"

"Good pick," Giselle cut her off. "What do we do?"

A moment. Then: "Come back," Azleena told her. "I can fabricate a polycarbonate suit and respirator to cover your entire body. Then you go in."

"How long will that take?"

"Six minutes. It's already printing."

"Good enough." Giselle turned to Farrington. "You've got lead. Wally, explain to Sheriff Dipstick over there that sending any speed-sters in will kill them. Hopefully, he'll listen to a polite young white man more than he does me. Nat, link. Will, home. Celeste—"

"You still want me to try mole?" the faunamorph asked, looking hopeful. "I could go real big?"

"Hold that thought," Giselle ordered. "The terramancers too, if they're considering tunneling inside. I guarantee if this guy has black-market anti-speedster tech, he's got landmines."

"Agreed."

"Agreed."

Will gripped Giselle by the arm and closed his eyes. As they turned away, the girl took one last look at the complex.

"Hang on, Matt," she swore. "We're coming."

* * *

The darkened basement closed in around him, and the room spun in time to Matt's heartbeat.

"What . . . ?"

Slowly, Fredericks rose, his shoulders slumped, his head drooping slightly, as if some great weight had been lifted from his shoulders. He stretched his neck to either side, giving the bones in his spine a little *pop* and staring down at Matt with crazed indifference.

"For the longest time, I didn't know what to do," the pastor continued, idly shaking his head as though they were talking about inclement weather. "I thought I knew the pieces, see, what I'd need, what I had to do. Captain Dawn, of course, he was obvious. Waiting, waiting, ready, and then the twins I eventually discovered . . . Turn over enough rocks. There are so many secrets," he hissed, "so much supposedly kept hidden in this world that you can learn with sufficient coin. And then I had two. But then, of course, Klaus Heydrich turned out not to be dead, and I was as shocked as anybody, and I thought for a moment he might be a good candidate. Cruel, true, but it does not matter; not the temperament, only the goal . . .

"But then she came. Then she came. Wreathed in gold. And I knew—in that moment I knew—I knew as I gazed upon her, where I had despaired mere moments before, mourning Dawn's loss. But there she was, and she had it. And she was one of them—a blessed vessel—and I knew, and I knew she'd found another one. Because I'd always suspected. Tinkerer, tailor, watcher, weaver, spin your little web. A glaring oversight, seemingly, in the allotment of gifts; it hardly made sense. But then *Jane*. I knew. That lie about the hair could not hold water; it was shockingly obvious . . . Sir Arthur Conan Doyle: 'Once you eliminate the impossible, whatever remains, no matter how improbable, must be the truth.'

"One more test, on national television, and it was proven. There was no way she could have seen that shooter; yet suddenly, she turns away the gun." The pastor motioned with his hand before his lips, the kiss of some deranged chef. "Only one explanation. Only one now. She went back. She stopped it. The power of time. The power of time!

"Then, of course," he continued briskly, voice dropping its husky fervor as quickly as it had been raised, "all that remained was moving pieces. Break her home. Make her fear for you. Expose the twins." The pastor scoffed. "Their asynchronous complementary manifestations were clearly a distribution of an original unbroken whole, though those Harvard incompetents remained blind. It was clear an empath could combine them. Split pieces of a single orb. I tested. I tested."

He clicked his tongue. "From there, it was just a matter of synchronization. A situation she could not yield from. A situation you could not live through. The power of time is incredibly hard to account for, but the Child was there; the Child guided. He knows she is an amateur. Though that will change . . ."

The madman paused. "It's simple, really," Fredericks said. "Less complex than you might think. Just four pieces. Four."

"Four pieces of what?" Matt whispered, the darkness spinning, lightheaded. He almost feared to understand. But Fredericks didn't seem to hear him.

"The power to control time," he murmured, unfurling his back, rising to his full height, staring at the empty shadows with eyes full of grim, determined madness. "Limitless energy. The power to control matter. The power of life and death. Four abilities. Four pieces of the Divine. I told you, Matt Callaghan," he said, and with swaying delirium, Pastor Fredericks looked down at him and smiled. "I told you this was not about you. I told you."

The darkened world stood silent.

"There is no God," the man of faith repeated. "There must be a God."

Matt's breathing stopped.

The pastor laughed, peeling away, swinging his arms in circles either side of his broad shoulders like some demented swimmer warming up. Matt sat in the darkness, eyes wide, head pounding, trying to think, trying to move his brain. So much didn't . . . But it didn't . . . It couldn't . . .

"Wait," he said slowly. He raised his head to look at Fredericks as his kidnapper bounced on his heels in the cellar corner. "Wait. You said control over matter. Jane can't control matter. That's only three."

In the darkness, the false priest smiled. "We're at the end now, Matt Callaghan. Dawn of the final day."

Suddenly, reverberating through the basement and the entire complex, a booming voice rang out.

"PASTOR PHILLIP FREDERICKS. COME OUT WITH YOUR HANDS UP."

"Oh," the madman muttered, and for the first time since he'd started speaking, since he'd launched unbidden into his rambling insanity, he actually looked mildly surprised. Fredericks shuffled over to a far wall and lifted up the louver, peeking out through a vent into sudden rays of sunlight. The pastor paused, frowned, then snapped the vent back into place and strode once more over to Matt. He gazed down, his mouth split into a knowing, giddy smile.

"Well," the pastor said lightly, "sooner than we thought."

"If these disasters could stop happening in such quick succession," Natalia muttered to Wally as they stood watching the SWAT team move into place, a slow, black-clad circle shrinking around the East-borough Baptist residence, "that would be fantastic. My pores are dreadful."

"Hush," snapped Wally.

"Hush yourself. I actually care about my appearance."

"Yeah, that's all you—" The words suddenly dropped dead in his mouth. "Someone's coming."

The front door of the complex opened, and from the depths of the house, a man emerged. Towering, stone-faced, he walked forward slowly, his hands in the air, unarmed, showing no hint of powers.

"Azleena," Wally whispered, "you seeing this?"

"Yes."

"And?"

"Nothing on him."

"HANDS IN THE AIR!" one of the police officers shouted. The line of SWAT troopers edged closer, rifles raised, powers bristling. "PALMS FORWARD! DO IT NOW!"

"Do we know what he can do?" Wally whispered, leaning over.

"No," Natalia replied, keeping her voice low. "Religious exemption to registration. Could be anything."

"For Christ's sake."

The looming figure of Pastor Fredericks kept walking, step by step, slowly onward, his hands upstretched, his upturned palms facing the police around him.

"Maybe he's surrendering," Natalia whispered. "They've got him; the jig is up."

"Maybe."

"I mean, what the hell can he do?" the English girl swore under her breath. "He might get off a lucky shot, but he's surrounded. The entire effing Legion's . . ."

"Almost. Giselle." Wally touched his earpiece. "I don't know how that new outfit's coming, but we're getting to the fireworks here."

"I know."

"Any sign of Jane?" Will asked.

"Not yet," Natalia answered under her breath, warily eyeing the skies. "I can't believe I'm saying this, you useless prats, but this may all wrap up nicely."

"ON YOUR KNEES!"

In front of his unremarkable suburban home, Pastor Phillip Fredericks stopped in the center of the lawn. He held his head high, his hair neat, dark brown and streaked through with gray. His eyes were vacant. He carried no arms or armor, wearing nothing but gray pants, a plain black shirt, and a russet felt jacket. He stood stock-still, holding his hands above his head. His palms faced out.

He did not kneel.

"ON YOUR KNEES, NOW!"

"Careful," Farrington's voice echoed through each of their ears, linked up through the comms. "Eyes sharp. First sign of a power, restrain him."

"I do not like this," Wally whispered.

"DO IT! NOW!"

Alone in the middle of the empty lawn, ringed by a dozen black-clad men with a dozen black metal guns, the tall man closed his eyes. Then slowly, deliberately, he removed and folded his glasses. His lips began to murmur, barely, the sound of his words whisked away by the soft breeze that ruffled through his hair and the thin green grass. He bowed his head ever so slightly, keeping his hands held upright, still mumbling, like he was in prayer. The ring of officers around him tensed as they crept an inch forward, flexing their powers, fingers twitching on their triggers. For a moment, the entire world seemed to lean in toward Pastor Fredericks, on the breathless brink of some precipice.

Then, without warning, the prayer stopped, and the priest's eyes flew open.

And they were, in their entirety, the deepest crimson red.

"OPEN F—!"

The SWAT leader never finished that sentence. In an instant, the barest flick twitched through Fredericks's hands, and an unseen force shot out around him in a ripple, racing not just through the air but through reality itself. And to the horror of every onlooker, the ring of men around him simply evaporated. Turned to dust.

"Holy—!"

Wally barely knew what he was doing, but suddenly, instinctively, he was sprinting back with Natalia, his arms around the tiny British psychic, hauling her off her feet while she could do nothing but stand there, eyes wide, mouth gaping, as the siege erupted into chaos. He dove behind a squad car, pulling them both into cover as all around them descended death.

"FIRE!" the sheriff screamed, and the police officers fired, bullets flying from every direction. They could not miss; their aim was true, and Fredericks made no attempt to evade them. Yet, nothing hit. Staring wild eyed over the back of the car, Wally could only look on in horror as a thousand bullets became nothingness mere feet from the pastor. Disintegrated.

"FIRE!"

Only now, it seemed, did the police remember they had superpowers. Torrents of fire and ice and lightning streamed toward Fredericks, but the priest's crimson eyes merely twitched, and the air around him was suddenly not air but crystal, great walls of impossible glass erupting into existence, absorbing the energy harmlessly, appearing from nowhere to—

And suddenly Fredericks was rising. The earth beneath him tremored and burst with diamonds the size of school buses, roiling sheets of marble and granite, waterfalls of liquid metal sweeping suspended through the air as he rose, gazing imperiously down, as whatever powers came near him disappeared, reformed.

"Back!" shouted Wally, Azleena, Farrington, someone, a terrified voice in every Acolyte's head. "Back!"

People were screaming—civilians, onlookers, media, Fredericks's own followers, tumbling handcuffed, screaming, scrambling out of the back of now unguarded police cars. The officers surged forward, yelling wordless panic, terror or pressure or training making them just keep shooting, keep advancing with their useless guns—

From his outcrop of shining stone, Fredericks swept his gaze down over the mortals, over everyone. He reached out his hands, his lips still moving, a conductor poised to command a symphony. Everywhere he turned, disintegration followed, rolling in a wave without distinction, without mercy. The police, the media, the Baptists—their voices all suddenly gone, swallowed by silence, their bodies turned to ash.

"Run. Run!"

Spread far back from the homestead, some Acolytes were firing, attempting to bring their powers to bear. Wally saw Gabbi hurtling shards of shining steel with razor precision, but the moment they got within three feet of Fredericks, they were no longer steel but raindrops. A tornado hurtled down from an unnatural gray cloud, but the wind did not so much as ripple the priest's hair, instead drifting harmlessly to floating snowflakes. Farrington's fire met inch-thin barriers of obsidian swirling into existence with almost indifference.

All of a sudden, Fredericks rose, his feet no longer touching the ground, his palms down and outstretched as he lifted through a hurricane of swirling black and white and silver, spiraling stones and sheets of diamond, the earth beneath him bristling, breaking, and reforming into man-size crystals of a dozen different colors, clear and chrome and cobalt, rippling squares of interlacing fractals, the boiling landscape of an alien world.

Suspended ten feet in the air, his maroon, listless eyes turned back to the stumbling crowd, where they found Monique, the dreadlocked, force fielder Acolyte, holding a champagne-colored hexagon between Fredericks and a camera crew. The pastor's left hand flicked toward her, his finger making the barest twitch—but suddenly, a black blur shot in front of the girl, and Monique was gone, dustless.

Wally felt Giselle's mind reconnect to their psychic network, felt the speedster race, wordlessly, covered head-to-toe in black nanofiber, desperately grabbing members of the Legion, hurtling them clear. In his mind, Wally heard her breath coming hard and fast, panting beneath the helmet and respirator as she desperately sped, racing in a blurring circle, hauling her Acolytes out of the way one after the other—

Suddenly, Giselle split, and faster than a bullet, she was running, leaping step by step through the surreal hurricane surrounding Fredericks, feet pushing off disks of stone and shards of diamond, faster than the eye could follow, hands gripping titanium blades.

But Fredericks did not even glance at her. Giselle leapt, plunging the daggers toward his neck, only for the metal to turn to salt before they got anywhere close. Giselle did not wait, did not waver, but instead sped off, running back to the Legion's perimeter—but now, Fredericks's eyes followed. Wally watched in horror as in the space of a heartbeat, his demon-blood gaze traced the blur of Giselle's speeding form, as his lips moved, as his right hand followed—as he pointed his forefinger.

And suddenly Giselle was screaming. Pain, incomprehensible pain, exploded in Wally's head as all of a sudden, in the far parking lot, Giselle tumbled, dropping out of superspeed, skidding like a stone across the pavement, and Wally was racing, loosing wordless cries, springing over the curb as Natalia sprinted beside him to find—

Giselle's body slid to a stop, her chest spasming, her hands desperately tearing at her helmet, ripping it free, her hair and cheeks caked with sweat, and she was wailing, sobbing in the morning air, screaming as Wally slid beside her, eyes wide with horror because—

Her legs were gone. Not burned, not broken, not severed, simply gone beneath midthigh, sheared in perfect lines to tremoring stumps. They didn't bleed. There was no bone or blood or muscle, just this creaseless black line, like the wound had been cauterized, flat and perfect—

"Giselle," he whispered. "Oh no, hang on, we've got to—*MEDIC! MEDIC!*"

And just like that, it was pandemonium. Panic surged through the Legion's psychic connection as everyone started running, as everyone started screaming—

Suspended in the center of the field, Fredericks's gaze no longer moved in a sweeping arc but person to person, flicking, a boy who had poured gasoline into an ants' nest squashing one by one those with the temerity to survive. Wally felt Adam's mind scream and go dark, Monique and Cameron not just vanishing but dying horrible, violent deaths. A sudden gasp as a chest was pierced from six directions by fist-size diamonds. A sudden heat, an inhuman shriek, as blood turned to boiling sulfur. A group of voices wailing as their bodies dissolved into the ground in fusing, hardening puddles, pain switching to choking gasps as the air around them became chlorine gas.

This was not fighting. This was not self-defense. Wally saw it in the flash of Fredericks's crimson eyes, the small smile playing on his lips. This was vindictive. This was pleasure. This was cruelty.

The pastor's eyes turned to Sheriff Brady and his senior staff, who were stuck standing still beside a police truck, eyes wide and hands shaking, seemingly unable to move. The police chief's mouth moved wordlessly beneath his mustache, whispering some inaudible plea, while around him, a few of his sergeants reached for shaking guns. Fredericks waved toward them with a lazy flick of two fingers, and then the men were coughing, gurgling, collapsing, clawing at their faces—their eyes, their ears, their mouths overflowing with silver trails of liquid mercury.

"God," Wally whispered. The word trickled from his lips in soft, desperate terror. "God."

Fredericks hung suspended in the twisting, shimmering air, his hands outstretched, surveying the destruction before him. Nothing lived within a hundred feet. A radius of surreal devastation, of pillars of salt and twisting metal talons, floating diamonds and velvet silver spread out around him; an alien hell made real. His eyes left those beneath him, and once more, Fredericks's gaze turned up toward the heavens. The ground rumbled and the earth shifted, rising as though giving birth to a great, awakening monster.

Ten feet below Fredericks's legs, there erupted trunks of glistening diamond, crystals bigger than houses shifting and rising underneath him and interlocking with shaking, resounding screams. Fredericks rose, borne upward by this impossible mountain, a castle of frozen rock and liquid diamond. And as he stood, it melded itself around him, grew forth to cradle him, his back and arms and feet. With a lazy turn, he flicked one hand, and the homestead below disintegrated into splinters. Within an enveloping spiral of silver, Matt Callaghan rose, wide-eyed, bloodied yet alive, carried upward atop the mountain on lifeless eddies of chrome.

Barely a minute after Phillip Fredericks stepped from its door, the Eastborough Baptist Church was annihilated. In its place, brought forth from beneath the churned ground in the heart of docile suburbia, stood a crystal citadel, a seamless diamond ziggurat with neither edges nor ends, shining curves untouched by tools of man. It gleamed in the morning sun, an impossible pyramid some six stories high—and there, at its summit, sat a being, a towering man with scarlet, empty eyes, his body splayed atop a crystal throne, king of all he surveyed. And beside him, bound by diamond chains, a prisoner. Matt Callaghan, who could do naught but gape in horror at the devastation before him, who could do naught but helplessly stare.

The crimson faded from Fredericks's eyes. The priest sat silent, smiling at the world beneath him, and waited without a word.

He didn't have to wait long, for at that moment, a figure dropped from the sky in a hail of blazing gold, slamming into the Earth, cracking the ground around her. Her eyes, clear gray-blue, burned with unspeakable fury. From the base of his kingdom, she stared up at Phillip Fredericks, fists clenched, teeth bared.

Jane.

"Let him go."

Jane strode through the destruction—through piles of ash and cars half vanished, roads erupted with crystals and spiraling metal lightning. None of it mattered. None of it would be spared.

"Jane!" Behind her, some fifty feet away in a parking lot, she heard Wally's voice. She didn't look back at him, didn't so much as glance. She had only eyes for the priest upon his mountain, and the figure chained at his side.

Slowly, atop the steps of his crystal citadel, Fredericks rose from his throne.

"You want him?" the old man asked. A small, deranged smile played over his mouth, and his voice sang out with a ringing peal. "This one?"

"Hurt him, and I'll tear you limb from limb," Jane swore.

The priest laughed. He took a step forward, then another, until he neared the edge of the precipice. "You cannot beat me. Look around you. No power on Earth can stop me."

"Yeah?" snarled Jane. "Wanna bet?"

"Jane!" Matt cried. On top of the mountain, beside Fredericks's crystal throne, she could see him struggling, pulling against his glittering chains. "Don't! It's a—"

"Silence," Fredericks hushed, and instantly, bands of iron swept over Matt's mouth, leaving him to fruitlessly struggle, unable to do anything but moan.

Jane bared her teeth. "I'll kill you," she hissed.

"I'd like to see you try," the man answered mildly, and said no further.

BANG! An explosion, a cataclysm of light, rendered the very air as Jane shot toward Fredericks, a blinding golden comet that slammed into his mountain, pulverizing it, shattering it into a million glass pieces. But as the diamond fell, Fredericks leapt forward over her, the air turning to obsidian platforms, carrying him down and away. He spun in midair, facing back toward the crumbling castle and Jane, and in an instant, his right hand flicked, the mountain of broken shards turning to boiling silver, a tsunami of molten metal that collapsed upon Jane even as Matt was hurled free, landing in a chunk of lawn that slid to liquid stone, binding him in place.

The pastor chuckled, but inside the smothering silver shone rays of gold. In an instant, the metal exploded, blasted out in a searing rain. Fredericks shielded his face, paling as Jane shot toward him, raising one, two, three, four, five—wall after wall of barriers between him and her, diamond and marble and ice and titanium, stumbling backward as his hands desperately flailed, but Jane roared and just kept coming, demolishing one after the other with hammering golden fists.

The last barrier shattered and Jane's fingers lunged, an inch from Fredericks neck, but the priest dropped at the last second, sliding into liquefied stone down beneath the Earth. Jane launched back into the sky, cupping her hands down, preparing to raze everything with a titanic golden blast—but before she could unleash the energy, the ground disgorged Fredericks beside Matt, and the rock encasing him flew between the pastor and Jane, shielding the priest from view.

Jane roared, the light in her hands vanishing as she dropped from the sky, strafing low and rapid as all around her, giant bladed spears of steel and crystal erupted, cutting at her cape, aiming for her heart—

BAM! She snapped into place an inch from Matt and the pastor, feet carving tracks in the ground, fierce arms smashing through and grabbing Matt's shoulders, spinning him into her with her momentum, carrying them both off, carrying them through—

Beneath her, the pastor's eyes blazed, and before Jane flew ten feet, he pointed and shouted some strangled yell. To Jane's bloodcurdling horror, Matt gasped, his body slumping, and he turned to ash in her arms.

Jane dropped, her chest shaking, dust streaming between her gloves. She stumbled to a halt, sinking in the mud, unable to see anything but the emptiness in front of her, unable to breathe. Behind her, she heard the pastor chuckling, then laughing, then cackling, because he knew, she knew, they all knew. Dust could not be healed. There was nothing of Matt to bring back.

No. NO!

Jane screamed and hurtled back through time. The strain from the New York City time travel attempts, the danger, the pain of it, everything lay forgotten as she threw herself into the cosmic chaos, the howling lifelines snapping all around her, threw herself—unyielding—back through the technicolor darkness, refusing to let it claim her, only seconds—

BAM! She snapped into place an inch from Matt and the pastor, feet carving tracks out of the Earth, having shot forward low to the ground and dodged the erupting razor columns. But this time, instead of reaching for Matt, she kept going, fist blazing toward Fredericks, lunging for the kill—

BOOM! A sudden wind, a sudden explosion, knocked Jane back, but in moments, she skidded to a halt, fingers clawing gouges in the rock, and saw Fredericks, too, stumbling, sprinting away, swallowed up by walls of glass closing around him; a box folding out in replicated fractals, a sudden square maze spreading up from nothing through which the pastor's reflection spread like a drop of blood.

Jane turned to grab Matt, but he shot free from the earth, bound in silver spirals, dragged inside the crystal maze where his reflection joined Fredericks's. Jane snarled and shot forward, slamming fists into the panels, shattering one after another, the shards dissolving into thin air and hissing, odorless gas, but the substance could do naught but burn against Jane's barrier, and she had no need to breathe.

Crash! Crash! Crash! The maze was sundered, and there, in the middle, on a white stone dais, eyes wide and reeling, stood Fredericks, one hand grasping Matt.

"Back!" he demanded. "Back!" He threw up his free hand, and a wave of diamond blades descended from nothing, aiming for her eyes, but Jane threw forward her hands and let loose a torrential blast of gold, vaporizing the projectiles and racing toward Pastor Fredericks, who at the last second uttered a wordless scream—

And again, Matt disintegrated.

The pastor's body twitched and stumbled, the left side missing, little more than a blackened corpse. But his hand still clung to where Matt had been an instant earlier, the human still gone, turned to ashes.

Again, Jane screamed.

Back, back again now. She did not care about the possibilities that sang to her, the roiling cosmic night or the yearning infinite. She did not want to understand; she did not want to see, did not care about the colors. She simply hurtled through, fury unwavering, back along the twisting threads, until—

Crash! Crash! Crash! The maze was sundered, and there, in the middle, on a white stone dais, eyes wide and reeling, stood Fredericks, one hand grasping Matt.

"Back!" he demanded. "Back!" He threw up his free hand, and a wave of diamond blades descended from nothing, aiming for her eyes, but Jane held up a defiant hand in a shining barrier, and one after another, they crashed and broke against the unstoppable energy in front of her. She stood there, silent, shoulders heaving, teeth bared, golden light wafting from her eyes.

Fredericks stumbled back two steps, the white stone evaporating so he was standing only in mud. His eyes bored into her, at once searing and terrified. He shoved Matt roughly away, who fell, still bound and gagged in metal.

The combatants stood there, facing one another, dwarfed on all sides by towering crystal ruins, flanked by colored earth and misting steel, ten paces apart, feet planted. Neither moved.

"Nothing you can do can stop me," snarled Jane, fixing the priest with a gaze of pure fury.

For some reason, the pastor laughed. "Yes. I see it now," he said, wide mouth split in a madman's smile. "I cannot win. You will kill me." Yet his teeth were still bared in a demented grin, and his hand rose toward Matt. "But you cannot save him."

"I'm faster than—"

"No!" Fredericks cried, the word ringing out between a mindless wail and an insane shriek. "You're not faster than thought. Not you; not anyone! All I have to do is think—*think!*—and he is gone. Scattered to the wind. Nothing."

"If he dies, I'll kill you," Jane swore, gloves balling into fists. Away from her, still gagged and bound, Matt stared at her, his eyes watering, pleading.

"Yes," the priest replied, his smile manic. "But he'll still be gone."

The world lapsed into silence. For the longest time, Jane and Fredericks just stood there, an inhuman stalemate, eyes never leaving each other, while all around them, unnatural winds swirled and sirens wailed in the distance, though neither paid it any heed. Five feet away from Fredericks, Matt squirmed against his restraints, straining to break free, but he could not budge the iron encircling him. Jane's glare met the priest's wordless smile. Her fingers clenched, unclenched, clenched again. The pastor's hand remained pointed at Matt.

Slowly, his lips split into a grin.

"The great Lady Dawn," he spoke, and the words rang high with mockery. "The supposed savior of humanity, beaten into submission, brought low by a mere man. What good does all your power do you? All your fury, your impotent rage? I have your measure," he crowed, "I know your weakness. And you will be mine; this world will be mine, and it will know me, and it will worship."

Jane said nothing. The priest's smile widened.

"Fool!" he shouted. "Fool! Thief of powers not meant for you; gifts given the chosen of God! You spit in his face, you think yourself above his decrees, but now you see his power! Now you face his champion, a true champion, chosen by God the Almighty, the Father, the Son, and the Holy Spirit, bearing gifts you can barely imagine, powers you can barely dream! What can you do, despoiler? What say you, oh treacherous Eve? God has blessed me, his strength flows within me, and as long as I live, the boy will be mine, and with a thought, I will unmake him, remake, and reshape the wor—!"

Jane's mouth twitched. Her eyes flashed and narrowed. Suddenly, she knew what to do.

She leapt forward, racing toward the pastor, who abruptly paled and let his words drop midsentence, speech inaudible, pointing toward—

But Jane wasn't aiming for Matt. She flew straight at Phillip Fredericks, light burning away her gloves—

In an instant, she held him, bare fingers wrapped around his windpipe. And a second later, Matt turned to dust.

Jane's fingers squeezed, but the priest's eyes shone with triumph.

"You lose," he whispered. "You—"

Jane dropped her final coin and absorbed his power.

A second too late, Fredericks eyes flashed in understanding. He wriggled and squirmed, face flushed with panic, trying to escape—but Jane did not waver. He would not move.

In the depths of her great consciousness, a desert of red satin spread and wrapped around Jane's ring finger. Beneath it rolled existence, countless and infinite, an endless sea of crimson sands. She felt the world move, felt herself move it. A trillion shifting grains, shapes infinite and ever changing. Hers to remake; hers to command.

With a scoff, she dropped Fredericks into the dirt. She hurled him to the ground, and the priest went sprawling, fumbling into the mud. Jane paid him no heed—only turned her gaze toward Matt's ashes, raising a trembling hand. Her eyes blazed red.

Slowly, slowly, like leaves swirling in an eddy, the particles before her spun and spiraled, drawing in together, reassembling once more into a man. Legs, then arms, then torso. A perfect body, reformed from ashes, lying on the ground, the undoing undone.

It was over in the space of moments. Matt Callaghan lay before her, pale and lifeless, yet whole. Lacking only one thing.

Jane's eyes flashed white. With a gasp, Matt woke up.

"No," he murmured, arms twitching with sudden movement, hands moving weakly over his face. His eyes glistened, unfocused, and he writhed weakly on the ground. "No. No."

Jane left him to his confusion. He probably needed a few moments to collect himself, she reasoned, his understanding of where he was, what had happened to him. She'd give him that. Jane turned back to Pastor Phillip Fredericks, the old man lying splayed in the mud, filth clinging to his simple clothes. She marched toward him, her eyes cold and hand open.

Beneath her gaze, the priest's shoulders were slumped—but his face bore no fear or resignation. On the contrary, his eyes shone as he gazed up at Jane in soft, heartfelt wonder, trails of joyful tears streaming silently down his cheeks. His mouth moved, summoning bare whispers in the air, and when his words finally trickled out and reached her, they held only tranquil madness and quiet, sobbing relief.

"It's done," he whispered, tears cascading down his face, glittering streams of diamond. "I've done it. Jane, oh Jane, you have to understand, I—"

Jane disintegrated him. Her eyes flashed red, the whites and the irises, and Pastor Phillip Fredericks became dust, never to speak or move again.

"Fall," Jane spat. And the dust was silent.

From a place no one could perceive, a blue-eyed child stood silent, watching. All around him, lines of color swirled. Infinite possibilities. All twisting together, bound and unbound, enslaved endlessly to this point.

Destiny pivoted.

It had to.

Please.

Behind her, in the muddy ruins of the Baptist compound, Jane heard Matt cough. Slowly, she turned away from Phillip Fredericks's ashes and walked over.

"Hey," she whispered, kneeling down beside him. "Hey. You okay?"

Matt's breathing came quick and shallow. His eyes, wracked with pain, seemed to be having difficulty adjusting to the light.

"What happened?" he whispered, his voice wavering, anxious and urgent. "Where am I?"

"You're safe," Jane promised. "You're safe. It's over."

But for some reason, Matt's distress only grew. His hands shook, his cheeks pale, and droplets of sweat beaded on his forehead.

"MEDIC!" Jane shouted, standing up and turning around. She surveyed the devastation, the chaos now fallen to stillness—the man-size shards of diamond embedded in craters, cracked plates of obsidian and marble littering the ground, veins of metal hardened like silver wax on the Earth's cold crust. Currents of dust blew atop the wind, police cars lay sheared cleanly in half, and in the distance, she saw the red figures of Acolytes crawling tentatively from cover. Jane strode through the wreckage, muttering under her breath in disgust.

"Medic!" she shouted again, annoyed that they would make her wait. Across, in the nearby parking lot, she spied the back of Wally's head next to the Legion healer, Editha, both crouched on the ground leaning over something. Neither answered her calls. Scowling, Jane marched toward them to find the focus of their crowding was Giselle. Her legs were gone, like they'd been cut off and dipped in black wax.

"Medic," Jane repeated. Her shadow loomed over the group. Beneath her, Giselle whimpered, her breathing coming fast and shallow, eyes swimming in pain.

"Jane," the speedster begged, the words pure agony.

Jane gazed down at Giselle's stunted form, the anguish on her face and the consternation on Editha's.

"What's wrong?" she demanded. She could see the healer pressing her hands into what remained of Giselle's upper thigh. "Why aren't you healing her?"

"It's not . . . It's not working," Editha snapped, flashing Jane over her shoulder the barest furious glance. She returned to Giselle, bending down lower, working her fingers as close as she dared to the injury site while the leader of the Legion writhed and moaned. "I can't . . . I can't heal it. Her legs aren't injured—they're not there!"

The corner of Jane's lips twitched. "Move," she said, and without waiting for Editha to reply, she clicked two fingers. The pavement the healer was kneeling on shimmered and slid backward like a sheet of breaking ice, carrying the small woman clear. Everyone around her stared with a mixture of terror and trepidation, but Jane didn't care. Instead, she loomed over Giselle, gazing down at her blackened stumps. Jane's lips twitched as she raised her hand, and the black lines flew open, muscle knitting back together from the surrounding air. Flesh blossomed downward like a time-lapsed growing of skin-colored icicles. In a little under three seconds, the speedster's legs had reappeared. Giselle gasped, and abruptly ceased her sobbing.

"There," said Jane, indifferent. "Fixed. Now, can you please come check Matt out. I want to make sure I didn't miss something."

She turned on her heel, gold cape flapping in the wind, leaving behind a wake of stunned silence. She strode back across the street, passing the desolated trucks and ruined sidewalk to where Matt continued to lie. Jane was pleased to see he had managed at least to sit up, and that his eyes seemed reasonably clear.

"You okay?" she asked again. Matt did not immediately nod, though he didn't shake his head either.

"Jane," he whispered, breathlessly. He turned to her, his eyes fearful. "What happened? Where's Fredericks? What did you do?"

Jane was not in the mood to repeat this conversation. She crouched down, wrapped her arms underneath Matt's shoulders, and helped him stand. "I love you," she told him.

"I know," he murmured—but he still did not sound reassured. Slowly, though, his arms moved around her in an embrace.

They stood like that—Jane holding on to him, her head buried against his cheek; Matt hugging her in a loose grip, his breathing shaky and uncertain—until Editha arrived. The small healer said nothing, merely glanced at Jane with an expression of anxious fear, then moved in to look at Matt. Jane pulled back to let her approach.

"Open your eyes," Editha requested. Matt obeyed. "Your mouth. Say *ahhh*. Good. Glands are fine. Temperature normal. Pulse . . . high."

"That's fine," Jane assured her. "He'll be home soon." The healer did not look at her.

"Pupils are normal. Reflexes fine. I'm going to prick your finger. There. How'd that feel?"

"Ow."

"Good." She paused, and the way she stared at Matt reminded Jane of a trapped bird squirming behind cage bars. "How do you feel?" There was a trembling in her voice, and perhaps . . . some hidden significance?

"Physically or mentally?" Matt asked, and though in Jane's view that was not particularly helpful, the answer nevertheless caused Editha to let loose a sigh of release.

"Any pain?" she murmured.

"No." Yet, Matt's eyes dropped as he said it.

"You see fine."

"Yes."

"You hear fine."

"Yes."

"Taste, smell?"

"Normal."

"I—" Editha's voice cut out midsentence. "Let me feel you." She glanced at Jane, who nodded, and then pressed her dainty hands into Matt's skin. The healer closed her eyes for a few seconds, then opened them.

"He's okay," she murmured—yet, for some reason, that bit of good news made the small woman look scared. "There's no room for healing. Everything's alright."

"Good," Jane replied matter-of-factly. "Good to know."

For a few moments, Editha seemed to be struggling for words.

"I . . . I was watching," she managed finally. She stared up at Jane, her small frame trembling. "I saw. You . . . You put him back together?"

"Yes," Jane replied curtly.

"How?" Editha whispered.

"Does it matter? Go identify the missing. Once Matt's back to safety, I'll see what I can do."

Editha opened her mouth—maybe to question, maybe to argue, maybe to thank—but after a few seconds, it seemed she could not find the words. Her mouth closed, and for the first time since Jane had known her, she gave a little bow. The healer shuffled quickly off.

"Jane," Matt murmured. "I need to talk to you."

"Shh. It's okay. Not now."

"No, it has to be . . ." He put his hand on her shoulder, turning her away so she was no longer facing the Legion, the crimson figures of the Acolytes slowly gathering around Giselle and the rest. "Fredericks. You don't understand. He was crazy."

"Yeah," Jane scoffed. "Obviously."

"No, you . . ." Matt's fingers dug into her shoulder, though from difficulty standing or simple stress, Jane couldn't tell. "It was all a trick."

"What was? Using you as a hostage? I know." She shrugged. "But I found a way around it. Just like before. I beat him."

"You took his power." It wasn't a question.

"Yes."

"The power to control matter."

"Ye—" Jane hesitated, feeling the new band of crimson satin sitting warm against her ring finger. Yes. She leaned into the sensation, and yes, she could feel it. With any movement she made, at any moment, she could plunge her arm deep into an endless pool of soft, warm sand, and the grains would change their shapes for her. "Yes. I suppose that is what it is."

"You have to get rid of it," Matt said. "I'm begging you, Jane. Listen to me, this is exactly what he wanted. He wasn't trying to win; he wasn't trying to hurt me—he wanted you to take his power."

Jane's brow furrowed. She turned to Matt, peering at him with a skeptical frown, but every line of his face was pleading, earnest.

"Why the hell did he want—?" she began.

"Because he was insane," Matt pleaded. "He'd gone crazy, had some existential crisis, and he thought . . ." Her boyfriend paused, sucking in heavy, shaking breaths. "He's been behind everything. Just him, not the government. There's no . . ." Matt shook his head. "The assassination at the studio. He was testing to see if you could really travel through time. The attacks, the assault on the apartment, the hit squad, he orchestrated all of it. He was trying to force you into absorbing the twins. And now, this here, it's the same plan; it's the same mad obsession, because he was trying to make you . . ." Matt's voice dropped so low Jane couldn't hear the final words he whispered.

"What?"

"A god." Matt leaned back, looking desperately to either side of him before staring up at Jane, his eyes wild. "Don't you get it? With the power of time, the power of Dawn, control over life and death, and the ability to control matter . . . you could do anything. Literally, that's . . ." He was at a loss for words. "The keys to divinity."

The world seemed oddly light and silent. Jane tried to speak, but whatever she was trying to say kept catching in her throat. She paused, swallowed, and gazed down at Matt, her brow furrowed.

"Does that . . ." she began, the words stumbling. ". . . Would that even work?"

"How the hell would I know?" Matt replied, throwing up his hands—though he kept the movement small, clearly keen not to be seen displaying too much distress. "Jane, we've seen what happens when these powers are used incorrectly, and now you've got not one but four?" He grabbed her right hand in both of his, though her own grip remained limp. She felt his powerlessness. "There's still time, Jane. I know, I know it's a lot to take in, but we can still make things right. Here, we can still—"

Matt's words kept coming, but Jane found it increasingly hard to listen. The world around her seemed strangely quiet, her own thoughts bright and pressing as this feeling of disbelief flowered within her, a mingling sensation of curiosity and awe. Slowly, she looked down at her hand, the one Matt wasn't holding, turning the palm over, seeing the bare pristine skin, scoured free of any impurities. It was as if she could feel them now, could almost see them in the gaps between her fingers—the spaces where powers could be—the impossible forces churning, wrapping heavy and around, binding to her body more tightly than ever before.

Four rings. Four fingers. Red of endless sand, blue of bottomless ocean, twisting black and white, and eternal burning gold.

A god, she heard Matt whisper.

Was it possible?

In the beginning, there was the word. How could she know? Where had the old God started? Distantly, she remembered sitting beside her overbearing grandmother in church, barely more than four or five, a memory from another lifetime, the one time her dad had relented to her grandma's belligerence. In the beginning, God, then light and earth and water, and then . . . a garden. God had started with a garden.

Slowly, Jane held out her free hand. Beside her, Matt's pleas fell suddenly to silence, and he looked on, eyes darting in fear between Jane's palm and her quiet, curious expression. Beyond him, a few yards away, some of the civilians, the remaining Acolytes, had begun moving cautiously forward, drawn toward her, her shining presence, to witness her inhuman acts. Jane paid them no heed. She paid none of them any heed. Her thoughts lay only in her outstretched palm.

Be, she thought, and in her mind's eye, she imagined a single image—a delicate magenta flower. Not something that she'd seen, just the quiet musings of her imagination. Instantly, Jane felt the rings shift and respond.

And from windswept nothingness, lines of color began to grow.

All this time, Jane wondered as she watched. All this time, the power of Dawn had hummed to her, the power of time had whispered, and she'd felt overwhelmed by their presence, their intangibility, their endlessness. Yet, she heard it now; the twisting sounds. Not inconceivable—a melody. Four living pieces; separate songs each distinctly their own, but impossible to truly grasp until they were put together, until they sang together in harmony. It was like clockwork; one turned, the other moved. One gave, the other took. The red ring pulled pieces from reality all around, but the instant that grew detrimental, the gold ring hummed and offered its power for conversion.

All matter was energy, all energy was matter, and she had endless, she could be endless. And she knew—instinctively, she knew. No, not instinctively. Her fingers floated across the surface of time, soft and cool yet never breaking the water's tension, and she flowed where she saw she needed to be, a thousand past and present microadjustments. *Do not go. Do not think. Be.* She knew the way. She had done it before, she realized, with Matt's body, with Giselle's legs—it was the like the power of time; if you did not pause, if you just *did*, then the thing was done.

How do you balance footsteps on uneven stone? How do you know how to sleep, to breathe, to catch a ball? Overthinking destroyed ability. So, Jane just did, like she'd always meant to do. She didn't think. She just made life.

The third ring surged, and the flower in her palm bloomed into existence.

"Jane," she heard Matt whisper.

A hush had fallen over the crowd. For a few moments, Jane simply gazed upon her hand, taking in the flower, marveling at her own handiwork—the delicate green stem, so thin it looked as if it should collapse under the weight of the petals, which hung in a long bell, a swirling, beautiful magenta hue. Tiny roots fanned out from its base, trailing between her fingers like spiderwebs; gently, Jane knelt and placed the flower on the ground. *Grow.* She smiled, feeling the silken tendrils extend, anchoring this small piece of life into place against the Earth. Amidst the stem, two small leaves unfurled. It needed a name, Jane realized. Clara.

Slowly, she rose.

"Jane," Matt whispered again. The empath turned and glanced at him, at the living flower at her feet, saying nothing, her face unmoved.

"Please," Matt begged her. He leaned in closer, desperate, though his hands held back from touching, hesitated from clutching her wrist. "Stop. You've got to give it up. Let it go, get rid of his power, now, before you—before . . ." His eyes flicked to the flower. "I don't know, but this is dangerous," he whispered. "Jane, can't you see? We're beyond crazy here. The line's been crossed, we crossed it ten miles ago, and we've got to go back; we've got to . . ."

His voice trailed off. For a time, Jane just looked at him, and then she turned and stared into nothingness, her eyes not fixing on Matt nor the crowd nor anything else around her. Her mind churned. She glanced up, and it was as if she saw the world they were forced to live in for the very first time. There was Matt, and in the distance, Giselle and the others, and in the periphery, the Clara's color, beautiful and enduring . . . but around that, so much darkness. So much brown and gray, so much ruin and pain, devastation, destruction . . . The police cars, the ambulances approaching, people injured, their sallow faces, screaming, weeping, loss . . .

And beyond that. The city of Sedgwick and roads flowing ever onward. The state of Kansas. America. The Earth. So many people. So many cities. So much pain and grief and suffering. So much that could be prevented. So much . . .

"Jane," Matt whispered, and this time, he took both her hands, craning his face up to try and hold her gaze. "Please. Please. Let's go home."

"Home," Jane murmured. Home, where men had tried to kill them. Home, where for so long, she'd been hated, hunted. Home, where the Black Death had slaughtered millions. Home, full of suffering, cruelty, sickness, hurt. Where could they go to escape that? Where was free from stupidity and violence? From injustice? From death?

Once more, Jane glanced down at her flower, and once more, she slowly raised her palms in front of her, both hands now, though Matt still held loosely to her wrists. *Orb of stone*, she thought. Beyond simple. And indeed, as she imagined it, a white, flawless sphere appeared, barely bigger than a bowling ball, where it hung in impossibility, floating gently above her palms.

We will do what we must, we few, we great. We, who have the power to save the world, and who will not, cannot, stand idly by while its peoples suffer.

Would she stand by? Jane's mouth twitched, and a thousand seams and patterns etched themselves into the stone before, in an instant, it cracked and vanished.

Slowly, she pulled free from Matt's grasp.

"Jane," Matt whispered, more urgent than ever.

"He wanted me to be a god," she murmured. She turned away, staring out over open sky.

"Yes," Matt said urgently, misunderstanding. "He was insane. He thought that if the world didn't have some sort of deity, some guiding hand completely in control of it, that it was all just pointless; everything was doomed. But, Jane," Matt pleaded, "you can't listen to him. You can't give him what he wants."

"Who cares what he wants," Jane replied mildly. "What do you want? What do I want?" And she turned to him, gazed at him, in quiet contemplation. "I want a better world."

"Jane!" Matt hissed. "Listen to me! Listen to what I'm saying! You have to let go! You can't be a god!"

But two steps away, Jane turned slowly to face him, her face a calm, inscrutable mask. She fixed her lover with an unblinking gaze—her irises gliding through all the colors of the rainbow, the *E* on her cheek shifting steadily from black, to red, to blue.

"Why not?" Jane replied.

And in an instant, she vanished.

TERRA ALBA

"I have seen the face of God, and she terrifies me."
—Graffiti on a bathroom wall, New Hampshire

Giselle could walk. She could walk.

The leader of the Legion of Heroes, if there was such a thing anymore, shuffled in a dreamlike trance, wandering between piles of ash where her companions once stood and pillars of diamond worth more than some countries. Giselle did not talk—she could not engage anymore. She did not speak to the trucks of fresh police as they arrived, swarming and yelling, to the ambulance officers wheeling out their beds and kits and trying to salvage the wounded.

What could she do? What could she possibly say? One man had opened his hand and rewritten reality. He had turned people she knew and cared about to nothing. He had disintegrated her legs—maybe, if she'd been slower, he would have disintegrated the rest of her. She had been crippled. And then, Jane had fixed it. Stood above her, glanced down with the expression of someone unclogging a dirty sink, and then simply . . . restored her. Giselle could walk again. She would run again. Her legs were bare, the protective suit disintegrated from her midthigh down—but they were whole, remade, as strong as ever.

But they were not hers.

She found Matt standing in a muddy field, staring off into the empty distance.

"Where's Jane?" the speedster murmured. Only with him, it seemed, did she find her voice.

For a moment, the human didn't speak.

"Gone."

"She flew away?"

"No."

"She . . . She teleported?" Giselle asked, confused. She glanced around. "But Will's still here, and Enrique—"

"No one teleported her," Matt mumbled. "Unless she teleported herself." He finally raised his head, and she saw that his eyes were trembling. The boy's face swam with an expression which unsettled Giselle to her core.

"I didn't know she could do that," Giselle said quietly, and they both knew exactly what she meant.

Matt nodded. "We need to talk," he said. "Privately."

"About what?" asked Wally. The pair turned as the psychic strode over toward them, making his way around a giant crystal shard. He stopped a few feet away and pointed. "Is it about that?" Matt and Giselle followed his finger, staring up into the sky where, in the low blue of the horizon, the moon's pale figure rose.

"The moon?" Giselle asked, confused. But beside her, Matt blanched.

"Anyone got the time?" he murmured, not glancing at either of them.

"Yup." Wally nodded as if pleased he and Matt were finally sharing the same very vivid hallucination. "It's about eight thirty."

"AM or PM?"

"AM."

"I don't get it," Giselle spoke up, still feeling dazed and like she was missing something. "What does that mean? Why does it . . ." Her voice trailed off, and she peered up at the white orb looming high and distant. "Wait."

The three of them fell silent, staring up at the sky, their feet stuck firmly in the mud. Around them streamed rescuers, survivors, camera crews, all eyes fixated on the surrounding carnage. Still focused on the chaos around them. Still yet to look up.

"Alright," said Wally, laughing with forced, almost delirious lightness. "Who's going to say it?"

"That's no moon," Matt mumbled.

"The sphere appears to be growing steadily, and we can confirm it is indeed within the farthest reaches of Earth's upper atmosphere . . . It is pale, and we do not yet know—"

"—solid white stone in appearance, yet seemingly neither affecting nor affected by Earth's gravity and—"

"—any attempts to approach the object resulting in failure and baffling displacement, with the International Teleportation Council describing the area surrounding the sphere as possibly quantum in nature—"

"—as Pope John Paul calls for calm, stating the object is likely a natural phenomenon similar to the Aurora Nirvanas, and that all practitioners of faith should take solace in—"

"*Te dije que la luna era falsa. Te dije. Ni una sola persona me creyó, pero aquí estamos. Hay una falla en la simulación y—*"

Will clicked off the TV and threw away the remote. It landed, skittering somewhere off atop the black-and-white tiles in one corner of the bar, causing the back to pop off and the batteries to scatter out.

"I hate the news," he muttered.

The four bedraggled friends—Matthew Callaghan, Wallace Cykes, William Herd, and Giselle Pixus—sat at a square wooden table in the middle of an abandoned Kansas alehouse, their arms and occasionally heads slumping alternatively atop the smooth, droplet-stained tabletop. Nobody had any idea where the owners or regular patrons had gone; probably off screaming down the street or running home to go pray like the rest of humanity. Will had switched off the

Disruptance so he could teleport back and forth behind the bar, and was now freely pilfering the display wall of spirits whenever one of them needed another drink. If anyone came, if anyone even cared anymore, Giselle would charge it to Morningstar as a miscellaneous catering disbursement. Which was, at this stage, a big if.

Giselle lay with her head on her hands and her hands on the table, her tumbler freshly emptied of scotch. Matt was just sort of slumped back in his chair, arms hanging limp by his sides, gazing listlessly into the broken bar mirror, which had splintered in a series of cracks where Wally had thrown an empty bottle of tequila at it. The psychic, sitting opposite Giselle, was already onto the next one, his wobbly hands pouring all four of them plus the table shots of *Patrón*.

"Well," he said, sounding perhaps a tad deranged, "let's recap. Half the Legion's dead. Only, you know, maybe death doesn't matter anymore." He made as if to shrug, and the bullet-size glass he'd been squeezing between two fingers sloshed tequila all over his shirt. "*Aaaand* Jane is God. The girl I used to eat sushi with while we talked about boys has ascended to become Shiva, all praise her sacred name. Fantastic. Just peachy." He clapped his hands, glancing between each of his companions in turn. "Are we a hundred percent sure Morningstar didn't accidentally mix up the orange juice yesterday and swap it out with, oh, I don't know, *two hundred gallons of LSD*?"

Giselle said nothing. Will said nothing. Matt said nothing, though he did take another shot. The horrible yellow liquid burned his throat as it went down, joining the empty contents of his stomach and a whole lot of existential dread.

"Are there any beer nuts?" he mumbled, glancing over at the bar.

"I just . . ." Wally spluttered, ignoring Matt's request, seemingly content to carry on by himself if no one was willing to engage with or cease his rambling. "Okay, Jane can travel through time. That's a new one; that's one I would've liked a nice Sunday afternoon to process. But oh, look, she also controls life and death. That was a big deal yesterday; now, I guess it's old news. Now, every man and his insane,

Baptist dog is burrowing up out of the woodwork, coming out as a—What'd you call them?"

"Divine," grunted Giselle.

"Divine. Fantastic. What a stupid, prophetic name. Bad enough that Captain Dawn can destroy cities, now we have Chinese twins who can resurrect you, and the world's worst landscaper moonlighting as a priest. Oh, and sorry! All those powers are now in the hands of one person. And that person is god."

"More tequila," Giselle mumbled, pressing her forehead against the table. "Please."

"Sure," replied Wally, pouring another shot and only spilling about nine-tenths. "Why not? Let's all just *drink* and forget our responsibilities, because Miss I-can't-cook-toast-correctly is out there creating a new moon, for reasons beyond our . . . God knows why."

"Jane knows why," Will corrected.

"Thank you. Yes, thank you, dear. Where would I be without your continued riveting insights?"

"I think it's technically a new Earth," Matt added, running his tequila-tipped finger around the rim of the glass. "I think that's what she's making. Building utopia."

"Of course," said Wally, throwing his hands up. "Utopia, handmade by an emotionally unstable nineteen-year-old girl. Outstanding. Simply outstanding." He rounded on Giselle, snapping his fingers at her downcast face. "Hey. You. Woman. Aren't you the leader of the Legion of Heroes? Shouldn't you be out there saving us from all this, figuring out what's going on, doing stuff?"

"I quit," Giselle muttered, turning her head away from Wally, resting her cheek in a tequila puddle. "Natash—Natalia can do it. She push—She put her hand up."

"And she was roundly voted down because everyone agreed that was a terrible idea and may God have mercy on our souls."

"Jane have mercy on our souls."

"Darling, I swear—"

"She couldn't be worse than me," Giselle groaned, ignoring the bickering.

"I think out of everything we can say," Wally declared, tearing his narrowed eyes away from Will to fix the beautiful speedster with a withering glare, "we can pretty safely say that none of this is your fault." Matt gurgled a sound approximating agreement, and without meeting anyone's eyes, swigged another drink. Giselle didn't seem to hear him.

"It should've been Farrington," she lamented. "Or you, or . . . anyone. Celeste, even. No." Giselle sat up slightly, lips pursed and thin eyebrows narrowed as a single drop of tequila trickled down her cheek. "Not Celeste."

"Farrington would never take it," said Will, shaking his head and wading in. "He's too . . . What would you call it? Sad?"

"Mournful?"

"Yeah. Just the wrong fit."

"He's doing a pretty good job now," Giselle mumbled, lowering her head back down into the puddle and not looking at them. Beside her, Will made a face.

"He's stepping in because he has to. Him and Nat both. They'll hold down the fort; doesn't make them captain."

"Why are we even talking about this?" exclaimed Wally, waving his shot glass around like a deranged choir conductor, rounding incredulously on the pair. "Does any of this even matter? Jane is a *god*. She is up there creating a new planet! Is the world even going to exist tomorrow? Screw the Legion of Heroes! Screw our little club!"

"Matt, dude," Giselle mumbled, one side of her face still on the table. "You really should've told us about the time travel."

Matt had by now told them about the time travel. He'd told them everything. How Jane had really beaten the Black Death. The true source of her Dawn powers. The Time Child and his enigmatic bullcrap. Pastor Fredericks and his plan.

"Yeah," he sighed. He pinched the bridge of his nose. "Sorry."

"Where did we land on the whole blond-kid-trying-to-kill-you thing?" Will asked, turning to him. "Is that still something we need to worry about?"

"I don't know," replied Matt, squeezing his eyes closed and massaging his temples. "Maybe I overthought it. Maybe he never was trying to kill me. Maybe this was all part of his plan. Maybe he was trying to help Fredericks, and he screwed up. Maybe Jane went god up into time-space and murdered him. Who the hell knows."

"I know I need another drink."

"I mean, maybe if we knew," the speedster murmured, "maybe if we'd nipped it in the beginning, maybe we could've prevented this."

"Prevented this?!" Wally threw his hands up again, sending drops of tequila flying all over them and the floor. "Do we even know what *this* is? Do we know what Jane's doing? Do we know what her godly plans are?!"

"She's going to make a better world," muttered Giselle. "She's going to prevent bad things from ever happening. And she can do it. Time, matter, life, energy; she's got everything she needs."

Will turned to Matt. "You said this time travel stuff is dangerous, though, right? Like maybe she could hurt herself?"

"Perhaps." Matt shrugged, his face blank. "But she's been doing it more and more lately. Like it's been getting easier."

"Okay," Will said. "Okay." He lurched drunkenly in his chair beside Wally, leaning his arms across those of Matt and Giselle. "Let's think this through. How do we stop her?"

"Stop her?" laughed Wally. "Honey, she can time travel. She controls life and death and the building blocks of reality. Oh, and also the power of the sun. What can you do—what can you really do—to stop her?"

"We just gotta get up there," Will insisted. "I teleport, or we get flown up, and"—he snapped his fingers—"Giselle's neutralizer— Giselle's backup empath neutralizer—we get them, and I don't know, we get near her, or we trap her . . ."

"You can't trap a time traveler," Matt sighed, resting his forehead on the table's surface, feeling the cold leech up into his weary brain. "Future sight. Causation."

"You don't know—"

"Dude, I swear to you, I have spent *so long* thinking about this—"

"Okay, but..." Will continued, struggling for words, "there's got to be something. What if there are more Divines out there, huh? Ones we don't know about. We put a team together, like a really good team, and we go up and stop her and—"

"Do we want to stop her?" Giselle asked suddenly. She sat up. The bar fell silent. Will and Wally turned and stared at her, their expressions stunned. Matt just kept looking down.

Giselle sighed and her shoulders slumped, almost as if she was ashamed of the words that were coming out of her mouth. "I don't... really know if I want to stop her," she said, averting her gaze. "Jane."

"Gizz, are you serious?" asked Wally. "Absolute power corrupts absolutely, and Jane—"

"We've all read *1984*," Giselle responded, not quite rolling her eyes. "This isn't a story. This isn't some metaphor or, like, an axiom. This is real. This is really ... God." She fell silent for a moment. "I mean, I know this Fredericks guy was crazy, but are we sure he had it wrong? Is direction ... is oversight ... bad?"

The other three sat in silence. Giselle glanced around the table, her face wracked with guilt. "Jane healed my legs," she said. "Like it was nothing. If I'd been dying, if I'd had cancer, she could've cured that too. Would have. Think of all the horrible things ..." Her voice trailed off, but after a moment, she gathered her strength and pushed on. "All the horrible things happening in the world right now. Rape, violence, murder. Disasters, accidents, disease ... Is it so bad to imagine someone getting rid of them all?" She looked at them, her eyes pleading. "I mean ... she could change anything. Everything. What if we didn't have to get old? What if we didn't have to die?"

"Those things are part of being human," replied Wally, aghast.

"But what if they didn't have to be?" argued Giselle. "Think about it for one second, put aside all those nice sayings and 'all good things must come to pass,' and 'it's the journey, not the destination.' Aren't those just things we say to ourselves because we don't truly have another option? Because death is inevitable? What if it wasn't? I-I don't want to die," she admitted with a shaky, semihysterical laugh. "I don't want to die! Is that so wrong? I almost . . . A few times now, and I . . . I like living! Screw me for saying it; I like being alive!"

"Death gives life purpose," Wally countered.

"Does it?" asked Giselle. "Or do we just say that to make ourselves feel better?" She paused, glancing between the teleporter and the psychic. "There is a god. A real god. A benevolent . . . ish . . . omniscient, all-powerful god. She wants to help us. She's trying to help us. She's out there literally building a better world right now. Do we really want to try and stop her?"

"I don't like the idea of god," said Wally. "The idea of someone controlling me, judging me, watching my every move."

"It's that age-old question," noted Will, shaking his head. "If god is all good and all powerful, why does evil exist? Well, now there's a god who is good—"

"Good intentioned," Giselle corrected.

"Right, and what does she immediately do?" Will paused, looking at each of them. "Day one. Better world."

"She's not god," Matt murmured. The conversation around the table suddenly ceased, and three sets of eyes turned to look at him. He didn't glance up. "She's just Jane." Matt shook his head and straightened slightly. "It doesn't matter how many powers she gets or what she does with them. She's just a person."

The bar was silent for a few moments.

"Matt," said Wally, "I hear what you're saying, and I appreciate it, I really do. But I also see the literal second Earth forming in the sky above us, and I have to say, appeals to 'we're all human after all' just aren't cutting it for me right now."

The other three lapsed back into argument—talk of what Jane's new world might be, whether to stop it, whether they could stop it, powers, combinations, ideas. Matt found himself increasingly unable to listen, or unable to bear listening. Maybe both. After a few more minutes and a few more throat-burning shots, he excused himself, claiming a need to go outside and pee. The others let him go without a backward glance, still enmeshed in their discussion.

Matt stepped out behind the bar onto a small dirt courtyard adjoining a patch of grass and a broad, hanging birch tree. The wind whistled through his hair, and he stared up at the moonlit skyline, the whispering heavens, the new white world, and the watching stars.

"Jane," he murmured. The moment before he'd uttered it, Matt had been afraid it'd feel stupid. But it didn't. They were well past feeling self-conscious. "Jane," he said again. "I know you're up there. I know you're trying. I . . . I really need to talk to you."

Wind whispered through the leaves.

"I . . . I don't know whether you're angry at me. If you think I'm trying to stop you. But I'm not. I'm not angry. I'm scared. And I don't want to be scared, and I don't want us not to talk to one another; I don't . . . Whatever you're going through, whatever you're planning, I don't want you to have to go through it alone.

"Because we're partners, aren't we?" he continued, his voice breaking. "Through all the stupid stuff? And I know you've never done anything to hurt me, and I'm never going to do anything to hurt you . . . So please. Let me in. I just want to talk."

For a few moments, Matt remained silent, staring up at the new moon shining pale in the night sky. The wind moved gently against the tree, swaying the birch's branches, the bark glistening like silk in the distant streetlights.

Nothing happened.

After a minute or so, Matt sighed and hung his head.

"I don't know why I keep thinking this'll work," he sighed, turning back toward the bar.

* * *

By the time they mustered the mental fortitude to return home, it was almost midnight, and the three Legionnaires and Matt were utterly paralytic. It took Will three minutes with his eyes closed just to plot a trip back to Morningstar, and since they all had to join hands and no one seemed to be able to stand up straight for more than about ten seconds, those three minutes were filled with lots of stumbling, swearing, and everyone collapsing in a heap as one person pulled the whole group over. When the four of them did finally reappear at the edge of the Academy grounds, they were all spat out from the crushing, nauseating black teleportation tunnel in different directions: Wally appearing in a tangle of limbs atop a pine tree, Matt dangling from a separate branch midway up, Giselle popping in from nothingness twenty feet up in open air and Will arriving with a heavy *Oof* face down in the mud.

All immediately threw up.

"Oh God," Will gurgled, pushing himself upright and wiping his mouth free of pine needles and vomit. Matt's grip immediately gave out, and he dropped the five or so feet to the ground, falling onto his butt and getting winded, while Giselle blurred around in an expert fall-breaking spiral, only to trip over as soon as her feet touched land. Wally's voice echoed from atop the pine tree.

"It's 'Oh Jane' now, darling," he called. The next five minutes was spent with the other three trying to regain their bearings while Wally gingerly climbed down.

"Let's leave out this part," Giselle mumbled as they staggered back up the hill toward Morningstar, arms linked together in a lurching human chain for support. "Let's leave this—*urp*—out of the report."

To no one's real surprise, Azleena was there to meet them when they finally staggered through into the entrance hall, her hands on her tiny hips and looking for all intents and purposes like she was about to slap each of them with her shoe.

"With me," she commanded, then without another word, the furious little genius force marched the four stumbling Legionnaires up to the infirmary. As they passed, Matt saw that the mansion's hallways remained abuzz—students running, frantic talking, lots of people still in armor. Matt had difficulty following what anyone was saying, so instead focused resolutely on putting one foot in front of the other. The others seemed to be experiencing the same struggle.

The moment they made it into the infirmary, Azleena led the four of them straight into an empty consultation room, only to leave and return a minute later with both Editha and Delores in tow.

"Purge them," the genius ordered. For the next ten minutes, the four inebriates sat in increasing shame and sobriety as the two healers supernaturally laid on hands and one by one flushed the alcohol from their bodies.

"Thank you," Giselle said finally, once they were all clean and sober. She looked at the healers and the genius with an expression of not insubstantial shame. "Sorry."

"You're lucky I didn't give you the hose," scowled Azleena. "Is it all out of your system?"

"The booze?"

"The self-pity."

"Oh. That."

"Yes, that." The genius muttered a rapid flurry of something Matt could only assume was Bangla. "Everything's crazy, boo-hoo. Harden up. The world continues to turn."

"World*s*," corrected Wally.

"Shut up," corrected Azleena. Giselle sighed, and with a begrudging nod, leaned forward in the doctor's chair she was sitting in and began rubbing her temples.

"Status report," she said with a long, defeated sigh.

"Do you want the good news or the bad news?" the genius asked.

"Good news," replied Giselle at the same time Wally said, "Bad news," and Matt muttered, "I literally don't care."

Azleena glanced between the lot of them. "Well, let's start at most normal and work our way up. Bad news: lots of Acolytes are MIA.

Seems your reactions to death and supernatural crises are not particularly unique or original."

"We get it; we were drunk!" complained Wally.

"Okay," mumbled Giselle, distractedly waving the psychic to shush. "Go on."

"Good news," continued Azleena, "Farrington, Natalia, and Enrique are tracking them down. They've found most of them. They're trickling home."

"Great. What else?"

"Bad news—there's no sign of Jane."

"I mean, there's at least one sign," countered Wally, indicating vaguely skyward. Azleena rolled her eyes but ignored him.

"Good news," she continued, powering on, "We've taken into custody one Levi Eller, sixty-two-year-old, former adjutant of Phillip Fredericks. Eller turned himself over to us once he saw Fredericks's televised rampage. Seems he was the go-between for a lot of his dealings."

"And?"

"And he confirmed pretty much everything our dear disintegrated pastor told Matt. Fredericks was working alone."

"That's good, at least," said Will.

"How did he pay for it all?" asked Wally. Azleena fixed him with an incredulous stare.

"How did he pay for it?" she repeated. "The man who could create gold and molecularly perfect diamonds out of thin air, who could rewrite the atomic foundations of reality? How did he fund the purchase of sensitive information and his overall illicit affairs? How do you think?"

"Alright, sorry, jeez," muttered the psychic, leaning back in his chair and folding his arms. Azleena shook her head and muttered under her breath a steady stream of profanity before returning her attention back to Giselle.

"Most of the work went through Eller," she continued, "who then parceled jobs out to individual contractors, one hand never knowing what the other was doing, yada-yada-yada. Eller himself has a long, sordid history, but I think seeing his boss disintegrate policemen on national TV might've tipped him off that it was time to throw in the towel. That and the new moon." She paused. "Small comfort, but at least it wasn't all a government conspiracy."

"Yes," Giselle replied heavily. "And on that topic—where do we stand with the military?"

"Well," replied Azleena, her lips tightly pursed, "this is where 'good-news, bad-news' sort of blends."

"Blends?" asked Giselle, her voice steeped in concern.

Azleena took a deep breath. "Jane killed a lot of people," the genius said bluntly. "And while one could argue all day about whether any-one's truly innocent in the military industrial complex, these people were at least completely innocent of the crime she was purportedly killing them for."

Nobody had an answer for that. Matt held his head in his hands. Despite the weight of her initial statement, however, Azleena's words did not remain macabre for long.

"Conversely, however, they are now all back alive."

"What?" yelped Giselle, sitting bolt upright. Wally swore, Will's eyes widened, and Matt peered up through his fingers. The two heal-ers just looked grim.

"Yep," Azleena confirmed. "As of . . . oh, about four hours ago. Everyone's back alive, actually: our dead Acolytes, all the people Fredericks killed. Disaster recovery teams were just hanging around and then poof! All of a sudden, one by one, people just started pop-ping back into existence on the old Eastborough front lawn."

"*Poof?*" asked Wally, crossing his arms and leveling Azleena a withering gaze. "Is that the technical term?"

"I'm sorry, is there a better word for it? Some term of art only pale ginger drunkards know?"

"Jane," Matt murmured under his breath, ignoring the sudden surge of argument.

"I just think, maybe, it would be more professional if—"

"Well, I think it'd be more professional if you didn't smell like a Mexican whorehouse, so—"

"Jesus, enough, you're both pretty!" Giselle cried. She glared at Wally and Azleena, and the psychic and the genius fell into reluctant silence, though they continued to simmer and scowl at one another. "Can we please just . . . focus on the matters at hand."

"Fine." Azleena glowered, turning back to their leader, though she continued to shoot Wally the odd stink eye. "As I said. Everyone's back into existence again. So, on balance, good for them." She worked her jaw. "Minus some lingering existential dread and confusion, of course, and who can say what it means long term for humanity, but I imagine at the very least there'll be several families tonight who are substantially less distraught."

"Holy hell," Will murmured. Like Matt, he was hunched over, hands clenched in front of his lips.

"Well, nobody I've heard interviewed so far has reported that," Azleena replied, very nonchalant. "So, you know, the great questions remain unanswered."

"How's the government taking it?" Giselle asked.

"Similarly to the rest of us," the genius answered. "Shaken, scattered, and confused. No longer on the warpath now that their soldiers have been unkilled, but I don't know if they're quite elated about the whole affair just yet. For now, though, they're more focused on the new planet."

"Right," muttered Giselle. "Understandable." She kneaded her fists into her lap, rubbing midthigh, where her protective leggings abruptly ended and exposed flesh. "Where do we stand on that?"

Azleena shrugged. "It's big. It's a ball. It looks like white stone. Most people on the news are calling it 'The White World,' because, apparently, originality died with Phillip Fredericks. I'm calling it *absolute bullcrap* because it's doing my goddamn head in. It's impossible."

Across from her, Wally muttered something inaudible and derisive.

"Wally," Giselle warned, fixing him with another icy glare. The telepath rolled his eyes but held up his hands in apology. Beside him, Will's brows furrowed, and he continued as if deaf to his partner's backbiting.

"What do you mean?" the teleporter asked. "When you say impossible, what—"

"I mean it's impossible," replied Azleena, cutting him off with a scowl. "Something that big, that close, should be having a gravitational impact on the tides, let alone everything else, let alone being pulled in on a collision course with Earth. But it's not. And with the proximity—I mean, you can see it; it's right there—you should be able to get clear readings or bounce light off it or zoom in with a telescope or something. But you can't. You can't land anything on it; you can't teleport to it. I think Russia even tried shooting a missile, but nothing gets through. Nothing. We have broken directional consistency."

"Broken what?" asked Matt.

"Objects existing in fixed relation," replied Azleena. "Used to be a universal constant, you could go between two places, A to B, in a straight line, or I mean, sometimes space curves, but"—she waved a hand around distractedly, clearly forcing herself not to get sidetracked—"basically, forget about it. Point is, a direction is a direction. You could go places. Except now, we can forget that supposedly universal law because if your A to B goes through the White World, screw you, you're going to point C."

"Okay, so that's weird," said Giselle, chewing her knuckle. "But I mean, weird's good, right? Weird's not damaging?"

"It *is* damaging," the genius protested. "It is damaging my calm." She paused and glanced between all of them. "I have nothing to support this," Azleena continued, biting her lip as she said it, "but I suspect we're being somewhat deceived. I don't think whatever it is that's up there is actually made of rock."

"What do you mean?" Will asked, frowning.

"The White World. I don't think it's a world. I don't think we're actually seeing white stone, regardless of what the scanners say or what it looks like on a telescope. I think we're looking at some kind of quantum field, some kind of barrier surrounding . . . something. Maybe a planet. Maybe . . . who knows what. Nothing. Jane. A great cosmic baby. A hole in the fabric of time and space with a seething horde of eldritch horrors behind it, preparing to descend and consume us all."

"Why would Jane make eldritch horrors?" Matt sighed, exasperated.

"I don't know!" cried Azleena, throwing her hands up and rounding on him. "She's your girlfriend! Why does she do anything?"

"We think she's trying to make a better world," said Giselle, sounding tired.

"Yes, I heard that theory amid your drunken ramblings."

"Excuse me." Wally frowned. "That's eavesdropping."

"Turn your earpieces off, then." Azleena scowled back. Giselle pinched the bridge of her nose.

"Okay," she repeated. "Okay. Lots to do, little to no information. Okay." She sucked in a deep breath and sat up straighter in the doctor's chair. "Az. Good work. Really well done. Good job holding down the fort. I am sorry I—*we*"—she gestured at the four of them—"handled this suboptimally. We are good; we are here. It is out of our system." She sounded as if she was trying to convince herself as much as anyone. Nevertheless, Giselle squared her shoulders and continued.

"Get on the horn," the speedster ordered. "Let's do what we can. Let everyone know I'm back on board, and I want all hands on deck. Natalia, Farrington, and Enrique can stay on stray duty. That's good; that's a good fit for them: good tracking skills, sufficient gravitas. Everyone else, I want everybody mobile: I want teams, I want quarantine established around everyone who's resurrected, and I want them monitored around the clock. Let's get them here if we can. If that's not practical, let's have them buddy up, powers counterweighing powers. We do not know if coming back to life has side effects, and I have seen enough undead surprises to last me a lifetime."

"Amen," said Wally.

"You weren't even there!" complained Azleena, incredulous.

"Azleena," Giselle continued, powering through before the psychic could dive back in with a rebuttal. "I want your full attention on that moon. Planet, egg, quantum ball of nonsense—I don't care. *I want you to study it.* I want to know about it. I want to understand if it poses a threat. Wally," she said, turning to the telepath, "assemble a team, get whoever you need, and liaise with the Pentagon. See if they're willing to quarantine their resurrected men. Hopefully, they're still willing to listen. I don't think Jane would deliberately bring back anyone messed up, but if we're talking about being reassembled from atomic dust, it just feels like we're working with a very low margin of error. Matt." She turned to face the human, and her gaze, though sympathetic, was firm. "I'm afraid that means you."

"It's fine," Matt sighed.

"I've looked him over," said Editha, piping up.

"I'm not saying anything," replied Giselle, holding up her hands. "I'm just saying, you were recently disintegrated. We don't know what that means long term for your . . . everything."

"I mean, even if you factor in an error of, like, point one percent," agreed Wally. "Forget undeath, what if you get like . . . cancer? Aneurysms."

"It's really fine," Matt said again, with absolutely no objection to just staying in a room somewhere and lying down.

"Do you think she might've improved him?" asked Azleena, peering at Matt with fresh interest. "If she did, I wish she'd have consulted me. I have a lot of thoughts about the human knee."

"I mean, she clearly didn't make him any taller," noted Wally.

"You'd think if you were remaking a human from scratch, you'd tinker a little," agreed Azleena.

"I wonder what it did to your gut flora?" Delores asked, staring at Matt and sounding legitimately enthused. Beside her, still sitting, Will tilted his head to fix the healer with an incredulous gaze. To her credit, Giselle didn't even blink.

"We also need to keep you out of harm's way," the speedster continued. "Now more than ever. I hate making those gun nuts right, but there's a chance before this is all over we might need some permanent neutralization."

"I thought you weren't sure whether you wanted to stop her," said Will.

"I'm not," Giselle replied. "But we have to consider our options. Besides, putting aside his blood, Jane genuinely does care for him. That might mean something in the long run." She fixed Matt with a sad look. "I'm sorry to say, but if push comes to shove, you might be our only leverage."

"If we go down that path," Wally added. Matt remained silent. Eventually, Giselle shook her head.

"Forget it. For now, let's just hole up, take a breather, try to sort the other problems out. One thing at a time."

"One thing at a time," a few of the other Legionnaires echoed. Matt just nodded and drew a deep breath.

"She wouldn't try to hurt any of you," he tried to reassure them. "Jane. I know this is all completely crazy, but at the end of the day . . . she's still the same person." He swept his gaze around the room, moving one by one across the sea of blank faces. "She wants to do the right thing."

"I know," said Giselle. She sounded serious and sad. She flicked Matt a small, kind smile. "We'll get through this," their leader said, turning to the others. "One way or another. I promise. We can do this. The world's faced impossible before. This is what the Legion is—this is what we do. I believe in you. I believe in all of us." Giselle rose from her chair, standing to her full height. "Let's go do good."

There were murmurs of resolute agreement followed by the clatter of chairs scraping on linoleum as, all together, the Legion got to their feet. The consultation room suddenly felt very crowded. Matt likewise stood, sticking his hands in his pockets and letting a long breath run out between his teeth.

"So, do you just want me to hang in one of the dorm rooms?" he asked, turning back to Giselle as the group started filing out. "I mean, I don't mind wherever, really. Just give me, like, a book or something. My Game Boy. Although, I'll marry the first person who brings me some pancakes."

"Yeah, God, I'm freaking famished," Giselle agreed. Matt fell into step behind her as they filed out the door and into the greater infirmary. "Twenty thousand calories a day normally, and now, I'm drinking on an empty stom—"

Abruptly, Giselle's voice cut off. Matt frowned and glanced up from where he'd been unthinkingly staring at the floor.

Only to find that the girl was gone.

And he was surrounded by white.

"—drinking on an empty stomach." Giselle kept walking, waiting for Matt's reply, but the next few moments brought only silence.

I wasn't blaming you, she thought irritably before she caught herself and sighed. She had been getting less and less tolerant lately. Or maybe it was just the last few days. After all this was over, Giselle promised herself, she was going to go to a full day spa; one of those places where some tiny-handed masseuse could put rocks on her back and massage her legs until she forgot they weren't original.

She pulled her half-distracted mind away from thoughts of hot springs and saunas, trying to ignore in its place the constant nattering of Wally and Will, who'd gone out in front of her and struck back up again about strategy and the unenviable prospect of defeating a Divine. Not really thinking, Giselle glanced back over her shoulder to where Matt had been mere moments earlier, only to find the space behind her empty. That was odd. She frowned and came to a complete stop. Where'd he get to? Giselle turned, throwing quick looks to her left and right, then stood on her tiptoes and peered back into the consultation room. Empty.

"Matt?" she called. Giselle swept her gaze over the rest of the infirmary, the rows of beds and high ceilings, the far-off entrances to the healer's stations and washrooms. All the doors were closed. A lot of beds were occupied, but she couldn't see Matt's head anywhere among them. Neither did she see him hiding or sprinting off. The speedster turned on her heel, her frown deepening.

"Matt?"

Matt stood in a chamber of infinite white and wondered if he was dreaming. The transition had come without light, noise, or warning. He had not blinked; he had not been blinded. He had simply turned his head, and he was no longer anywhere he recognized. He was not in Morningstar. He was not in Sedgwick, Kansas. Instead, he was somewhere white. Endless, unbroken white stretching as far as the eye could see without crease or curve or corner.

Matt glanced down at the floor and then up again, gripped by a sudden sense of vertigo, feeling with his feet, searching with his eyes. He was standing on something solid—some kind of stone, maybe, and he thought inside, because up high, maybe a hundred feet above him, he could just make out the slightest change in angle, which he thought might be the curvature of a roof. But the color of the stone was so bright and pure, with light seemingly coming from everywhere with no visible source, that it was impossible to make out where the walls were, or where the room started or ended. He stood inside a cathedral. A cathedral of infinite white.

"Hey." A soft, familiar voice spoke from behind him, and Matt spun around.

There, in the still, white glow, stood Jane.

She looked older somehow. Not physically older, not gray haired or more developed or showing any signs of greater aging, but in the way she held herself. The way she smiled, calm, almost motherly, the light soft upon her body, never changing. Her face, her limbs were free of any dirt or tarnish, and the uniform of Dawn was gone, replaced by a long white sleeveless robe falling in gentle folds across her shoulders and down her frame. Matt had not heard her arrive, yet there she stood, barely three feet away from him, smiling, serene. Her hands were clasped, her bronze hair falling long and loose down behind her shoulders. Her eyes were human, showing no signs of change or color. Yet the *E* tattoo on her cheek was now white—changed from tattoo black to the color of pure, unblemished marble.

"Jane . . ."

For a moment, Matt wondered if he'd fallen over; if he'd hit his head falling out of a pine tree or passed out back in the restroom of the Kansas bar, having dreamed the last hour and was in reality now pantless and enjoying a big drooling snore. But as he considered his surroundings and the sight of Jane in front of him, Matt felt completely sober.

Okay. Matt didn't take a step back nor let himself panic, though his pulse did quicken a few paces. But the look on Jane's face was so calm, so composed and self-assured, that the sense of panic he'd been expecting to come rushing in never eventuated. He gawked at her, then gaped at the world around them.

"Where are we?" he asked her, his voice low, almost reverent. "How did we get . . . ? What happened to you?"

"Come," Jane said simply, taking his hand with a warm, caring smile. Their fingers intertwined, her hand soft and warm. She led him gently through the endless white hall, in the direction she had appeared from, though if she'd disappeared again, Matt would've found it hard to keep track. His gaze wandered over Jane as they walked, taking in her long straight hair, the change in her demeanor, the light and happiness in her eyes, her utter, implacable calm. Somehow, though their footsteps swept across unblemished stone, the sound did not echo throughout the cathedral's halls.

"Are you . . . older?" he asked. It hardly seemed like a rude question given the circumstances. Jane laughed, and to Matt's unexpected relief, it was not some divine, tinkling chime but her usual biting bark.

"I guess," she answered. She squeezed his hand, and the calm smile she held twisted into a bit more of a grin. "I have been . . . living a lot, lately. Condensed down. Not aging specifically. I don't think that's happening anymore."

"Oh," Matt replied. He was unsure how to respond to that. "How much time . . . ?"

Jane laughed again. "How many thoughts are there in a second? How much light streams in from the sun? At some point, you miss the point by counting. What matters is the warmth, the sunshine, the love." She squeezed his hand again. Matt didn't know if the answer made him feel more or less reassured.

They continued walking.

"What is this place?" he asked eventually as they continued down the endless white hall. "Is this inside that sphere?"

"Correct."

"Everyone back on Earth is freaking out over that, by the way." He paused, momentarily reassessing with some discomfort the fact that he'd just had to say *back on Earth*.

Again, Jane only laughed. "I know. Let them panic. It's not going to do anything. Might do them good to instill a little reverence and awe."

There was a lot to unpack in that sentence. "They're worried they're in danger."

Jane shrugged. "People have held false beliefs for millennia. Another few days won't hurt."

They ambled on, and Matt thought he saw a distant rectangle of light down the very, very far end of the hallway. "How did I get here?" he asked her. "Can you teleport now? How did you make this place?"

"Fredericks was right," Jane told him, her voice calm, confident, without the slightest hint of fear or resentment. "I am a god. Or like a god. How do you draw the distinction? Anyway." She brushed the question away with a wave of her hand. "These things I can do. These four pillars. They're not just powerful on their own; they work in tandem. Like they were made for each other. Like missing pieces."

She raised her right hand, the one not holding Matt's, out toward the wall and ceiling, and to Matt's amazement, a trail of green plants and buds suddenly blossomed along the pure white.

"Matter and energy are two sides of the same coin. I have unlimited energy, and so I can make limitless matter. Create, control everything at its most basic level. Time and space go in tandem. I mean, you've seen the Child appearing where he wants to. Every moment's a back door. So I can go and make and see and be, and then things I want to live can just live; I can give them that spark. So anything I want just sort of . . . exists."

She gently twisted her hand, and the green buds bloomed into a thousand flowers of every color. "Time's the key. I can go back and forth now; it's easier to do it. Not so much to rewrite things but to"—she contemplated her words—"*see* where the lines are. See what's going to work. The Child is enmeshed in time, deep beneath the surface, but I just sort of . . . skim." She turned and smiled at him. "It's all just practice. Attempts to get it right. Keep your mind calm and don't let it consume you, and it can show you where to go. And I can undo." She paused, lowering her hand, and the line of flora ceased appearing. "Unlimited trial and error. If something doesn't work, I just roll it back and do better next time."

The opening from which light poured was moving closer.

"You're redoing things?" Matt asked. "Over and over?"

"Foresight and hindsight." Jane nodded. "After a while, it's just seeing. I think that's what the Child was trying to tell me at some point. Existence isn't so, you know, *linear* when you can just endlessly predict and redo."

"And is it just creating things you're doing over?" Matt asked, not sure if he wanted to know the answer. "How many times have we had this conversation?" To his surprise, Jane cocked her head, and for the first time since he'd entered the white room, her brow furrowed, and she stared at him with something resembling hurt.

"I would never do that," she told him. "I'm not . . . These powers aren't to manipulate you or win an argument. I love you. I want this to be real with us."

"Okay."

"I'm serious. I promise."

"Okay. I believe you." Matt tried to force a smile. "I'm just trying to wrap my head around this."

"That may take a while." Jane laughed, turning back to face in the direction they were walking, her auburn hair flicking free, all trace of consternation forgotten. "There's a lot to take in."

As she said it, they reached the door. Because Matt could see now that that patch of endless white they'd been walking toward, through which blinding light seemed to be streaming, was indeed a door: an enormous, hundreds-of-feet-high rectangle opening in the stone walls, floor to ceiling; a titanic gateway to the world beyond. Jane led Matt forward, and like ants wandering across the floor of a temple, they walked toward it, Matt gazing up in wonder at the impossible structure's flawless seams and towering height.

As they approached, Matt felt the soft brush of wind on his face, heard the tinkle of distant running water, and caught the smell of fresh rain, the scent of pollen and deep earth. Light streamed through the doorway, and as Matt stepped through, he had to use his free hand to shield his eyes. Then they were out on the balcony, and slowly, Matt's vision adjusted. His heart stopped.

"Welcome"—Jane smiled—"to my world."

It was all Matt could do to keep breathing.

"What the fu . . ."

Paradise.

Actual, stereotypical paradise. Before him, from atop the white stone balcony on which they were standing, stretched an endless expanse of radiant nature: glistening blues and golds, earth tones, and fields of green. Long grass hills undulated and rolled out into the horizon like waves across an ocean; forests stood hundreds of feet tall; streams flowed unbroken through lakes and cascaded into glistening waterfalls. There were flowers everywhere—fields of pinks and reds and yellows—mighty cliffs of rough-hewn stone, and above it all, the cosmic sky stretched eternal, glistening with stars, sweeping green and purple clouds of galactic dust and nebulas.

And among it all—*animals*. So many moving animals: deer grazing in herds, flocks of bright parrots flapping and squawking, elephants, giraffes, peacocks strutting about, and on the far side of the hills, a pack of sandy lions prowling around as if they owned the place. Yet these were just the beginning. Between them, between all these familiar, Earthly animals, moved other creatures, impossible creatures, things that shouldn't exist, that existed only in stories or people's imaginations. Flying feathered snakes with scales of every color. An eagle-faced, lion-legged griffon gliding casually through the clouds. Matt saw a rabbit made of pure gold, some sort of white, six-legged flying oxen, and a great copper dragon the size of a school bus lying curled up beside a shimmering pond, tiny gray-and-black plover birds picking between its scales and teeth.

"Are those freaking *dinosaurs*?" he asked, breathless, unable to help himself, leaning over the balcony and pointing; a child again enamored, enraptured at the zoo. Jane laughed.

"Yep," she said. "They took a few attempts. I think I've got them right. There'll probably be a few modifications."

"Holy . . ." Matt whispered. The words died beneath his lips. He gawked down across the vibrant, color-strewn paradise, the rolling hills of Eden brought impossibly to life. Far off over snowcapped mountains, a pterodactyl circled. Rainbow-scaled fish swam just beneath the surface of a river. Distinct orange tigers paced next to a family of mottled green triceratops, the predators giving a wide berth to the three-horned dinosaurs as they plodded through a sea of grass.

"Do you want to go see?" Jane smiled at him. Matt felt as if he was in a dream, and he turned to look at her, his hand holding on to the rail to prevent his collapse. Jane's smile beamed, radiant.

"Do I want to go see dinosaurs?" Matt replied, knees and voice both weak. Jane nodded. "I . . . I don't . . ." He swung his gaze back weakly around. "How do we get down?"

Again, Jane laughed, and it was so refreshing—such a happy, vibrant sound—that he couldn't help but smile at her, couldn't help being swept up.

"However we like," she told him, waving her hands. Suddenly, his torn, muddy clothes were loose white linen, soft and unimaginably comfortable, and like her own, flowing gently in the cool summer breeze. She leaned forward and wrapped her arms around his waist. "But I thought we could try this."

She bent forward and pressed her lips against his forehead. Suddenly, Matt's whole body grew hot, and all of a sudden, it felt like he was glowing, like after years of being in the snowy wilderness, he'd suddenly plunged into a blissful steaming bath. He gasped, his eyes widening. A light surged through him, a lightness, a sudden singing in his veins. It was the most exhilarating feeling he'd ever experienced.

"Go," Jane whispered, and she released his hand and floated gently up off the balcony. Matt watched her rise, his heart pounding, and he glanced over at the distant ground. It was a long, impossible drop. But suddenly, Matt wasn't afraid of falling. He glanced upward, at the white, rippling folds of Jane's cloak—

And flew.

"HO-LEE SHI—!"

Matt was flying. Slowly at first, unsteady, his legs kicking wildly out from under him, but an instant later, his heart surged with confidence, and he took off, rocketing like a shot, racing through the air, tumbling, hollering giddy with laughter, rolling in an ungainly tangle of hair and limbs then spinning, stretching out straight as an arrow, shooting up into the clouds, shouting with pure glee. He rose above the verdant world, slingshotting through the clouds and above the skyline, then plunged, falling—no, diving forward, racing toward the ground at breakneck speed before pulling up, whooping with joy, flying back above the rolling emerald hills. He heard a bark of laughter and looked up to find Jane soaring above him, specks of gold trailing behind her, staring down at him with shameless satisfaction.

"You're a natural!" she shouted, and as Matt rose back up, she shot down past him, a white-tipped golden arrow, cackling as the rush of air sent Matt tumbling, his own face splitting in excitement as he turned and shot off after her a moment later. They flew fast and lithe, a hundred feet above the rolling landscape, over glistening lakes and migrating herds of buffalo, over fruit-strewn orchards, azure lakes, and sandy shores.

Jane led him into a forest, between a maze of high-rise tree trunks, and together, they twisted and turned beneath the suddenly cool, mottled canopy, weaving so fast through leafy boughs and hooting monkeys that there were moments Matt was sure he was going to crash. But always, at the last second, he managed to turn and right himself, racing at breakneck speeds behind Jane's golden trail. After a minute or two, he heard her whoop and shoot straight out through the topmost branches. He followed her up, and they ascended into the clouds, breathless, where he found her waiting for him, grinning from ear to ear, wind blowing through her hair, sunlight shining through her dress, this impossible girl floating above an impossible planet.

Matt slowed, leaning his body back so he was drifting, staring upside down among the blue and open sky, gazing with wonder at the majesty below. The colors swirled and blurred, and Matt realized he was crying, wordless tears flowing down his cheeks and onto this incredible world, the dark specks of animals moving in their herds, the distant drift of eagles, the long-necked brontosaurus shuffling in slow herds across the plains. He turned to Jane, and their eyes found each other, their beaming, almost aching smiles, and as though guided by the clouds themselves, they drew together and embraced in the celestial sky. His lips found hers, soft and warm, his hands running through her hair, her fingers rushing against his skin—

And they stayed there, joined together beneath the cosmos, as daylight faded into night.

Matt lay in a bed of white stone and swimming silk and stared up at a ceiling that never ceased. Around them, the endless hall flowed cavernous and eternal, an empty cathedral steeped in never-ending twilight. A night that never truly darkened; a dawn that never truly came.

Jane's head rested against his chest, and his finger wrapped around a strand of her hair as she murmured to him of her visions.

"I'll make cities of glass and marble," she whispered, her smooth skin warm and restless, their bare legs intertwined, "with green veins running through. Leaves and flowers growing everywhere, on every surface. Avenues and avenues of trees; hanging vines. There'll be no pollution; no war. Nobody will ever go hungry; nobody will ever get sick. Kids will play in the streams and pick fruit from the orchards, and in the night, fireflies will light up the darkness, everything like stars." She paused, leaning her head into him. "What are those cave worms called? The glowing ones?"

"Bioluminescence."

"That's them. I'll put that on the bark of trees. Or maybe the worms underneath it. On buildings. And in the lakes, there'll be blue, unstinging jellyfish. When night falls, the entire city will glow."

"I can see it."

"People can work, if they want to," she told him. "They can make things or they can write or they can teach or invent. But they won't have to. Whatever they need, I'll give it to them. Everybody will be rich. Nobody poor."

Matt was silent.

"I'm going to make saddles for the pterodactyls," Jane continued. "I'm going to domesticate them, I think. Just change their brains a little to be more like horses, and then, when the kids are old enough, they can ride them."

"Sounds dangerous."

"If anyone falls, I'll catch them."

"Sounds like an incentive to let go."

Jane laughed. "I can keep making the world bigger, I think, as big as I want to. Shuffle things around. Space for those who want to be left alone, you know. Beaches where it's never cloudy; mountains always covered in snow. People won't have to live in cities, but I think a lot of them might want to. They might be used to it. Or might want to change between them, one after the other."

"I imagine it'll be where most of the good food is."

"The food will be good everywhere." Jane laughed.

"What, are you god of the kitchen now, too?"

"Hilarious." Jane smirked. She paused. "I'll make the atmosphere high enough to fly in, but beyond that, keep gravity low. Won't be long before people can travel out into space, if that's where their hearts take them. Or into the caverns below, or the jungles. Our own world is so big, but I could make this one bigger. All unknown; all unexplored. A whole new world of discoveries. I'll make that for them."

"Can you make Pokémon?" Matt asked. "Actual, working Pokémon?"

"You are such a nerd." Jane cackled, rolling over on top of Matt to tickle him, breathless and bare as the new day. After a moment of Matt's laughter and resistance, she rolled off, and he ceased his squirming.

"What color will the flag be?" he asked eventually. Beside him, her autumn hair splayed out over the white down pillow, Jane pursed her lips.

"I'm not sure," she admitted. "What color do you think it should be?"

"Green."

"Ew, no, green? Gold. Definitely gold."

"A gold flag? What are you, an Arab dictator?"

"It's my world." Jane laughed, giving him a light push.

"Is it?" said Matt. "I thought it was everyone's."

The goddess waved her hand. "It will be everyone's. But it'll be mine first and foremost. And yours." She rolled over onto her stomach, fixing him with a grin. "Come on. What do you want?"

"Breakfast?" Matt's own stomach grumbled. "I think it may have been legitimately two days since I've eaten anything."

"Sorry," Jane laughed. "I forget you need to eat. Do you want me to take care of that for you?"

"As in order something in?" Matt glanced at the endless white hall on the impossible utopia planet currently circling in low orbit around the Earth. "I think we might be outside the usual delivery radius."

Jane rolled her eyes and punched him lightly on the shoulder. "No, as in make you something. I could just snap my fingers and—" She broke off, clicking her fingers to demonstrate.

"Is there a risk your planet would burn down?"

"Hilarious. Again, just hilarious. You think you're so funny."

"I *am* so funny."

She kissed him on the cheek. "Or I could just take away your hunger."

Matt's smile faded slightly. "What?"

"Yeah, I could just make you never be hungry. Put, I don't know, some self-sustaining energy in your system, replace your stomach. It'd be pretty easy."

It took Matt a few moments in silence before he was able to respond. "No . . . No, thank you," he said quietly. "I . . . I think I like the way I am."

"Your loss," said Jane, rolling off him onto her back. She propped herself up with her arms to look at the endless twilight darkness and the ceiling, not bothering to keep beneath the sheets. "It would be pretty easy."

"You can just change people like that?"

"Gave you the ability to fly, didn't I?" She raised her eyebrows. "It's just atoms. Tinkering. You can sort of reach in and see how people work, and just . . . change things. It's complex, but not *that* complex. No more than making a stegosaurus."

"What if you get something wrong? What if you break something?"

"Then I undo it." Jane shrugged. "A thousand times in a single instant, until I get it right. It's easy, though, once you get the hang of it."

Matt said nothing, and the room lapsed into silence. After a moment, Jane turned and leaned on her elbow to look at him, frowning slightly.

"Is everything okay? Are you alright?"

"Sure," Matt replied, though he wasn't quite sure he believed it. "It's just . . . a lot, you know. I've never not been hungry. Or, you know, not needed to eat. It's a strange thought."

"Hunger," said Jane, waving an errant hand, "fatigue, sleep, aging, death. They're all just things, you know? Things that happen in our bodies; a biological process. There's no magic to them; they're not vital. If I can get rid of them, why shouldn't I?" She turned again, staring up at the ceiling, her eyes bright. "Just imagine never growing old. Never having to worry about dying. Never being afraid of losing anyone. Of having to say goodbye for the last time."

"I think a few folks probably have people they wouldn't mind saying permanent goodbye to."

"Of course." Jane shuffled back down onto her side again, seeming restless, unable to stay in one position long. "Nobody will have to see anyone if they don't want to."

"What are you going to do once people start starting wars?"

"*Pfft*, wars over what?" Jane scoffed. She fixed him with her gray-blue eyes. "Everyone will have everything they ever wanted. There'll be no scarcity. There'll be no reason to hurt or steal or go to war with each other."

"Except all the stupid reasons people have always hurt and stole and gone to war with each other throughout the whole of human history."

"Like what?" demanded Jane.

"Jealousy. Anger. Hatred. Betrayal. Person A loves Person B, who loves Person C. Disagreements about the correct priorities in life, the right books, the right songs. The right god."

"Please," scoffed Jane. "By the time people come here, that debate will be settled."

"What if it's not?"

"What do you mean?" she asked him, sounding a tad annoyed, though not quite angry. "I'm right here."

"So was evolution. People still don't believe in it. People still believe in angels and astrology and demons and all kinds of stupid stuff." He paused and tilted his head on the pillow, looking over at her. "Are you going to let them keep believing in that if they want?"

"They can believe in whatever they like," Jane replied with a small frown. "I don't care."

"So, if they want to build a giant statue of an angel in the middle of your tree city, you'll be alright with that?"

"I—" Jane hesitated, brows furrowing. "I mean, I guess. It's just a statue."

"What about if another city makes a statue that they think is better?"

"Then we can have a best statue competition and goddamn settle it," Jane growled, a little irritable.

"What if they don't believe it was you who did this? What if they call you the Devil?"

"I don't care." She laughed again.

"What if they do believe it was you, but different groups have different interpretations of your rules?"

"I will literally appear and correct them."

"What if they don't listen? What if they don't believe you? What if they want to start fighting?"

"I'll make them stop." She scowled, then paused, propping her head up with one arm, her face creased as she looked at him with a frustrated frown. "Are you trying to pick holes in this?"

"No," said Matt. "I'm just asking questions."

There was a long pause while Jane stared at him. "Are you . . . Are you not okay with this?" she asked, sounding a little taken aback—maybe even offended.

"No," Matt insisted. "I'm fine. I just . . . I don't know if it's going to be that simple. I'm just trying to understand how it'll work."

"Do you . . . not want me making utopia?"

"Do I have a choice?"

"Of course you do." Jane looked taken aback. She recoiled, sitting up straighter in the wide white bed. "You're my partner in this. In everything. I'm doing all this for you."

"Are you?" Matt asked. "Is this really about me?"

"How can you ask that?" said Jane. "Of course it is. I-I'm trying to make a world where we can be . . . where we can live . . ."

"As kings," Matt finished for her. "As deities. Ruling over everyone."

"I . . ." Jane sounded flabbergasted. "Yes! Is that bad? Are you *complaining* about the thought of being king of utopia?"

"Is it annoying?" Matt asked, gazing at her. "Is it illogical?"

"Yes!"

"Do you want it to stop? Do you want me to stop not doing exactly what you want, being petty, unreasonable, and human?"

Abruptly, Jane fell silent. For about half a minute, she just stared at him, her face blank and eyes narrowed.

"I see what you're doing," she eventually muttered.

"Were you tempted to look forward in time to see if I was going to do it?"

"I . . . No," she grumbled, though her words and gaze were dark.

"Will you be?"

"Will I be foreseeing our conversations?"

"Yes."

"No. I told you that already."

"So you're not going to redirect the future? You're just going to let conflict occur?"

"Matt." Jane gave a heavy sigh and sat up, the sheet falling off her, her hands moving in frustration down to her hips. "Why are you being like this?"

"You tell me."

"You know I can't read your mind."

"Can't you?" Matt asked. "Because you can make me fly. You can teleport. You can change a living creature's brain. You can do anything." He let the words drift out into the empty, yawning silence, watching their ripples make their way across Jane's frustrated expression. "And a part of me can't help but wonder how long it'll take before you get sick of people disagreeing with you, get sick of them having their own opinions, and stop giving them a choice."

"Please." Jane stood up, rising from the bed, not bothering to drape herself in the covers—the air was perfectly temperate, and with the barest touch of her hand, white silk appeared from nowhere and wrapped itself around her torso. "This is ridiculous."

"What? What of what I'm saying is ridiculous?"

"You're arguing with God," she snapped. "What isn't ridiculous?"

"You're not God," Matt replied. "And if you were, you could beat me in an argument."

"Well, I'm the next best thing." She stared at him, her face hard and disbelieving, her arms crossed over her white-clad chest. "Why are you doing this? Why are you being this way? Why can't you just be happy? Why can't you get out of your own way?"

"This isn't going to make me happy," Matt countered. "It isn't going to make you happy, living like this, domineering everything, getting angry at everything you can't control."

"I thought you said I could do anything," Jane snapped.

"You can," said Matt. "But that doesn't mean everyone's going to do everything you want them to. And eventually, people are going to start making choices you don't agree with. Choices you think damage things. And you're going to be faced with the option of taking away their ability to choose or letting them do things which hurt people."

"I don't . . . This is absurd."

"You're making heaven," Matt pushed onward. "Alright. What if everyone's version of heaven is different?"

"Everyone can have whatever they want," Jane answered, throwing up her hands. "I don't care. I'll make new planets. Separate planets. It'll be huge."

"The Klaus Heydrichs of the world? The white supremacists? The religious fanatics? The pedophiles?"

"They're not coming in!" Jane almost shouted, rolling her eyes so aggressively she practically rolled her head.

"So some people are getting left behind, then?"

"I . . . No! Maybe! I don't know." She scowled, though there was something troubled behind the expression, a look not necessarily directed at Matt. "There'll . . . Obviously, some people are monsters. They . . . I won't bring them over; I can't, because then they'll just hurt people; they'll just . . ."

"And where do you draw the line? Who gets into paradise, who stays in Hell?"

"I . . ." Again, Jane's words failed her. "I'll look into their pasts," she finally told him, though the way she said it sounded less like a foregone plan and more like something she'd made up on the spot to get Matt to shut up. "And their futures. I'll see . . . if they're truly irredeemable. If they were always going to end up like that."

"Are there many evil children?"

"You know what I mean!" she yelled, again throwing up her hands. "If they can't be fixed, if they can't be changed—"

"And you're going to change them?" Matt asked, sitting up. "What bits of their pasts are you going to alter? What bits of their personalities are you going to remove?"

"No!" Jane cried, and in the twilit room, the faintest white glow began creeping along the edge of her tattoo. "I . . . You're twisting my words. I'm going to . . ." She suddenly stopped, her jaw clenched, her nostrils flared. "You know what?" she said. "Enough of this. If you want to complain, to nitpick and find flaws in everything I'm doing, that's on you. That's *fine*. But I'm not going to stand here and listen while you do it. I've got work to do. Important work." She turned away. "The most important work in history. I'm making a world." She sniffed. "Our world."

"What if I don't want it?" Matt murmured.

"Then you're an idiot." Jane scowled, and this time, the anger in her voice was real and directed squarely at him. "A selfish fool and an idiot who doesn't realize what he's got and everything I'm trying to do for him."

Suddenly, the nothingness in front of her folded like paper, and Jane was gone, leaving Matt lying in an empty bed in the halls of a great, vacant cathedral, surrounded by empty whiteness, all alone.

When Matt rose from the (admittedly absurdly comfortable) stone bed, he found a set of clothes waiting for him. Dozens of sets of clothes, actually. By the look of it, every set of clothes Matt had ever owned or thought about owning, or even looked at. He struggled not to roll his eyes and picked out the same white linen shirt and loose pants he'd worn yesterday, which admittedly were very light to the touch and inherently soothing against his skin.

He set out walking down the formless, wall-less hall, glancing with some trepidation at the hundred-foot-high ceiling, the seemingly endless expanse of now morning sun—morning sun?—infused stone. Matt had no idea how the lighting worked in this place, or how Jane had made the space feel so boundless. Maybe she'd spent a lifetime taking classes in interior decorating. Maybe it was micro-LED lights. Maybe she'd invented some new kind of rock.

After a few minutes of wandering, Matt was surprised to see that what he'd assumed—or what he could have sworn had been yesterday—was a long straight hallway leading to the outside balcony, now abruptly curved off to the right. Matt hadn't even noticed the corner from a distance because of the towering white walls' uniformity, but as he got closer, his sense of sight began tingling, and he stopped a few feet short of colliding with the stone.

"Okay," he murmured, turning the now nonoptional corner. He advanced down the slightly narrowing high-ceilinged hallway, still surrounded by white on every side, following it as it again expanded. In the distance, his eyes fell upon something in the middle of the chamber, rising flat and white, the same texture as the floor but covered in splotches of color.

"Of course," Matt sighed to himself as he got closer. It was a table of food. A huge table of food, a flat stone bench waist height, and about half the length of an Olympic swimming pool covered with every kind of cuisine imaginable: lobsters, crab, roast beef, fish, turkey, bacon-wrapped chicken, about fifty different types of cheese, a dozen pizzas of varying flavor and thickness, truffle mac and cheese, baguettes, bowls of lentils and pasta, steak, lamb chops, Christmas ham, fried eggs, waffles, pancakes, crepes, ice cream—an entire literal slab of multicolored ice cream—hotdogs, a variety of hamburgers, potatoes mashed, roasted, fried, and baked, a bunch of meat and vegetables on skewers, donuts, chocolates, candy, salad (what kind of sick bastard would sit at a table like this and eat salad?) long loaves of garlic bread, cheesy garlic bread, about twenty cakes, Jell-O, those little biscuit candies Matt liked with the pandas on them, a pile of extra crispy bacon as high as his leg, berries, hot toast, hash browns, ramen, fried rice, pad Thai, sushi, and Indian, an entire circle of different curries. Matt struggled not to roll his eyes.

"I know you didn't cook this!" he called out into the white nothingness all around him. "God or no god!" Nevertheless, Matt was nothing if not practical and a firm believer in the old saying about gift horses and mouths, so he sat down at one of the long stone benches in front of the table, which of course had on top of it the softest, most comfortable cushions he'd ever sat on.

He ate in silence, heaping a little bit of this and that and everything in turn on a white porcelain plate until he was full to bursting, though he'd still only managed to try maybe a quarter of the food. Matt got up, grumbling about needing to use the restroom, only to find that off to the side of the table, down a narrower white alleyway, was an outhouse (in-house?) with the most luxurious toilet imaginable. The seat heated to the perfect temperature when he sat down, it sprayed warm water and hot air when he finished, and everything washed away in a soundless, stainless flush.

Overkill. Matt scowled, walking away without looking backward, but it was clear complaining wasn't going to do much.

He continued on past the table and down the huge white corridor, which after another minute or two, turned ninety degrees to the left again. This time, Matt found himself staring at a pen full of golden retriever puppies.

"This is absurd—" he began, but the puppies just continued whimpering, oblivious to his indignation, and though they had food and water, Matt—with a defeated sigh—had little choice but to climb into the pen and let the warm fluffballs scurry all over him, pawing and licking passionately at his face.

"Hey!" He laughed as the baby dogs continued to swarm. "Come on. Come on. Hey, come on, ha-ha. Oh God, that's so tickly; oh God, that's my ear—"

Matt didn't know how long it had been by the time he clambered free from the puppy pit, staggering forward in a stumble, his clothes a mess, covered in golden dog hair and swaying like he was drunk. It was difficult for that much cuteness and affection not to overwhelm the human mind.

"I see what you're trying to do!" he shouted, and again, Matt just assumed Jane by virtue of having created everything within a thousand nautical miles could hear him. "It's not working!"

It was working a little, Matt admitted internally. He rounded the next corner, again to the left. This time, he came face-to-face with a saddle-mounted triceratops. Matt sighed and leaned his hand up against the wall, staring at the very calm and docile dinosaur. For crying out loud.

The stretch of hallway went on for what felt like several kilometers, and Matt's dinosaur took some time with its steady plodding to carry him all the way to the end. On two or three occasions, Matt kicked his heels in and brought the beast up to a reasonable canter, but it felt a bit mean making it put in the extra effort when they were only really charging at empty walls.

"Whoa, Hildy," he soothed, pulling on the reins of the triceratops as they approached the next corner. "Whoa, easy, girl." Matt swung his leg around, sliding off her back, careful not to catch his loose pants on his companion's bony frill. "You stay there. Who's a good girl?" He scratched underneath the dinosaur's chin, used the reins to turn it away, and slapped it on the hindquarters to send it plodding back to where it had started. Not that this was probably necessary—Jane would doubtlessly ensure no harm came to the beast—but Matt was a well-bred, respectable dinosaur owner. Good people put away their toys.

Matt rounded the next corner to find, finally, the halls of the cathedral opening up into the titanic white doorway, and to see Jane standing out on the curved balcony, her back to him and the hall. Her arms were bare like yesterday, though the fabric she had wrapped around her was a slightly darker shade of white, if that was possible, and maybe a touch more formal.

"Did you enjoy your morning?" Jane asked, looking over her shoulder to fix him with a smug smile as he strode the last stretch of hallway. Matt stepped through the enormous rectangular gateway onto the terrace, struggling once more not to be blown away by the sight of sprawling paradise.

"I feel a bit condescended to." He managed to scowl, eventually tearing his eyes away.

Jane fixed him with a deadpan stare. "Don't," she warned. "I'm sick of fighting."

"I'm not trying to start anything."

"And yet, you always seem to."

"It takes two to tango," said Matt, but he held up his hands in a gesture of conciliation. "I was just saying. I don't know if I should be offended that that's what you think I'd enjoy."

"But did you enjoy it?" asked Jane, raising an eyebrow.

"Oh, immensely," he answered without a trace of a lie. "I just am a little sad I'm so predictable."

Jane smiled, but the expression slowly faded. The two stood there in silence.

"I'm just trying to show you that you can be happy," she mumbled. Matt stepped forward and took her hand.

"I am happy. I'm with you. I don't need all this."

"But why not have it, if you want it?"

"It's not my happiness I'm concerned about," he said. "Truly. It's everyone else's. I'm just worried about what will happen when you start bringing other people in."

"I don't have to," Jane said quietly. "If you wanted. It could just be us."

"What about my mom and dad, though? Jonas and Sarah? I want to see them again. Your dad. Don't you want to see him?"

"Of course," Jane replied. "I can bring them over. They can come."

"But they're going to have people they can't stand living without either. Friends who have families, who have . . . you know? Endless. Forever. Even if they don't, are we going to keep them from ever meeting anyone? Is Sarah going to be the only twelve-year-old in the world?"

Jane was silent. Matt pressed on.

"It's this endless chain," he continued. "Humanity. And not every piece links to every other, but ultimately, we're all bound. It's all or nothing. Or you're hurting both those coming and those left behind."

Jane rubbed her eyes with the heel of her hand. "I don't understand why this has to be so difficult," she muttered. "I'm not trying to do anything wrong."

"I know you're not. But something like this"—he gestured out across the verdant, shining landscape—"needs more than just good intentions. You're upending people's worlds."

"So it might not be perfect," Jane admitted, "in every way, in every facet. But shouldn't we not let perfection be the enemy of good?"

"Shouldn't we not destroy good in pursuit of better?"

"You are infuriating," she snapped. "You talk to me like I'm a baby, like I'm an idiot—"

"I talk to you like you're a person," Matt replied, refusing to be baited, staring at Jane head-on. "Like you're capable of thinking through the things you're doing and changing your point of view."

"I'm not moving on this," Jane told him. "I am going to right wrongs. I'm going to help people. Even"—her voice rose to preempt Matt—"the ones who don't want it."

"Including me?"

"What?" scoffed Jane, turning back as the sun rose over her kingdom. "You don't want paradise?"

"No," Matt answered quietly. "I want to leave."

"I want to leave," Matt repeated.

Jane's heart stopped beating.

"That's not funny."

"It's not a joke."

"You want . . . You want to leave?!" Suddenly, Jane turned on him, her dress spinning, the balustrade cracking where her hand clenched around the stone. "Is this not good enough for you?! Is all of this not good enough for you? Am *I* not good enough for you?!"

"That isn't it."

"What more do you want?!" she cried. "What more do you need? What possible, imaginable thing do you not have here that I cannot give you?! How much better could it possibly get somewhere else?!"

"It's not about that."

"Then what do you want?!"

"I want you to let go."

Jane stared at him, her chest rising and falling, her breathing heavy, feeling like her eyes were going to burst from her skull and bore through Matt's head.

"Let go."

"Yes. Let go of this." He took a step forward and grabbed a hold of her hand. "Come back with me to the real world."

"The real—?!" Jane spluttered, eyes wide and incredulous as she spun, tearing free from his grasp, gesturing at the land she had created, the paradise. "The real world?! Is this not real?! Is this not real enough—!"

"This is a fantasy!" Matt cried, shouting over the top of her. "A make-believe realm where nothing you don't want ever happens, and nothing is ever outside your control!"

"I'M DOING THIS FOR YOU!"

"I never asked you to," Matt replied quietly. The way he stood there, his face blank and unemotional, made Jane want to rip apart the very fabric of the sky.

"Give me one good reason," she demanded, finger shaking as she pointed at him. "One good reason why you should go, and I'll let you."

"Because I should be able to."

"THAT'S NOT A REASON!" she roared, and suddenly, the sunset sky spun thick with choking rainclouds, lightning thundering down and cracking across the land. Matt flinched, but he didn't recoil—only stared at her with that blank, unrelenting, infuriating stare, hands clasped quietly in front of him. Jane wanted to strangle him.

"You want to go?!" she shouted, rage swelling in her chest. "You want to leave?!"

"Yes."

"FINE!" she shouted. "FINE! YOU DON'T NEED ME? YOU DON'T NEED MY HELP? GO BE BY YOURSELF! GO BE ON YOUR OWN, SEE HOW FAR YOU GET. YOU'LL HAVE NOTH-ING! YOU'LL—*ARGH!*" With a wordless roar, she swung down her fist, and the balcony shattered into a million pieces, collapsing underneath them, sending Matt plummeting downward with a cry as she stayed flying, thousands of feet above the darkened ground.

The world swept gray and storming, and she glared, leering as he tumbled through the lightning-stricken sky, and it was only at the last moment, in her final, barest shred of mercy, that Jane wrenched her hand up and cut the impact from his fall. She watched with Divine eyes and sneered with Divine lips as far beneath her, Matt struggled to stand, shivering against the howling wind and sudden, driving rain, and her words thundered down atop the roaring tempest.

"Go then!" she bellowed. "Leave if you can! See what doing every-thing yourself gets you. See how your precious freedom tastes!" she spat out, and a flash of lightning split the heavens. "And don't bother trying to fly! Don't come to me for anything! I'm done with you. We're over; you'll get nothing from me!"

Jane glared down from the summit of Olympus.

"Walk on your own damn feet."

ALPHA & OMEGA

Human beings in a mob.
What's a mob to a king?
What's a king to a god?
What's a god to a nonbeliever?

—"No Church in the Wild,"
JAY-Z, Kanye West, and Frank Ocean

Matt Callaghan trudged through the dark, freezing rain.

He did not know where he was headed, where away was, if there was even a way off this planet, or if there was, whether it could be found or safely used. *Low orbit*, his brain kept nagging at him, and a part of him wondered if Jane would be so vindictive as to move the White World farther out into the deepest reaches of space so that even if Matt somehow did find an exit, it would lead to naught but asphyxiation and death.

If there even was a way out. This was a planet, spherical, with gravity. There was no escape hatch from Earth. Jane wouldn't have needed one to get in, so there was no reason to suspect she would have built one to get out. Still, Matt pushed on, if only because it was his choice to do so.

The rain was coming down hard, the ground squelching wet, the ankle-high grass buoyant and mobile atop sodden earth, mud sucking at his bare feet with every step. Matt's thin white clothes were soaked through, and before long, he'd had to remove his linen shirt to prevent the damp from sticking. Though the weather was warm, the rain temperate, it was not quite humid enough to be tropical.

About a mile in, he took cover under the branches of a large sequoia tree and ripped the shirt in half with a sharpened rock, tying each piece around his feet as many times as he could to make some form of makeshift shoes. They were beyond flimsy, as far as footwear went, and he had no idea how long they would last, but they might deflect the odd stone or bramble. It was better than nothing. In the current situation, they were the best Matt was going to get.

He kept walking, not throwing more than the occasional glance back at the tower, which was what he was mentally calling the impossibly high structure of pure white stone that jutted up and over the wall of the distant cliffs, the edge of Jane's utopia. The tower rose in a single, sheer flat surface, ninety degrees straight up, almost to the clouds, without so much as a bump or deviation, its flawless white now drenched in the storm clouds' shadow. Jane liked minimalism, he guessed. Or preferred her presence intimidating and stark.

Lightning flashed overhead, illuminating a herd of creatures moving in the distance, a slash of water off to his left, and the outer edge of the sequoia forest. The clouds were so dark, the rain's pounding so heavy that Matt could not tell what time of day it was meant to be, or whether the entire world had changed. If this place even had regular day-night cycles. For all he knew, the sky literally changed according to Jane's mood. Which was currently stormy, if you could pardon the pun, judging by the tempest crashing all around him.

Matt wiped rain from his hair and set off in the direction of the herd, having no real goal or direction. If all he could do was explore, then he'd explore. If he found some other genius thought or some other way, he'd take it. But he had to leave.

It'd been his only choice.

*   *   *

Jane hung, robes billowing in the storm-wracked sky, and glared with gritted teeth down at her fleeing lover.

How dare he? How dare—A thousand acts of cruelty and violence leapt, snarling, to the forefront of her mind, pain and fitting punishments she could inflict on this maddening imbecile for making her feel so damn enraged. *Leave? Leave?!* She'd break his nose, coat him in ceaseless white-hot flames, cut out his tongue, and sink his legs into stone for daring to . . . for having the audacity to . . .

No. Jane hissed to the churning storm clouds, her entire body trembling with seething, fervent anger. No. This was just what he wanted; he was trying to aggravate her, prove she was some petty, vindictive little girl, unstable and incompetent, incapable of creating utopia, unable to do anything right. Hurting him wouldn't do anything—pain would just prove his point.

High up in the thundering heavens, Jane clenched her fists and ground her teeth. Stupid, closed-minded idiot. Ignorant, infuriating man. She'd show him; she'd show all of them. She'd—*Argh!* In a rush of rage she spun and lashed out, sending a shudder through the earth, watching in the distance as her fury annihilated some far-off mountain range. *Fine. Fine!* He wanted to go, then let him. See how long he lasted, weak, soft fool. He'd get it out of his system— questioning her, being like this—the ungrateful little . . . *Argh!*

I don't care, Jane snarled, sucking storm-lit air between her teeth. *I don't care, I don't goddamn care.* What was he going to do, anyway? Where was he going to go? She had eternity—endless, endless eternity—and all the power in the world. He'd come back. He always came back.

To hell with him. Let him have his little protest; let him come crawling to her a week from now begging, pleading that he was wrong. She could almost hear him, see him, feel the immense satisfaction of being right. *Oh, really? Oh, this* is *the best you could've hoped for? What a goddamn shock. What an absolute revelation.* Maybe she wouldn't even punish him. Maybe she'd just smile; maybe she'd go straight to embracing him, just to show how righteous she was—make him see her benevolence as a god.

Still. The sheer nerve. It rankled her—it absolutely rankled her—and the more she turned and turned it over, the more she just wanted to tear fissures in the sky. Leave?! He wanted to leave?! Leave all of this; leave everything she'd built for them—leave *her*?! Unacceptable. No, she wouldn't have it. You don't get to leave perfection. Happiness wasn't *optional*. Nobody left her paradise.

You don't get to say when we're finished, Jane snarled at the wind—and in the dark, stormy distance, she watched a speck of a person struggling away from her into the night.

Matt sat shivering in a cave, watching the rain continue to fall.

His teeth chattered a little, and he kneaded his hands together, though it felt less like hypothermia and more just like his body trying to make itself warm. He'd be okay. He'd eaten a lot that morning, and this place was just wet, not cold. The rain would let up sometime. He could try to make a fire, find food. He'd be okay.

What am I doing? a part of him wondered. *Just go be happy, give in to her, get off your high horse, and get out of your own way.* But it was a strangely surface-level thought, not extending into real feeling or conviction. Deep down, Matt knew what he was doing was right.

Jane was going to end up hurting people, and he couldn't stop her, but he didn't have to help.

In the end, he knew, it might all become too much for him. The part of Matt that was afraid, that yearned for peace and a sense of comfort, might win out over abstract moral convictions, and he'd end up convincing himself that resistance was hopeless, that giving in was simply making the best of his current lot. Maybe, eventually, hunger, weariness, the deep-seated animal needs of his body would exert their irresistible power and force him to relent. But he hadn't gotten there yet. And just because you might not be able to do the right thing later wasn't a reason not to do it now.

Step by step. Choice by choice. I will do the best I can where I am, not just do what's best for myself.

Jane sat on a throne in an empty hall and glowered as she swept across her kingdom with her mind.

There were things to do—land that needed shaping. Yet, with Matt gone, it seemed all Jane could summon the energy for was to scowl and to occasionally throw inanimate objects, sending them shattering into the endless white stone walls. Things that broke she could repair with the barest glance, and time she had in limitless abundance, so it was not waste nor loss that gnawed at her. It was this boiling anger she was still feeling, searing beneath her white mark and silk vestments, the sensation so crude, so childlike, so revoltingly *human*. She hated Matt for making her feel like this. She hated herself for her unbidden silent retort that maybe he wasn't in charge of her feelings. She hated wondering if anything he said might've been true.

This frustration, too, was compounded by a splitting headache. Jane at first hadn't noticed the painful tightness creeping in under her forehead or the stinging beneath her temples, so rooted was she in the assumption that she was above such mortal displeasure. Yet, the pain continued to grow as if from a sleepless night or dehydration, which only made Jane grit her teeth, as obviously, she needed neither sleep nor water.

It did not take her long reflecting to find the culprit. A glaze of the eyes, a glance toward the shimmering tapestry of time, brought Jane face-to-face again with the paradox, the waiting jet-black maw consuming everything that ever was and ever will be. A choice, the Time Child had called it, back when he'd appeared to her in Morningstar. Every time Jane brushed the surface of time in concert with her other powers, she felt it lingering there, this darkened haze inching ever closer. It frustrated her more than frightened her now, because with her newfound Divinity, the idea of fear was laughable. There was nothing she could not overcome. And yet . . .

The darkness stared back at her, insentient, empty.

What the freaking hell was it? What could possibly be so wrong with the world, with the universe as a whole, that she couldn't destroy or correct it with all the powers at her disposal? What goddamn challenger could now possibly present itself that the power of a god could not overcome?

Yet, try as she might, think as she might, the blackened void still persisted, its gaping mouth an abyss swallowing all of reality whole. She had time, Jane thought. Literally, she should have had unlimited time. Yet every time Jane turned her eyes to the thing, she swore it inched closer. Grew larger. Consumed more of the glowing life threads.

What had the child said? "Someday soon, you will have to choose between Matt Callaghan and the world"? Something along those lines. But that was nonsensical now; she didn't have to. Matt and the world were still perfectly fine, their existences perfectly compatible. Every time she'd faced an instance where it'd seemed like she was going to lose one of them, where it'd looked like she'd have to make a choice, Jane had overcome it. And now, here she sat, godlike, with limitless power on a divine, unbroken throne.

So why was the singularity still looming?

"Go away," she growled at it. The pending collapse of the universe at the edge of her extratemporal vision did not hear her, instead continuing to mindlessly consume the sum total of reality. Jane balled her hands into fists. She was tempted to dive into time, to fly headfirst at the thing and blast it into nothingness, pummel it with enough golden light to tear the stupid thing asunder. But a small, quiet part of her knew that wouldn't work. And although she hated listening to that small part, for now, she resentfully heeded its words.

Work. She just had to continue the work. The problem was that the concept hadn't been clear enough. If she could just push on, create more, really show Matt her vision of a functioning paradise, then maybe he would snap out of whatever crusade he thought he was on and bring his stupid ass home.

Jane closed her eyes and envisioned the cities: towers of glass and silver and marble, waterfalls flowing from rooftop lakes, and sidewalks blossoming with flowers. She imagined the underground caverns, cities of stone never needing the sun, stalactites ringed with gold lighting, deep and cool and flowing serene into the earth's calm heart. She imagined floating metropolises, towers and domes on metal wings soaring adrift rising thermals, skies of glass and latticework, souls never touching the ground. She imagined it all—she imagined everything—and then, when Jane reached down with her hands, she created it, her four rings alive and singing, spinning all the complexity she could dream.

The night sky opened before him, and Matt Callaghan gazed in quiet wonder up at the drifting celestial clouds.

Green and yellow. Purple, blue. A painted rift of stars and galaxies spun above him, so close he could almost touch them, their soft colors illuminating the world below.

It had been three days now. The rain had stopped, the clouds finally parted, the sun rising, and the sun setting. Matt was not completely confident that it did so in the same place every morning and every evening, or that that place was west or east or that such directions even existed here. He was not sure if the days were twenty-four hours long and constant, nor that time moved the same way it did back on Earth. He suspected maybe it didn't. Yet, he kept counting sunrises all the same.

For three days, Matt had just kept walking. The thin linen "shoes" he'd fashioned had predictably disintegrated in short order, but the grass was soft in most places, and he soon found the soles of his feet turning hard. At first, Matt had been worried about going hungry and about the animals, but those two fears were soon revealed to be baseless. There were ripe, overabundant fruit trees hanging thick with apples, pears, and oranges scattered in groves as he passed, and bushes of mulberries and blackberries growing wild around every hill and corner.

The predators—lions and tigers, crimson-green and sometimes feathered velociraptors, and a pack of what looked like giant three-headed wolves—all seemed to avoid him, simply skirting out of his way, their eyes glazing over him, or their approaches being deterred by his uniquely human scent. The smaller creatures conversely showed no fear at a person approaching, and Matt had been able to very easily catch fish by standing in a stream and letting them swim between his outstretched hands. This was a world devoid of danger, he soon realized. He'd scaled the fish with a bit of obsidian he'd found among the stones on the shoreline, and cooked it beneath a rocky overcrop on a fire of broken branches and paperbark, watching as, in the distance, a dragon frolicked and dived. Matt had never been very outdoorsy, but his mom had taken him and his siblings camping a few times and shown them a couple of things. It wasn't luxury, but he could make do.

Matt continued, often, to wonder what he was doing—or maybe, what Jane was doing, if she really was actually through with him, resigned to letting him wander the wilderness forever until he died of old age. Maybe this was her giving him the life she thought he wanted; maybe this was her idea of punishment. Maybe she was genuinely ignoring him, and once she felt like he'd had sufficient days in the time-out corner, she would magically appear, and he would be transported back to the palace. In a way, though Matt didn't know, it didn't matter. He couldn't predict nor control Jane's actions. He could only control himself.

Matt stuck to the shade during the daytime, meandering slower in most instances or resting on beds of soft grass beneath shady trees. Despite this, by the third day, the skin on his arms and neck was becoming more golden, and his legs stronger and more certain. His beard was starting to grow. He walked mainly at night, the path illuminated by the blanket of stars and the irregular path of the moon, which strayed much closer than it did on Earth, hanging huge and silver in the sky. He still did not have a destination, only a general sense of purpose, a desire to wander and be free.

It was on his fourth night, when he stopped in a cave overlooking a river to rest and take shelter, that Matt found the dog. He had just lit a fire—getting better at it each day with practice—and was warming his hands when, from the back of the cavern, he heard a whimpering sound. Matt turned around, peering curiously into the darkness, then pulled a smoldering stick out from the fire and made his way cautiously deeper inside. In the back, among a pile of fur and bones, a puppy sat whimpering, white and stringy haired, with splotches of black and brown, floppy triangular ears, amber eyes, and a fat stomach. Matt wondered how it had come to be there, but then, he saw one of its feet was twisted, and it was struggling to walk. Maybe the mother, for whatever reason, had moved on, forced to leave the runt.

"Hey, little one," Matt whispered. He bent down and scooped up the whimpering puppy, who was shivering with cold and terribly scrawny. Matt brought it back to the fire, holding it firm against his chest. "Here you go."

He waited for several hours with the little dog in his arms before it stopped shaking, feeding it morsels of fish and talking to it in a calm voice about everything, anything in the world. By the time the sun rose, the puppy was sleeping. The following day, Matt searched around until he found a plant with strong-looking leaves of a sort he'd repeatedly come across, and with much trial and error, jerry-rigged a kind of rudimentary harness. From there, the little pup stayed strapped to Matt's chest, bobbing as he continued to walk. They carried on, past wide, mist-covered lakes where huge, finned serpents stirred while flocks of gray dodos squawked on rocky shorelines, heading toward a distant mountain rising up into the sky.

"Dammit."

Jane rolled back a few seconds in time, glaring at Ironleaf City's wireless networking system, which continued to resist her attempts to fix it now and for all eternity. It worked in the present well enough, but Jane could see the lines of reality twisting around to indicate that in a few months' time, the network would inexplicably slow down again. She was a god. A freaking god. It was Wi-Fi. Why was it so hard to make the freaking Wi-Fi work?

The work was continuing—the cities built, the planet expanded to a size she believed was currently adequate. Beautiful, empty metropolises dotted the land, atop and beneath oceans, among the jungles, the snows, and the heavens, each one as unique and different as she could make it, and each one ready to receive all those who strove to reside there. She would make modifications once the people came, of course, to adjust for whatever they needed beyond what the silhouettes of the life threads told her. Humanity would want for nothing. Or so she'd initially thought.

The first batch of humans she'd imported had been a source of near-constant frustration. The first city done, the other work unfolding, Jane had reasoned she needed randomized test subjects, so had simply ascended up to her planet a random subway carriage of New Yorkers. All had arrived simultaneously, with only what they were wearing and carrying, and all had been told they were now children of paradise, congratulations. They would want for nothing; they need only ask, and they would receive, would be provided for entirely. They would live long, happy lives free from pain and suffering. They were unchained, limitless, free to do as they wished.

For the majority of people she'd transported, this news had been met with understandable shock, confusion, and excitement, followed mostly by joy and acceptance. A few people had asked for their dogs, and one long-haired Russian man for his bird, all of which Jane was fine with, all of which was perfectly doable. They settled in to explore the city, the world and its many wonders, marveling at the majesty all around them, searching out places to call their home.

Yet there were some, Jane found as she scowled, who were being nothing but difficult. Some inexplicably lurching toward idiotic, mean, or self-serving behavior even when there was a literal god in front of them, paradise at their beck and call, and an entire planet open and ready to provide pure luxury and happiness.

There was one sleek-haired man in his midthirties who, about five minutes after the transportation hit, ran straight up to the tallest of the unoccupied city towers and began tearing off metal sheeting to hastily scrawl signs, claiming it as *his* private property. He did that to three other entire skyscrapers—to the point of yelling at other people stopping by that they couldn't come in unless they rented from him—before Jane teleported him into the middle of the desert. He was a faunamorph, able to turn into a snake, so Jane knew he would get out of there eventually, but she couldn't see his behavior changing, and she wasn't certain what she'd do when he got back.

There was another woman who complained about the food and a lack of a movie theater. Jane, appearing incorporeally before her, asked her to describe what it was she wanted to eat, and offering to transport it through to her. Yet, everything the woman requested and Jane delivered, the hag for some reason deemed "stale," "unacceptable," or "fake" by virtue of some issue not even Jane's omniscience could divine. The woman's dietary requirements also seemed to change daily, and even with the ability to perceive both past and future, Jane struggled to placate her and struggled to keep up.

She made her a movie theater, no problem, which the woman soon came to perpetually occupy, but within a week, she and another resident almost came to blows over his desire to watch something other than the woman's soap opera, which she sat gawking at all day, transfixed by the inanity playing out on the silver screen. Jane had been forced to transport the pyromancer man to the opposite end of the city and extinguish the fire he'd started in the cinema curtains, which he'd not been happy about even once she'd manifested him a theater of his own, and even when she'd assured him he could burn this one down to his heart's content.

Then there was Mister Abdul Aziz al-Maliki, penitent Muslim, who refused to settle in at all, instead wandering around the city refusing food, water, and shelter, crying Arabic phrases and wailing, "I worship no god but Allah!" Despite Jane literally appearing in front of him and performing miracles, he refused to even so much as go inside, and his screaming soon began to annoy the other residents. After three days, Jane was finding it hard to resist the urge to drop a boulder on his legs and see if his precious Allah lifted a finger to intervene.

Then there were Mr. and Mrs. O'Brian. Although initially ecstatic at the time of landing, the couple soon had come into serious dispute after it was revealed that Mr. O'Brien, who possessed superbreath, had viewed his transportation to paradise as rendering his vows of monogamy obsolete. Mrs. O'Brien, who had supersenses, had, upon finding him gleefully entangled with another woman, repeatedly tried to stab him.

Jane had, naturally, seen the whole thing coming, yet felt hand-tied to do nothing but intervene at the time of conflict to prevent bloodshed, transporting the O'Briens a couple of hundred miles apart. Yet, Mrs. O'Brien had held on to the knife and swore every night to the starry heavens that she was going to track that man down and murder him. And she was, to Jane's displeasure, slowly making good on her promise, every day narrowing the distance between them as she trekked relentlessly across Jane's world.

Then, finally, there were the children. A small excursion of schoolchildren had been on the subway, who Jane had expected, maybe hoped, would delight in a world of abundance and openness, free from rules. Yet many of them just screamed for their parents. Okay, Jane allowed, that was understandable. She'd brought in the children's parents. Then those parents wanted to bring their friends. And their friends had their own children. And soon, what was initially meant to be a small proof of concept had blown out in number threefold, and Jane was spending half her days in the timestream trying to correct and anticipate every need.

"I miss my home," some people kept crying. Eventually, Jane got so angry she just started sending them back. *If you want to leave, fine, no one's stopping you. No one's keeping you in paradise.* She seethed with every one she transported back, refusing to admit the irony.

And so, the nights swam ever onward, and day after day, Jane found her gaze inevitably drifting back to Matt—back to the small, stubborn human and his new companion as they wandered her wonder-strewn world. Day after day, she watched them, night after night, for glimpses, then minutes, then hours, as Matt hummed to himself, as he talked to the dog, as he sometimes sang, and as they made their way slowly across the wilderness, bearing no destination save *on*.

"Come on, bud."

Matt smiled and beckoned a hand to the black-and-white puppy. The dog scampered out from behind a thick chicle tree, having been chasing a bright, quick turquoise lizard, tongue flapping and tail wagging happily in response to its master's call. It was able to run on its own now, the swelling in its foot subsided, and was growing bigger by the day. Matt had named it Scraps.

They wandered through a jungle-spun city, a dense forest of temperate, flourishing green so lush and verdant Matt often found himself wanting to stop and just run up and rub his face all over it. The city, too, was an engineering marvel—quite impossible, he suspected, without a Divine hand's guidance. The buildings were not built next to trees but around them, trunks and branches swept into walls and rooftops, soft whites and muted silvers matching the wood's natural twist and flow. There were no roads, only leaf-strewn paths, and up above the city streets hung a thousand vine-linked bridges and canopies. Birds sang in every color, monkeys swung outside glass domes. It was exquisite. It was more beautiful than Matt could have ever dreamed. He marveled once more at Jane's imagination and all the wonders still yet to see.

The city had also, happily, supplied him with a couple of new shirts, some packaged food, and a backpack, which had been sitting unattended and clearly awaiting eventual human consumption in a number of green-tinged stores. Matt had plucked out a few without hesitation, secretly glad to no longer be seminaked and getting a bit sick of fish and berries. For Scraps, too, he found a little bowl and some filtered water, a red ribbon, and for his fur, a children's comb. One night, they slept in a penthouse suite, with the dog splayed across the bedspread, utterly alone and watching the dawn mists drift over the city's green and living canopy.

It was not quite living off the land, but in this strange world, the cities seemed just as alive as the animals, the forests as man-made as they were organic. It was a beautiful place, and still, Matt kept on walking, looking for a way to leave. Searching for the edge of paradise. Looking for the way back home.

The city functioned. People had moved out into estates, into farms. The lakes, the rivers, the mountains. There was peace, prosperity, order. In her empty hall atop her white stone tower, Jane sat unmoving in her seamless throne, eyes flickering from white to blue to yellow to red to white to blue to black again. Her lips mumbled, her eyes slow and sightless, her fingers only occasionally twitching, yet she moved more than anyone could ever see. She was submerged—sunken deep within the color-woven waters, between the ripple and the rock, the darkness and the light. Soon, she would not dwell on this throne, in this reality, but sink to where the threads were deepest, disappear into the world between the walls. She saw everything her people were, what they would be, what they would ask for before they wanted it. She knew their needs, gave them fulfillment—purged disease, kept the world in balance. Kept everything in bloom.

Jane prevented now, rather than cured. For desolation, anger, every kind of human affliction. Problems were fixed before they ever manifested, and the problems stemming from those solutions she then resolved separately themselves. If a soul required fulfillment of one kind, she gave it. If thus fulfilled, they yearned instead for something different, that too was met. Yet sometimes, as Jane found herself looking ahead through turn after turn of action and reaction, satisfaction and desire, her blue eyes found no way to permanently resolve their problems. No actual answer. She had every kind of key, yet using them changed the shape of the lock.

She tried not to dwell long on the futility of the helpless. There was so much to do, to control, in her test city, now test country, as her initial subjects spread. There was the constant maneuvering of their lives, the minute twitching of small coincidences, keeping that person from ever running into this one, preventing this emotional response, or provoking this negative thought. If two people were incompatible, she twisted their roads so they would avoid each other. If someone would one day yearn for something someone else held, they were guided subtly to a substitute. Nudges and bumps, sudden rains, untied shoes, and flocks of birds. Those who could not cope with paradise, mentally, she transported back to Earth, returned them to their original location. She would deal with them—the obstinate, the absurd, and the simply mentally ill—when her initial utopia had been mastered.

Today was like any day. People moved, gifts were created from thin air, and mountains rearranged themselves. Jane diverted the path of a wife who would look jealously upon another woman so she need not ever see beauty that would trouble her, would never feel that sting of hurt. Jane had already changed the woman's body as she'd requested, but it was still insufficient, and there was something about the happiness of this other person that would cause Rachel Malley a deep and piercing grief.

An older regenerator, Percy, ran staunchly, outspokenly conservative, and so Jane directed him away from an elasticisable, dreadlocked man to prevent triggering a violent argument. Both men fancied they would make good mayors of this new colony; both would turn violently angry if they lost. So, Jane had created another separate city, divided along ideological lines, to be ruled by the second man.

Her time's eye turned to a young couple then. A man and a woman, their names unimportant, who would meet and have a future. Jane wandered through their lifelines, seeing the relationship sour, seeing it cause pain, lifeless, gray. She moved her hand to stop them meeting—yet, as she did, she hesitated. Before her, their lifelines untangled, but now she felt less in them; less happiness, less color. She waved her hand backward, letting them meet. The joy returned. But then, again, the conflict. Jane flicked forward, trying to prevent it, remove the onset of rot. Yet, they were doomed to failure. Yet, they were happy after it happened. Yet, the loss brought pain. Yet, never meeting brought loss.

And suddenly, alone in the throne room, in her white eternal hall, Jane found herself crying. Silently, openly weeping, tears flowing quietly from her shifting colored eyes. She saw the couple's life together, and it was beautiful, felt their heartache and their grief. Saw the pain fade but never truly heal; watched them age and grow. He met someone else and found happiness, grew into a better man, a loving parent; she did too. But without the pain, the joy, the experience, it happened for neither of them. Darkness begot light begot darkness. Hurt led to change led to growth.

And suddenly Jane was staring back, remembering, looking at her own timeline, her own immutable path. She saw every failure and defeat, every slight and setback. Not all of them had made her stronger—but they had all made her *her*. They were cracks and chips in porcelain that one by one she'd filled with gold. Beaten down, so working harder. Falling for a false man so she knew what it was to love a real one. She remembered standing in the center of an arena, beaten, broken, and bloodied, yet utterly ecstatic, delirious with pain yet not wanting to change anything for the world. Without loss, without struggle, there never was that moment. In the streets of Detroit, a lifetime of pain and resentment pressing down, it had not been her strength that turned her from Klaus Heydrich. It had been her mother's face. The strength of loss.

Alone as soft rain began to weep over her cathedral, Jane released her hands from the timestream and allowed the couple to meet, knowing the pain before them—and returning them their choice.

The aurora washed over starlit skies, and Matt marched on atop the snowfall, singing tunelessly as he walked. Scraps, near full grown, nipped at his heels, and Matt turned the song toward him, singing senseless, nothing tunes of light and life and love. Around them, snowflakes fell in a gentle dusting, the muscles in Matt's legs burning as they ascended the mountain further and further up, heading to nowhere within understanding, still simply searching for somewhere left to go.

"Oh-ho my love . . . Oh-ho my . . . silver moons and handkerchiefs . . . and little puppy dog tails . . ."

The words sang gently out, swirling up to meet the aurora—a normal one, not a magical one—flickering lines of green and blue. It was beautiful, and again, Matt marveled. The light, the being, the experience. The pinch in his lungs, the aching cold. He was alive, he had a song, and he had chosen to be here. Tomorrow, he might choose to come back down. Or chase dreams of freedom hidden high within the clouds.

His boots crunched, the snow not much more than an inch or so thick. They were still relatively low down. Higher up, he might have to hope this was one of those places where Jane built a colony. Or he might have to hunt a deer, find some furs.

Possibilities.

"Matt."

Matt stopped and turned his head, swearing he could have heard his name whispered in the wind. He glanced around, seeing only fir trees, a stony trail, snow-dusted boulders. He frowned, wondering if hallucinations signaled the onset of frostbite.

"Was that you?" he asked, glancing down at the dog.

"It was me."

Matt spun around, and suddenly, he was in the white room again, staring at Jane, clad in shining white.

Matt looked back over his shoulder. The mountain had entirely vanished, like it had never even been there. His face puckered in annoyance.

"Was I getting close?" he asked, though more lighthearted than irritated. At his feet, Scraps barked, growling at the sudden change in their surroundings from mountainside to eternal hall.

Jane sniffed. Her eyes were red, but not the crimson kind. "Not even a little," she murmured.

"Darn." Matt glanced down at Scraps, then back at her. "Thanks for bringing the dog."

"He seems to like you."

"He goddamn better," Matt said, glaring down at the black-and-white puppy, who met his gaze and cocked its head.

They were silent for a moment.

"Can we talk?" Jane whispered.

"I never closed the door on that," Matt replied.

"You walked a long way away."

"From my girlfriend, who has no concept of distance."

Jane hiccupped. "So we're still dating?"

"I am if you are," he said. "Again, it's just been me and the dog."

Jane let out a snort; a small, short laugh. The sound of it faded, still against the whiteness. Jane sniffed. Matt's features softened.

"What's wrong?" he asked her.

"I don't know," she whispered. "I'm seeing things; I'm feeling things I don't want to . . . It's all too much." She shuddered and closed her eyes, and when she opened them, Matt saw that they were flashing through with colors, one after the other, over and over and around.

"I feel so alone," Jane whispered. "I'm so many things to so many people. Why do I feel so alone?" And she sobbed as she said it, really, truly crying, the first time Matt had ever seen her do so. Instinctively, he moved toward her. Without thinking, he folded her within his arms.

"It's okay," he murmured, cradling her soft, warm head; the goddess. "It's okay." For a moment, they just stood there, the weight of Jane's soul leaning into him, her limbs heavy and helpless. Matt moved his hands to her shoulders and forced them apart, held her upright, looking into her flickering eyes.

"Stop," he said.

"I can't."

"You can. You have to. It's okay if you can't do it. It's okay for it to be too much."

"That's the thing, though," Jane mumbled, and her eyes continued churning with colors as fresh tears leaked from the sides. "I *can* do it. I know I can. If I let myself, if I fall back. But I . . . I can feel it, Matt. It's never going to stop. It's never going to be enough. I want to help them, stop their pain, but the more I control . . ." She trailed off into a sob. "It's too late. I'm too deep. I'm going to become God. For all of them, for everything. And I will force this world to be perfect. And I will force them all to be happy. It feels so wrong."

She stared at him, her eyes trailing starlight. "Please. You can help me. I . . . I can give you my powers. You can be a god too. We can do this together. Always. I want to be with you. I want us to be happy."

"Then come with me," Matt murmured.

"Where?"

"Out. Away from here. Away from this world."

"Matt." Jane's face was pained. "In here, you won't be hurt. Nothing will ever harm you."

"And I'll never be harmed," Matt said quietly. "Never know loss, never know pain, never feel sad. Never feel the weight of failure and know I have to do better. I'll be a god, but I'll never be a better person—just stuck, divinely forever, in this beautiful snow globe. And you'll be stuck with me, never failing. Never changing. Never growing."

"Would that be so bad?" she whispered.

"It would feel good," he answered truthfully. Then, after a moment: "It would be wrong."

For a few seconds, Jane said nothing. Then she sniffed, and an edge of hardness crept back into her voice.

"I could stop you," she murmured. "I could stop you leaving. I could keep you here, forever, with me, and we'll never be alone or apart."

"If you do that," Matt told her, "I'll leave you."

Jane's shoulders slumped, and she stared at him with such pain it was as though he had just driven a knife into her heart.

"What?"

"I'll leave you," Matt repeated. "Even if you try to stop me physically, I will run away from you, with my body and my soul, for the rest of my days, until all the stars go out."

Jane's throat clenched. She could barely squeeze out words.

"But why?"

"Because it's the only thing I can do," said Matt, and though he spoke the words kindly, he did not flinch from them nor the pain that uttering them caused. "Look around," he said to her gently. "Look at me. You are so incredibly powerful. Beyond anything I can ever accomplish. Beyond anything I can dream. What can I do? There is nothing I can do to stop you, literally nothing I can do or say or offer that you can't simply brush aside. You're a god," he urged, "and I'm a man. And I can tell that all this"—he waved his arm around at the cavernous chamber, at the waiting door to the impossible world—"is wrong. Worse, it's hurting you. Destroying who you really are. Who you might be.

"I have nothing left to give," he told her. "No way to fight; no card to play. Save one. Only one. I can leave, and I can deprive you of the only thing I can offer: my heart, my care, my love. And you can stop me. That's the thing, you know; I understand it. You can stop me. You can reach into my mind and change my choice and strip away my free will. And you can force me to love you and never leave and be with you forevermore. And I'll never know it was done."

He fell silent for a moment and stared up at her. "But you will."

Jane let out a wretched sob, her shoulders shaking. "Please. Please." And she twitched toward him, her hands reaching out, only to stop, her face a tapestry of loneliness and pain.

But Matt was not there to hurt her. And in an instant, he stepped forward and wrapped Jane in his arms, her eyes drowning in colors and tears.

"Listen to me. Listen," he begged her. "I love you. I don't want to leave you. I don't have to. But you cannot be a god." His voice wavered, and he averted his gaze. "No; you can. But you shouldn't. Because a god's not who I fell in love with. And being a god won't make you happy. Being a god won't save mankind."

"But . . ." Jane hiccupped, "without me . . ."

"The world will keep turning." Matt leaned back, cupping her tearstained chin, and gently took Jane's face between his hands. "I've been thinking about it a lot," he said softly, "as I walked, as I strayed. About God and gods and humanity and purpose. Wondering what I was doing; wondering ultimately what the point of it all was. Whether I should just accept unnatural happiness here, whether I should try and embrace it, whether I'm being a fool to fight this change. Clinging to the notion that what matters as a person are your choices."

Matt gazed out as the white walls slid down around them, revealing the glowing, windswept land. "Maybe there was a God once," he said quietly. "Maybe there was some being who created the universe, created us, shaped our world. Maybe they guided our every step, truly wanted what's best for us, like all loving parents should. But I think—I think I've realized now, if there was a god, then they released us. Because they realized they were doing wrong. Because they realized that loving something isn't the same as controlling it—that the greatest gift they could ever give mankind was the power to choose."

They stood atop a palace of white impossibility, all walls crumbled away, hands in hands, gazing into each other's eyes as lights danced across the heavens.

"Maybe," said Matt, "that's what the Aurora gave us. Maybe that's why it came. Because we're growing up now. And God wanted to give us potential. They wanted to give us a choice."

And suddenly Jane's heart surged, and she felt the universe calling, loud and deep within her very bones. Her eyes filled with every color between the stars, and when she looked up, the sky danced not just with aurora but a trillion lines of light and life, shining bright and intertwined. They sang to her, their spinning lives—every sound a melody. And beneath them hummed the maw—that yawning, gaping vortex that threatened to swallow all of existence, from the end of time to the beginning, without malice, without knowing, a consequence, a cavern's heart. And it was her choice now, her head on which the universe swayed, poised to tip, poised to sing forever into radiance or collapse eternal into the dark.

And Jane knew what she had to do.

On an impossible world, a paradise of her own creation, where sunlit buildings scraped the heavens and the world hummed and gleamed with life, she let go of Matt's hands and wrapped her arms around him, pulling close the man she loved, kissing him long and soft and deep. They stayed like this, like it would last forever.

Then, she let go of his arms, and they parted. Matt gazed at her with confused eyes.

And Jane disappeared into nothingness.

The girl sank back through light and dark, through the shining web, the spinning cosmos. She sank backward into time, through the clear black water, until it covered her chest, her neck, her head, her hair drifting cool and free and silent. Farther and farther down beneath the surface, where eternity waited. Soft rush, soft glow. For once, the life threads did not pull at her as she slid through, instead simply rippling softly, a forest of glistening kelp shimmering gently all around. Her body sunk, deeper and deeper. Down, down, down into utter, clear-glass blackness—into the very tapestry of light.

The cold, soothing water washed against her eyes, and the colors stopped flickering, fading back, releasing. They melted together, and it was her own eyes that awaited. Eyes that finally knew the path once traveled. Eyes that saw her circled footsteps. Eyes that saw the world.

She lifted her head and righted herself, the veil of time spinning free from her. She stepped out, unseen, into a moment, onto a swath of verdant grass. A willow tree. A parking lot. Garbed in flowing white, her eyes clear, her lips closed, soft skin glimmering in the sunlight.

She drifted with silent steps into the hospital: angel, wraith, and godmother. Come to take; come to bless.

Bare feet padded on the linoleum, down corridors and around corners, free from sight, unintrusive, flowing in soft white waves. When the nurses turned, when the doctors glanced, their eyes found only space emptied by seconds; perhaps a shimmer, the air left faintly aglow. But her trail hung no more than dust suspended in sunlight, a feeling of warmth for them—of safety.

Jane glided through the world as if a vision in a dream, ceaseless songs singing softly inside her.

She found them in a room behind the glass—a viewing panel. Two dozen lives; two dozen lights. Here was one who would love many. Here was one who would soar among the clouds. Here was one who would carry others' burdens. Here was one who would keep faith.

Little soul. Little light. She drifted through the window like it was never there, and she stood, eyes floating over the rows of cribs, auburn hair and white robe waving with the kiss of wind and unseen stardust. She gazed down at them—at all of them—as she waded between the rows, one by one, until she found him. The one she had chosen. She surveyed him, soft and loving. Unseen, she bent down and kissed him, the barest touch of her lips against his tiny, soft-pink forehead. For a moment, the child glowed. Then, the glow faded, gone but never vanished. Merely hidden. Hiding fate.

The goddess rose. She turned, drifting from the nursery and back out into the hospital, as if she was never there. She left no footprints, no ripple or change behind her.

Save one.

A tiny, pink-skinned baby, shifting beneath a cotton blanket, bearing the barest wisp of newborn hair, its tiny fingers curled. Looking, for all the world, completely normal. Distinguished from others only by the label on the bassinet.

Matthew Callaghan
August 24, 1982

Outside, in the sunshine, her bare feet stepped once more atop the grass. And then all she had to do was look. Look up. At the sky, the sun, the clouds—

And suddenly, Jane was flying. Soaring, free, heart racing, white cloth whipping around her, flickering against the sky.

She rose, farther and farther, through layers of white and blue and indigo, back through the singing darkness, the star-spun shining sea. The endless expanse opened to greet her, and there was music waiting in the abyss; a song of purpose, life, and joy. She rose into space, and the currents of time rose with her, the life lights spinning, swirling heavens as her guide. There was no more sadness. There was no more grief. Only an aching sense of purpose and a fulsome life well spent.

She knew what she must do. She would do it. It was already done.

With eyes open, she flew forever into the abyss, to weightlessness, to tranquility. Bathed in distant sunbeams, her head swum with infinity and oblivion, with togetherness and solitude. She flew and flew and flew, a floating shining pinprick, until all sense of place was lost to her, until she was but another speck, drifting out among the stars. Alone, but never alone, against the great cosmos. Flying farther than any man had flown.

Finally, she stopped. Finally, her journey ceased. The returning road, the destiny, stretched starlit behind her. And a million miles away, the Earth. A mote of dust, suspended in a sunbeam. Hers to love. Hers to keep.

In the deepest reaches of space, Jane Walker closed her eyes, her white robes rippling in the void, hair floating out in silent wisps. Free from constraint, free from longing—free to save the world she'd always known.

Jane's shoulders clenched, and she hunched in on herself, hands clutching to her breast, curling into a fetal ball. Her fingers tightened around the light in her chest, and from between them, in a ball of barest threads, a power began to grow. A golden orb, smaller than a thimble, yet dense—thick and molten—shining brilliant like the sun. Her hands clenched, the ball grew, and her body shook with power.

And for the last time, Jane Walker's eyes shone gold. A gold the world would know.

Everything Jane had, she poured into it. Everything she'd been; everything she was. Every hope and dream and passion, tearing from her chest into the sphere, a light that grew ever larger, on and on, spreading between her hands in opaque waves of liquid gold, impossibly powerful, impossibly dense. Her hands drew back, the power growing, and the very fabric of space rippled and shimmered as Jane unleashed into this power every fragment of her soul.

The golden orb grew. And in the center of the white fabric flowing atop her heart, Jane's body began to fade. Inch by inch, atom by atom, pieces broke off from the core of her, leaving a growing, drifting hole, a pit deepening in her center. Yet still she gave. Still, she poured every piece of herself into the orb. And when the pain of it became too much to bear, when the song became too loud, Jane ripped back her hands with a wordless roar, and the cosmos exploded in light.

A titanic veil, a rippling cloud, like a sheet of golden fabric, billowing and transparent, a hundred feet high, a thousand, shot out from the shining figure at its center in waves of radiance and joy. It spread and spread and spread until you could barely see the girl within it, her arms held aloft, light flowing from her hands, every piece of her consumed. In the depths of space, there swelled a wave of shining brilliance, greater than anything ever imagined—

And in an instant, it was set free. Hurtling off into the nothingness, no trace of its creator remaining. Only motes of light, ash, among the stars as the goddess's work rushed forward, now and forever done.

The Earth stood unaware.

Silent and alone, a blue-green marble floating in the black. Across its surface teemed humanity and everything humanity brought: chaos and noise, movement and life. But out here, from far enough away, mankind's machinations faded into irrelevance. Watched from afar, the Earth was peaceful.

A silent sphere swimming through an ocean of stars.

The date by human time was July 6, 1963.

And a wave of golden light was billowing toward the Earth.

EPILOGUE
THE ASHES

Giselle Pixus stared quietly out of her office window, slowly tracing her gaze across the cloudless sky. A thousand emails cried out from the laptop in front of her—a thousand problems, a thousand requests. Giselle sat silent, opening none of it. Her fingers shifted, and a pen slid idly over and around her knuckles, looping in pointless circles, petty and inadequate.

W. Reid, the engraving read, carved into the silver. An heirloom or a collectible, arguably. Giselle toyed with it regardless.

An outdated relic from a bygone era, some might claim. The wrong tool for the job: outmatched, dried out, empty. Yet, she held it all the same. The pen remained mighty, and though the world's troubles grew ever greater, with time, it might surmount them. Surely, she mused as she turned it slowly between her fingers, hope could still prevail.

The world churned with problems. Jane Walker and Matt Callaghan remained missing, vanished without any trace or explanation. Word of Pastor Fredericks, the resurrected soldiers, and New York had leaked, though thankfully, not of the Cao Duan twins, who remained safely contained in the Academy for study, therapy, and guard. Yet, the greater social crisis loomed. The notion of undeath did not go easily back into the bottle. There was rioting in the streets; not since the Year of Chaos had the superhuman world been so wracked with violence, with panic, stemming from a new discovery, a fundamental rewriting of basic laws. Freaking Divines; freaking celestial phenomena. Although this time, it seemed to mainly be the religious and the spiritual rather than the ignorant who were having trouble settling down.

Then there were the missing. An entire subway car—a quarter train of unremarkable people—had vanished into nothingness like they'd never even gotten on. That would have been enough of a headache on its own had the bastards not then started reappearing. In drips and drabs at first, irate busybodies and crazy people, only for others connected to the missing to inexplicably vanish. And then, all of them returned at once. In their hundreds. Speaking of a world, a goddess. Impossibilities that sparked international inquest and concern. A thousand more questions unanswered. Every knot untied entangling a dozen more.

Peter Walker had disappeared. Giselle had no idea what that was about. Had he likewise been abducted, or had he simply learned of his daughter's disappearance and set to walking? Him gone, but not the Callaghans. What in the flaming hell was Jane playing at? What was she doing? Why wouldn't she communicate?

If she was even still out there. Jane Walker absorbed the powers of a god and then vanished, and not twenty-four hours later, Matt Callaghan vanished with her, neither seen nor heard from again.

The pen spun around and around Giselle's fingers. *Is your perfect world still up there, Jane the God? Are you still taking your time to build it?* It'd been months now, almost a year. The disappearances had stopped, the vanishing hand unvanished, returned wide-eyed and drenched in stories. All quiet on the transcendent front. Had Jane given up, Giselle wanted to know. Had Matt talked her out of it? Or had she broken under the strain. Had she snapped, and the poor, defenseless boy finally fallen victim to her explosive temper? Were there forces more sinister at work—other gods jealously guarding the cosmos—and her friends' bones now lay broken among nameless stars, solar winds scattering their ashes?

Or maybe Matt, maybe, bearing blood mundane and human, had pulled off the one thing that could stop her . . . the most unlikely, remarkable play . . .

Giselle no longer knew what to think. There was work to do, constantly, and though damaged by the storm of mysteries swirling around the late Lady Dawn, the Legion endured. It had pulled the world from crisis once; it could do it again. Even better this time. One by one, these problems would be beaten.

And then. And then.

Her hand slowly closed the thin laptop, her mind racing far afield from mundane tasks. Giselle Pixus rose to her feet and walked quietly to the window, gazing out at the sun-drenched land beyond. The Academy lawn bristled with the tips of rockets, receiver dishes, and unlaunched satellites. Teleporters trying techniques in custom-built chambers; flyers testing polycarbonate space suits. Azleena's war machines stomped around the grounds, eyes soulless and unblinking, enough room for a person inside.

Answers weren't forthcoming? Fine. They'd take their own. Earth was the start of the Legion's jurisdiction, but it wasn't the end. For so long the world had never looked beyond itself, convinced without convincing that everything worth watching was already happening here—hopes and needs and dreams; families, neighbors, nations. They had all stared sidelong at their sideways little problems, rarely looking beyond their homes, rarely watching beyond their lives.

But everyone looked up now. Everyone paid heed.

Giselle Pixus, leader of the Legion of Heroes, stood against the fourth-floor window, spinning the pen of a dead Divine, staring up into the sky.

The White World stared back at her, silhouette pale against the clear blue.

Giselle's face remained steady. Her lips twitched into a smile.

Soon, she whispered to no one. *Soon.*

The sphere stood silent.

EPILOGUE
THE WORLD AS WE KNOW IT

Matt Callaghan sat alone at a KFC and stared quietly out the window.

It was a nice KFC, as far as KFCs go. Adapted from an old, refurbished building, with gold fans hanging from high ceilings and textured millwork patterns on the walls. The booth he sat in, opposite a small polyplastic table, was comfortable, the red high-backed seating firm yet forgiving enough. It was midmorning, a little after ten, and there was a steady enough stream of customers, although nothing ever approaching what you'd call crowded or busy. Matt sat alone, facing the red chair opposite him, unnoticed and unremarkable, idly fiddling with a white receipt.

There came no rush, nor sound or movement. No gust or flash of light. Yet suddenly, without Matt even blinking, another person sat opposite him. A pale, school-age boy with remarkable blue eyes and a shock of white-gold hair.

Somehow, Matt was not surprised.

"Nice of you to join me," he said. The Time Child stared at him. Today, for whatever reason, it was wearing a school uniform.

"*I never left*," it replied.

"Yeah," sighed Matt. "I got that impression."

They lapsed into silence.

"What're you doing here?" Matt asked eventually. The Child gave a tiny, deceptively adult shrug. Its small face remained emotionless, yet Matt couldn't quite shake the feeling that it was trying not to smile.

Just keeping an eye on you. Two of them.

"Well, I suppose someone has to," Matt sighed. He paused for a moment as a teenage girl in a KFC uniform with mousey brown hair and braces approached and set a red tray with his meal on it down in front of him. It took Matt a few seconds after she left to realize why that bothered him.

"I didn't know they did table service," he said to no one in particular—or he guessed, the Child, since it was the only one sitting there. The boy reached over with a small hand and took some of Matt's French fries.

"Ah." Matt rolled his eyes. "I see."

"*I like the salt,*" the Child said mildly. "*It's the little things.*"

"Sure." Matt fell silent. "I've just realized," he continued after a moment's pause, "this is the first time I've heard you speak."

The Child helped itself to another fry. "*Does it align with your imagination?*"

"Few things ever do."

"*Understandable.*"

"I suppose you don't really have that problem."

"*Less so, now,*" the Child replied.

Once more, they lapsed into silence, the soft hum of the air conditioner, the sizzle of frier oil, other people's distant chatter, and the occasional rush of cars outside the window melding together to create a soothing background hum.

"You were never trying to kill me, were you?" asked Matt, his eyes narrowing slightly. He tried not to sound too put off.

The Child's face remained utterly innocent. "*Whatever made you think that?*"

"I never thought it," Matt countered, perhaps a little petulant. "I wondered. Hypothesized." He paused and sniffed, scowling at the boy across the table. "It was all just nudging."

"*Mm-hmm. To prevent the paradox.*"

"Right. Did Fredericks know?"

"*Some,*" answered the Child. "*Not all. He wanted to believe in destiny, and for his life to mean something, and I played into that.*" The boy paused. "*He was a very unhappy man.*"

"I got that."

A longer silence this time. Slowly, Matt's shoulders fell.

"Was I an idiot?" he asked finally. "For not giving in? Did I destroy paradise?"

"*Paradise,*" the Child mused with an air of incongruous philosophy, waving his small hands over his school uniform and speaking between mouthfuls of French fry, "*is rarely in grand schemes, and rarely where we expect. You were right to hold true. At least in my opinion.*"

"Yeah, well . . ." Matt rested his elbow on the table and listed his head to one side, gazing blankly out the window. "Doesn't feel like it."

"*The feeling will pass.*"

"I'm having a hard time imagining that." The words were soft, sad and resigned. He turned back to the Child. "Is she really gone?" he asked.

"*Not everywhere,*" the Child answered. "*Not always.*"

"Not helpful," said Matt, rolling his eyes again and turning back to the window.

The sky was gray, autumn leaves blowing in the wind. A bus drove past.

"I don't know what I'm going to do," Matt admitted eventually. "This . . . This is all new to me. Well . . ." he added with a faint look at the people and the fast-food joint around him, "not quite all."

"*They remain, fundamentally, the same.*"

"Yeah," Matt mumbled. "I suppose they do."

He paused, watching the people with quiet eyes.

"The tech is what I find the weirdest," he said after a while. "Everything's so old."

"*The Aurora gave everything a jump start,*" the Child noted. "*Give it time,*" he said with a shrug. "*It'll catch up.*"

"Yeah, maybe." Matt turned back to him and made a face. "And traveling everywhere?"

"*You did that before.*"

"I know, but . . . at least I had options. Airplanes, ew. My kingdom for teleportation." He shook his head. "I'm going to have to relearn modern history."

"*I can recommend some excellent textbooks.*"

"You're quite enjoying this, aren't you?" Matt stated, fixing the Child with a narrow stare. The boy made no move to deny it.

"*I like it when things come full circle,*" it shrugged. "*When an old day dawns on new potential. Cheer up,*" the Child told him, "*things are brighter than they seem.*"

Matt let out a deep sigh, the corners of his mouth twitching into a frown. He took a bite from his burger. "Where there's life there's hope, I suppose."

The Child smiled.

"*My father used to say that,*" he said, reaching his little hand once more across the table.

"Did he also tell you to get your own goddamn French fries?"

"*Not regularly.*" The boy chewed and swallowed, then reached into the pocket of his gray baggy school pants and withdrew a plain white envelope. He slid it across the table to Matt, who opened the unsealed lip and peered inside.

"What's this?"

"*Money. Documents. To help you fit in.*"

Matt glimpsed the tip of a driver's license, a birth certificate. *Matthew Callaghan.* He tilted his head, his brow furrowed. "Are you looking after me?"

"*I've always been looking after you,*" said the blue-eyed boy. "*I always will be. It's what we do. It's what she would've wanted.*"

"You miss her," Matt said, puzzled.

The Child nodded, and for the first time since he'd arrived, he looked, if anything, a little sad. *"Yes and no. It's lonely out there, in eternity. It was nice to have someone to talk to, even if only occasionally, even if only for a moment."*

Against his better instincts, Matt felt a small surge of pity. "Well, you can always come talk to me if you really get bored. Help me figure out everything that's going on here."

"It's not that difficult to understand."

Matt scoffed. "Easy for you to say, time traveler."

At that, the little boy smiled. *"Our paths take us many places,"* he said, *"but ultimately, all we are ever searching for is home."*

Then, without a blink or a word, he simply vanished, and once more, the booth opposite Matt sat empty, as if he had never been there.

"Thanks for the money," Matt mumbled, still a bit resentful. Though at least the boy had, in a roundabout way, paid for his food.

He continued eating in silence and alone, staring out into the world. Across the road, people walked and chatted along the sidewalk, passing his face in the window with complete obliviousness. An old couple in felt overcoats sat waiting for a bus. A man in a suit stood with one finger in his ear, talking animatedly into a flip phone. Across a minor road, on which the KFC sat on the corner, a group of teenage girls emerged, laughing, from a store.

Matt finished his meal and wiped his mouth, then stood and took his trash to the trash can. He smiled and waved a quick thanks at the people behind the counter, pushed through the heavy old wood-and-glass doors, and stepped out into the brisk autumn streets.

Where to now, he wondered. What did he do; where did he go. The envelope the Child had given him weighed snugly in his pocket, a small weight of security and comfort. Matt stood at the crossroads, gazing up at the light gray sky, thinking.

A bark of laughter broke him from his reverie. The girls who had come out of the shop across the road had stopped on the sidewalk, pausing to compare notes about something or contending where to go next. Matt watched them inattentively—then suddenly, the group shifted slightly, and a figure caught his eye.

A tall girl with long auburn hair and sharp features.

Face bright with laughter, she leaned back from her friends, staring confidently out across the city, gray-blue eyes clear and confident. Just at that moment, the smallest gap in the clouds opened, and a weak beam of sunlight shone through.

Matt's heart skipped a beat.

Across the road, the girl turned toward him, daylight shining on her clear, unblemished face.

Their eyes met.

Matt's soul leapt.

And she smiled.

Now, his mind whispered. *Now*.

ABOUT THE AUTHOR

Benjamin Keyworth is an Australian author with a master's degree in creative writing from the University of Technology Sydney. A lawyer by day, Keyworth wanted to be a writer since he was five years old (before which, he wanted to be a dinosaur). In his spare time, he enjoys baking, playing basketball badly, and playing video games pretty well. Born and raised in Newcastle, New South Wales, Keyworth currently lives in Canberra with his wife, dog, infant son, and many plants.